EXODUS 2012

A Mission to Save the Earth

Carol Richardson

Babienge Productions
Washington, DC

Exodus 2012: A Mission to Save the Earth
Copyright 2012 - © Carol E. Richardson

ISBN-13: 978-0615658834
ISBN-10: 0615658830

Printed in the United States of America

Babienge Productions, Washington, DC

Dedication:

This book is dedicated to my two children, who are beautiful, brainy
young adults who amaze me
and who have already made the world a better place,

And to all children of the world;
May they be blessed with peace and love forever.

I also dedicate this novel to Jesus Christ,
who inspired me throughout the writing of this book.
Jesus welcomed the children and blessed them,
and invites us to do the same.

Author's note:

Hu Jing Sheng is a name I developed with the help of On-Line Chinese Tools and Behind the Name to approximate the name Jesus Christ. Hu is the last name of many people who live in the Hubei Province of China. 'Sheng' means 'spiritual'. One of the meanings of 'Jing' is 'essence, or perfect'. So putting together Jing and Sheng can result in the name meaning: 'Perfect Spiritual Essence,' or 'Perfect Essence of Spirit'.

Table of Contents

1. THE BURNING BUSH

ALL THAT GLITTERS IS NOT GOLD, FOR THE LIGHT OF LIFE DWELLS AMONG US. WHO SEEKS GOLD AFTER FINDING THE LIGHT OF LIFE?

She had to connect. The summer Olympics in Beijing were on, and her TV was not. Balancing a large plate of mostly raw, vegetarian food in one hand, Liz Cooper pushed the power button on her antique (20 year-old) television with her other hand, which also held her cell phone. The Olympics flooded into her living room – the noise, the excitement, the international flavor, the excellence of human achievement, the drama of uplifting stories, the grace and beauty of human movement, and the peaceful hope of the world all rolled into one. What a gift!

Praying the cell phone would not ring, she also gave thanks as she sank into her chair after a long day of running a wellness center complete with yoga classes, energy healing, meditation sessions, a bookstore, and a health food restaurant. At last she could enjoy the great combination of her flavorful food creation and the joy of watching the Olympics. What a contrast the Olympics were to her setting in Kalamazoo, Michigan, a small city with a great sense of community, and some wonderful diversity, but still, a small city kind of lost – partly on purpose – in the great outdoors of Michigan. For Liz, the Olympics were a relief connecting her with the larger world of human achievements.

Ten minutes later, when she had just relaxed into the flow of commentaries on the current beach volleyball game, someone knocked at the door. Her dog barked, and beat her to the door, making welcoming anyone a challenge.

She looked out the front window beside the door, only to see an Asian man, smiling at her, and holding up a sign that read:

"What on earth," she thought, but having once been a door-to-door community organizer herself, she willingly opened the door to express kindness to strangers. (Besides, her dog would protect her, if necessary.)

"Hello," he said, with an Asian accent, yet very clear enunciation.

"My name is Hu Jing Sheng. Please call me Jing Sheng. I wonder if you know the significance of the year 2012?"

"Well, it's the end of the Mayan Calendar for one thing," she managed, surprised by the directness of his deep question, not feeling eloquent enough for this stranger, and uncomfortable with her ignorance about what was happening here.

"Yes, it is the end of the Mayan Calendar," Jing Sheng replied, re-stating her obvious commentary as though to comfort her. "Do you know why that date is important?"

"Well," Liz tried again, "I read one book that said that either humankind needs to make a shift in consciousness by then, or we'll destroy the planet – something to that effect."

"And is humankind making a shift in consciousness?" Jing Sheng asked.

Wondering if this was 20 questions leading to enlightenment or serving no particular purpose at all, she looked at him, to try to read him and connect with him. She appreciated his use of the word 'humankind' rather than 'mankind' – which gave her significant hope that maybe he was not as sexist, or at least not as androcentric, as most men.

Jing Sheng was dressed in a blousy white shirt and somewhat baggy black pants, with a soft black sash pulled tight enough to show off his trim figure. He looked like - she did not know what - maybe a Tai Chi Master? He was well-built, obviously worked out (made her feel very insecure about what he thought of her almost fifty-year-old body), and had an aura of peace and love about him that she could actually feel. And his smile was irresistible. Somehow, it seemed natural to launch into a full-blown conversation on a deep topic with this perfect stranger.

"Some people are making a shift in consciousness, but many are not." She finally answered, knowing how disappointing that must sound. Liz was trained as a therapist, with a master of social work degree, and she knew how challenging it is to ask any human being to make even a slight shift in consciousness.

"And will the planet be saved or destroyed?" Jing Sheng persisted.

"You know, some scientists predict that 60 percent of species will be dead – extinct – by the end of this century, even if we slow global warming, so I don't know; it doesn't sound very good."

"What about your children and their children – is this the earth you want them to inherit?" inquired Jing Sheng, as though standing outside her door, asking her these questions, was the most usual event in the world – to be expected, really.

Feeling as though someone should be standing outside everyone's door asking these questions, Liz answered, "no, of course not, it's just that it's hard to know what's really going to happen, and how to change anything – what to change – how to convince people, how to make anything different at all."

Jing Sheng looked at her with compassion. She remembered her door-to-door community organizing manners, and asked, "Look, do you need a drink of water, or to use the bathroom?"

Jing Sheng responded, "No, thank you." He paused, smiling directly into her eyes. "I see that you have not forgotten to do unto others as you would have them do unto you. You are doing well in the eyes of God. Bless you."

"Thank you," she managed, feeling bewildered and wondering if he could read her thoughts. He spoke as though he knew her and her deepest faith issues. "Are you with some group – a religious or environmental group?"

"No," Jing Sheng answered, "I've come to start a group. A group of people who will change the world by 2012, and save lives at the same time as they save souls."

"Wow! That's ambitious; is anyone helping you?" she wondered out loud.

"The Spirit of God is helping me, and I trust that you will help me, because my prayers have led me to you." Jing Sheng replied.

"Your prayers led you to me?" She knew better than to feel pride about this, yet felt some anyway, then immediately realized this may mean a lot of work, rather than fun and games. She also remembered that she had sworn off being a part of any religious group precisely because they never seemed to practice what they preach. Unlike so many church people she knew, that was the one thing she was determined to do: live according to her beliefs and values.

"Yes, that is precisely why you will be perfect for the job," Jing Sheng pointed out, as though reading her thoughts. "Will you help me, please?"

"Thank you for acknowledging my free will," she answered, ever the stubborn feminist who cherished freewill and the exercise of 'power with' rather than 'power over.' She treasured this sacred, egalitarian use of power the way some people treasure salvation.

"You are welcome. Nonetheless, God has sent me to you, and I must ask: will you help me?" Jing Sheng smiled his encouragement as he spoke.

"I don't know – maybe? I *am* pretty busy." She wondered what she would be getting herself into. She wasn't entirely sure that she trusted either the faith with which she was raised, or the faith that she was trying to create – or discover, or whatever one does when one is secretly hoping that God will show up on one's doorstep and suddenly make sense of the universe. Why was Jing Sheng so sure of what God was saying to him? Most people would think he was crazy, but for some reason she could not name, she felt she needed to trust him.

"I see this is not an easy decision for you," Jing Sheng reflected softly.

"No, not really – I mean, I don't know just what you're expecting me to do, but I do have a lot of responsibilities and a busy schedule," Liz almost whined, but instead managed to sound firm.

"I shall return soon, giving you some time for prayer and meditation," Jing Sheng suggested.

"Okay, see you later then. Good night," she added, softly.

"Good night," Jing Sheng bowed, with his hands joined in front of him.

Liz recognized the prayerful bow as 'Namaste,' the bow which essentially means: "I bow to divine presence in you." Namaste recognizes the spark of the divine within all people, an idea which Liz cherished as representing the original goodness of everyone's soul, or that part of humans that comes from divine spirit. She wasn't sure why a Chinese Tai Chi master would bow in Namaste, since the custom was practiced mostly by Hindus in India, but she loved it.

She slowly closed the door, and returned to her healthy food and her beloved Olympics. Only then did she realize that her dog, Comet, the neurotic border collie who always insists that people throw sticks or balls or squeaky toys for her while they are talking in her presence, had just lain there, looking up at Jing Sheng and panting contentedly the whole time they spoke.

"Wow, Comet, is Jing Sheng some kind of holy man, or what?" Comet wagged her tail and lay down, as though the matter was settled.

2. LEAD MY PEOPLE OUT OF EGYPT

WHY DO YOU DOUBT YOURSELF?
CAN YOU NOT SEE GOD WITHIN YOU?
GOD IS INDEED IN EVERYONE.
LET LOVE BE YOUR EYES, AND YOUR HEART WILL GUIDE
YOU ALONG THE HIGHEST WAY.

Two weeks later on a Saturday, Liz was in the middle of mopping the kitchen floor when the doorbell rang. Comet barked, but as the door opened and Jing Sheng bowed in Namaste, Comet stopped barking and wagged her tail, looking unusually happy to see this man whom they had just met.

"Hi, come in," Liz invited.

"Thank you, it's good to see you, Liz," Jing Sheng said.

"Wait, how did you know my name?" Liz asked.

"Do you believe me if I say I just knew?" Jing Sheng suggested as much as he asked.

"Um, sure," Liz replied, thinking that the internet might somehow be the answer to this mystery. "I'm sorry the place is a mess – I'm in the middle of cleaning, but come on in, if you don't mind a mess."

"Cleanliness may be next to Godliness, but God also made dirt, and I came to see you, not your house," Jing Sheng replied. "Have you prayed about my offer?"

Liz hesitated, thinking, *dear God, why can't we have some small talk before I have to deal with this – whatever happened to how's the weather? – oh, he's probably not into small talk if he's been sent by God; it would be a waste of time.*

She finally answered: "Yes . . . and I'm sure God wants me to listen to you and help you, but I just can't let it interfere with my job – I run a wellness center you know."

"Yes, I do know that you run a wellness center, but you can let this project interfere with your job, you just don't want to," responded Jing Sheng, not judgmentally, just matter-of-factly.

Seeing that Jing Sheng's truth barometer was perfectly accurate, Liz realized that not being 100% honest with Jing Sheng was like not being 100% honest with God. She always felt a little nudge from God, or maybe it was from her guardian angels, when what she said was not perfectly on target with the truth. Some people might call that their conscience nagging at them, but Liz's life journey had led her way beyond 'normal' spiritual experiences into a variety of esoteric practices and experiences, including awareness of her guardian angels.

"Is there some way you can help me keep the wellness center running while I help you on your project?" Liz counter-offered, wavering between insecurity and boldness.

"Good question. I believe there might be ways to make that possible. In fact, that would give me a cover to begin the work we need to do together," Jing Sheng spoke thoughtfully.

"What can you do that would help a wellness center?" Liz asked.

"I teach Tai Chi, and would be happy to lead Tai Chi sessions daily. I also have the gift of healing, and could practice the spiritual energy healing that you do. And, as far as the intuitive spiritual coaching that you do, that would be something I could do as well."

"So you *are* a Tai Chi master – I knew it!" Liz exclaimed.

"I was trained in Hubei Province, at the monastery on Wudang Mountain, in the line of the ancient masters," Jing Sheng's demeanor glowed as he answered, bowing in Namaste to acknowledge this blessing. "But the teachings I bring, beyond Tai Chi, come from myself, and in no way reflect the teachings of the monastery."

"I see, well, I guess we could advertise having Tai Chi classes, but I don't know about adding your name to our brochures," Liz thought out loud.

"Not necessary – we have more pressing matters to attend to."

"Like what?" Liz sat up in her chair, and threw a ball for Comet, who had grown impatient with not getting attention for herself.

"We need to visit some key people who will help us," Jing Sheng answered.

"Like whom?" (Perfect grammar was important to Liz.)

"We will visit people who need to be aware of the needed shift in consciousness, and people who already are."

"When did you want us to start?"

"Tomorrow," Jing Sheng stated simply but emphatically.

"Sunday?" Liz wondered skeptically. She was thinking to herself that most people will either be in church being indoctrinated with dogma about saving souls while neglecting to save the earth, or home enjoying what little peace and sense of sanctuary they could find in this sometimes scary world.

"Yes, we will go perform Tai Chi with some others in Bronson Park, and then we will hold a time for speeches."

"And what are you expecting me to do?" Liz asked.

"You could introduce me as the new Tai Chi master at your wellness center, and then simply follow me in the performance of the Tai Chi."

"I hope you have a permit."

"There are ways to take care of these things," Jing Sheng replied.

Liz's cell phone rang – a jazzy ringtone that announced her son was calling.

"My son is calling me – what time do you want me there tomorrow?" She asked, while flipping open her phone. "Hi, honey, how are you? . . . Can you hold on a second for me?"

"11:00 am" Jing Sheng said, bowing in Namaste, and then gracefully moving to the door.

"Okay, I'll be there, but I'm not sure I'm ready to say anything," Liz agreed, opening and closing the door as Jing Sheng departed.

"Hi, honey, how are you?" She spoke into the cell phone.

"I'm fine, Mom, how are you?" Her son, Cliff, was considerate, but brainy and sometimes resistant to being empathetic.

"I'm good, Sweetie. What's new with you? How's school?" Liz was inquiring about St. John's College, in Annapolis, Maryland. St. John's was her son's first choice of schools, a 300-year-old classical education referred to as "The Great Books School," and it certainly had caused him to become a very polite, self-controlled, and well-read young man. The next year he would be continuing on for a Ph.D. in economics.

"It's good. I was just thinking about coming up to Michigan with some friends, and thought we might swing by Kalamazoo and see you for a night, would that be okay?"

"Of course, honey. When do you think you'll be here?"

"Next Saturday night."

"I'm sure that will be fine, although I just made a commitment to this very interesting man to help prevent global warming."

"Sounds interesting, Mom, you can tell me all about it when I get there." Phone calls with her son were usually short like that. Liz always had to fight disappointment when they were. But, he was growing, and becoming more spiritually aware, and that always gave her both comfort and hope. She just hoped that working with Jing Sheng would not prevent her from having at least a little time to be Mom. *We'll see*, she thought. In the meantime, I have a lot of work to do before tomorrow.

3. GOD'S COMPLAINT AGAINST PHAROAH

WOULD YOU KNOW THE TRUTH?
WHAT IF THE TRUTH I SPEAK TO YOU SOUNDS FOREIGN,
AS THOUGH SOMEONE ELSE WAS MEANT TO UNDERSTAND,
AND YET I ASK YOU TO TROUBLE YOURSELF
TO LISTEN TO THIS SOMEONE, TO HEAR THEIR TRUTH,
INSTEAD OF DEMANDING THAT I SPEAK TO YOU?

Sunday morning was one of those perfect fall days in Michigan: brilliant blue sky with the sun angled low and yet golden, reflecting gorgeous shades of reds and yellows, greens and amber on the leaves of vibrant trees. The crisp morning air had given way to a sunshine-warmed, chilly breeze kind of day, the kind in which Liz always preferred designer fleece and stretch-yoga pants even though she felt a little self-conscious at not being quite as fit as she used to be.

She arrived at Bronson Park in downtown Kalamazoo at 10:45, searching for a parking place among all the church-goers' vans, cars and SUVs. Downtown Kalamazoo is pretty quiet for a city, but then most of the buildings near this square were 'white' Protestant churches of nearly every stripe and hue. The predominantly African-American churches tended to be on the north side and east side of town. The 'white' churches were mostly dwindling drastically in attendance, or at least no longer drawing the large crowds for which they were built.

Liz found a parking spot, got out, locked her purse in the trunk, and then looked around to see the usual assortment of economically disadvantaged folks strolling by or sitting in the park. Liz had earned her M.S.W. years ago, hoping to make a difference in the lives of both well-to-do people and socially marginalized folks. So far, she hadn't really helped the marginalized ones very much, so she felt a pang of guilt at seeing them on park benches on a chilly Sunday morning when they could have been inside a warm home somewhere. After all, *they* were not wearing designer fleece . . . '*Let go of the guilt, you can't save the world*,' she told herself.

Following the sidewalk around the band shell, she discovered Jing Sheng doing some Tai Chi, looking like some god who descended from the sky in order to dance on earth for a little while. Joy somehow seemed to be radiating from his presence, and people were beginning to be drawn to him, like an audience in awe of something holy. A handful of people were dressed in Tai Chi attire as well, and they stood patiently together in a cluster, respectful, peaceful, looking wiser somehow than everybody else – or maybe it was Liz's imagination.

Church-goers glanced at the group as they hurriedly made their way into their own safe havens away from the confusion of whatever might be happening in the world on any given day, including today's 'weird-looking' group gathered in the park.

Jing Sheng Hu stopped, bowed, and addressed the small crowd.

"Good morning. My name is Hu Jing Sheng, and I am a Tai Chi master from the Wudang Monastery in the Hubei Province in China. In a few moments, we will begin the ancient practice of Tai Chi. Perhaps those of you with experience will set the example for those who have none. Everyone is welcome to feel the reverence, to allow the energy of life to flow through you, coming from its source, balancing you, and bringing you into balance with all life. First, I will demonstrate a few movements."

Jing Sheng began teaching as though the present moment was all there is, and as though the people who were there at the present moment were all that mattered to him. Liz thought of books she had read about the importance of 'being in the now,' and realized Jing Sheng was a master of this in ways she could barely imagine.

Jing Sheng led the group in the ancient art of Tai Chi, and Liz joined in, hesitating a lot because she really did not know Tai Chi; she was a yoga person herself. But as the group moved more or less together, a harmony filled her, maybe even filled the air, and somehow, slowly, the crowd grew.

Twenty minutes later, Jing Sheng was closing, and then he bowed, saying "Namaste" to the crowd. He stepped into the bandshell and addressed the people present. There, propped up beside him, was his sign which read, "Exodus 2012."

"Thank you for being a part of creation today. Thank you for bringing inner balance and harmony into yourselves so that you might bring more balance and harmony into the world. I have come here today, to invite you to live more harmoniously with the earth, and with the Divine Creator who asks us to care for the earth and her sacred beauty."

Jing Sheng paused to let his invitation sink in. People smiled, looked perplexed, nodded, shifted to a more comfortable stance. Knowing that people did not come to the park for a sermon, Jing Sheng continued carefully.

"Humankind is killing the earth, and in doing so, we are killing ourselves. Some call it global warming, but it is more than that. Some call it climate change, but it is more than that. The ancient Mayans predicted a cataclysm in the year 2012, and they were right. Christians have long predicted the 'end of the world,' but the way they conceive of it is inaccurate. The Mayans were more correct. What Christians call the 'rapture' is really meant to be the raising of consciousness to a higher, more spiritual level. What the Mayans predicted is that humankind would either make the shift in consciousness which is necessary to attain balance and divine harmony on earth, or humanity would fail, and the earth herself would die, and all life with her."

Murmurs went through the crowd, heads nodded, and then a hush that could be felt moved among them, harmonizing and uniting them. Somewhere behind Liz, a homeless man started singing a crazy-sounding song, and then went quiet. The breeze felt a little too cool, but somehow all that mattered was listening to Jing Sheng talk. Everyone unconsciously acknowledged their need for words that would bring Life.

Jing Sheng Hu offered them just that.

"For those who can hear what I am saying, I have returned to help raise the consciousness of humankind. We need to organize ourselves to gain understanding of what is necessary for life in this universe, and then we need to live according to the guidelines the earth requires of us for harmony rather than for greed and self-interest. Our children's children need to know there is a better way. Video games may appear to them to be the way to the future, but the true Way to the Future is in the peaceful consciousness of a Spiritual Warrior.

"Why do I use the unpeaceful-sounding words, 'Spiritual Warrior'? A Spiritual Warrior is someone who achieves self-mastery within, thereby bringing peace, love, and harmonious action into the world in balance with the natural processes of the earth and of Life itself. The Muslims call it winning the Greater Jihad, the inner struggle between good and evil. Hindus call it Self-Realization. Christians call it sanctification, although most of them ignore that invitation from God to live in divine balance both within and without, for the Christian tradition has largely lost sight of the true teachings of Christ about the purpose of their own lives."

"What!?" Liz's mind shouted out, or maybe someone else actually said it – she wasn't sure. Anyway, she was sure Jing Sheng had just created enemies for himself by putting down the Christian faith.

"Who are you to speak against Christianity?" a woman shouted, and even shook her fist at him.

"*WHO ARE WE* NOT to live in relationship with God and one another in a way that brings love and life for creation as well as for future generations of human beings?" Jing Sheng's answer was to the crowd.

"Why separate ourselves from one another through any fear-based thought pattern, whether it is religious thought patterns that divide us, or national and political thought patterns that divide us?" Jing Sheng was presenting a new thought that sounded so obvious and down-to-earth, that Liz couldn't imagine why human beings had never figured out this problem before.

"It is our thoughts and even some of our beliefs that separate us," Jing Sheng went on. "Humanity's consciousness needs to be unified around the essentials of divine life on this earth."

"What do you mean by 'divine life?'" someone ventured boldly.

"Divine life is the presence of God in creation. What some people call God or the Holy Spirit is God's mind, which is present everywhere on earth and throughout the universe. One cannot separate God's heart from God's mind, and so divine life may also be understood as the Sacred Heart of God. It is helpful to think of divine presence as Energy, as Consciousness, as Wisdom, and as Love. Love is a powerful life-giving and life-sustaining force – indeed Divine Love is the most powerful force of consciousness in the universe." Jing Sheng made sense to Liz, but she was sure others would think he was crazy.

"What do you think you are talking about?" the woman tried again, less antagonism in her voice, but lots of distrust. "Are you saying the Bible does not have all the answers we need for life?" She was somewhere between fear and tears.

"Thank you for asking," Jing Sheng's voice sent her a calm comfort. "The Bible has many answers indeed, but often those answers have been mis-interpreted, mis-translated, and mis-understood. The ancient writers were limited by their own scientific knowledge and the biases of their own culture when they wrote, so they brought through what they heard God saying the best they could –very faithfully, but sometimes slightly off the mark. And now, translations have often, especially in English, lost the flavor of the original languages. Most importantly, sexism and other cultural values such as economic values and materialism have skewed current Christian understanding of the *original* divine messages in ways that do not harmonize with all life, especially not with Mother Earth."

'*Wow!*' was all Liz could think. '*Wow, why hadn't anyone talked this way before?*' This was a sermon she wanted to hear.

"But what about sexism in Islam?" Liz surprised herself by asking out loud about what really bothered her.

"What about Islam? One cannot dominate another human being and call it harmony. And yes, women are human beings equal to men. In fact, the Genesis story in the original Hebrew makes it clear that *Adam* (Jing Sheng pronounced it in Hebrew) was not man, but human: originally both male and female which were one harmonious being, and then split into two – man and woman became separate, but equal. Clearly the Genesis text specifies that both man and woman together image God. Man alone does not fully image God, but male and female together fulfill the image of who God is."[1]

---

[1] For scholarly explanations of the original Hebrew meaning, please see the writings of Phyllis Trible, author of God and the Rhetoric of Sexuality (1978).

"That's not how the story goes!" The woman who yelled at him earlier yelled again.

"Not if you take it literally as you read it in English, but then Genesis one and two actually contain two creation stories, neither of which was meant to be taken literally. They tell about what God was doing, but not literally what happened.

"Returning to Islam, we also find the idea of the lesser Jihad, which has become the fight against infidels. But again, domination of other human beings, especially to the point of killing them, is antithetical to the Greater Jihad, which is the struggle between good-and-evil within oneself. The lesser Jihad is rather meant to be self-sacrifice as a loving invitation to others to choose the Greater Jihad – the struggle for goodness and love and self-sacrifice within themselves.

"We asked, 'what about Islam,' but we also need to ask: 'what about Christianity?' Christians cannot live in harmony with God while dominating other species as though animals and plants exist solely for the sake of the survival of human beings. That is not what having 'dominion' means. Notice, please, that in the ancient story of Adam and Eve, God placed them in a garden, and the story tells us that Adam and Eve did not have to work until they were kicked out of the garden. When we live in balance and harmony with God, with creation, and with one another, there is no need to work hard to dominate anyone else. Only in being cast away from divine presence, as well as from the divine sense of balance in creation, did Adam and Eve begin to experience the need for hard work and domination of the earth and of one another. But that is not God's original plan for the earth, nor for humankind.

"I have come . . . that we might rediscover God's original intentions for humanity and the earth. Only in this way can we be freed from our own domination."

After a moment of bewildered and awe-stricken silence, Jing Sheng bowed. "I will be offering Tai Chi lessons on a donation basis in the evenings this week at Spring of Life Wellness Center, as well as early morning practice sessions at 6:30 a.m. every weekday. I will return here to the park next week, weather permitting. God bless you." Jing Sheng bowed again, adding, "Namaste."

'*Wow*!' was all Liz could think. '*Wow*!' Her head was spinning. She went and sat down on the seat of a picnic table. She realized then that the crowd had been more diverse than the usual Sunday morning crowd; after all, thanks to Christian churches, Sunday mornings in America are the most segregated times of the week.

Then she realized that this made Jing Sheng Hu even more of a hero to her. First, he was a hero because he was not afraid to speak the truth about the failings of religion and religious people. Second, he was her hero because he cared deeply about the earth and the survival of all life on the planet, including, but not limited to, humans. And in her heart of hearts, she felt an incredible fondness and longing for Jing Sheng because he spoke against sexism publicly. Having a man do that made her feel so good she didn't know how to express it. To top it off, he drew a crowd that was ethnically and economically diverse – hardly appropriate in the minds of most upper-class white people.

And most exciting of all, he had just announced that he was leading Tai Chi at her wellness center! She wondered how he knew that the 6:30 time slot was open on her center's schedule.

She looked up from the ground at which she had been staring, lost in thought, and saw Jing Sheng pick up his 'Exodus 2012' sign and begin to walk over to her slowly.

"Where are you staying?" she asked.

"Good morning, Liz." (She felt an inner pang for forgetting her manners.) "I am staying in an apartment on the east side of town."

Well, that explained the racially-mixed group, since the east side of Kalamazoo is mostly African American in population. Liz lived on the west side of town, never even having been shown the east side of town when she moved here as a white person looking for a home long ago.

"Why didn't you explain the sign?" She couldn't help asking.

"Ahh!" He sighed. "Not even you have figured out the full meaning of this sign."

"Do you mean that it represents a scripture, as well as a date?" She replied.

"Yes, but there is more to the combination of date and name, just as there is more to the scripture than first meets the eye." Jing Sheng sat down beside her.

"Well, I looked up the scripture," Liz continued, partially sure of herself and yet humbly knowing that Jing Sheng apparently knew spiritual things that she did not yet know.

"And?" Jing Sheng encouraged.

"Well, it's one of the Ten Commandments, of course, in Exodus chapter 20 – it's the one about honoring your father and mother." Liz spoke with a touch of exasperation, since she could not see the point of this. "The only curious part of it is that it says, 'so you can live long in the land.'"

"I need you to write a book with me, so that we can explain the meaning to people," Jing Sheng said gently, yet firmly.

This was unexpected. Liz could not see how writing a book could possibly fit into her life.

"What do you mean explain it to people? I still need you to explain it to me!" Liz exclaimed.

"Yes. We will do that. How about over lunch somewhere?" Jing Sheng suggested.

Liz's two young adult children were in college, so she could eat most of her meals anytime she wanted, anywhere she wanted, money being the only limiting factor.

"Would you like to eat out, or would you prefer that I fix something vegetarian and mostly raw at my house?" Liz offered.

"Which one is better for the planet?" Jing Sheng responded.

"My house it is," affirmed Liz. "Do you need a ride?"

"I have my motorcycle," answered Jing Sheng.

"Wow! What do you plan to do in winter?" asked Liz, thinking about how impossible it could be to ride a motorcycle through six inches of snow and ice in ten degree weather.

"I will walk, ride the bus, or ask for a ride." Jing Sheng said calmly, as though living the way economically-deprived people do in America made any sense as a good choice, which, in small cities like Kalamazoo, is rarely an easy choice. Buses in Kalamazoo were rarely convenient in either their timing or their route. Most people had to depend on cars. "The transportation system in most of America is designed for greed, convenience, material pleasure, and the destruction of the planet. Perhaps people can begin to see that all these things go hand-in-hand."

Thinking that she might need him to explain that comment, and slightly embarrassed that she was thinking like a privileged white person, Liz remained silent a moment.

"Would you like to follow me? Oh, that's right, you've already been to my house."

"I will meet you there," Jing Sheng affirmed.

4. I AM THAT I AM

OUR TRUE IDENTITY IS HIDDEN IN THE FOLDS OF TIME;
ONLY IN THE NOW OF ETERNITY
CAN WE SEE WHO WE REALLY ARE.

Liz arrived home and realized she needed to fix something more than just a salad and a power bar – one of her low-cal meals. So, she looked for the recipe for a veggie loaf that she had planned to bake, and got out the pine nuts, mushrooms, eggplant, oatmeal, eggs, parsley, tomato sauce, red wine, onion, green pepper, olive oil, basil and oregano that were her favorite ingredients. The doorbell rang.

Liz went to the door, following Comet, who was barking, of course. They looked out the window to see that it was Jing Sheng, and let him in.

"Come in! I've just started to fix a veggie loaf. Are you very hungry?" She asked.

"Do you remember the line, 'One does not live by bread alone but by every word that proceeds from the mouth of God?'" Jing Sheng answered as though every moment of life were a spiritual learning opportunity.

"Oh, I get it," Liz answered. "Every moment is an opportunity to grow closer to the divine, whether we're hungry or not. So, I guess you can wait while I fix the food?"

"Yes, of course," replied Jing Sheng. "I will take Comet in the back yard and throw a stick for her while you prepare lunch."

"Oh, thank you!" exclaimed Liz, excited that Jing Sheng respected her dog and her dog's needs. Border collies become unbearably bored when they don't have a job to do. If they don't have sheep to keep track of for you, they need something or someone else (often children) to keep track of for you. They have an interactive mindset – they're keeping track of something *for you*, not for themselves, so they can't do their jobs alone.

The veggie loaf was baking, the salad was prepared, and Liz was making iced tea when Jing Sheng and Comet came back in the house. Jing Sheng also held the back door open for Liz's cat, Picasso, who cautiously ran past Jing Sheng and Comet, jumped up on the kitchen counter and meowed at Liz for food. She petted him, filled his bowl, and placed both the food and the cat on the floor.

"Come on and have a seat at the table. I hope you will eat vegetarian food."

"Vegetarian food respects the body, the soul, and the planet, and is therefore best for all three," replied Jing Sheng peacefully yet enthusiastically.

"I think so, too," Liz echoed him. She placed a raw salad on the table (she doesn't count 'pasta salads' or 'Jello salads' as constituting real salads), along with some sliced bread with herb-seasoned olive oil.

"I do need to wash my hands, however, before we eat."

"Sure, the bathroom is just past the front door. … Is iced tea ok or would you like water or hot tea – herbal, green, or black?" Liz inquired as graciously as she could when Jing Sheng returned, while hoping he did not want coffee or Coke or Pepsi or some such unhealthy stuff.

"Iced tea or hot tea, either one is fine, thank you," Jing Sheng responded.

Liz poured the iced tea, and then took her turn excusing herself to use the bathroom upstairs.

When she came back down, she took the veggie loaf out of the oven and sat down with him. "Do you say grace before meals?"

"I would be happy to pray for the food," Jing Sheng answered.

"Yes, please." Liz was already grateful many times over but had no idea how to express it appropriately in his company.

"O Guiding Spirit who gives us life, we thank you for blessing us with this food. Nourish our bodies, that we may nourish our souls through your Spirit, and send forth your life across all the earth. Amen." Jing Sheng prayed deliberately and reverently.

They ate a few bites in silence.

"This is good," Jing Sheng ventured politely. "The reason I'm here, though, is not just to share your food."

"Why *are* you here?" Liz wondered out loud.

"I came to earth to bring a message of salvation – a hope for humankind to survive this devastation that they are bringing upon themselves and the planet earth." Jing Sheng replied.

"And why have you come here to my home?" Liz asked.

"You are meant to help me," Jing Sheng paused, "and you know it."

"Yes, I suppose I am, but who are you?" Liz really wanted to know the answer to that question, because she had a feeling Jing Sheng was much more than just a wandering Chinese Tai Chi master.

"I am Jing Sheng Hu, or more properly, Hu Jing Sheng."

"Yes, I know that is your name, but I get the feeling you are someone else, too, or more than just a mystery man – oh, I'm sorry, I don't know how to convey it – but, Comet thinks you're someone special and I feel like I know you."

"Do you know who I AM?"

"Well, aren't you a Tai Chi Master?" Liz stalled.

"Yes, of course. But, do you know who I AM?"

"Well, you remind me of Jesus Christ, but that doesn't make sense, does it?"

"What do you think?"

"Well, I mean, Jesus is supposed to come again, but on the clouds, not knocking at my door, and well, Jesus was not Chinese."

"But Jesus was not American, either, was he?"

"No, he was Jewish, so how could Jesus be a Chinese Tai Chi Master?"

"Does it matter?"

Feeling more confused than ever, Liz replied, "I don't know, does it?"

"Liz, what is God telling you about me?" Jing Sheng helped her focus.

Liz thought about her prayer and meditation time – her most sacred time of the day each morning. "I know God is telling me to listen to you, to trust you, and to follow you or serve you or something. And this morning, when I talked to Jesus in my prayers, I saw you. At least, I think it was you – first you looked Jewish, then you looked Chinese, and you looked more and more radiant and holy and – and – so handsome!" Liz couldn't help herself – it had to come out that she thought this man was absolutely gorgeous.

"Thank you. Of all those things that happened in your mind, which one really mattered?"

"Wow! You're more like a Zen master or something!" Liz objected to the difficulty of the assignment.

"Liz, you have to achieve self-mastery to attain full connection with God. I know you think of yourself as bad at self-mastery, AND I know that you think of self-mastery as something brutally masculine and therefore unloving, but self-mastery is necessary on the path to full embodiment of divine love," Jing Sheng explained with a mixture of loving patience and the sheer force of absolute truth.

"Self-mastery is a means to an end, not the end in itself, which is what you rightly object to. Rather, self-mastery is a tool for incarnating divine love."

"There are no kindergarten lessons with you, are there, Hu Jing Sheng?" Liz inquired, laughing nervously as she desperately tried to make life feel normal instead of spiritually heady and totally unreal.

"What good would kindergarten do for those who seek God, for those who love God and seek to dwell in God's presence? What good would kindergarten do for saving the earth – who is our mother, a divine treasure, and our home in this universe?"

"I see. So, the most important thought I've had about you is that I need to listen to you, trust you, and serve you …   I hope lunch was okay."

Jing Sheng laughed with delight. He looked at her with inescapable truth and love that made her know she was in the presence of God – there was no doubting that Jing Sheng was God in the flesh. He did not lust after her; he did not look down on her; he did not objectify her in anyway. With Jing Sheng, Liz felt more like a whole person with a God-given purpose than she had ever felt in her life.

"How does he make me feel that way?" She wondered. Maybe he reads my mind and plants his thoughts in my head. *"Yes,"* she heard. *"Oh, boy, I'm not ready for that,"* she thought. *"Why not?"* Jing Sheng mind-spoke to her.

"Liz," Jing Sheng said out loud, "the biggest obstacle to peace on earth is that people have made me or someone else their savior. Instead, it is time for people to step up and commit themselves to spending enough time with God that they too can have the mind of Christ the way Paul wrote that Christians should. When people achieve having the Divine Mind, which can also be called the Sacred Heart of God, then they will be able to live the Reign of God here on earth."

"I believe that, but I always end up messing up sooner or later." Liz actually had boat-loads of guilt hanging out in the back of her mind, because she was raised by missionary parents in Malaysia. Once she came to the U.S. in high school, she found Christian churches in America to be boring, judgmental, and hypocritical, as well as anything but diverse. Despite being a disappointment to her parents, she only barely stayed connected with the church by getting married there, baptizing her children there, and then attending on those high-holy holidays. She knew that her great-grandmother would consider her a heathen for being a "C & E" Christian – a person who attends church only at Christmas Eve and Easter.

Nonetheless, her childhood was full of stories of the life of Jesus, and she did find him to be fascinating. So every now-and-then, she would re-read the gospels, and wonder how she could ever be like Jesus.

"That's where the idea of self-discipline is so crucial." Jing Sheng reprimanded her, or maybe led her – it was hard to tell which, because he was so gentle and yet so right.

"Self-discipline is essential to manifesting divine presence – divine love – within oneself, and through oneself. And manifesting God's presence within each person and through each person is the only way to wholeness and peace for all the earth.

"The Greek word used for 'salvation' in the Bible means 'wholeness' which is what I came to bring before. Now I have come again now to help everyone understand that this inner wholeness makes each person 'one-with-God' and 'one-with-one-another' and 'one-with-life on earth.' That is the 'at-one-ment' that the Jewish idea of atonement sought to achieve. Or another Jewish word for that which we seek is 'Shalom'. Shalom, properly understood, means reconciled and peaceful relationships among all people, all creation, and God."

"Don't Christians call that the kingdom of God?" Liz asked.

"Yes, Christians call this Shalom or at-one-ment the Kingdom of God, but when they reserve it just for heaven, they've missed the point. That is why I told them that the kingdom of God happens among them and within them - Luke 17:21 is where my quote can be found."

"Wow, Jing Sheng, are . . . are you really Jesus?" Liz was tearing up – unable to contain all the emotions and awe that overflowed from within her.

"Liz, what does it mean to be born again?" Jing Sheng softly queried her.

"I never was quite sure about that, although some people seem so certain they know what it means." Liz looked and sounded sad.

"Precisely: the phrase "to be born again" could have more than one meaning, correct?"

"I suppose that would have to be true, literally speaking, and metaphorically speaking." Liz sounded slightly more hopeful.

"One meaning of "to be born again" could be a spiritual rebirth within this lifetime, is that not so?" Jing Sheng prodded gently.

"Yes."

"And another meaning could be to die and to be born again as one does when one is reincarnated, is that not so?" Jing Sheng kept his eyes steadily on Liz's eyes.

"Yes, of course to be born again could refer to reincarnation." Liz shifted herself to sit up a little straighter.

"And so, if Christ chooses to come again, does Christ have the power to come again anyway that Christ chooses?"

"Of course!" Liz sounded definite this time.

"So there is nothing to prevent Jesus Christ from choosing to return to earth reincarnated as a Chinese Tai Chi master, correct?"

"That's true." Liz smiled slightly at Jing Sheng.

"So perhaps Jesus Christ chose to return, but preferred to avoid the clouds, so that people would not mistake him for a space alien and kill him."

Liz did finally smile.

"Perhaps Jesus Christ chose to return, but to be born in a foreign land so that American Christians would learn not to "have any other gods before me," such as their country, and no idols such as the American flag."

"Good luck with that one!" Liz laughed a little, relief so needed from this overwhelming sense that God was dining in the flesh at her table. Jing Sheng smiled at her.

"I AM, I was, and I always will be the kind of savior who calls all people to attain this wholeness within their own being through their own relationship with God. That is why I repeatedly told people that their faith has made them well. This salvation as wholeness is for people of all faiths. We can also call this wholeness or at-one-ment the Greater Jihad, Shalom, Spiritual Enlightenment, Christ-Consciousness, Buddha-Consciousness, or Self-Realization."

"Wow! Well, I noticed in scriptures that you always told people that their own faith healed them. I've always really liked you for that line – the fact that you affirmed people as having their own direct connection to God . . . " Liz paused.

"When I do energy healing work, the people who have some kind of faith that God will heal them, or that the energy will heal them, they always receive so much more than the ones who are not sure, or who doubt." Liz paused again, and then added emphatically, "But I always tell people that all healing comes from God."

"Yes," Jing Sheng answered simply. A good savior has to let people do their own self-discovery, not just preach at them all the time.

"Thank you for the lunch – it was as it should be. Now you may go take care of your responsibilities at Spring of Life Wellness Center. I will wash the dishes, let Comet out, and then let myself out the back door. I will return at 8:00 p.m.. We will start planning what we are going to do together," Jing Sheng finished with this helpful explanation, as though that made turning her life upside down all okay.

"Thank you for washing the dishes. Would you be willing to play with Comet again on your way out?" Liz was afraid she was being too bold – but her dog's sanity depended on staying busy.

"Comet and I have been playing already – dogs can mindspeak if you know how." Jing Sheng smiled at Comet as he spoke.

Comet wagged her tail and looked at Jing Sheng contentedly.

"Okay, well, maybe you are real, and maybe angels are real, but I just don't know about this mindspeak stuff – I feel as though I'm losing my mind when you talk about it." Liz sounded exasperated. Having a stranger walk into her life, and knowing that this stranger must somehow be Jesus Christ made no sense to her and yet felt so true that it was really stressing her out.

"I'll see you later – thank you." Liz kind of curtsied, kind of bowed to Jing Sheng, as he bowed with his hands conveying 'Namaste.'

Liz returned to the healing center where she had an energy healing scheduled, a yoga class to lead, and a pile of paperwork. She thought about skipping the paperwork, and then remembered what Jing Sheng had said about self-discipline. *"You're going to have to help me then,*" she thought, "*because you know I'm no good at getting the paperwork done.*"

"*No problem,*" came the answer to her prayer, except the answer she heard was in Jing Sheng's voice. "*Wow! You mean that 'mindspeak' is a form of prayer?!*" Liz exclaimed in her head, hoping this thought/prayer was addressed to Jing Sheng.

"*Of course. God is everywhere, and God loves and connects us all.*" Jing Sheng ended her prayer with "*Amen – so be it.*"

5. GOD GIVES MOSES A STAFF

JUST BELIEVE THAT WHERE YOU INTEND TO STAND
IS IN FACT
WHERE YOU STAND.

At 8:00 p.m., Liz walked into her living room, only to find Jing Sheng already sitting there. "How did you do that?" she asked.

Bowing in Namaste, Jing Sheng replied, "How did I do what?"

"Get into my living room without my knowing it." Liz was confused.

"When the wind does not blow, where is its sound?" Jing Sheng replied.

"I don't think that's an answer," Liz shot back.

"The mind can retain what the air holds within, yet the air knows more than the mind."

"I don't think Americans are going to like you," she announced, as though it mattered.

"Is being liked so important?" Jing Sheng responded.

"Of course not, unless you need to be popular to get your point across," Liz stated with all the assurance of her American high school upbringing.

"The truth is often unpopular, although it is one of the three greatest gifts of God."

Jing Sheng went on, as though Liz had asked what the other two greatest gifts of God were: "The other two greatest gifts of God are Spirit and Love. Spirit is also wind, breath, mind, wisdom, consciousness, intelligence, word, light, energy, reiki, chi, or qi – it means all those things."

"I thought Paul wrote that faith, hope, and love were the greatest," Liz replied.

"Faith and hope are not so much gifts of God, as they are states of being, or energies of a consciousness which is necessary for human life to go on. They are choices that humans must make for themselves. Although, truly spoken, everything is a gift from God." Jing Sheng paused, as Comet came over to him and obviously asked to be petted.

"Oh, would you like some tea?" Liz asked.

"No, thank you, I would like you to explain to me what energy healing is, the way you explain it to other people."

"Oh." Liz wondered if this was a test of their relationship, because she had once had a vision in which Jesus had spoken to her about healing energy – and she deeply hoped she had not imagined that conversation.

"Well, it depends. Some people are really limited in their spiritual experiences, so they are not usually open to an explanation. Others are ready to accept how amazing God is and can be in our lives."

"Yes," Jing Sheng encouraged, "go on."

"Well … energy healing is asking for God's energy to come through the healer for the other person – it's a form of prayer, kind of like a laying on of hands, and the healer becomes a vessel for God's healing energy. When the other person receives the healing energy, it can bring a renewed sense of well-being, it might be a cure, or it might not, but it feeds and balances the person's mental, physical, spiritual, and emotional well-being."

"That's nice," Jing Sheng responded. "It sounds pretty Christian. What do you tell people who are not Christians?"

"I tell them that God's energy is everywhere, that the Japanese call it Reiki, the 'universal life force,' and that the Reiki energy can feed and balance their energies emotionally, physically, and spiritually."

"And what did I tell you when you had that vision?" Jing Sheng said as though of course the vision was real and he knew her personally and she knew him, too.

"You . . ." Obviously, Jing Sheng was aware of the vision, but Liz realized that if she accepted that Jing Sheng had spoken to her in the vision, then she committed herself to recognizing that he was indeed Jesus Christ.

"You told me, 'this is the living water of which I spoke,'" Liz quietly replied with a catch in her throat, for the first time being truly reverent to Jing Sheng. Tears formed in her eyes.

"Good. And what did I mean by living water?" Jing Sheng went on.

"Oh, Jesus, I mean Jing Sheng, you told me that the Reiki healing energy is living water." Liz was crying, knowing now beyond a doubt that this Chinese Tai Chi Master sitting in her living room was the living embodiment of Jesus Christ.

"That's okay, you may call me what you wish, but in front of other people, please call me 'Jing Sheng.' He was silent a moment.

Beams of love radiated from him to her, and she was able to stop crying. "And what do you know about this living water?"

"I went to the Bible, of course, after I had my Reiki training – after . . . after you spoke to me in that vision. Well, first I did an online word search, so I found John chapter four, the story of you with the woman at the well. And you told her that people are meant to have streams of living water come out of them – so I believe that you were telling me that we are all meant to be springs of living water – healers – filled with God's healing energy of love."

Liz felt as though heaven itself were pouring into her living room – almost with a glow. A sense of peace descended as though a healing was taking place, and, she guessed it was – she was healed of doubts and fears, and felt right about life in a way she never had before.

"We need to share this truth with others." Jing Sheng spoke with a smile, as though that might be easy or fun.

"I hope you don't think that will be easy or fun," Liz challenged him out loud.

"It will be an adventure, and adventure can be fun, if you let it be."

"Why is he so smart?" She thought, and then realized, *"of course, he has the mind of God."*

"Liz, we are going to expand your gift of healing to include two things: The knowledge of what is wrong with someone – person or animal, and the ability to cure it instantly."

"Oh, Jing Sheng, that's going to make me seem like even more of a freak than I already am in so many people's minds," Liz objected to the very gift God would give her. "Besides, what if I really can't do it?"

"What is up to God is not necessarily up to you," replied a distracted Jing Sheng, whose attention seemed to be directed in prayer as he moved his hands above, behind, and around her body.

Liz felt a jolt of energy shoot from her feet all the way up to her head along her spine. After that, she felt as though she was barely standing on the floor.

Jing Sheng floated up to the ceiling and sat cross-legged there like a Mary Poppins character in the old movie.

"I've always wanted to be able to do that ever since I saw Mary Poppins as a little girl!" Liz exclaimed.

"Come on up," Jing Sheng answered.

Liz felt herself lighter and lighter on her feet, until she realized that she was, indeed, in fact, floating above the floor. She thought about floating up and sitting near the ceiling, and suddenly she was there. She crossed her legs, and relaxed into what felt like an amazing amount of energy holding her up, like an ocean of water.

"Does this mean we can walk on water, too?" Liz asked.

"Of course. Mind works over matter every time you put faith and love and God's will together as one."

"But how do you explain this to the scientific lot out there – you know, the people who don't believe in miracles because they are too intelligent to be suckered into anything they can't understand with their rational minds?"

"Quantum mechanics has shown us that, at the quantum level of reality, the mind, or consciousness, plays a role in determining what will happen. Most Americans are stuck in Newtonian physics, the physical laws of cause and effect. But at the level of quantum physics, reality is malleable. Not only chaos, as in chaos theory, occurs at this level, but also miracle. Quantum chaos leaves room for miracle, at the level in which matter and energy are interchangeable and often indistinguishable.

"What we think of as random coincidences are hardly that – they are miracles created through the interconnection of our minds through the curve of space-time. Miracles are real, and you can make them happen." Jing Sheng looked at Liz, placed the palm of his hand on her forehead and the top of her head, and instantly, she felt a shot of energy go from the base of her spine through the crown of her head.

"Now, unfold your hand and see the light there." Jing Sheng instructed her.

Liz looked at the palm of her right hand as she unfolded it, and it glowed. Golden light pooled in her hand and glowed outward.
"Wow! What is it?" Liz managed as she stared at the pulsing glow of light in her hand. She opened her left hand, and the same glow was there.

"This is the healing energy that has always been with you when you have been healing people – now it is just intensified because you are ready."

"Ready for what?" Liz asked.

"Ready because you are purified through your faith in me. But now, because I am the kind of savior who helps you attain salvation with God yourself, I have granted you your prayer to have the power of God within your own hands to help and to heal. This time, even to cure in one session. This is the energy of the prayer, 'I can do all things through Christ who strengthens me.'"

Liz stretched herself out and 'flew' slowly around the living room. "This is so cool!" She cried out. "I've always wanted to be able to do this."

"As with all gifts from God, this Christ-energy which you have been given comes not only as a blessing for you, but as a gift which transforms you into a blessing for others. You must give thanks for the gift, and you must serve God by helping others with the gift, or you will lose it."

"Oh, I am grateful! Thank you, God!" Liz enthusiastically proclaimed. She bowed in Namaste to Jing Sheng. "What would you like me to do right now?"

"Now, we will walk and then meditate before bedtime. Tomorrow morning we will do yoga and Tai Chi, then we will speak with your co-workers, and we will create the schedule we need and arrange the payment for my services."

6. GO AND ASSEMBLE THE ELDERS OF ISRAEL AND SAY TO THEM: 'THE LORD HAS APPEARED TO ME'

THE PURE IN HEART SEE GOD PRECISELY BECAUSE THEY SEEK TO BE VESSELS OF LOVE, AND NOTHING ELSE. THOSE WHO SEEK GOD WITH THEIR WHOLE BEING WILL SEE GOD EVERYWHERE, IN EVERY SETTING, AND IN EVERYONE, EVEN IN THEMSELVES.

As the alarm went off at 5:30 the next morning, Liz realized she felt her age, and wasn't sure that she could pull off this following Jesus/Jing Sheng Hu lifestyle. She dragged herself out of bed, made tea, let the dog out, fed the cat, took the tea upstairs and took a shower. She sat on her meditation seat and prayed a few moments, sipped her tea, took her vitamins, fed the dog, and got in the car. 6:05 a.m. was so early for her, but she had to beat Jing Sheng to the wellness center, which was 5 minutes away by car.

Liz wondered if anyone would show up for the Tai Chi lessons. As she pulled into the parking lot, she saw Jing Sheng Hu beside his motorcycle, talking with a young African American man who was holding a helmet as though he just got off the motorcycle with Jing Sheng.

"Good morning, Liz," Jing Sheng greeted her.

"Good morning," she managed with a smile.

"Liz, this is Darnell Williams, who will be my apprentice in the Tai Chi classes. Darnell hopes to become a Tai Chi master, and will need to take your meditation class as well."

"Hi, Darnell," Liz extended a hand.

"Good to meet you," Darnell replied, shaking her hand somewhat tentatively.

"How did you two meet?" Liz asked, wondering if Darnell was a spiritual prodigy who would quickly advance to being Jing Sheng's star pupil. *Oh my gosh, there's my ego again*, she thought – *feeling insecure and dreading competition, afraid I'll 'lose.'* Then she realized that Jing Sheng could probably hear her thoughts, and that made her feel worse.

"We were shooting some hoops, when Jing Sheng came by and asked if he could challenge us to some one-on-ones," Darnell replied, "and he stole the ball before I even realized he was coming at me. Then, he managed to make sixty straight shots in a row. We knew he must be someone special, but I'm the only one who really realized who he IS."

"So you know who he is?" Liz exclaimed as she unlocked the doors to the wellness center.

"Yeah, I mean, I was brought up in church and all, but I never expected anything like this to happen in my life."

"Yeah, me neither," Liz agreed.

"Ok, you two," Jing Sheng re-directed them, "Let's get centered."

"But I need to get ready to register new students and to charge them for the class. How much am I charging them, anyway?" objected Liz.

"Liz, come get centered first, please, and then we'll get to the details." Jing Sheng drew them into a circle and had them bow in Namaste to one another, to him, and outwards to God. "Now, take a couple of clearing breaths, and we will pray."

As Liz breathed in through her nose, and out through her mouth, she realized it sounded strange that Jing Sheng needed to pray, but she just let him lead.

"God we are grateful for your bountiful goodness and for this opportunity to serve you together. Bless us and guide us, we pray, that we might serve the needs of the people whom you send to us. Let those who need you to appear to them through us be drawn here this day. Amen."

"Amen," Darnell echoed.

"Liz, why not charge each person $5 a day or $20 for a week," suggested Jing Sheng as Liz moved towards the welcome counter.

"Ok, how much of that do you need to receive?"

"$25 should do per class," Jing Sheng replied, "and $10 for Darnell, while he's in training."

Just then, a new student walked in the door. "Is this where the Tai Chi class starts?"

Ten students showed up, all of whom seemed to have at least met Jing Sheng before. Only one was a previous client of Liz's wellness center – a yoga student who occasionally scheduled massages, maybe four times a year.

The class went quickly, with Liz learning, but not at the pace Darnell seemed to manage. Of course, he was significantly *younger* than she was, Liz realized.

When it was over, Liz realized that the center had only earned $15 for the whole forty-five minutes, after she paid Jing Sheng Hu and Darnell. $ 15 doesn't go very far in paying heat and electricity and a salary for her. She frowned. *Well, maybe this is not about income, she thought. At least it's fifteen more than I would normally have by this time of day. And if we get the word out, we may get more students.* She felt a little more peaceful.

"Would you like some tea and fruit before my 7:30 yoga class starts?" she asked Jing Sheng and Darnell.

"I'd like some fruit, please," answered Darnell.

"Please," answered Jing Sheng.

They followed her to the café, where she fixed them flavored green tea along with a plate of fruit topped with slivered almonds and a dollop of yogurt. She added a squeeze of fresh orange juice to the tea, and placed the fruit on a few fresh spinach leaves.

Having looked at the overhead menu, Darnell and Jing Sheng each gave her $6, and Liz realized this might work out after all.

They sat at a table, sipping tea and breakfasting on fruit, mostly silent as they enjoyed the peaceful, yet energized feeling that came from doing Tai Chi.

"Are you coming to my yoga class?" she asked them both.

"I've got to go to work," Darnell replied.

"Oh, where do you work?" she asked.

"Right down the street at the hospital – I'm a med tech."

"Oh, that's wonderful – you're so close," Liz enthused. She was good at being enthusiastic as a way of encouraging and affirming people.

"Yeah, I'll see you later for the lunch meeting," Darnell replied as he headed out the door.

"Lunch meeting?" Liz inquired of Jing Sheng.

"Yes, we'll need to meet with your staff and go over some game plans together," Jing Sheng answered.

Not sure what he meant, Liz nonetheless trusted that Jing Sheng knew what he was doing and what needed to happen, so she kept her mouth closed and went to turn on the lights in the yoga room.

After her yoga class, Liz stretched out her yoga mat in her office, closed the door, and promptly fell asleep. Her cell phone alarm went off at 9:30 am, and Liz went to get some herbal tea before preparing to do an energy healing. Andy, the massage therapist was in his therapy room, so she stopped in and asked him if he had heard that they were having a meeting at noon.

"Yes," Andy answered, "I really like Jing Sheng Hu, but there's something puzzling about him."

"Yes, I think there is," Liz mused. "Well, thanks for being willing to take time to meet. I'll see you later."

Noon came, and the central gathering room was full. Twenty people sat around the tables, but only six were practitioners or staff of the wellness center, not counting Liz. Other than Jing Sheng and Darnell, then, eleven people showed up whom Liz had never met.

Jing Sheng calmly stood, bowed in Namaste, thanked everyone for being there, and then chanted a single, sustained, "OM" for about twenty seconds. "Holy One, be among us now, we pray, that we may serve the highest good, according to your divine will. Amen."

Liz realized that Jing Sheng naturally never ended his prayers with "in Jesus' name." He didn't have to, so his prayers sounded as though they could be Jewish. *Oh, right, Jesus was Jewish*, Liz moaned inwardly at her own limited reality. *Then again,* she thought, *his prayers sound kind of New Age-like, or Hindu or something. But I guess that makes sense, really, since he must be here to reach people from several religions.*

"Let's go around and introduce ourselves, if you will please," Jing Sheng requested, as he gestured to Liz to start.

"Hi, everyone, I'm Liz Cooper, the owner of Spring of Life Wellness Center."

"Hi, I'm Darnell Tanner. I'm a med-tech at Bronson Hospital and a member of Tabernacle Church of God."

The others went around and gave their names and occupations, some adding religious affiliation. Liz was astounded at the diversity of the people present. The group included a variety of races, men and women, two wealthy business people, one Jewish rabbi, two Buddhist monks, one Hindu woman, and a Muslim Imam. How Jing Sheng managed to draw such a group, she was not sure, nor could she imagine why.

"Thank you for your introductions," Jing Sheng continued, "As you may have noticed, we are a very diverse group of people – different ages, different races, different genders and orientations, different religions. This is what the kingdom of heaven will look like. It's not going to look like our neighborhoods here on earth, nor even our churches, synagogues, mosques, or temples, where we separate ourselves out as though we are holier than others. No, the kingdom of heaven has diversity of every kind. A kind and helpful heart will get you farther in the kingdom of heaven than anything else.

"Many of you may be wondering who I really am. Who I AM may be different to each one of you. So, at any time, the important question may be: what do you know or believe about me?"

"I know you're a Tai Chi Master," cheerfully ventured Daniel, a bronzed, Greek-god-like middle-aged man who looked like one of the original disciples of Jesus Christ in Liz's way of thinking.

"On an obvious level, yes, but let us go beyond the obvious, who do you believe I AM and does it matter?" Jing Sheng persisted.

"It matters who we all are," proclaimed a woman whom Liz found herself expecting to be a Lesbian.

"Of course," replied Jing Sheng, "but I believe you will find it helpful to answer the question."

All of a sudden, Liz realized that she and Darnell might be the only two people in the room who truly knew who Jing Sheng was, so she looked at Darnell, caught him looking at her, and raised her eyebrows. Darnell shook his head.

"I believe that you are Jesus Christ, returned to earth, not on the clouds, but instead, reincarnated as a Chinese Tai Chi master," Liz answered, just like a star pupil.

Gasps and utterances of surprise, maybe even objections, were heard around the circle.

"Thank you, Liz, but giving that answer does not earn you brownie points, you know. Remember that you, like all of us, are simply a servant of the Most High God." Jing Sheng paused.

"And would it matter IF I AM the reincarnation of Jesus Christ?" Jing Sheng inquired of everyone.

"Maybe you need to set the record straight," answered an older white man, who looked fairly scholarly, yet sounded quite agitated. "At least, I hope you're here to say that Christians got pretty messed up along the way. I can't stand organized religion; it's done more damage to the human race and to the planet than anything else!"

"Thank you, Warren," Jing Sheng responded calmly to Warren's outburst. "Please remember, though, that while Christians have often gone astray, killing in the name of God, and denigrating the worth of the natural world to the point of near catastrophe, nonetheless, Christianity has done a lot of good for people's souls."

"Well, they'd better start showing it, before they ruin the planet and kill off everyone they think is destined for hell!" Warren just couldn't let go of his point. *It was, after all, a good point*, Liz thought.

"While that is a good point, Warren," Jing Sheng replied as though he could hear Liz's thoughts, "all of our opinions about others must be expressed with love and understanding, or else we also are judging them and in effect damning them to hell as well."

With that answer, it became apparent to everyone that Jing Sheng truly was a spiritual Master, and therefore someone nobody wanted to cross for fear of looking foolish, as Warren had, despite his good point.

"We are gathered here to begin a world-wide movement to raise the consciousness of humankind so that, together, we can save the planet and ourselves from both physical and spiritual extinction." Jing Sheng spoke with authority, as though this was the most natural and obvious thing to do.

"Why Kalamazoo?" Sylvia, one of Liz's massage therapists, wondered aloud. "Why would you start a world-wide movement in a little city like Kalamazoo?"

"Good question, Sylvia," Jing Sheng affirmed. "Kalamazoo, as you know, in its original Native American language, means 'boiling water,' so it is an apt name for a movement that seeks to stop global warming, don't you think?"

"Oh, yes," Sylvia sighed.

"And also, there are both wisdom and energy here in Kalamazoo that seek to preserve life in its many forms, as evident in the numerous preserves around town. There's also a movement already to work together across racial and gender boundaries. There are many people in the Kalamazoo area who already know the importance of letting go of their egos in order to accomplish a greater good. These three aspects of wisdom: care for creation, celebration of diversity, and setting aside of ego in favor of divine love, constitute the essential components for our movement.

"Furthermore, the only way this movement will succeed is by achieving a sense of unity among human beings. In Kalamazoo, so many people already understand the fundamental concept of unity in human existence: we are one. Kalamazoo has the Kalamazoo Promise; Kalamazoo has an ordinance that seeks fairness for all people including gays and lesbians; Kalamazoo has pastors and NAACP leaders and organizations that reach across racial and religious differences. This community models for the world that we are not fully human until we live in one community in which all people are valued, and all people have opportunities to live well, be well, and do well."

Jing Sheng smiled, looking around the circle at everyone. "That is God's idea, and God desires that community for the whole world."

"Well, what are you expecting us to do?" asked an older, white lady with wild, white hair and a garish, multi-colored wool sweater.

"What are you willing to do?" answered Jing Sheng. "Wanda, what are you willing to do to help save the earth?"

"I have thought for fifty years that we all need to live in communes so that we'll save space and use fewer resources," Wanda proclaimed. "I'm willing to live in a commune – is anyone else?"

"Ooh, I like that idea," Liz found herself chiming in. "I've always wanted to build a commune."

"Several of you are neighbors," Jing Sheng observed. "I chose you because I was thinking that you could combine your homes and yards to create a commune especially since your homes are near Kleinstuck Preserve."

"What a great idea!" Wanda exclaimed.

"Yes, but that means that you will need to get rid of many belongings, and invite people to live in your homes, and tend your gardens together," Jing Sheng pointed out.

"We could be the Kalamazoo Commune," Wanda exclaimed again, obviously excited.

Liz worried a little about setting some rules or something so that everyone could get along.

"Jing Sheng?" she asked hesitantly.

"Yes, Liz?"

"Could you help us set some guidelines that everyone would have to agree to in order to live together peacefully and preservingly, if I may coin a word for taking care of the environment?"

"Of course, Liz," Jing Sheng assured her. "Let's set a meeting for this Saturday for all those who would like to try communal living. Jerry, would you please get word in the Gazette, so that the meeting is open to the community?"

"Sure, Jing Sheng," replied an older African American gentleman.

"What else can we do?" Darnell asked, since he wasn't yet convinced about living in a commune with a bunch of white people.

"Find some faith, Darnell. We're building the kingdom of heaven on earth, and you're going to have to trust that it will work, or there will be no kingdom," Jing Sheng answered Darnell's unspoken doubts more than his spoken words. No doubt, Jing Sheng's answer confronted other people's lack of faith as well.

"Does everyone understand that this is going to take all you've got?" Jing Sheng addressed the whole group. "Your faith, your patience, your ability to stay spiritually-centered, your resources, your time, and everything you've worked for so hard in life. Just like the rich young ruler, whom Christ told to go and sell all of his things 2,000 years ago, some of you are going to have to give up a lot. All of you will have to give up fear.

"Some of you will have to give up possessions and possessiveness. Remember, all good gifts come from God, and so all good gifts are meant to be shared. In the meantime, everyone please take a look at your belongings to see what can be sold, what can be shared, and what can be thrown out. It will be good to travel more lightly in this world."

Jing Sheng must have realized that that amount of spiritual teaching was enough for everyone to try to absorb for the day. It was almost one o'clock; time for Darnell and others to get back to work as well.

"Time to break. Everyone please take a deep breath and just sigh it out. Breathe out your fear; breathe in God's love. Now, go forth in the light and love of God, and trust that this is real, and that all will be well." Jing Sheng bowed in Namaste.

Liz and a few others bowed in Namaste as well. The room cleared.

Liz realized that she needed to pay attention to the needs and activities of the wellness center, but she wished she could just sit and talk with Jing Sheng.

"After dinner," Jing Sheng suggested in answer to her thoughts. *Why not dinner?* She wondered as she replied "Okay."

Just then, Daniel came back, standing in the doorway, and asked, "Am I interrupting anything?"

"No, I was waiting for you to return," Jing Sheng answered and then added, "I am just leaving."

"Could I interest you in having dinner with me at the Oak Centre Bistro?" Daniel looked at Liz with his god-like face beaming a positive glow towards her.

"Tonight?" was all Liz could manage.

"Sure, if you're available around 7?" Daniel raised his eyebrows and smiled.

"Yes, I guess I am. I just have to meet Jing Sheng later," Liz answered.

"Can I pick you up here, or would you prefer to meet at the Bistro?"

Thinking that she had only just met Daniel, Liz realized that normally she played it safe, so she answered that she would prefer to meet him at the Bistro.

"Sounds great. I'll see you at 7," Daniel smiled and exited.

Liz was alone with her thoughts. *Wow, I haven't been on a date in two years. Wait, where does he work? Oh, yeah, he owns the local bookstore. Wow, that's cool. Daniel...oh, I forgot his last name. Maybe Jing Sheng remembers. Wow, he's so good-looking!*

At 6:00 p.m., Liz headed home to pay attention to Comet and Picasso, and then change into some clothes that were more suitable to dinner, or a date, or whatever was about to happen.

Wait, she thought, *maybe Daniel isn't really interested in me; maybe he just wants to get closer to Jing Sheng, and he thinks he can accomplish that by getting closer to me. Oh, why can't men make their intentions clear up front, so there's no doubting, wondering, or feeling insecure involved? Oh, I guess the feeling insecure part is my responsibility. But, he's so gorgeous!*

When Liz walked into the Oak Centre Bistro, Daniel was sitting at the bar up front, with a glass of white wine in hand. He immediately stood up, reached for Liz's hand, and held it gently.

"I'm so glad to see you!" Daniel exclaimed, smiling broadly.

"Thank you. I'm really glad to see you, too." Liz felt like a school girl, grinning from ear-to-ear. She tugged at her dress as if that might possibly improve her appearance somehow.

"They've got a table open for us at the back. Why don't we go sit down, and we can order you a drink from there, unless you need one now?" Daniel was smooth and in control.

"No, thank you. I meditate; I can manage without alcohol just fine, although I might enjoy a glass of red wine with dinner."

They sat down, enjoyed discovering that they both were vegetarians, and then ordered two different dishes so they could share. After ordering, they all of a sudden both looked up, and really looked into each other's eyes. Liz felt mesmerized.

"Wow!" Daniel laughed. "You have stunning eyes!"

"Thank you, so do you," Liz managed. *So, I guess this is more than just about Jing Sheng,* she mused.

"Where are you from originally?" Daniel inquired.

Liz explained her upbringing in Malaysia, then asked Daniel where he was from.

"Well, my father was Greek. He and my mother met when she traveled to Greece after World War II, because she had served in the Red Cross in Europe, and then decided to see a little more of the world before returning home to New York. I grew up in Greece and then just outside of Detroit in Farmington Hills. My father owned a law firm there, and my mother was head of the ER nursing staff at Botsford Hospital. I studied law at University of Michigan, and opened my law practice here, because I yearned for more wide open spaces along with less of the hard-driving competition of big city life."

"What kind of law do you practice?" Liz wondered out loud.

"Family law – I handle divorces, custody issues, wills and trusts, that sort of thing." I went into law not only because of my father, but also because I realized that lawyers can make such a difference in people's lives right when they're going through the worst times. I decided that, for me, practicing law would be about practicing compassion. It's not easy, but it can sometimes be done. I opened up the bookstore just as a hobby and community service." Daniel smiled, gazing happily into Liz's eyes.

"So, how did you get drawn to Jing Sheng?" Liz asked.

"Well, I've been studying Eastern spirituality ever since I got divorced myself ten years ago. After the divorce, I traveled to India to find answers to the mysteries of life that suddenly seemed to become so much more important when I found myself alone and pushing forty. That's partly why I opened the bookstore. When Jing Sheng showed up at the bookstore, I found myself really drawn to him, although I had no idea why. Maybe I intuitively sensed that he is Jesus Christ. Although, did you notice that he did not exactly say that he is Jesus Christ?"

"Yes, I noticed that he said, 'IF'. But it doesn't really matter to me, because I know, for myself, beyond the shadow of a doubt that Hu Jing Sheng is Jesus Christ." Liz sounded completely confident.

"Really? And how do you know that?" Daniel inquired with eyebrows raised.

Liz explained about her vision of Jesus during her Reiki attunement, along with how Jing Sheng made reference to what he told her in that vision.

"Well, if this isn't the most fascinating thing that could have ever happened in my life." Daniel spent a moment seeming contemplative.

They talked for a long time over dinner, until Liz remembered that she was supposed to meet Jing Sheng. She and Daniel hurriedly and therefore awkwardly parted ways. Liz then rushed home, hoping that Jing Sheng would not be too upset.

When she arrived home, she found Jing Sheng and Comet playing ball in the front yard, waiting for her to arrive. Comet didn't care that it was getting dark out; she would chase a ball in complete darkness if she could.

Liz greeted them tiredly, and Jing Sheng followed her into the living room, where Liz asked Jing Sheng questions about life and spirituality and why he chose her and the others.

"What I really want to know is if reincarnation is real, because it doesn't fit with the Christianity that is taught in churches." Liz's doubts seemed self-evident to her, but then she was surrounded by a culture that treated life as though you really do "only go around once."

"Actually," Jing Sheng replied, "Reincarnation was a part of the beliefs of early Christians, including Jesus himself. You may have noticed references in the Bible to John the Baptist as the reincarnation of Elijah. In the gospel of Luke, there is also mention of the spirit of Elijah on John as a baby in the womb as well. Finally, in the letter of James, who was actually "the Lord's brother" as Paul refers to him, he mentions the wheel of birth, as it is correctly, though not often, translated.

"The concept of reincarnation was accepted by many early Christians, until the doctrine of the immortality of souls, especially as pre-existing before birth, was declared heresy by a church council. Historical records of the concept of reincarnation in the Middle East are limited because of the burning of the library at Alexandria. Christians as well as Muslims have destroyed and repressed both writings and knowledge that might disagree with their sacred texts. Too often, that has included killing people, as in the case of the notorious Inquisition."

"So did Jesus really teach about reincarnation, then? And if so, what did he teach?" Liz inquired.

"Ah, Jesus was operating in a context in which Jewish religious leaders had created such an unjust system of redemption, along with severe judgment on the sick, poor, and marginalized members of society, that Jesus lovingly focused his message on loving one's neighbors as the route to spiritual perfection.

"That is, indeed, the most loving route to incarnating God, who is Love, on earth. When Jesus mentioned statements such as "I AM the Way" or "I AM the Truth," he meant that the Christ-Consciousness which can arise within us all is the Way and the Truth. The Christ-Consciousness, or Buddha-Mind, is the Tao, or the Way of Enlightenment. Jesus brought fullness to the Self-Realization of God on earth, by emphasizing the incarnation of divine love through the unconditional love of others. He meant for his followers to do the same."

Liz reflected that Jing Sheng seemed oblivious to the verse John 3:16 that so many Christians love to spout as proving that Jesus is the only way to heaven. Always worried that they might be right, she finally got up the nerve to ask: "What about John 3:16?"

"For God so loved the world that God sent God's only child into the world that whoever believes in Christ shall not perish but have eternal life – that verse?" Jing Sheng rattled off his version of the text.

"Yes, but Bibles never use gender inclusive language for both God and Christ the way you did – that was awesome!" Liz glowed.

"Bibles are written by men who fear the sacred feminine, and believe that Jesus only spoke of a heavenly Father. However, if they could go back in time, those same men would discover that Jesus gave thanks for our Earthly Mother and her angels of the air, water, and sunshine.[2]

Again, it is the birth of God through each person that gives rise to the Christ-Consciousness within, and that, of course, brings salvation, or wholeness, which leads to eternal life. The very next verse is that God sent Christ into the world not to condemn the world, but so that the world might be saved. This aspect of Christ was manifest in Jesus, but the point is to let that Enlightened Mind manifest within us all."

Jing Sheng's answers created in Liz a sense of completion, a sense that life really did make sense somehow, even in so vast a universe. She realized that those people who, like her, responded right away to following Jing Sheng were spiritual seekers who cared about the earth, and who had not found answers in conventional religion.

By the time they finished their discussion, Liz was so tired, she yawned 'good night' in Jing Sheng's direction, and then dragged herself up the stairs to bed. Jing Sheng let himself out.

Liz took her tired body and sleepy head to bed. *Maybe I'll see his miracles in action and everything will somehow make sense*, Liz thought longingly. She fell asleep with a smile on her face, thinking about Daniel and remembering that giddy feeling of looking into each other's eyes.

♥ ♥ ♥

---

[2] For this concept, I am indebted to <u>The Essene Gospel of Peace</u>, edited by Edmond Bordeaux Szekely.

7. O MY LORD, PLEASE SEND SOMEONE ELSE

AVOIDING SUCCESS, LIKE AVOIDING RESPONSIBILITY, ALLOWS FEAR TO ROB YOU OF THE INNER GIFT OF YOURSELF TO YOURSELF – THAT PART OF YOU WHICH IS A GOD-GIVEN MIRACLE OF BEING AND OF POTENTIAL BEING.

The next day was Friday, Liz's 'day off,' if you ever really get one when you own a business. She was sleeping in – well, drinking tea in bed and re-reading her favorite inspirational book and then settling in to doze off again. She started wondering what would happen if she introduced Jing Sheng to her son, who was so smart in a philosophical kind of way that he made Aristotle look average.

Cliff wouldn't be intimidated by Jing Sheng, and Liz decided she would have to let both her kids (who were actually young adults) decide for themselves who Jing Sheng is. She knew her daughter would be interested, but not want to admit it.

Just then, the doorbell rang. Comet ran barking to answer the door, and Liz realized she was not yet dressed. She hurriedly threw on something – not entirely decent, and descended the stairs as fast as she could. Jing Sheng was standing inside the front door when she got to the entryway.

"Has Comet learned how to open doors?" She asked, lamely.

Jing Sheng chuckled, "It is easier to walk on water than to teach a dog to act like a human being, because dogs have a higher purpose. Dogs are here to demonstrate unconditional love to folks who often cannot grasp what it means."

"I'm sorry I was not expecting you – this is my day off," Liz apologized.

"Perfect. Then we are free to go around town and begin to teach people the importance of life on earth." Jing Sheng asserted.

"We-ell, I need to rest, and I have to clean house, and I have to pay bills," Liz said timidly.

"Yes, you do, but that can wait," Jing Sheng insisted.

"I see. Well, do you mind if I take a shower, eat breakfast, meditate, pray and exercise, the way I usually do, before we go?" Liz asked.

"I cannot stop you." Jing Sheng answered, tilting his head downwards, but smiling peacefully as always.

"What do you want me to do?" Liz realized she should ask.

"I would like you to hurry up," Jing Sheng said, smiling and laughing.

An hour-and-a-half later, they got in Liz's car and headed downtown.

"Where are we going?" Liz asked.

"Let's go to the mayor's office," Jing Sheng replied cheerfully.

"You're kidding!" Liz sputtered. "You know you'll need an appointment to see the mayor!"

"We shall see," Jing Sheng said calmly.

They arrived; Liz struggled with where to park, feeling ungracious, out-of-the-flow, and practically stumbling over her own feet with uncertainty and anxious feelings.

"I thought you meditated," Jing Sheng remarked.

"I did."

"Well, since you are so nervous, why don't you breathe deeply, relax, and trust God and the universe, and get back into the divine flow of life?" Jing Sheng suggested.

Liz breathed, prayed in her head, and looked around to try to become one with whatever was happening – whatever was needed now.

They arrived outside the mayor's office, and Jing Sheng addressed the mayor's administrative assistant.

"Excuse me, will you please tell Mayor Bliss that Hu Jing Sheng would like to see him?"

"Mr. ...?"

"Mr. Hu," Jing Sheng offered helpfully for the obviously non-Chinese speaking assistant.

"Mr. Hu, I don't believe that you have an appointment," was the assistant's courteous but firm reply.

"You are correct; however, I am hoping that Mayor Bliss will grant me a moment to speak with him." Jing Sheng replied.

"One moment please." The assistant, whose desk name placard identified her as Cindy Hartwell, spoke into the phone, "Mr. Mayor, excuse me, but there's a gentleman here named Mr. Hu who would like to see you for a moment. I don't know, sir, but he is quite persuasive. Yes, sir." She turned and addressed them, "You may enter." Her face looked truly puzzled.

Perplexed, Liz whispered, "How did you do that?"

"Mindspeak," Jing Sheng replied. "Soul-to-soul communication. You'll learn it – you already know how to, really, but you haven't used it the many ways you could."

They knocked on the mayor's door, listened for permission to come in, and entered.

Mayor Bliss rose from his seat and came around his desk to shake hands with them.

"How do you do?" He asked, shaking hands with each one.

"I'm Hu Jing Sheng, and this is Liz Cooper. Thank you for your time, Mayor Bliss."

"Certainly, certainly. Have a seat, please. What brings you to my office today?"

When he got around his desk and started to sit down, he jumped right back up.

"What the -!" He cried out, as he saw Jing Sheng levitating in the cross-legged lotus pose just above the leather arm chair on which he was supposed to be sitting.

"I've come *in answer* to your prayers. I understand that you have been asking God to send you someone who can help you figure out how to deal with the multitude of problems facing this community today. I heard you praying in church, and I am glad to meet a man of such great faith." Jing Sheng smiled solemnly.
"How could you possible know what I prayed in church?" Mayor Bliss sputtered.

"Well, that will be just between you and me and Liz, Mr. Mayor, but I think you know to whom you addressed your prayer on Sunday."

The mayor sank into his chair, muttering, "It's not possible, it's not possible. You're …?"

"I AM WHO I AM," Jing Sheng replied. "I'm Hu Jing Sheng, and I've returned to earth to help humankind shift to Christ-consciousness so that it will save all life on the planet rather than destroying it."

"You don't sound like you do in the Bible," Mayor Bliss objected.

"No, of course not. That was then, and this is now. Why would anyone say exactly the same things to different people living in different times with different spiritual needs? But in case you need further proof, I forgive you for what you did last week, although you really need to take your wife out to dinner and start treating her better. Do I make myself clear?" Jing Sheng spoke calmly but with a power like no one either Liz or Mayor Bliss had ever heard before.

Mayor Bliss stared at him, flabbergasted and open-mouthed, hemming and hawing before he could manage to sputter, "Of course, of course." Mayor Bliss cleared his throat and pulled himself together. "Now what are we going to do for this city?"

"Well, first, I suggest you call a press conference and announce that you would like to have a contest for the best environmental solutions for zoning, transportation, building and energy usage possible for this city. And second, I suggest you announce that this city will become the city of Future Promise – a place where people live in harmony with the environment. I know that you work with other city commissioners to start initiatives, but please start immediately with the ones who will automatically support these ideas, and let them know there will be funding."

"I'll have to lay a lot of groundwork before I can just announce those things," the Mayor replied. "And *will* there be funding?"

"Have faith, please, about the funding. While you work on the groundwork, I'll work with you on your spiritual life. First, I'm asking you to pray daily – at least in the morning and at night, and preferably every time you're confused or uncertain in between. And if you don't hear God's answers to your prayers, just call me." Jing Sheng finally let himself lower slowly and sit in the leather chair.

He rose, invited Liz to leave with him, and bade the mayor good-day. Mayor Bliss sank back into his chair and stared straight ahead in a daze.

As she and Jing Sheng walked out to the car, Liz felt uncomfortable.

"You know," she said, "Following you around like this I look like your bimbo or something. I really don't like doing the dumb blonde routine here. I know I have brown hair, well, grayish brown hair, but I just don't want people thinking you're sleeping with me."

"Liz, joy of my soul, people may think whatever they want. You are with me as my assistant, are you not?"

"I guess so, but it's kind of embarrassing. I don't want people to think I'm crazy, you know."

"I do know that, Liz, and I have no fear that anyone will think you're crazy except people who also think that I am crazy. Won't that keep you in good company?"

Liz had an 'ah-ha' moment. She realized that, if even Jesus had people think bad things of him, as they did, no doubt people would think bad things of her and Jing Sheng.

"Well, if these were Biblical days, I'd be in the best company I could possibly have!"

Jing Sheng smiled, and bowed slightly in Namaste to his assistant.

"So where are we going?" Liz asked as she opened her car door.

Jing Sheng sat down in the passenger seat and directed her: "Let's go pick up Darnell from work, and take him with us to a lunch speaking engagement I have with the Rotary."

As Liz pulled the car up in the entrance of Bronson Hospital, Darnell walked out the front door, waved, and climbed into the back seat.

"Hi, Darnell, were you expecting us?" Liz asked with a smile.

"You know, Liz, Jing Sheng just has a way of letting me know where we are going today. You know?" Darnell shook his head in wonderment.

"I do know," replied Liz.

"So, where am I driving you two gentlemen?" Liz glanced the question at Jing Sheng, who sat with his eyes closed and hands folded, appearing to be in deep meditation or prayer right there in the front seat of the car.

"Please take us to the restaurant beside the downtown hotel."

Liz was pretty sure she knew what Jing Sheng meant by that, so she headed towards the parking garage across from the Radisson.

They found the Rotary luncheon, where they were warmly welcomed.

I wonder if they will feel so warm and welcoming towards us when we leave, Liz thought.

Stop worrying. She heard Jing Sheng's thought/command in her head. *Okay.*

They sat down and ate lunch, which is often challenging for three vegetarians eating American cuisine as someone else's guests. Darnell had apparently made the arrangements, and so it all worked quite smoothly.

When it was time for Jing Sheng to speak, the Rotary president introduced Liz as a local business owner, and invited her to introduce Jing Sheng.

Oh-oh, thought Liz. *I haven't practiced this yet.*

"I'd like to introduce my friend and mentor, Mr. Jing Sheng Hu. If we were in China, I would introduce him as Hu Jing Sheng. Jing Sheng is a Tai Chi master who studied at the Wudang monastery in Hubei Province. He has come to America on a mission to help us save the planet from global warming, or climate change, if you prefer to call it that. His mission is called 'Exodus 2012' which is both a verse in the Bible, and a remembrance that the Mayans thought that life on earth might end in 2012."

Liz sat down as Jing Sheng stood up, and bowed in Namaste. Applause politely greeted him in response. Wearing his black Tai Chi uniform and looking very Chinese, he could get away with bowing in Namaste, and people just chalked it up to him being foreign, rather than questioning the spiritual significance of his bow. Of course, Liz and Darnell knew better, recognizing Namaste as a bow in recognition of the presence of God in the person or people to whom one is bowing.

Jing Sheng smiled, and explained the meaning of Exodus 2012. Polite smiles faded around the room; puzzled and concerned faces took their place.

Suddenly, a wave of peaceful, loving energy settled on the room like a big security blanket dropped out of the sky by God. Jing Sheng stood beaming his sunshine-y smile at everyone, hands folded in front of him, looking at each person as if he knew the true depths of their soul. *Oh, he probably does*, thought Liz.

Some people sighed, faces relaxed, and Jing Sheng continued.

"We have a responsibility to care for the earth; she is our mother. Scientists speak of the delicate balance of nature, of homeostasis and the web of life. What biologists study is the very sensitive nature of life on earth, balanced carefully in a harmonious blending of taking life, renewing life, and sharing habitats which have to be maintained just as they are for all their native species to survive.

"Survival is a spiritual issue. In the story of Adam and Eve in the Garden of Eden, we have a beautiful metaphor for human life on earth. Metaphorically speaking, God did not put Adam and Eve in the Garden of Eden to despoil it. The story tells us that their sinfulness led to their being expelled from the Garden of Eden. This expulsion represents the fact that human willfulness leads us into living out of balance with the garden of life on earth. It is our responsibility to restore the Garden of Eden, and to learn how to live there harmoniously once more. That is the purpose of Exodus 2012, to call us all to live in spiritual harmony with one another, and with all life on earth, so that we may live long in the land.

"I will be speaking soon on national television to unveil the full mission. In the meantime, please contact either Darnell or Liz for more information. I believe they have fliers they would like to hand out."

Jing Sheng bowed in Namaste; people clapped politely if somewhat uncertainly, and Liz and Darnell passed out fliers. Two or three people seemed very interested; a couple of people seemed to feel drawn to Jing Sheng, wanting to shake his hand and saying things like, "I feel as though I know you, somehow." Darnell and Liz both knew what that meant. They'd be seeing those people again soon enough. Darnell announced a talk that was taking place that night; several people nodded their heads as though they would be there.

♥ ♥ ♥

Later that evening, Liz picked up Jing Sheng to take him to the local health food store which had a classroom where guest speakers are invited to speak from the community and even from around the state. The usual entry charge is $10, and tonight, the room was packed. Liz had no idea how Jing Sheng had gotten the publicity. She suspected that, while she was Jing Sheng's chauffeur, Darnell was his publicity and scheduling specialist.

"Good evening, I have come to speak with you about the importance of allowing a new spirituality to lead us in saving the earth from global warming. I have come to help us synthesize both Eastern and Western spiritualities into a unified whole; that is the only way we can make our planet whole. Every right approach to salvation, whether of ourselves, or of the earth, begins with right spiritual understanding. We will begin with the importance of understanding who we are and who we are meant to become.

"We are spiritual beings embodied in this lifetime as human beings. We are incarnated souls, with personalities, bodies, and egos. There is a tension between incarnation and dissolving of the self – the ego self. Buddhists understand correctly that humans need to dissolve their egos into nothingness. The Christian West needs to learn this lesson from the spiritual masters of the East. And yet, the Christian West correctly understands the importance of the incarnation – that is, God coming to earth and dwelling in the midst of human life, to bring wholeness, to alleviate suffering, and to enlighten with the truth. In other words, the incarnation of divine love is a necessary aspect of human life.

"When we combine the spiritual philosophies of East and West, we dissolve ego into nothingness, and we merge our own consciousness with divine consciousness. We then incarnate that divine consciousness here on earth. There is no longer us and God, there is only the All."

"Do you mean that those bottles of Dr. Bronner's Peppermint soap have it right? That God is the All?" A listener interjected flippantly.

"Oh, flippant one, how God loves your sense of humor, but rather than letting it take you closer to God, you wrongly think that God doesn't like your humor, and so you substitute it for God.

'The answer to your question is that truth may be found anywhere, but always in measured doses, and Dr. Bronner fails to recognize the sacred feminine, does he not? How can All be All if it is only masculine and not also feminine?"

Waves of love for Jing Sheng as her ultimate feminist hero washed over Liz with such force that tears streamed down her face in gratitude for his taking on the issue so directly for her, and all other women.

"One must dissolve ego, including that clinging one is tempted to make to one's own gifts, such as humor, and instead one must see that all ability comes from God. Letting go of taking credit is the biggest chore of getting rid of ego. Few people truly want to give God credit for who they are, but God is the Source of all abilities, all strength, all goodwill, including that powerful force called a 'positive attitude.'"

"Oh, come on," objected a philosophy Ph. D. student present in the crowd, "Each of us makes choices out of our own free will. It makes no sense to say that we have free will and that God enables us to have abilities. When I make a choice, it is my own mind that makes the choice, and I freely choose it. No one makes me, and no one enables me. I just choose it."

"And do you have everything figured out, including God and what God does? What makes sense to you is what you know with your rational mind. Rational minds are wonderful things – God did an amazing job creating such wonderful repositories of conscious thought. And yet, with a rational mind, we cannot know God. With a rational mind, we can only posit free will, we cannot know it or do anything but posit how it comes to us.

"With our spiritual insight, however, we can know that God provides not only the free will for us to make choices, but also the energy coursing through our neurons, through our neurotransmitters, even through the calcium and other ions that cross over membranes during the firing of neurons as we make decisions with our brains. God designed the very processes by which we become human, express our humanity, and pass it on to the next generation. God's energy is part of these processes all the time.

"It helps if one does not assume that God is separate from the process. The kingdom of God is at hand all the time, because God is always present in every level of reality."

"Oh, really, must you quote that Bible crap about kingdoms of God? How offensive that is to us women. Heavenly Fathers with no Heavenly Mother and some masculine king dominating us all the time. Christianity is nothing but a boatload of patriarchal oppression!" The woman speaking stood up and shook her fist as she continued, "women have taken enough oppression at the hands of men through their religions. It's time we women had religions of our own. That's why I'm a Wiccan! We protect ourselves – no male macho power structure needed!"

"Is it any more acceptable for you to reject men and followers of male-dominated religions than it is for them to reject you and your path? Good for you, though, for taking religion into your own hands but better yet that you place your religion in the hands of the Infinite Divine. The Divine Infinite holds in its hands unconditional love for all people. So it is that, on the path to Self-Realization, or union with the Divine, it is important that *one causes no offense*. Just as men have caused offense by subjecting women, you also cause offense when you deny the spiritual truths which have freely evolved within the male-dominated religions, despite their patriarchy.

"The phrase 'God is no respecter of persons' means that no matter who is looking down upon whom, God sees all people as needing to evolve to a higher consciousness, because only God is God. It also means that God blesses all people equally, despite any egotistical consideration of worthiness or unworthiness."

Silence ensued for a few moments. Some felt humbled. Some felt confused and afraid. The woman felt humiliated, but outwitted by this obvious spiritual master. She realized that Jing Sheng had nailed her with the truth that she looked down on others for their patriarchy. That was her spiritual progress for the day. Some people were embarrassed by the confrontation. Others actually listened and received tremendous spiritual insight.

Jing Sheng continued, "Jesus often said, 'let those with ears to hear, hear.' What he meant by that is that not everyone is ready to hear a deeper level of truth. In the universe, there are many levels of truth, just as there are many different frequencies of waves of light. Particles of light blip momentarily into existence – that is what we perceive as the reality of being, although it is the wave behind the particle that comes from the light source. Just so, all being comes in different wavelengths from the one true Source. So, reality has different frequencies of being, which are different levels of truth, and each individual is in a different place from which they perceive a particular level of truth. The rainbow prism represents different perspectives and abilities to perceive various aspects of Truth."

A woman sitting near the front quietly asked, "Why do you quote Jesus so much?"

Jing Sheng replied, "Jesus often told people, 'I AM.' Just so, I AM WHO I AM."

The woman, again speaking quietly, responded, "Are you saying that you are Jesus Christ?"

Jing Sheng repeated, "I AM WHO I AM."

"Hey! That was God's name given in the book of Exodus," cried out one young man. "Are you saying that you are God?"

Jing Sheng calmly, patiently, enunciating every word carefully, replied, "I AM WHO I AM. Let those who have ears to hear, hear the truth. Let those who have eyes to see, see the truth. Let those who hunger and thirst after righteousness be filled."

"I am the President of the local Association of Atheists. We work for freedom of thought and speech in the community. How can you possibly make all these claims for and about God as though you know that God is real? And if you think you are God, you're just crazy."

"Have I forced anyone to think a certain way? No, of course not." Jing Sheng answered the man's hinted at accusation, then continued, "Atheists have generally done a great job rejecting a lot of bad ideas about who God is. As for certainty about God, our consciousness is either open to the divine, or it is closed. Do you have an open mind?"

"Of course," the man vehemently answered.

"How is it that you have an open mind, and yet you have closed your mind to God? Do you know for certain that there is no God?"

"God makes no sense – Marx was right that religion is the opiate of the people!" Angry at someone, or at his life, the man raised his voice at Jing Sheng.

Calmly, quietly, Jing Sheng spoke: "The only way to allow God to make sense in your mind is to allow God into your life." Jing Sheng paused, then continued, "Religion has sometimes functioned as an opiate, but also sometimes as the motivation towards greater justice.

"There is also a difference between religion and true spirituality. The point of spirituality is to grow close enough to God so as to incarnate God with one's mind, one's heart, one's soul, one's words, and one's actions. Since God is love, the point of life then is to celebrate love, to circulate love, and to incarnate love. *Everyone* who does that, embodies God within themselves, and births God into the world."

There was silence. Someone breathed an awed, "Wow!" There was a collective sigh that passed around the room. Somehow, the energy of love swooped around the room with Jing Sheng's words, and touched everyone's heart with warmth and affection.

"I invite you, therefore, to celebrate love, to circulate love, and to incarnate love . . . Thank you, everyone, for being here. That is all for today." Jing Sheng bowed in Namaste. The crowd responded, some with Namaste, some with applause, some with both.

"Wow! What a mystery man you've found, Liz!" whispered her friend Beth in her ear. "Do you get to keep him? He's hot, too!"

"Beth, stop drooling – you can't become a spiritual master with questions like that!" Liz wavered between agreeing with Beth, and knowing that something far more important than anything else in her life was going on here.

People were crowding around Jing Sheng, hoping to get a word with him, but Jing Sheng simply bowed, excused himself, and came straight to Liz. "We must go now," he said.

"Okay, I'll get the car, unless you'd like to walk with me around the block to the parking lot."

"We will walk," Jing Sheng affirmed.

A wise master knows when the students need to struggle with their own questions, rather than clinging to the master, and so Jing Sheng left the building with Liz, leaving behind some puzzled people, some true students of divine spirit lost in wonder, and a couple of jaded people just as angry as ever, because life had delivered them salmon instead of beef, as it were. Self-mastery over our thoughts may truly be the hardest lesson of all.

"I just can't do this anymore, Jing Sheng," Liz blurted out as she drove him home. "I don't know who I am anymore, and I don't know why you gave me the gift of healing; I'm afraid to use it. No one wants me poking in their business healing them, anyway, and I can't just make an announcement: 'everyone who wants a healing, please line up.' Why did you choose me anyway?"

"Are you learning anything?" Jing Sheng calmly breathed the question at her.

"Of course! But who wants to learn this way when it makes you look like a crazy person who's starting a cult!"

"What are you learning, Liz?"

Liz realized she was going to have to center herself to stay at a soul-level of discussion with him. She breathed, noticing her breath, feeling grateful for her breath, choosing to be calm, choosing to accept 'what is' along with the gift of breath.

"I'm learning all sorts of things about God, you, myself, others, the universe, faith…"

"That is why you are with me, Liz. Of all the people I could have chosen to help me start this mission, which is a mission, not a cult, I needed you because you learn spiritual truths like a sponge soaking up water. Nothing is more important for this mission to succeed than finding people who will learn, and who can then understand what it is all about. To do that, some people have to be willing to understand me, a task which my original disciples found very challenging indeed."

"Why Darnell?" Liz wondered out loud.

"Do you not think that is between me and Darnell?" Jing Sheng replied.

"Well, of course, I just wondered. I mean, it seems as though you expect Darnell and me to work together, and I just can't see that we have much in common except a strong desire to be close to you."

"That is all any of my disciples ever need in order to work together: a strong desire to be close to me, and to become closer to God, who is love. You and Darnell need to learn to work together. Call him, please, tonight."

"Okay, I will," Liz answered sleepily, wondering how she was going to add Jing Sheng and his agendas into her life. *Oh, yeah, I have the gift of healing; maybe it will help me by healing me so I need less sleep. I'll try that later before I go to bed.*

Pray for what you need only; all else is greed. God knows what you want, and joyfully grants loving requests to God's daughters and sons; you will be blessed by letting God know what you prefer, but asking devotedly only for what you need. Jing Sheng's thought-lecture passed into Liz's sleepy mind like a wise dream floating through her consciousness.

♥ ♥ ♥

8. AARON, GO INTO THE WILDERNESS TO MEET MOSES

TO TRUST ONE ANOTHER, ONE MUST LOOK FOR GOD IN EACH OTHER. TO WORK TOGETHER, EACH ONE MUST CONFESS THEIR EGO-SELF IN EACH AND EVERY DIFFICULT INTERACTION, AND LET GO OF ALL THAT IS NOT LOVE.

Liz managed to call Darnell and they agreed to meet for lunch after the Saturday planning session for communal living.

Saturday morning started out gray and chilly; not an uncommon start for a day in Michigan. Liz bundled up in layers topped by a cheerfully bright sweater and some yoga pants, and headed out the door quite early to lead her Saturday morning yoga class. After that, she had a healing scheduled at 9 a.m., so she would just be able to make the 11:00 a.m. meeting. She trusted that Jing Sheng somehow knew her schedule, (mysteriously enough, he always did), and that she could just show up by herself.

Fifty people filled the room when she arrived. *This many people would like to live communally and we just had no clue about each other, or maybe lacked commitment, until a Chinese Tai Chi master showed up and brought this out of us?! Oh, yeah, he's not just a Tai Chi master – he's Jesus Christ, who can, of course, do anything!* Taking a seat at the back of the room, Liz pondered in amazement this newly energized sense of commitment to communal living.

Jing Sheng went to the front of the room and invited everyone to get up and do a few stretches and breathing exercises. Then, he invited the Muslim Imam, who had also shown up, to pray. Next, he invited the Hindu woman to pray, then an African-American pastor (*probably Darnell's pastor*, Liz thought), then the Jewish rabbi, and last-but-not-least an Episcopalian priest, also a woman. Finally, Jing

Sheng invited everyone to bow in Namaste to God and to one another, and to have a seat.

Both he and the Hindu yogini[3] sat in lotus posture on their cushioned seats.

Liz kind of faded out of the conversation, feeling quite on overload, as Jing Sheng led a discussion of ideas that people had about how and where to live together communally. She glanced around the crowd, and discovered that Daniel was also there, although she had not managed to talk with him except briefly once after they ate dinner together. Now she really had trouble concentrating on the flow of the conversation as she sat dreamily thinking about Daniel.

Joy of my soul, Elizabeth, please let your mind stop wandering. We will need your input shortly. Liz heard Jing Sheng's plea as if it were a voice in her head, but oh, so quiet, just like that still, small voice in scripture. She looked at Hu Jing Sheng, blushed as his smiling eyes caught hers, and nodded.

She realized that they were discussing living arrangements as far as cooking together was concerned. Liz raised her hand.

"Could we suggest that the communal living respect the idea of being vegetarian, as a way of saving the planet?" She asked a little uncertainly when called upon by Jing Sheng.

"Excellent suggestion," responded Jing Sheng. "Can anyone explain to us why eating vegetarian is important for the planet?"

Daniel volunteered. Liz's heart did a flip, she blushed, and found

---

[3] A yogini is a woman yogi, or individual who seeks union with God through the practices of various types of yoga, which include meditation and selfless service.

herself hoping that maybe, just maybe, she had found herself a worthwhile companion.

"Eating vegetarian respects the energy of life. Eating lower on the food chain also preserves more food to be available for human consumption. If we feed grain to animals and then eat the animals, more land and grain and fuel are required to provide us food than if we just eat the grain directly ourselves, and raise fewer animals for food or milk or eggs. Also, the energy of Ahimsa, or non-violence, will bless us and the earth herself." Daniel sat down, bowing slightly in Namaste to Jing Sheng.

Ooohh – yes, a man after my own heart, Liz thought hopefully.

"Thank you, Daniel," Jing Sheng nodded and then turned towards the crazy-looking old white lady with yet another wild sweater. "So you see, Wanda, that the gardens which you would like us to plant will be so important – they save fuel and transport costs, reducing our carbon imprint, as well as respecting the natural balance of nature, eating locally, and growing only organic produce. This is all so important for the earth, as well as for the survival of human life on earth.

"We will also need meditation rooms. Liz, will you make your meditation room at Spring of Life Wellness Center available to anyone who lives communally at no charge?"

"Um, well, I'd be happy to, as long as I continue to have enough income streams to run the center," Liz answered, feeling guilty about sounding fearful and greedy.

"Liz, you will have more business than ever before, because people who live communally will need to get regular healings and do yoga together in order to maintain harmonious lifestyles together." Jing

Sheng tilted his head, smiling sadly at her for her fear-based greediness.

Liz bowed in Namaste to him, "As you command me, Jing Sheng, I will gladly do. Thank you." She felt both heart-warmed by Jing Sheng's call for generosity and harmony and like a freakish groupie on display at the same time.

"Please do this because I request it, and because you choose to do so of your own free will. What kind of God would want cookie-cutter followers who simply obey orders instead of offering variety and ingenuity in service to Divine Love?"

Murmurs of approval ran through the crowd. Next, they considered practical issues of how to decide who would live with whom, and came up with the idea of rotating living spaces, forming families together for two years, and then switching to a new home. That way, people could both get relief from each other's annoying habits, and stretch in new ways while living with people with a new set of habits that they might need to overcome.

By noon, Liz felt very ready to go get lunch with Darnell, who remained pretty quiet throughout the whole event. Liz noticed that only a few African-Americans showed up. Liz wondered if Darnell felt lonely. Then she realized that he was sitting next to a young man who seemed to be very good friends with Darnell. *Oh,* she thought, *maybe that explains it – could Darnell be gay?*

When the meeting ended, Liz found Darnell and his friend, and suggested that they both go to lunch with her. Darnell's friend started to object, but Liz said, "Wait, please, I have another friend I'd like to invite, and then there would be four of us. I'll be right back."

Liz rushed over to where Daniel was talking with the Hindu woman, said hello, and introduced herself to the woman, whose name was Rahima Patel. Some of us were just going to go to lunch together, would you both like to join us? Ms. Patel excused herself graciously, but Daniel accepted the invitation.

They walked back over to Darnell and his friend, and Liz gushed, "I'm so sorry, I forgot to introduce myself, I'm Liz." She offered her hand to Darnell's friend, who replied, "I'm Adam."

"Nice to meet you, Adam. This is Daniel; Daniel, this is Darnell." The men shook hands. "Where shall we eat, you guys?"

"How about the new Middle Eastern place on West Main – we can find vegetarian food there," suggested Daniel.

"Sounds great," said Liz. "Do you like Middle Eastern food, Darnell and Adam?"

"We love it," replied Adam.

Twenty minutes later, Liz, Darnell, Adam, and Daniel all sat eating hummus and pita bread.

"So, the reason we're here is that Jing Sheng wanted Darnell and me to talk," ventured Liz into the food-satisfied silence. "I think he wanted us to talk because I'm feeling very uncertain about my role here."

"Well, I feel uncertain also," Darnell responded.

"What do you mean?" Daniel asked.

"Who, me or Darnell?" Liz managed between mouthfuls.

"Both."

"Well, I feel like a freak at a side show. Sometimes I just follow Jing Sheng around like some kind of Bimbo, and I don't want people to think I'm his lover – that just seems all wrong, not that I think people would think I'm attractive enough or young enough, but I just don't want people to wonder." Liz blushed.

"And then, there's the fact that he tells me he gave me the ability to know what's wrong with people and to cure it instantly, but I haven't even tried to see if that's true, because I don't want to become a real freak in this sideshow, if you know what I mean." Liz glanced anxiously around the table, searching the men's faces to see if they understood her point-of-view; she felt definitely unsure about finding support.

"He gave you a gift that amazing and you don't want to use it?!" Darnell seemed flabbergasted.

"Jing Sheng has not given me any gift except the gift of acceptance, although, coming from him, that's huge," Darnell admitted somewhat sadly.

"I mean, I'd love some kind of supernatural gift, but I guess, now that I listen to you, I realize that would make me even more of a freak at a sideshow."

"Don't you think about yourself that way," Adam insisted. "You're the cats-meow in my book and if Jing Sheng accepts you, then you know God must think you're perfect just the way you are."

"I know, I just wish I didn't have to be so public. At some point, the issue is going to come up, like, probably tomorrow when he speaks in a church, and then I won't be able to hide, and who knows how big this is going to be? He plans to go on national TV."

"National TV audiences will be much more accepting of you than any local church group is likely to be," reassured Liz. "But what am I going to do when he expects me to heal someone in front of an audience?"

"Jing Sheng is not like that – he would never put on a freak show, as you call it. I would not worry about having to perform in public if I were you – or if you do, it will feel so necessary that it will also be and feel like an amazing blessing," Darnell took a turn reassuring her.

"Thanks, I guess you're right, Darnell. So, I'm the chauffeur, student of this amazing Master, healer, and yoga instructor, and you're the scheduler and PR guy?"

"Yes, and I have my lessons with him, too! You can't hang around Jing Sheng and not be required to learn something about serving God and becoming more loving!" Darnell laughed despite the frustration. He knew it was just his old ego hanging on, refusing to let go so that Darnell could just love others unconditionally, the way he longed for God and others to love and accept him.

"You two seem incredibly blessed, if you ask me," chimed in Daniel. "I would love to get to be one of Jing Sheng's sidekicks, but I guess I'll have to settle for distant admirer."

"You never know," said Liz.

"That's for sure," added Adam. "I was just minding my own business, being Darnell's friend, never going to church with him, and now I'm supposed to go to the church meeting tomorrow, too. I'm just glad it's not Darnell's own church we're going to."

"Why's that?" asked Liz.

"Darnell's church won't accept gays and lesbians for about another thousand years. As long as they take their Bible literally, gays are going to be damned to hell in their eyes!"

"Is it still that bad?" asked Daniel. "I guess that's why I don't go to church, but now that Jing Sheng's around, I feel like I need something. I hope I can find a place for me with all my questions, doubts, and interest in interreligious dialogue."

"The adventure is just beginning, you know. I have a feeling we're all in for quite a ride," Liz observed for all of them. "I guess I'm in, you guys – are you in for the Jing Sheng wa-hoo express: Exodus 2012-here-we-come-mission?"

"I'm for sure in," Darnell replied.

"Me, too, then," said Adam.

"It's the most interesting spiritual game in town." Daniel added, "I wouldn't miss it for the world."

9. THE PEOPLE BELIEVED

*THE ENERGY OF FAITH IS LIKE THE ENERGY OF A LIGHT
WAVE; AS LONG AS THE WAVE IS CONSTANT, FAITH AND
LOVE CREATE HARMONIOUS INTERACTIONS TOGETHER.*

Sunday dawned a brighter day, cooler still, but sunshine promised
for later in the clear, powder blue skies of Michigan. Liz woke up
and sat up immediately, thinking, *oh-my-gosh, where am I supposed
to be today? Oh, yeah, church.*

She started to say her usual 'before-I-get-out-of-bed' prayer, and
found herself feeling confused, because she could no longer pray
without addressing part of it to Jing Sheng. *Well, I'll see you later,*
she found herself thinking, as though that settled anything, and then
rushed to get ready.

She picked up both Jing Sheng and Darnell, who did not want to
attend a predominantly white people's church unescorted, expecting
that he would be treated differently. They all walked into Howard
Street Christian Church together, where they were greeted by an
older white couple, who effusively helped them with hanging up
jackets and otherwise getting settled in.

As they were entering the narthex to go into the sanctuary, Pastor
Mary Ellen McLean came along and shook hands with them.
"I'm so excited that you're here," she said. "We have a very
mainline congregation, with both conservatives and liberals and
everyone in-between. It will be interesting to see what they think of
your message today."

At that point, Adam arrived and joined Darnell and Liz, who
introduced him to the pastor.

A camera crew was setting up at the back of the sanctuary, and a channel 3 news reporter came over to meet Jing Sheng.

"Hi, I'm Mike Adams with channel 3 News and I'd like to schedule an interview with you after the service, if I may."

"Of course, Mr. Adams," Jing Sheng replied, "If that is alright with Pastor McLean."

"Certainly, although I'm counting on you to mention the name of our church in your news broadcast," Pastor Mary Ellen added hastily with a grin. "We do need to get started, if you'll excuse us."

Jing Sheng and Pastor Mary Ellen walked up to the chancel, while Darnell, Adam, and Liz chose seats somewhat near the front in case Jing Sheng needed them. As the service began, singing surrounded them in four-part harmony, and Liz tried to relax. She noticed that Darnell looked uncomfortable. Adam just looked curious.
When it came time for the sermon, Pastor Mary Ellen rose and introduced Jing Sheng as a Tai Chi master "who has come to bring a message from Jesus Christ, or so I hear. Please welcome our Chinese guest who has come so far with a message of love and environmental concern for the people of America."

"Thank you, Pastor Mary Ellen," Jing Sheng bowed slightly to her as he spoke into the microphone. Liz thought he was in trouble already for bowing in Namaste in a Christian sanctuary.

"Thank you all for accepting this opportunity for us to receive the word of God together. Please pray with me . . . Divine Love, you are Father and Mother to us all, and we thank you for your gift of life. We thank you for sending Jesus Christ to show us the way to wholeness in our lives individually, together, and with you. Lead us forward now, speaking to us the word we need to hear, so that again, we can be made whole in your image, from within the inner soul of our beings, to our minds, to our churches, to our communities, and to all the world together, that your way will be known upon the earth, and your saving grace among all nations. Amen." Jing Sheng looked up, smiling.

"What does it mean to be made whole? Let us talk for a moment about salvation. It is taught that Jesus Christ came to save men – that is, people, from their sin, and to bring them safely into heaven where they will dwell in eternity with God.

"Do you have any idea what heaven looks like?" Jing Sheng paused between each question. "Do you have any idea what salvation really means? Why did Christ die on the cross? What did Jesus really mean when he said that he came to show the way, the truth and the life?

"First, let us begin with salvation. Salvation is not simply about individuals making it to heaven, as though they were just handed a first-class travel ticket, with no activity or consciousness-raising required.

"Christ came to teach the way to be made whole. All people are children of God in that all people have souls. When Christ talked about being born again, he meant that we need to let go of our ego's way of taking control of life, and live instead by our soul's guidance.

"When we live according to the leading of God's Spirit within us, with our souls blending our wills with God's will, and our minds becoming more and more aware of the mind of Christ within, or what one might call the Consciousness of God, then we are made whole.

"In Islam, that is when one wins the Greater Jihad, the struggle between goodness and evil within oneself: one becomes perfectly attuned to the true, merciful, and loving will of Allah. In Judaism, one becomes a prophet, faithful to God's covenant, preaching and living out God's truth with one's whole life, and one's whole being. In Buddhism, one attains enlightenment through letting go of the ego-self and attaining complete non-attachment and even-mindedness. In Hinduism, one attains Self-Realization and God-realization: that state of Samadhi bliss, or nirvana, in which one becomes perfectly one with God.

"This enlightened state of conscious being and doing is also what Jesus Christ referred to when he said 'Be ye therefore perfect, even as your heavenly Father is perfect.' Perfection comes from letting go of our egos, and becoming attuned with the mind and heart of God at all times. The mind of God may also be called the mind of Christ and may be experienced as either the Holy Spirit's or the higher Self's intuitive guidance and awareness.

"Christians rightly call this being filled with the Holy Spirit. However, Christians mostly mis-understand what this means, because many Christians have not yet learned to let go of their ego-selves. Our egos like to stay in control."

A few people laughed nervously at this remark. Jing Sheng paused and smiled, looking around at everyone.

"Jesus Christ was an Enlightened Master, just like many enlightened masters in many religions. He was called, as the Bible says, a high priest in the order of Melchizedek. Melchizedek was a Persian king, mentioned in Genesis, who lived long before the physical time of Christ, but who was also an Enlightened Master. The eastern influence which came through Persia from Asia included belief in reincarnation. For instance, Zoroastrians in ancient Persia believed in reincarnation. Indeed, Christ and his disciples believed in reincarnation as well.

"This is why many people said that Jesus was Elijah, or expected Elijah to come first before the Messiah, because reincarnation, while not part of traditional Judaism, was nonetheless familiar to many people in Palestine and Judah at the time. Christ himself referred to John the Baptist as the reincarnation of Elijah, as his disciples understood him to say. Reincarnation was a common understanding among first century Christians, until the so-called Church Fathers began writing letters decrying it as heretical. The main reason they felt they had to write against it was the simple fact that so many Christians believed in it, and the concept of reincarnation reduced people's need to receive salvation through Jesus and the church.

"Now, the main reason we do need Jesus Christ for our wholeness, or salvation, is that all of us start out really bad at letting go of our egos and getting them out of the way. Because we so often fail to get our egos out of the way so that we can incarnate Love, we need the grace which only an Enlightened Master can bring us when we get lost in the darkness of fear and pain which Christians call sin. We have to get our egos out of the way so that we can become fully attuned to the will of God – the will of Divine Love and Life, if you will.

"Until we become enlightened ourselves, we all need an enlightened master to lead us on this journey of discovery of our True Selves, our souls or higher Selves, which is what it means to be born from above. Born from above is a better translation for the Greek, and for what Jesus meant, than is the phrase 'born again.' When we are born from above, we live out the reality of our higher Selves, the Truth of our Being from a spiritual realm.

"Until we are fully enlightened, or born from above, no matter what our faith may be, we need an enlightened master to guide us. In the East, such enlightened masters are called 'gurus.' The word 'guru' properly understood in the original Sanskrit means dispeller of darkness – a guru brings divine light to his or her followers.

"That is precisely what Christ did. Christ also died upon the cross. Only a true child of God would give him or herself for others in such a way. Christ's action was both a spiritual as well as a political action, because the poor people at the time were excluded from forgiveness of sins if they could not afford to buy a pigeon. To do so, they might have to go hungry, or keep from feeding their children that night. So, Christ's choice to die on the cross was in part a political statement against the ruling religious authorities to say that poor people had the same right to both food and forgiveness as do all other people, because all people have equal rights in the eyes of God.

"Christ's act of dying on the cross also forgave karma – what Christians refer to as forgiveness of sins. Karma is, in part, the cosmic debt or gain that we acquire through our actions, our thoughts, and the energies of our intentions and beliefs. All gurus are capable of forgiving the debts of their followers by taking on karmic energies for them. By giving up his life in such a painful way, Jesus Christ took on karmic debt for *everyone* who asks for his help.

"Christ desired to show that God forgives everyone who truly repents of their hurtful ways. No matter what a person's religion, they can be forgiven by God if they repent, but their karmic debt may still remain. For Christians, Christ often removes the karmic debt, depending on what is needed for their spiritual growth, and for the balance of life and love for humanity.

"Following Christ is not simply a matter of saying that Jesus is your lord once and then forgetting to explore what that means. Christians often say that Christ is their lord, but have no idea what that entails. Get to know Jesus through the gospels, if you will, because that's important, but please don't stop there.

"When we say that Christ is lord but then never get to know him personally, it makes no sense. Do you start your day talking with

Jesus? Do you turn to Jesus throughout the day when you need guidance, or when you need help, or better yet when you don't feel like being loving but you know God wants you to speak and act lovingly anyway?

"That is the start of a relationship with Jesus Christ as lord and savior. To be made whole, you must have what the apostle Paul referred to as the mind of Christ. Another way of saying that is Christ-consciousness, a way of knowing and being and doing that characterizes all enlightened masters. Buddhists would call it having the Buddha-mind.

"Jesus neither set out to start a religion called 'Christianity' nor to have followers who are called 'Christians'; rather Jesus Christ called people to be Christ-like. To be Christ-like, you must let go of your ego and let Christ rule over you. If you would have Jesus Christ as your savior, you must invite him into your mind, and definitely into your heart, and most certainly into your way of life. Then you will experience the Oneness of the Holy Spirit's presence within you – one with Christ and one with Divine Spirit.

Churches often speak of all Christians being one in Christ. However, the only way to attain this is for each and every one of you to allow Christ and God to reign over your will rather than letting your ego reign. It is only by being united with Christ as individuals who receive him fully as lord, that you as a church will be able to be one *IN* Christ.   It is necessary for everyone to 'have the mind of Christ' in order to BE 'one in Christ.'

"When we truly let Christ and the Spirit of God reign within us, the kingdom of heaven resides within – peace and joy and love will come over us. When we let Christ reign over us together, then the kingdom of God comes among us – it is always ready at hand, for those who do God's will, the way of Love.

"Salvation comes to us like a conveyor belt of white light; it is not that we have no work to do, but we must step onto God's conveyor belt of white light, which leads us closer to God. That is God's grace, that it draws us closer to God. As we grow closer to God, we find that we must also lay down our lives for others, and serve God in our own unique calling, giving over our whole selves to God. In this we see that faith and works are inseparable; for both convey the grace of God. By faith in grace we step into the light; through the grace of faith we do Love's work. As we turn our whole selves over to divine service and live our lives for the sake of others, we become more and more filled with the light and love of God, and God draws us ever closer and closer, until we become perfected, just like Jesus Christ." Jing Sheng paused and smiled at *everyone*. Everyone felt included in his gaze of love, as though the conveyor belt of God's love and light was drawing them towards Jing Sheng at the moment.

"So, today, we remember and celebrate and give thanks for the life of the Enlightened Master Jesus Christ – our Lord, our Master, and we give thanks for his teachings as well as his chosen sacrifice, which he made that we might approach God through Christ's grace.

"To God be the glory forever and ever, amen."

As silence engulfed the sanctuary, it seemed as though a wave of white light also engulfed the whole room, lighting up the crowd. Jing Sheng sat down.

Suddenly, applause broke out, and one or two people stood up, then more and more, until Jing Sheng had about half the congregation giving him a standing ovation. A couple of people walked out, never to return to that church. Some people were muttering audible objections. Some people were shaking their heads, confused and having hardly understood a word he said. "It just didn't sound like the gospel to me," one elderly lady 'whispered' loudly, "I don't believe that man was speaking the Truth," she said to the woman sitting next to her, who looked perplexed and perhaps a bit distressed.

The organist launched into the next hymn, and the mutterings subsided, as "Amazing Grace" filled the sanctuary, musically, at least.

After the service and following the interview, Jing Sheng, Darnell, Liz, and Adam all went to Liz's house for lunch. She whipped up some stir-fried vegetables and rice with cashews, her favorite addition to many foods.

"We have to plan the New York program," Jing Sheng announced.

"New York?" Liz almost squeaked.

"Yes, I will be speaking on American Morning News Hour, and then we have a speaking program followed by a concert of interfaith music at Central Park."

"Oh, my, are you expecting me to go?" asked Liz, looking around at Darnell and Adam to see what they seemed to be feeling.

"Yes, I will need you to hand out fliers and greet people who will want to volunteer with us at a shelter there in New York City. You will be sort of a volunteer coordinator, except that you will also collect donations and contact information from people who will want to become part of our mission. I promise we will get more volunteers to share the work, okay?"

Liz wasn't sure if she was really being given much choice, but she realized she would have to find some volunteers to cover for her at her wellness center. She wondered when and where and how Jing Sheng and Darnell managed to coordinate so much.

"As soon as I get my work at the center covered, it will be okay. When are we going?"

"Next week, but don't worry, a volunteer will show up within the next 24 hours," Jing Sheng assured her.

Well, that's that, then, she thought. *New York, here we come.* She didn't even think to ask where they'd be staying.

The morning of the concert and lecture in Central Park started so early that Liz couldn't believe that people normally got up at that hour, but they had to in order for Jing Sheng to be interviewed by Roberta Robins on American Morning News Hour, a popular TV news and celebrity show that lasts two hours, despite its name.

Roberta Robins opened with the line: "I'm sitting here with Jing Sheng Hu, or I guess I should say, Hu Jing Sheng, the proper Chinese way to say his name, a Chinese Tai Chi Master who is touring the United States with a very controversial teaching about Christianity, religion, spirituality, and even global warming.

"Good morning, Jing Sheng."

"Good morning, Roberta."

"Your teachings are causing quite a controversy. Perhaps the most controversial part is that people are saying that you are the reincarnation of Jesus Christ. I thought he rose from the dead – how is that possible?"

"Reincarnation is always possible; it simply means that a soul that is in heaven has chosen to return to earth in a physical body."

"That's a lovely theory, but people want to know, and I mean really want to know, are you the reincarnation of Jesus Christ?"

"I will make no claims about myself here," Jing Sheng calmly answered. "Well, I am a Tai Chi Master, but that is a fact of my training." (Jing Sheng smiled.) "People must realize for themselves who I AM. It will do no good for me to tell them."

"But what do you believe about yourself? Do you believe that you are the reincarnation of Jesus Christ?"

"Roberta, I am aware that here in America, if someone says they believe something about themselves that few other people believe, Americans label them crazy, lock them up against their will, and drug them until they become completely unproductive. So much for freedom, but that lack of freedom is the American way."

"Are you showing disrespect to the United States of America?"

"I merely speak the truth of the American way. The fact that it is contradictory to the myth of the American way is a fact, not a lack of disrespect. Those who worship God must worship in spirit and in truth. It never honors God when we live in denial."

"Wow! I think you covered about four weighty topics in three sentences. So, let's back up a little bit. Do you believe in reincarnation?"

"Of course, all souls that die either go to heaven, or go to the outer darkness because they are lost in negativity and despair, or stay tied here to earth because they are weighed down by earthly concerns. When souls go to heaven, they can choose to return to earth either to learn more lessons, which is the most common reason, or to serve the will of the divine."

"The will of the divine?" asked Roberta, clearly mystified by her interviewee.

"Yes, God's will, as some would call it."

"So you're saying that people choose to be reincarnated, but sometimes it's God's idea?"

"The most important thing to know about God is that God is love, and love never imposes its way on others without their soul's permission."

"Wow! Never?"

"Never."

"Well, so, let's say God has an idea that it would be good for me to reincarnate after I die, but I would get to choose whether or not to come back?"

"Yes. Truly enlightened souls return time and again to help other souls with their progress."

"What do you mean by 'their progress'?" Roberta queried a little slowly compared to her usual prompt questioning.

"The most important thing about life is that people learn to let go of their egos and grow closer to God. Sanctification, the traditional Christian method of doing this, works if people take it seriously. The problem has arisen that most priests, ministers, and pastors have failed to pass on the core teaching of Christianity, which is that we are all meant to become one with God, by dying to self and becoming Christ-like, thereby allowing the consciousness of God to reign in our hearts, bodies, lives, and minds every day all the time.

That is the coming of the kingdom, or reign of God, to which Jesus referred."

"Wow!" You said a mouthful, and I imagine that priests and theologians are going to have a heyday denying some of what you just said, or challenging you with all they've got. But many people really seem to be taking to your message. Why do you think that is?"

Jing Sheng smiled, and looked at the camera instead of Roberta, "because we know that the old ways have failed, and we must do something new if we are to save the earth. How can we save our souls if we cannot even save the earth?"

"Okay, that's a new message alright. So are you more concerned about saving the earth than you are about saving souls?"

"My message is the message of Exodus 20:12. 2012 is both the year that the Mayan Calendar ends, and a verse in the Bible, which says, 'honor your father and mother that you may live long in the land.' If we understand that the verse also means honor your heavenly Father, meaning God, and your earthly Mother, meaning mother earth, then we know how to save the earth by the year 2012, and we will save our souls as well."

"Well, I can see that it might be helpful to interview you for a whole week, but that's all the time we've got right now. Thank you so much for being with us today. Jing Sheng Hu, ladies and gentleman, will be speaking later today at Central Park. Stay tuned to this station for new updates throughout the day."

Jing Sheng met Liz and Darnell outside the recording studio, and they headed for the elevator. Just before they reached it, Roberta dashed down the hall calling out, "Mr. Hu!"

"Yes, Ms. Robins?"

"I'm so glad I caught you. Our producer just called me to say that we would like to host a special segment with you all next week called: "Hu Jing Sheng: Could he be the next Messiah?" We would interview you for 15 minutes, including questions from the audience. Are you available?"

"Yes, Ms. Robins, I believe I AM." Jing Sheng always managed to make that phrase sound like his name, at least to Liz and Darnell, who knew what Jing Sheng meant when he said it.

"Wonderful! Thank you so much – we'll have our assistant director call you and make the arrangements with you. Here's my card if you have any questions, otherwise just wait and Lisa Olinger will give you a call."

"Thank you," Jing Sheng replied.

"Wait," cried Liz, "Are you at least going to compensate Jing Sheng for his time?"

"Of course! Ms. Olinger will discuss that with Mr. Hu." Roberta Robins waved and positively sashayed back into the studio. "Next week, then!"

Jing Sheng, Liz, and Darnell descended in the elevator. Darnell started explaining the set-up in Central Park, and how there was just enough time to pick-up some tea and a light breakfast, if Jing Sheng would like.

So, they proceeded with that plan, Darnell acting as Jing Sheng's agent, Liz the ever-eager, but slightly confused assistant.

When the time came for Jing Sheng to go out on the stage, he handed Liz his cup of herbal tea, and Darnell went out first to introduce him.

"Good morning, everyone, I'm Darnell Long, assistant to Mr. Hu Jing Sheng. We'd like to thank everyone for coming out today…" Darnell paused as he realized that he was speaking to about 4,000 people in front of him, and on camera with potentially millions of people watching at home.

"Jing Sheng will be speaking in just a moment, and after he speaks he will take questions from either of the two microphones positioned towards the middle of the crowd. There will be people there to assist you in taking turns.

"First, however, we will have a word of prayer by the Rev. Jesse Handlon of Unity Park Church here in New York City, a church where everyone is welcome, and everyone is a child of God."

The pastor walked out on stage, smiled at the crowd, and with his well-known charismatic presence and booming voice, rang out, "Let us pray…

"Oh, God, Creator Divine, Source of Every Blessing, we thank you this day for the privilege of being in the presence of your greatness. Send your blessed Spirit to each of us and all of us we pray, that our hearts might be mended, our minds opened, our ears blessed with spiritual perception and our eyes blessed with spiritual insight. Let your wisdom, your love, and your peace prevail, not only here today, but through us and through your Spirit, everywhere on earth. Amen."

Liz wondered if he did not add a prayer in Jesus' name because Jing Sheng was here, or if Rev. Handlon was trying to be inclusive of all people of faith attending, or both. She decided he was clever enough that he probably was doing both.

Jing Sheng stepped out onto the stage, bowed in Namaste to Rev. Handlon, who bowed in return, and then, stepping towards the microphone, bowed to the audience. The audience responded by applauding loudly, and some people shouted "Praise God!" and other forms of acclamation.

To those who could perceive it, a white light emanated from or actually through Jing Sheng's whole being – he didn't need stage lights because he positively glowed. There were gasps in the crowd and then loud whispers as those who could see the glow expanding told those around them what they could see.

"I bring you greetings of love, peace, forgiveness, patience, kindness, gentleness, generosity, joy, faithfulness, and self-control from the Holy Spirit, who stands ready to pour out these fruits of the Spirit on all here who would now receive. If you would like to receive the fruit of the Spirit, simply lift your hands in the air and say, 'Oh, God, I am yours; we are One. I humbly asked to be filled with your Divine Spirit of Wisdom and Love. I thank you for this blessing. Help me to serve you this day and always. Alleluia, Amen.'" Jing Sheng paused between each part of the prayer, and thousands of people lifted their hands and prayed with him.

A tingle of electricity ran through the crowd, and then a feeling of peace descended on everyone, even though not everyone could feel it, or maybe just didn't realize *what* they felt. Liz knew that angels were present, spreading the peace of God all through the crowd. Sometimes, she could see the angels, although they just looked transparent and wispy to her.

"I have come to speak with you today to bring you the message of Exodus 20:12. The commandment 'Honor your father and your mother so that you may live long in the land' refers not only to honoring your human parents, which is important, but also to honoring your Heavenly Father and your Earthly Mother. God is both masculine and feminine, Alpha and Omega, beginning and end. God is also Spirit which transcends the known universe, as well as Spirit present throughout the entire universe creating, sustaining, breathing life and health everywhere it is possible to sustain the life of the spirit in physical form.

"There were many ancient peoples who passed on spiritual wisdom in many forms. The ancient Egyptians have an oral wisdom history that is tens of thousands of years old. The East has had many spiritual teachers, some recorded in writing, some whose teachings have been passed from Master to disciple for thousands of generations. When I say Master, I mean women as well, because there are women who are enlightened Masters.

The ancient Mayans stored much of their spiritual wisdom in their calendar, which ends in the year 2012. That date is a warning to humankind. It is a severe and urgent warning from Divine Spirit, saying that unless human beings get their priorities straight, they will kill all life on the planet in the next hundred years.

"Some people expect a cataclysm, but apocalyptic teachings are part of the ancient history of humanity – they come from a shared memory of an apocalypse that happened almost tens of thousands of years ago. Some ancient records share this cataclysm as the flood that covered the earth, as in the Bible and in the Gilgamesh Epic, as well as other records around the world, along with lingering stories of Atlantis being swept under the sea.

"The book of revelation teaches about an apocalypse to come, but such teachings contain more spiritual mysteries than actual prophetic content. It is the symbolism and the message of these apocalyptic messages that must be heeded.

"God loves everyone, and has no desire to bring about universal devastation of any sort. That is why it is important that we revere our Earthly Mother as divine. God's Spirit dwells on and in the Earth and all her life forms.

"We must cherish all life forms, including our own bodies, as temples of the divine.

"When we cherish all life, we will truly be honoring our Heavenly Father and our Earthly Mother, and only then will humanity be able to live long in the land.

"Notice that our wars still tear us apart. Our Earthly Mother would have us learn to care for each other. The myth of the capitalist world is that each person must take care of themselves.

"The truth of the kingdom of God, however, is that everyone is meant to care for others, and when everyone cares for others, everyone will be cared for by someone else.

"The Reign of God happens on earth when children and their well-being are put first, and afterwards, people care for one another so that no one is left out. Caring for others is the key to the Reign of God's will on earth.

"Caring for children must come first. So, it is important that we exchange our children, from one home to another, from one city to another, from one village to another, around the whole earth. It is only by exchanging children for one year, that communities will learn to live in harmony with one another economically, spiritually, and in all other ways as well.

"We have a vast organization set up to communicate around the globe to help this happen. God enabled people to create the internet just in time to save themselves together.

"Please go to one of the tables at the back to obtain more information, and logon to the website: **www.exodus2012.org** . By learning new ways of living together, you will save yourselves and the earth.

"If you would like to hire meditation teachers or spiritual guides to help your community grow in its connection to God and Divine Wisdom, please fill out a card at the back or send in your request online.

"Thank you, and God bless you. I will entertain your questions now."

An elderly woman stepped to the microphone. "Mr. Hu, if you really are the reincarnation of Jesus Christ, then why aren't you more worried about convincing people to be Christians than you are saving the earth?"

Jing Sheng smiled.

"Those who *already knew me*, and understood my message, now recognize that I AM WHO I AM. Those who think they know me but do not, are confused about me, resentful of me, or in denial. Those who don't know me don't care, or are merely curious, or are staying close to learn the Truth.

"Jesus' message was never that people should become Christians. He was about reforming Judaism, not about starting a new religion. Jesus' message was that people need to stop looking outside themselves for salvation, cultivate their own faith within, be the answer that they are looking for, and be Christ-like. Anyone from any religion can do those things.

"The message of forgiveness on the cross is a reassurance that people receive forgiveness when they repent; it is not necessarily the means of their forgiveness, but the message of forgiveness. Through *faith*, the message of the cross *can* be the means of forgiveness for people, but mainly it is the message that forgiveness is God's way of doing things. Forgiveness only happens when we do not fight back. It has always been important for One not to fight back, in order to bring the message of forgiveness more fully.

"Forgiveness is always available from God for those who repent. Just as a person who is shaking their fists cannot receive a gift until they stop and open their hands, so also forgiveness cannot be received by those who do not repent. God forgives, but we do not receive forgiveness until we repent, because forgiveness is for wrongdoing, but we cannot receive that gift until we *acknowledge* our own wrongdoing. Repentance and forgiveness can overcome both individual and group karma. It is Christ-like to forgive.

"So, please be Christ-like, loving and forgiving, not fighting back, generous, healing, serving, and merciful. Whatever your religion may be, that is the request of Jesus Christ."

A man with a clerical collar spoke up. "Who do you think you are to tell us Jesus' spiritual message? Have you studied theology somewhere?"

"I studied Tai Chi at the Wudang Monastery in Hubei Province, China. But these teachings are not what I learned there. These teachings are my own. I WILL BE WHO I WILL BE."

A young mother with a baby stepped up to the other microphone. "Are you serious about people sending their children to other families half-way around the world? You must be crazy! You certainly must not be a father!"

"You can only think the idea is crazy if you have a human view of children, rather than God's view of children. To God, all children are special – equally special. And to God, all children belong to the Divine Father/Mother, not just to human parents. To God, each set of parents is simply entrusted with the care of children for their well-being, and so it does not matter to God which children parents have, because all children must be loved equally. Do you love your children more than you love other people's children?"

"That's not fair! Of course I do, but you're trying to make it sound as though that is wrong!"

"Let me ask you a different question then. Who gave you your child?"

"My husband did."

"Really? Your husband implanted your child's soul in your child's body?"

"No, of course not, but he implanted his seed inside me."

"But without a soul, even sperm and eggs together cannot create a new life, so God implanted a soul in your child. Your child is a gift from God. *All* children are gifts from God, and we are *all* responsible for their well-being. That is the first lesson of the Reign of God on earth."

Silence ensued. For a moment, no one dared speak at the microphones. Then, a little calmer, the woman continued.

"So, are you serious about us sending our children somewhere that might be unsafe or they might get diseases? There's no way I'm willing to do that to my children."

"And yet you are willing that other children should suffer disease, malnutrition, and starve to death – tens of thousands die every day, and millions every year. Why do your children deserve a better life than do other children? Are your children better than the children of Somalia?"

"No, well, I don't know. Oh! Of course they're not better, but they're mine."

"But again, God gave them to you for safe-keeping, just as God gave you all children for safe-keeping."

"I don't have any way of taking care of all the children of the world!"

"Of course not. Not when you think of yourself as isolated and alone, as you do when you think your biological children belong only to you. But no one is isolated and alone, even though Western materialistic culture has made people that way.

"The truth is that everyone is responsible for everyone, and so none of you are alone, and no children are to go uncared for. Together, you are fully capable of feeding, clothing, sheltering, and protecting all the children of the world. When you get your priorities straight, you will do so.

"So, of course you can take care of all the children of the world, just as soon as every adult in the world, or at least most of the adults, decide they are going to do just that. Again, taking care of all the children of the world is the first goal of the Reign of God on earth."

Again, a moment of silence ensued as that thought began to register and make sense in people's brains. Some intuitively and instantly recognized the inevitable Truth of what Jing Sheng was saying; others had to think about it for awhile; others still thought that goal to be impossible.

A young man dressed in a suit stepped up to a microphone. He had a Bible in his hand, to which he pointed as he spoke. "Why do you speak of God's forgiveness for everyone who repents, when the Bible makes it clear that the only way to receive forgiveness of sins is by belief in Jesus Christ and forgiveness by his blood on the cross?" He sounded angry.

Jing Sheng paused, smiling gently at the man. Those who could see Jing Sheng's energy glow saw a portion of that glow spread to the young man, as it had for all the speakers, although not many could 'see' this happening. Few were aware of the spreading of Christ's love to those who asked questions. By this time, the glow was spread throughout all the people as a warm, peaceful sensation, like a gentle, loving hug from God.

"Are you saying that God cannot forgive people who are not Christian of their sins?"

"Well, no, God can do anything, but that's not the way God works. God sent His Son to bring forgiveness of sins, as the Bible says." The young man still sounded fairly confident, although somewhat unsettled.

"So, you agree that God is all powerful and that therefore God is able to forgive non-Christians for their sin if they repent?" Jing Sheng sounded steady and firm.

"Well, yes, of course God could, but again, that's not how God planned it. Salvation is only for those who accept Christ."
"So, are you so wise that you actually can stand here before thousands of people and tell us that you personally know how God planned salvation?"

"It's not me that knows – it's the Bible that says so." The young man seemed to realize that there was a weakness in his sounding so presumptuous.

"Ah, I see. Now, the Bible also says that God is love, correct?"

"Yes, in 1 John, the Bible states that God is love, and that those who love God must love one another. Well, let me read it so that I get the quote right: 'Beloved, let us love one another, because love is from God; everyone who loves is born of God and knows God. Whoever does not love does not know God, for God is love. God's love was revealed among us in this way: God sent his only Son into the world so that we might live through him. In this is love, not that we loved God but that he loved us and sent his Son to be the atoning sacrifice for our sins. Beloved, since God loved us so much, we also ought to love one another. No one has ever seen God; if we love one another, God lives in us, and his love is perfected in us."

"Yes, a beautiful quote isn't it?" Jing Sheng nodded his head and looked thoughtful, and many people assumed he was just thinking, although a few could see that a wave of peaceful energy emanated from Jing Sheng as his mind sent its gratitude to God for the beauty of that passage.

"So, if God is love, and God commands us to love one another, then can we love someone and fail to forgive them at the same time?"

"I'm not sure – I don't think so, unless they don't repent."

"Ok, assuming that our sister or brother repents, can we love them and refuse to forgive them at the same time?"

"No, of course not."

"So is it correct that God asks us to forgive our sisters and brothers?"

"Yes, of course, God asks us to forgive our sisters and brothers in the faith."

"What do you mean by qualifying it with sisters and brothers – 'in the faith'?"

"Well, does God really ask us to love and forgive the whole world? I mean, that's impossible, and well, we know that sisters and brothers who are Christian are forgiven by God, but we don't know about non-Christians."

There were audible objections in the crowd.

"My brother, I ask you, do you remember the Bible passage that says, "God so loved the world...?"

"Oh, of course I know that one! But you didn't finish it, it goes on to say, "that he gave his only Son, so that everyone who believes in him may not perish but may have eternal life. John 3:16."

"Yes, let's just consider for a moment that the Bible says, 'God so loved the world.' Now does the Bible say that God only loved Christians?"

"No, I guess that includes everyone."

"Good, and if you were reading this text in the original Greek back in the day that it was written, you would have known that it was obvious, because the Greek word for world is cosmos, and that meant the entire human world.

"So, if God loves the entire human world, does that not mean that God loves everyone?"

"Well, that makes sense."

"And so, if God loves everyone, can God love someone and refuse to forgive them if they repent?"

"Well, if they don't accept Christ as their Savior, God doesn't forgive them."

This time, there were gasps and shouts of outrage in the audience.

"I think you can hear that the audience includes some people who believe that God loves them and forgives them even though they are not Christian. Again, is it possible for God to love someone and yet to refuse to forgive them – is that really divine love, to refuse to forgive someone?"

"Well, I mean, it doesn't sound like it, but I'm not God, so I don't know."

"Ah, now we are nearer to the Truth – you are not God, so you don't know God's answers. That is obviously true."

Some people disrespectfully giggled.

"Although it is also true that no one here is God all by themselves, and so no one here knows the full Truth of God, including myself."

That brought a somber silence of reflection to the crowd.

"So, we have concluded that God is love, and that it is impossible for love to refuse to forgive those who repent, correct?"

Several people shouted out, "Correct!" The young man added, "I guess that's right."

"So God so loves the world, that God forgives everyone of every faith and of no faith when they repent of their hurtful behavior. That is TRUTH.

"Now, why does the Bible speak of atonement through Christ the way it does? Well, we need to remember that ancient Jews believed that God punished sinners by having bad things happen to them: they got sick, their animals died, a plague came, locusts ate their crops – something bad happened to those who sinned.

"That is the Jewish concept of karma – karma as punishment. It makes one feel guilty, and gets one confused about the actual causation of things.

"Let's look at the laws of karma. Properly understood, karma has two elements to it. The first Truth of karma is that what we put out, we receive in return. So, if we are loving, we receive love back. If we are angry and abusive, we receive strong negativity back. If we are anxious and afraid, we experience scary things in our lives. Our thoughts, our actions, our intentions, and our energy of love or fear create matching karmic reactions in the universe.

"The second element of karma is this: we have life lessons that our souls have chosen to learn in this lifetime, so that some bad things happen to us as learning opportunities. Some good things happen to us because our souls have chosen to receive our rewards in this lifetime rather than the next life, or our souls have chosen to have easier lessons for this lifetime.

"One person's karma is not another person's to judge, because they have no way of knowing what a person deserves, and what they have chosen for lessons. Therefore, do not judge one another.

"Christ came so that people could make spiritual progress faster by having some of their karma forgiven. If people spend many lifetimes just suffering the results of their hurtful behavior, it can be difficult for them to perceive all the spiritual lessons which they need to be learning. Any true guru, or Enlightened Master, can forgive karma for their followers, because they can sense when the easing of burdens is necessary to help someone learn."

"You are not Jesus Christ! Jesus Christ would never talk about karma and gurus and many lifetimes – you're a fraud!" The young man was waving his arm and thumping his Bible and spittle was flying from his mouth. He stormed away from the microphone, almost running other people down.

"As I said a moment ago, those who already knew me, and understood my teachings, recognize me now as I AM THAT I AM." The only sign of Jing Sheng's distress was a slight shivering of the Christ energy at the edges of the crowd. The loving, peaceful Christ energy around the young man tore in two as he made his way through it, taking negative, painful energy with him as exited the crowd.

Jing Sheng nodded his head at a woman at the other microphone.

"I'm sorry, Mr. Hu, that you had to experience that outburst," she said gently.

"Do not be sorry for the actions of others – you are responsible for your own energy, not his."

"Yes, of course, I just regret that he aimed such venom at you."

"Thank you for your kind consideration of my feelings."

"I was wondering if you believe in reincarnation, but apparently, from what you just said, you do?" She bowed in Namaste.

"Yes, we have many lifetimes to achieve the perfection of Christ-consciousness, or Buddha-consciousness or God-consciousness as it were."

"Thank you, Master, may I please study with you?"

"All are welcome who come sincerely to learn their lessons. It is not easy, however, to get our egos out of the way in order to attain complete attunement with the mind and heart of God."

"Yes, Master Jing Sheng; that is why I would like your guidance."

"For all those who sincerely seek to let go of ego and be made one with the love and peace and forgiveness of God, you may go to the table to my right, where my assistants will sign you up to receive e-mails, spend time with me, receive lessons, do community service and community organizing with us, and so on.

"And now, as it is our time for ending, we have a few announcements of community service opportunities right here in the city. We will have a moment of worship, led by the gospel choir of Christ the Holy Savior Church, and then please stay to hear the announcements and receive the flyers so that we can all serve God together by loving our neighbors right here. After the announcements, the Interfaith Music Concert will begin.

"Thank you for being here, God bless you all." Jing Sheng bowed in Namaste, and walked out as a choir filed in, and the band began to play "Great Is thy Faithfulness" with an upbeat air to it.

Liz gave Jing Sheng his cup of tea, now barely lukewarm, and asked if he would like her to give the announcements or hand out the flyers.

"Please make the announcements, and then join me at the homeless shelter where we will help serve lunch."

"Yes, of course, Jing Sheng, thank you!" *Oh, that means missing the interfaith music – I was hoping to hear the Buddhist monks blowing their large horns and OMing together. Well, I have heard them before, so I guess I'll just let go of that desire,* Liz reflected.

Good job, my little dove! Liz heard Jing Sheng's voice in her head.

♥ ♥ ♥

10. LET MY PEOPLE GO

TO BE CREATED IN THE IMAGE OF GOD MEANS TO LOVE UNCONDITIONALLY. UNCONDITIONAL LOVE REQUIRES EMPATHY, COMPASSION, AND NON-JUDGMENTAL UNDERSTANDING. FORTUNATELY, THESE VIRTUES ALSO IMAGE GOD MOST FULLY. YOU ARE INVITED TO IMAGE GOD FULLY AND COMPLETELY; TO DO SO, YOU MUST BE ABLE TO RECOGNIZE GOD IN OTHERS.

That afternoon, Liz was just finishing up a bite of lunch when her phone rang. She was sitting in the office of a local homeless shelter in New York, surrounded by a whole crew of people who were all somehow working for Jing Sheng. Some were on the internet receiving and transmitting messages around the world to would-be followers in half a dozen languages.

Jing Sheng was in the office making plans with the director of the shelter program. They agreed to do a press conference outside the shelter the following day, after the American Morning News Hour. That evening, he was giving a talk right there at the shelter.

Liz flipped open her phone to see who was calling. *Oh, Daniel,* she thought, *oh, boy, how do I have time to do this? God, if this is your idea, please help me!*

"Hi, how are you," she announced into the phone.

"I'm well, but I'd love to see you. I saw Jing Sheng's television appearance. That was pretty exciting even from here. It must have been really exciting up close and personal."

"It was. I'd love to see you, too, but really, I can't do this long distance, why don't you just come to New York? You wanted excitement – well, following Jing Sheng is a surprise a minute.

Apparently, we're sleeping on the floor at a homeless shelter tonight…"

Liz somehow persuaded Daniel to come to New York anyway.

Jing Sheng invited his followers to join him that afternoon for a group meditation at 3:00 p.m., so followers around the world were sent e-mails inviting them also to meditate at 3:00 Eastern Standard Time.

So, 3 p.m. found them sitting in a circle on the floor, some on cushions, some in lotus position, some on chairs because their backs or knees or age would not allow them to sit long on the floor.

Jing Sheng announced, "Let us open with a few clearing breaths, breathing in deeply through our noses … and sighing out through our mouths. As we breathe in, let us take in the goodness of God, and as we breathe out, let us let go of stress, anger, fear, resentment. And again, breathe in the hope of God, breathe out the negative. And again, breathe in the love and light of God, then breathe out fear, anxiety, and judgment.

"And now let us say 'Aum' (OM) together three times. Aummmmm … Aummm … Aummm.

"Now let us pray. Almighty God, we thank you for this sacred space, a place where those with no home get to sleep with a roof over their heads. We thank you for all those who serve here, both paid and volunteer, and ask you to bless them. We lift up all who stay here, and ask you to fulfill their needs. Guide them through a better way to find a better day. In your love and light we pray. Amen."

Quiet ensued; the hush sounded nervous at first with throat clearings, sniffs, and a few sighs. Then peace descended; Liz thought of the dove at Jesus' baptism, because she could feel peace descend upon her and upon the room as though a palpable spiritual presence had entered into their midst. She opened her eyes; reality struck hard at first, but after recovering from the drab harshness of the shelter, she realized there was an unexplainable brightness in the room.

For twenty-five minutes, they sat quietly. At 3:30, Jing Sheng rose and bowed in Namaste to the hasty altar they had laid with portraits of Jesus and other great saints of all faiths, along with some white Christmas lights entwined safely between in lieu of candles on top of a purple and gold cloth.

Jing Sheng sat back down and explained that this group of volunteers would be preparing and serving dinner that night, and that five or six volunteers could spend the night as chaperones.

After he spoke, the director came in and took charge, and the hustle and bustle began afresh. Liz slipped outside for a breath of fresh air with Darnell and Adam.

"Can you believe this?" She asked.

"No, I never dreamt about coming to New York and serving in a homeless shelter, but I guess it makes sense," Darnell replied, shaking his head as though his thoughts could not keep up with the reality in front of them.

"This is craziness, sheer craziness," chimed in Adam. "What do I know about feeding homeless people and hanging out with them? Jing Sheng wants us to eat and talk with them. I mean, what do you say to a homeless person? 'Hi, why don't you have a home?' I just don't think I can manage to be tactful enough!"

"I know," moaned Liz. "But guys, Daniel will be showing up tonight, even though I told him we'll be staying here. What am I to do?"

"Either you are Jing Sheng's disciple, or you are not. Right now, being his disciple comes first," Darnell wisely replied.

"But you guys are together – how do you do it?" Liz practically whined.

"It's not easy, honey, trust me, but we know who is the most important person around here. So, as Darnell said, Jing Sheng comes first." Adam offered little comfort, even though he obviously tried.

"Okay, well, so much for 'fresh' air here in New York. Let's go back inside and help. I'd rather help in the kitchen while you guys cover the computer mail, ok?"

"For sure," Adam answered.

"Right," replied Darnell.

So, the evening progressed. Soon, 60 homeless men, women, and children were seated around tables eating a vegetarian dinner for a change. Some of them complained about not getting meat. Others tasted the strange-looking food as though they expected it to taste bad, but were mostly pleasantly surprised.

Liz found herself at a table with a family, texting her business associates with instructions for her healing center while learning the family members' names and explaining why they were eating vegetarian food.

"Who is this Jing Sheng Hu guy?" asked the man, whose name was Lionel.

"Well, officially, he is a Chinese Tai Chi master, but he also is obviously an Enlightened Spiritual Master as well. Some of us believe that he is the reincarnation of Jesus Christ."

"Say-what!" Lionel nearly spewed out his butternut squash soup with cashews.

"Well, I know it sounds crazy, but Jesus did say he would come back someday, and he didn't specify the how, except maybe the 'on-the-clouds' idea. I think Jing Sheng could float in on a cloud if he wanted to – I've seen him levitate." Liz was determined to make her case.

"Get out of here!" responded Shawnell, the mother of three little ones, who were keeping her busy. "He can levitate? Maybe it's not that hard when you're so skinny."

"So what's he going to talk to us about? I hear we have to listen to him after dinner." Lionel sounded resentful, skeptical, everything you'd expect of a traumatically stressed out dad who spent his days looking for work and yet could not provide for his young family.

"I have no idea. He surprises me all the time. But I'm pretty sure he cares about poor people and injustice. He's not all that impressed with American capitalism, and I don't think it's just because he's Chinese. He really sounds like Jesus talking in the gospels some times. Not that I go to church anymore, but I used to." Liz started wondering where she could hear anyone who would sound as perfectly wise and divinely-attuned as Jing Sheng. She gave up, and started texting her two adult kids to let them know what she was up to. They both lived in or near Washington, D.C.

The child next to her became fascinated with her phone, and she showed her some of her photos and played some ringtones for her. That was enough for a two-year-old, who then started clamoring for more cake. (Chocolate almond cake with caramel-almond icing.)

"Wow, who made this cake?" asked Shawnell.

"I did. Well, it's my recipe, and a few volunteers helped make enough for 60 people," answered Liz.

"It's really good," observed Shawnell. "How did you learn to cook?"

"Well, my parents were missionaries, so my mom had to make everything from scratch. She taught me how to make things from scratch, and it just stuck with me." Liz put her phone away reluctantly, thinking she should have heard from or seen Daniel by now. And then she remembered New York City traffic, and decided to relax.

"Would you like me to help bathe the kids?" she asked Shawnell. "I loved bath time with my kids, and I'd be glad to help."

"Oh, thank you," Shawnell responded with relief. Off they went, three young children in tow or literally in their arms.

When Daniel arrived, he found Darnell and Adam in the office, and stayed with them a little while, learning how to add people's names, e-mail and snail mails into the database. He wondered how and where they had acquired four laptops, but it did seem necessary to have them all going at the same time, since apparently people were now following Jing Sheng from around the world.

Liz came into the office and a smile lit up her face.

"Hey there, stranger!" She greeted Daniel with a hug and a kiss.

"Hi, honey, I just couldn't resist a night in a homeless shelter with you; it sounded so romantic," Daniel laughed and hugged her again.

"We don't have much time – Jing Sheng is about to start talking at 8, and then people settle down for the night at 9." Liz sounded ready for bed herself already. She yawned, just thinking about it.

"As a matter of fact," Darnell interjected, "We'd better go see if we need to set the chairs in a circle or anything."

They all followed Darnell into the main room, where volunteers and guests were already rearranging tables and chairs into a circle. Jing Sheng always insisted on a circle. Liz did not really know why, so she inwardly hoped that he would explain it, and trusted that he would hear her 'prayer.'

By 8:00 p.m. everyone who was spending the night was seated in a circle, including the children, who had toys and books and video games to entertain them.

A news crew arrived from channel 10 news, and aimed the camera at the seat where Jing Sheng was to sit and speak.

Jing Sheng entered the room and bowed in Namaste, smiling to everyone around the circle. He looked so holy, so loving, Liz thought, as she sat next to Daniel and squeezed his hand, then released it to bow in Namaste in return to Jing Sheng.

"Good evening, everyone; thank you for joining me here. I am Jing Sheng Hu, or as we say in China, Hu Jing Sheng. I have come to America with a message, which is the message of Exodus 2012. I will not explain that here, because here we need to talk about justice, about courage, and about faith.

"First, let me open by explaining why I prefer that everyone sit in a circle. In a circle, we can acknowledge that God, who is Love, is in the middle. Please let love be at the center of all you do. Second, in a circle everyone is equal – no one is more important than anyone else. Third, in a circle, everyone is included; no one is left out of the circle of love. So, here we have a circle of light, a circle of life, and a circle of love. And now, let us speak of some concerns, which Love has laid on my heart.

"American society clearly has the haves and the have-nots. The haves clearly do not understand how they contribute to there being have-nots. It is complicated by hundreds of years of racism and sexism tagging along with the classism. But injustice can always be overcome by a people who make justice and equality their main priority, as this nation once intended to do. Many other priorities have held sway in recent years.

"Jesus preached a gospel of peace, but his gospel of peace hinged on bringing healing to the sick, and justice to the poor. Many Christians ignore this fact, as though forgiveness of sins was the whole of Jesus' message.

"But I tell you avoiding sin by avoiding exploitation of the poor was primary in Christ's teachings, as you can see some places in the gospels. 'Blessed are the poor,' Jesus said, and so I have come to tell you that, as liberation theologians around the world have discussed, God is on the side of the oppressed.

"What does that mean? 'God is on the side of the oppressed' means that God longs for every nation to create economic systems in which people are paid a fair and living wage, both within their own nations, and as a basis for international trade.

"Every human being deserves the dignity of a decent job, or the support while being a stay-at-home parent. Christ honors you, each of you here tonight, for who you are, for choosing life amidst the struggles you face each day, and for blessing others with your faith.

"Let's talk about faith. Sometimes we hope that if we pray for one specific thing, then God will answer our prayer. And God does answer our prayer, but not if the thing for which we are praying is more important to us than God is. To live prayerful lives of faith, we must become one hundred percent devoted to God, first and foremost, no matter what our religion, and *then* we can pray for something. God knows that we need food, shelter, dignity, and health, and God always helps those who connect with God through faith and loving devotion. Does God always pave the way so that our lives are easy?

"No, of course not. We know that. We know that life is full of pain and suffering and seemingly endless challenges. God cares about our challenges. God is love, and love always cares. But life is also about finding God; finding God in our own hearts and minds, and seeing the goodness of God in others. Sometimes we can only see a little of God's goodness in someone else, but there's always at least a little goodness and love in each person, no matter how wounded and warped they may have become.

"The challenges of life help us learn to let go of everything else until we see God. 'Blessed are the pure in heart, for they shall see God.' If your trials and tribulations are not helping you become pure in heart and see God, then the trouble with your life is *not* actually the trouble with your life. The real trouble with all of our lives is that we so often become preoccupied with the stuff of life that we forget that God is the most important aspect of every life, of all life, everywhere, all the time.

"Through our troubles, we need to choose to have faith, no matter how hard it may seem, to have faith that God is with us in the midst of our troubles, and that, if we stay calm, God will help us figure out a way out of our problems.

"Love will find a way. That is a true statement. It is important to use affirmations to change the way we live life. Here are some affirmations that may help, and I have had them printed up onto little cards that you may take with you:

God is love.
Love is real no matter what the world is dishing out.
Love is real no matter what comes my way.
Love will help me succeed in life.
Love knows a better way.
Love lights my path.
Love leads me home.
Love is the way, the truth, and the life for me.
Let love fill my heart, peace fill my mind, and hope give me strength.
Love will help me succeed.
God loves me; I have nothing to fear.
The very real presence of God is within me.
The very real presence of love is within me.
All I need I have within me.
God's wisdom shows me the way, in the quiet moments in my mind.
Peace, be still, I am love, says the Lord.
I love you, says God, who is like the best mother in the world.
God is love, and I am love's son (or daughter).
I will grow in God's love.
All is well in God's love.
So be it. Amen. Om."

As Jing Sheng read the affirmations, it was as though a lullaby swept around the room. Everyone grew more relaxed, and a faithful, friendly feeling spread like a calming good-night glow, comforting as well as a fire in a fireplace on a cold winter night.

"Thank you all for listening, please take a card if you'd like, and have a good night."

Jing Sheng rose, bowed in Namaste all around to those seated in the circle (and last to the news camera – or maybe it was more to the news crew that was present – Liz couldn't tell), and then walked out of the room and went into the office.

♥ ♥ ♥

At 5:00 a.m. the next morning, some of the volunteers began to prepare breakfast while Jing Sheng, Liz, Darnell, Adam, and Daniel all headed over to the studio of American Morning News Hour. On the way there, Liz learned that Jing Sheng had risen at 4:30 and created the first of what was to become many lessons in spiritual enlightenment for all people who sought The Teachings. She realized that his staff of mostly volunteers were going to have to send them out via e-mail not just across the nation, but also around the world. *Who's translating them?* She wondered, but as they were arriving at the studio, she did not have a chance to ask.

Roberta Robins enthusiastically greeted them with her ever-present, cheerful smile.

"Good morning, Jing Sheng, I'm so glad to see you. We'll be taping for fifteen minutes after you have had a session with our make-up crew. I'll meet you in ten minutes, ok?"

"Okay." To Liz, Jing Sheng always sounded more Asian when he said 'okay' than he did at any other time. She loved him for that, too. She loved him for every ounce of who he was, and is, and would be to come.

Once on the set, Jing Sheng sat opposite Roberta Robins, and looked particularly dashing in his Tai Chi master attire. The make-up did not make him look terribly pretentious, just gave his skin a warmer, non-shiny glow. For those who could see auras, he had enough glow of his own to transform make-up or a lack of it, either one!

"Good day to you, I'm Roberta Robins and I'm sitting here with Mr. Hu Jing Sheng from China, a Tai Chi master whom we introduced to our audience last week. Mr. Hu has kindly returned to be interviewed in a series of interviews all week long."

"Thank you, Mr. Hu, for returning to our show."

"You are welcome and good morning, Roberta, and all who seek."

"Speaking of seeking, Mr. Hu, I know I asked you last week, and you refused to answer, but apparently some people really do believe that you are the reincarnation of Jesus Christ; is that true?"

"Roberta, I AM WHO I AM, and those who know who I AM know the truth about me. Who I AM is not something that I can teach you or tell you." Jing Sheng smiled so genuinely and lovingly while sounding so mysterious. Liz thought that if his smile didn't captivate the audience, nothing could.

"I see. Well, I for one am still confused about who you are, so I'd like to ask you some other questions. First, why did you come to America?"

"My message is a mission of world peace and healing. My mission is Exodus 2012. Exodus 2012, as you know, is a scripture, and 2012 is the end of the Mayan calendar," Jing Sheng paused to allow Roberta to keep up with him; Liz thought that was a mistake.

"Exodus 20:12 would be one of the Ten Commandments – honor your father and mother, I think, is that right?" Roberta piped up quickly.

"Yes, however, the spiritual understanding of this text has been limited for roughly 3,000 years. A deeper meaning, in addition to honoring your parents, is to honor your heavenly Father and your earthly Mother."

"And just what do you mean by your earthly Mother?"

"Our earthly Mother is that aspect of God that pervades the universe – the omnipresent aspect of God that Christians might call the Holy Spirit. She is the mother of creation, just as the transcendent aspect of God, which is beyond this universe, is the father of all creation, and yet, they are of one substance – one God." Jing Sheng spoke slowly and certainly, but Liz figured only theologians would really get what he was saying.

"Fascinating," Roberta Robins replied. "So, would you consider yourself a Christian, or a Christian theologian?"

"I AM true to the teachings of Christ; you may call me what you will." Jing Sheng held his hands in prayer position in his lap, and opened them upwards as he spoke.

"Well, I'm not sure you sound like a Christian, but which teachings of Christ are you sharing in your message to America?" Roberta stayed on top of the interview, alright.

"Well, first let us consider that Christ's teachings did not all make it into the Bible, so I draw directly from his teachings, not just the ones in the Bible. And the most important lesson which I would like to share today is that all people are children of God. First and foremost, all people have a soul, which is that aspect of them which is born of God.

"Secondly, those who open up to the Spirit of God dwelling in their hearts and minds and directing them on their path, are truly children of God who are growing up into the fullness of the image of God. An Enlightened Master is a person who becomes one with the Spirit of God, letting go of their ego-self, and choosing to let their souls become one with the Spirit of God leading them and guiding them until there is a perfect unity between their higher Self and God – they have become One. Jesus Christ was one such Enlightened Master, or Son of God, but not the only one who walks or has walked the earth. There are and have been numerous Sons and Daughters of God who are Enlightened."

"Really? Name one or two for us, please, if you will." Roberta looked mystified, but leaned towards him, eagerly paying attention.

"Well, of course the Buddha was Enlightened. So also have been many Hindu gurus. The most well-known enlightened guru who has come to the United States was Paramahansa Yogananda, who founded the Self-Realization Fellowship, and who also wrote the book *Autobiography of a Yogi*. In that book, you can truly see the teachings of Christ, just as you can in the Bible."

"Wow, I'm sure many Christians will object to that teaching. Are you here to start a new religion?"

"As I said, I am on a mission to bring healing to the humanity, with peace and health for all life on earth as well. When we honor both our heavenly Father and our earthly Mother, it is the only way that we will be able to live long in the land, as the Bible says. So, now, we must care for the earth, and for one another."

"Thank you. Hu Jing Sheng, ladies and gentlemen. We will be interviewing Mr. Hu more tomorrow and all week. Please stay tuned."

"Well, that certainly was interesting, Mr. Hu. Tomorrow do you have anything particular in mind that you would like to share?"

"Oh, yes, I would like to address acceptance of people of all religions, instead of the myth that non-Christians will go to hell."

"Wow! That sure will be a page-turner for us, as it were! I look forward to seeing you tomorrow. And I understand that we will be taping the rest of the interviews tomorrow after the show so that you can then travel to Washington, D.C. Is that correct?"

"Yes, thank you for accommodating my schedule." Jing Sheng bowed in Namaste to Roberta, and she stuck out her hand to shake hands. He shook her hand very gently.

Liz, Darnell, Adam, and Daniel surrounded Jing Sheng and swooped him out of the studio.

"We have some questions for you," Liz spoke up assertively.

"Yes, my little dove," Jing Sheng made her feel as though she was the only person in the world, but then, he could make everyone feel that way, if they let him.

"Well, first, are you charging anything for these lessons you're sending out? I mean, we've received donations, I know, but somehow, we need to make money."

"And speaking of money, we need your help covering our time and expenses – I'm on unpaid leave from my job," added Darnell, who really meant more respect than came through because he had a little fear going on.

"Darnell, please do not let fear get between us. Thank you for attending to financial matters, both of you. Let us go to the Chase Manhattan Bank where there is an account we can draw on. I'll discuss the other financial details with you later."

So, that day was spent mostly in preparing for the expansion of the mission, hiring a few translators (New York City is a great place to find translators, what with the United Nations there and all). Liz found it very exciting.

That evening was spent offering prayer, counseling sessions, and healing to the guests at the homeless shelter. Liz finally began to use her gift of healing. The results were extraordinary, and one woman began to tell everyone that Liz had healed her of her gout, even though Liz kept insisting that God was the healer, and that she just showed up and prayed.

The TV crew came back, and when they got wind of the healings, they interviewed Liz, too. The commentator closed with these remarks:

"Tonight, we have witnessed a miracle, or several miracles. Right here at the homeless mission, Mr. Hu Jing Sheng and his followers have been praying for healing for the guests at the shelter. One woman reports that her gout was healed. An older gentleman reports that his cataracts are gone. A little girl says that her toothache went away. Could Jing Sheng be the reincarnation of Jesus Christ? That's what people are wondering down here at the mission, where miracles are occurring."

"Oh, great, that's just what we need – now people are going to come in droves to see us. I mean, this is New York City – the most populous city on the east coast. What are we going to do?" Liz complained to Daniel and Darnell.

"Let's hope Jing Sheng has a plan," Darnell responded.

"You've got a gift, surely God will not overwhelm you with demands to use it – or maybe Jing Sheng can turn more of us into healers so that you're not alone. That's a good idea, I'll go ask him," Daniel finally developed a sense of purpose and connected to the mission. Liz felt relieved, both at the thought of not having to do all of the healings (except of course, what Jing Sheng did), and at the idea that Daniel finally found himself a place in Jing Sheng's scheme of things.

Sure enough, Daniel returned fifteen minutes later, grabbed Liz and hugged her, saying, "He gave me the gift of healing – I can feel it! It feels like heaven on earth!"

"That's wonderful; I'm so glad," Liz effused, and gave Daniel a real kiss, which he gladly returned.

"Hey, hey! That's enough in here!" Darnell didn't want to have to deal with an office romance, as it were, but he couldn't complain too much, since Adam was with him. "Just make sure you two put the mission first, will you?"

"Oh, Darnell, please stop worrying so. It will be alright. Haven't you learned that yet from being with Jing Sheng?" Liz let go of Daniel and gave Darnell a shoulder massage. "Maybe you need to go do some Tai Chi. Oh, wouldn't that be a wonderful thing to do here at the shelter? Why don't you stay here and do that with folks tomorrow while Jing Sheng and Daniel and I go to the studio?"

"I like that idea," Darnell replied. "I'll check with Jing Sheng."

The next morning, Darnell stayed and led some early morning Tai Chi while Jing Sheng, Liz, and Daniel headed over to the studio. Darnell and Adam planned to join them after the initial interview, but before the full taping of the remaining three segments.

"Good day to you, I'm Roberta Robins, and this is Mr. Jing Sheng Hu here with me again today. Mr. Hu, since you were with us yesterday, we have heard some news that some miraculous healings took place last night at the homeless shelter. Is that right?"

"Yes, some would call them miracles, Roberta. Please call me Jing Sheng, by the way."

"Did you perform the healings, or did some of your followers?"

"Well, one of my followers, Liz Cooper, has the gift of healing – God can cure anything through her, if God wills it. She and I performed some healings on a few people. And I have shared the gift of healing with another follower as well, so that more of us can respond to people's needs." Jing Sheng remained as calm as ever, while discussing miracles as though they happened every day. Of course, around him, *they did*.

"What kind of healing did people receive?" Roberta asked, knowing full well that the show's ratings depended on such sensational news.

"One woman was cured of her gout. One man had his cataracts removed, and one little girl was cured of a toothache." Jing Sheng answered innocently enough, as though he had never considered that they would now be avalanched by requests for healing, in person and online.

"Wow, for real!? They were actually cured of those things, not just temporarily felt better?"

"God heals all wounds, inner and outer. It is up to us to choose to live according to God's will, whether we are healed or not, and someday, on this earth or in the next world, we will be healed."

"So now you're saying that people are not always healed of every disease when they ask God to heal them?" Roberta seemed genuinely disappointed.

"That is right. Prayer is not so much about getting God to do something for us, as it is about lining us up with where we are meant to be. All of us struggle to be in line with God's will, and we need to get ourselves in line with the will of love if we would be healed."

"What do you mean by getting ourselves in line with the will of love?"

"Well, God is love, and when we ourselves are neglecting to love God, to love others, or to love ourselves properly through good nutrition, exercise, and self-care, then we cannot be fully cured if we stay out of line with the fullness of God's love. Permanent healing and wholeness comes from being filled with Divine love for ourselves, for all life, and for God, God's Self." Jing Sheng paused and smiled at Roberta, who looked mystified.

"God, God's Self?"

"Yes, that is one way of avoiding the tendency to limit God to one gender, whether male or female. In different time periods, humankind has preferred either the female aspect of Goddess, or the male aspect of God. Really, our Divine Creator is both."

"So you use political correctness now in your faith, in religious language, too?"

"Of course. Political correctness at its best is about including all people with our language so that they will have equal power, equal affirmation, and equal inclusion. To refer to God as just 'he' leaves women and girls out of what it means to be holy and god-like, or divine. Men certainly are in *no way* more divine than women."

"Does that mean that you support women being priests, or ministers and pastors?"

"Of course. Jesus had female disciples, the men just refused to recognize them as such, because Jesus lived in a patriarchal culture. But many of the early priests were actually women. If you could read the New Testament in Greek, that would be apparent to you."

"So I have heard, so I have heard. Well, thank you so much for your enlightening, and I might say, controversial remarks, Mr. Hu. We look forward to having you on our show again tomorrow, and the rest of the week!

"You are welcome," again, Jing Sheng bowed to Roberta in Namaste, and this time, they showed him doing so on national TV.

"Oh, my, you realize that people are going to flood us from all directions with requests for healing, don't you?" Liz demanded abruptly as soon as she saw Jing Sheng.

"Liz, many people need healing, do they not?" Jing Sheng looked at her quizzically and smiled.

She knew there was no need to answer that one. She just bowed to him in silence.

The interviews went on after they had been served a lovely breakfast with tea and fruit and French toast. Jing Sheng had green tea, and skipped the butter and syrup, putting the fruit directly on the French toast instead. *Health nut,* muttered Liz in her own head, but she knew she should do the same, especially as she was now apparently a model of what it means to be a healer. So, she did likewise. Daniel, Greek-god look and all, of course ate like a health nut.

After that, they all three did some Tai Chi together, while they waited for Roberta to be ready to interview him. It is hard to do Tai Chi and receive text messages on cell phones, not to mention that Darnell kept calling him to warn him that people were lining up outside the door for healing. The homeless shelter just said that, if they wanted to make a donation to the shelter, they were welcome to stay. Only a few turned away. Jing Sheng and Liz ignored their phones.

Finally, after the Tai Chi, they began to respond to text and voice messages. They were busy until Roberta finally appeared, a couple of hours later.

"I apologize, but your segment has lighted up the phone lines with requests for healings, and our producer wants to take a new angle on the show. Would you be willing to do some healings live on TV? Or taped - I know you have to go to Washington, DC, but how about one more interview, and then we'll open up the doors to ten people for healing, and the Thursday and Friday segments can just show you healing people. Does that work for you?"

Liz moaned.

"Of course." Jing Sheng sounded pleased. "My assistants, Liz Cooper and Daniel Stavros are both healers, and we will need them as well, to save time. And of course, they will need to be compensated."

"Of course, I'll work out the details. Let me just speak briefly with my manager, and then we'll begin the final interview." Roberta whirled around and was hardly gone before she came zooming back in the room, excitement personified.

"We already have ten or fifteen people who really need healing; they're being screened for fraudulent stories while we do the interview, so let's get cracking." She led them back into the part of the studio where they taped interviews.

Jing Sheng sat, as before, while a couple of make-up artists touched up his face, and combed back his lustrous, straight black hair.

"Good day to you, America, I'm Roberta Robins, and I'm once again privileged to interview Mr. Hu Jing Sheng, a Tai Chi master from China, who tells me that Christians are wrong when they say that they are the only people who are saved and will get to go to heaven. Why on earth would you make that kind of claim, Mr. Hu?"

"Thank you for asking, Roberta. First of all, imagine living in China, if you will, with billions of other people, most of whom are not Christian. Imagine, just for a moment, that everyone you know and most of your fellow countrymen and women are supposed to go to hell. Billions of people that God supposedly does not love enough to save. Is that really a loving God? I do not think so. God is love, as the Bible says, so love is the primary goal of everything that happens in creation. Behind every act of evil and wrongdoing, love stands as a reminder that it is the preferred way, and the only eternal way of being."

"But Mr. Hu, Jesus Christ said "I am the way, the truth, and the life, no one comes to the Father but by me," quoted Roberta Robins, who certainly had her scriptures memorized.

"Yes, but that quote is found in the gospel of John, which, first of all, is a very mystical gospel. Most of its spiritual teachings are not meant to be taken literally; rather, they are to be understood mystically. When Jesus uses the phrase 'I AM,' he is identifying Divine Spirit or Christ-consciousness within himself. But that same Divine Spirit, or Christ-consciousness is available to everyone – everyone can attain what the apostle Paul referred to as the mind of Christ, or as I refer to it, Christ-consciousness, although one could also refer to it as Buddha-Consciousness.

"Jesus did not seek to have a bunch of followers who would be called Christians. He set out to invite people to become Christ-like, as in his remark, 'be ye therefore perfect, even as your Father in heaven is perfect.' There are many non-Christians who are very Christ-like. There are also many Christians who are far from being Christ-like in their thoughts, their speech, and their way of acting in the world. What saves all of us is finding the Christ-presence within ourselves, and living as that presence in the world."

"Wow, Mr. Hu, that certainly is a controversial view. Well, thank you for clearing that up. We have time now for one or two brief issues; is there anything else that you would like to state to our audience today?" Roberta was obviously uncomfortable, but kept smiling because she knew the ratings would be skyrocketing. She just kept thinking how lucky she was to get to interview him, instead of one of the other major networks.

"Yes, Roberta, thank you for asking. First, please allow me to speak to the issue of abortion."

Roberta's smile faded, though she nodded and said, "Okay."

Jing Sheng continued. "Long ago, Jesus Christ said, 'as you do it unto the least of these members of my family, you do it unto me.' Now, an unborn baby has a soul, and as such, is just as much a child of God as anyone else, and therefore, a member of Christ's family. So, if we abort an unborn child, we are treating Christ himself that way also."

"Oh, Mr. Hu, some people are going to love you for that, but what about a woman's right to choose?" Roberta stayed on top of this one.

"Yes, a woman does have a right to choose. God gives us free will in all things, and to take away a woman's right to choose is to take away a fundamental freedom that women deserve to have. Any man who is Truthful would acknowledge that, if he were a woman, he would also demand the right to choose. To treat a woman any other way is to treat her as less than a man, and that would be wrong and unloving in the eyes of God and of Jesus Christ.

"Some women choose to have an abortion, because it is the most loving choice they know how to make. No one else has the right to judge whether or not a woman is making a loving choice. As long as abortion is chosen as an act of love, and not merely for convenience or self-interest, then God, as love, respects the choice, and the unborn soul receives another chance to return to the earth. We should all pray for the souls of unborn children who are aborted, that they will be guided safely and lovingly back into the realms of God's Spirit, where they will be loved."

"I see, so Mr. Hu, apparently you are saying that abortion should be a choice of last resort, and only if it can be made out of love?"

"Yes, that's right, Roberta."

"Thank you. Is there just one more issue you would like to clear up for us today?" Roberta seemed a little uncertain what to expect.

"Yes, the issues of gay, lesbian, and transgender people."

"Another hot one – okay, that's alright, that's what we're here for," Roberta appeared to be trying to stay calm, while bobbing her head up and down and smiling a little.

"Let my people go."

"Excuse me? What do you mean by that?" Roberta now looked really confused, but still smiling slightly.

"Let my people go; do not hold them hostage as victims of your own moral self-righteousness. The Bible speaks of homosexuality the way it does because homosexual practices during the time of the Bible rarely had anything to do with consensual sex between two equal partners. Often, it was a cultic act in a temple, with a temple prostitutes serving as a representative of some god, or it was the Greek practice of a male teacher sodomizing his student. Neither of these were activities that God, who is love, had in mind.

"Consensual acts of sex between two equal and consenting adults (not teenagers, by the way), is what God has in mind. Teenagers are not ready for the responsibility of parenting; they should not have sex until they are willing to accept that possibility and responsibility. But two men engaging in loving sexual activity within a committed relationship is no less holy than a man and a woman doing so. The same is true of two women partners. God ordains loving, committed relationships between equal partners, just as God, God's Self, has both masculine and feminine aspects in equal partnership.

"Okay, well, that's a very clear statement. We have time for a brief statement about transgender individuals..." Roberta looked encouragingly to Jing Sheng to hurry up.

"Yes, often these individuals feel confused because their previous lifetime was spent in a body of the opposite gender. Everyone's soul chooses the specifics of gender, mother, and major life issues to be faced before they incarnate again into a human body. If you have chosen a male body or a female body with which you feel really uncomfortable, you alone can know what is the real spiritual issue that needs to be worked out in your life: whether to accept and live in that body, or to change it and deal with a different status in relation to other people who might judge you."

"Thank you, Mr. Hu Jing Sheng. Ladies and gentleman, you heard it here first on American Morning News Hour. We'll be right back."

"Wow! Mr. Hu, I don't think you're going to win any popularity contests, but I really appreciate what you had to say. I only wish we could talk longer. Perhaps you could return for a visit some day?" Robert offered her hand to him as they walked down the hall.

"I have no desire to win popularity contests, Ms. Robins. However, you are always welcome to join us on our mission."

"Well, thank you, Mr. Hu. Let's just check in here on how many people need healing, and then, after a little lunch, we'll tape the healing sessions, alright?"

"That's fine, thank you." Jing Sheng looked a little wearied. Liz felt a touch of worry for him for the very first time.

"Are you alright?" She asked him.

"Nothing a little prayer and lunch won't cure." Jing Sheng smiled.

"We will have to eat lightly, though, in order to keep our energy light for being vessels of God's healing energy."

"Yes, we will," Liz replied, and Daniel nodded.

The healing sessions went superbly. Jing Sheng laid his hands on the head of a woman who obviously looked ill; she had a tumor growing in her lungs and one in her brain. She was bald from chemotherapy treatments. Within moments, she not only changed skin color, looked radiant and energized, but also peach fuzz began to grow on her head.

"Oh my gosh! I feel so much energy!" She exclaimed. "Thank you!" Tears streamed down her face as she jumped up and hugged Jing Sheng. "My pain is gone! And there's hair on my head – peach fuzz – oh, thank you so much!" She hugged him again.

Liz had placed her hands above the head of a child with spina bifida. The child was not able to sit up properly. As the healing occurred, the child began to sit up straighter and straighter.

The mother, who was watching from behind, started screaming, "He's healed! He's healed! Look at that, he can sit up!" She jumped up and hugged her child, and then hugged Liz. The child smiled, stood up, and hugged his mother back. They walked out of the studio together.

Daniel placed his hands on the head of a man with diabetes, who was told he was about to lose one leg. He was also obese, had heart trouble, and was seated in a wheelchair. The man breathed rapid, loud, shallow breaths, which were clearly visible as his large chest rose up-and-down in an exaggerated manner. As the healing energy grew, the man started to breathe more slowly, and rubbed his leg, saying, "My leg feels better – all tingly … and now just right."

He stood up and shook Daniel's hand, wiping tears away from his eyes with his left hand.

"Thank you, thank you! I feel so good. I'm going to go out and get some exercise and eat the way the doctor tells me to. I have hope now; thank you, thank you, thank you!"

He looked at the wheel chair, waved it away with his hand, and walked out.

The next round came in, with similar results. Roberta Robins and the whole crew just watched, saying things like, "This is amazing." "I can't believe my eyes." "Are you sure this is real?" "I'm not dreaming, am I?" "You mean God is real, after all?" "Wow!"

Roberta closed the segment with these remarks:

"Just to be clear for our audience, these people are not getting paid to act as though they have been healed. As a matter of fact, they completely volunteered to come on the show to receive healing, and only healing; no monetary compensation has been allowed. This is the real thing, folks! Hu Jing Sheng, Liz Cooper, and Daniel Stavros of Exodus 2012: A Mission to Save the Earth! Thank you; we'll be right back."

♥ ♥ ♥

The rest of that day and evening was spent doing healings at the homeless shelter. Income flowed into the shelter as never before. Many people who were healed signed up to return as volunteers, because they were so grateful and touched by God's presence in the midst of the suffering at the shelter.

Early the next morning, Jing Sheng and his followers packed their bags. From New York, Jing Sheng, Liz, Darnell, and a few dozen followers traveled down to Washington, D.C., where the U.S. Congress was deciding whether or not to give billionaires another tax break. At the same time, congress had to decide whether or not to renew unemployment checks to millions of people who had been out of work for over 99 weeks because of the poor economy. So, what were the legislators with cushy benefit packages who never had to worry about income or benefits in retirement now doing? They were forcing nearly hopeless, jobless people to wait while they negotiated tax breaks for wealthy people.

Jing Sheng had something to say about this.

So, Darnell made arrangements, and Liz communicated with the followers. By train, they traveled to D.C., to save energy, and hence, the environment. Many of the followers traveled by train as well; while others chose their own means of transportation. Liz constantly had to schedule appointments for them with Jing Sheng, who taught many of them lessons on meditation and advancement of their souls. Fortunately, these appointments often led to large contributions to a growing bank account, of which Darnell had to keep track. Darnell and Liz both stayed very busy. Everywhere they went, people asked for healings, which meant that Jing Sheng, Liz, and Daniel all stayed busy with that as well.

Liz realized this was all just one big lesson in attaining and maintaining the Christ-Presence, no matter what else was happening in life. So, she accepted the challenges, and remembered to breathe in the light of Love as much as possible. Life, to her, felt amazing.

She still felt kind of doubtful about getting and keeping a relationship going with Daniel, but working with Jing Sheng was like an unreal dream. Somehow, everyone back at her wellness center was coping nicely; she would have to make it up to them one way or another, maybe with the help of Jing Sheng.

When they arrived in Washington, media found them as they arrived at the Washington Palace Hotel, one of the few hotels with rooms for under $200 anywhere near the White House. Darnell and Liz went into action, keeping the media at bay, but Jing Sheng leapt up onto a very high retaining wall, and addressed the crowd.

"Friends, thank you for coming."

Since when does anyone address the press as 'friends', Liz wondered.

"I have come to speak on the steps of Congress, but I understand I must receive a security clearance before we can receive a permit. I intend to speak Friday morning. Please come be my guests." Jing Sheng bowed, sprang down from the wall, and slipped through the crowd into the hotel.

Friday morning arrived, and a large crowd had gathered, several hundred people having converged on Congress that day. Somehow, a security clearance had been passed through for Jing Sheng, miracle enough in its own right.

Jing Sheng stood as close as he was allowed to the building, a portable microphone unit having been set up so that he could address the crowd. He literally had to stand on an old-fashioned 'soap box' to be seen.

"Friends, thank you for coming. I especially thank the congressional leaders who will hear what I have to say. It is to them that I address this speech.

"In America today, millions of people are unemployed or significantly underemployed, or significantly underpaid for the value of their work. Millions of people are struggling to keep roofs over their heads and to make ends meet. More and more children are living in poverty in America as millions of families are sinking financially. Millions of adults over 50 are unemployed and feeling un-employable, or are under-employed or are living on severely fixed incomes. Millions of Americans struggle to have enough food to eat; in fact, millions of children go to bed hungry, and go to school hungry as well. With so many people having a tough time, is it truly apparent to anyone that billionaires need tax cuts? Does that make sense in any way to you?

"I understand that you believe that America is built by the entrepreneurs who become rich, but I tell you, America is built by the underpaid working class – citizens of the world who contribute their energy and time so that others get rich off of their backs. Or you believe that America's wealth is built by the middle class, which is partly true, but again, I tell you, it is the underpaid poor people of the world who fund all the rest of you. The very people you look down on do the work you don't want to do or don't have time to do, and you pay them too little so that you can earn more and have more.

"Many of you have no business calling yourselves Christians, although you do. Christ said, "My sheep hear my voice, and I know them, and they follow me." Would Jesus Christ stand here in this capitol and recommend a tax-break for billionaires while so many people suffer? Let us listen again to Christ's voice today: "Feed my sheep!"

"With my apologies to those of you who are of other religions or of no religion, please know that I am aware that many non-Christians are more Christ-like than are many Christians. And yet, many of you Congressional leaders purport to be Christian, but have little idea what it means to be Christ-like. You arrogantly believe that having faith will save you, when in fact showing faithfulness is the only way to be made whole.

"Faithfulness depends on having faith, but having faith without showing faith's fullness is like giving birth to a stillborn child.

"Christ told the rich young ruler long ago that, if he wanted to be saved, he needed to go and sell all he owned and to give the money to the poor. Do you think he was kidding?

"Why is it that you believe that you can call Christ your savior, and then ignore what he tells you to do? It is for this reason that he said, "many will call me Lord, Lord, but I will tell them 'I do not know you.' "

"Why do you allow your neighbor to suffer, when these very neighbors are your own responsibility? Why is it that you allow the rich to get richer, pretending that their riches will 'trickle down' to the masses who are unemployed, or earning minimum wage and working two jobs just to pay a few bills and get to eat?

"Why do you turn a blind eye to the suffering you yourselves inflict on others?

"Christ told you to serve your neighbors. Go out and find out what is happening to your neighbors beyond your own rich friends. Go live like a poor person for awhile, and then, and only then will you be worthy to follow Christ.

"If you have not yet sold all you own and given the money to the poor, you are unworthy of Christ, and have no reason to call Him your savior. Do not pretend to be Christians while you choose to benefit the rich, and rob from the poor.

"What is more, you determine the economy by choosing dirty energy sources that ruin the environment. The earth herself is what maintains a solid, vibrant economy. Yet you destroy the earth. It is time for economists to realize that sustainability is the balance that creates a harmony of all economies – *and every habitat in nature is an economy.*

"Likewise, it is time for economists to realize that there is a natural limit on economic growth posed by the earth herself in the form of equilibrium. If equilibrium is maintained for all life on earth, all habitats will thrive with life forms living in balance, and then humans can also maintain a sustainable economy. The idea of a growth economy continuing indefinitely constitutes the idol of a people who thrive on greed at the expense of other people, and at the expense of the environment.

"Have you not yet learned the lesson of the honeybees? When the honeybees die, there will be no more food for humankind – or only about one third of the crops which you are now blessed to eat. How many of you can name which crops don't need bees to survive? Do you like fruit? Save the bees. Do you like summer squash? Save the bees. Do you like almonds? Save the bees.

"My message is the message of Exodus 20:12 – honor your heavenly Father and your earthly Mother so that you may live long in the land.

To do this, you will need to care for people, specifically for children – for all children, and not just for some. To care for all children, your economic policies must benefit not only white suburban children but also African-American and Latino urban children and Native American children. To care for all children, your economic policies will have to benefit children in Asia and Africa and the Middle East – children of all races, all religions around the world, including Muslim children.

"Followers of Christ must practice non-attachment, letting go of all greed, and living lives of service for the good of humanity. It is simple. Now do it. Please do it *now* while there is still life on earth to sustain. So be it. Thank you for listening to me."

Jing Sheng stepped off his little soapbox, and immediately the media swarmed in to interview him. Darnell and Liz and Daniel and Adam all did their best to intervene and to protect Jing Sheng, but Darnell found himself wishing they had hired a bodyguard for him. Jing Sheng placed his hands in Namaste, and Darnell and Liz slid to his sides. With Adam and Daniel taking the outer edge, they cut through the crowd in a V formation, with Jing Sheng at the center. When they got to the cab they had paid to wait for them, Jing Sheng turned and waved to the crowd, bowed in Namaste, and sat down in the back seat of the cab.

Daniel climbed in beside him, Liz swept to the front and asked the driver to drive them out of there as fast as he could. "Where to from here?" Liz asked.

"Let us return to the hotel. There will be media present to interview us. We will speak to them there." Jing Sheng spoke calmly, despite the turbulence they had just gone through to escape the media and others.

11. PHAROAH SAID, "WHO IS THE LORD THAT I MUST HEED HIM?"

WHAT IS SUCCESS? MANY DEFINITIONS OF SUCCESS HAVE NOTHING TO DO WITH WHO GOD IS. WHAT HIGHER GOAL IS THERE THAN TO FIND GOD AND TO BECOME ONE WITH GOD? IF YOU HAVE NO DESIRE TO FIND GOD, THEN HOW CAN YOU CONCEIVE OF YOURSELF AS A SUCCESS IN LIFE, WHEN GOD IS THE CREATOR OF YOUR LIFE?

As they approached the Washington Palace Hotel, they became aware that the media had beat them to it, and it was going to be particularly difficult just to get in the front door. So, they took advantage of the hotel's underground parking garage, and drove far enough in for the cab to let them out without being followed, then took an elevator to the 11th floor, where Jing Sheng, Liz and Adam got off, while Darnell and Daniel rode back down to meet and screen the press. Fortunately, the hotel allowed them to set-up an interview space in one of the hotel ballrooms.

Jing Sheng came down, looking blindingly handsome and glowing with energy. A few minutes of meditation had revived him totally, and he felt inspired, peaceful, and prepared. Liz, on the other hand, felt stressed, anxious, worried; all those negativities in which a yogi or yogini (practitioners of yoga) are not supposed to get stuck. She meditated a few moments also, and managed to go down feeling peaceful enough to believe in Jing Sheng's ability to handle the press.

The first interview took place with Tom Burns, of one of the national TV news shows.

"Mr. Hu, I appreciate this interview, and I don't mean to be rude, but I would just like to clarify for our viewers: who do you think you are?"

Jing Sheng laughed; a deep-bellied, smiling-Buddha type of laugh.

"Mr. Burns, I am a Chinese Tai Chi master."
"
Yes, thank you, Mr. Hu, but I understand your name may mean Jesus Christ in Chinese, is that right?" Mr. Burns tried a new approach.

"My name, Jing Sheng, means 'perfect spiritual essence,' which describes God, whom I love very much."

"Thank you, Mr. Hu. Now, today, you addressed Congress on the very steps of the Capitol building, taking them on for continuing tax cuts for millionaires and billionaires. Why was that so important to you?"

"Mr. Burns, long ago, the prophets of Israel made it clear that God is on the side of the oppressed. Jesus Christ, in the line of all the great Jewish prophets, continued to proclaim that message from God, taking sides with the poor over against the rich young ruler. I merely choose to follow in Christ's footsteps."

"I see, so would you say that you are the reincarnation of Jesus Christ?" Mr. Burns was pretty slick, through years of experience interviewing all kinds of political tough nuts.

"It is not for me to say who I AM; it is for others to discover for themselves. Truth that is spoken in simple words often gets mangled by those who lack understanding. Divine wisdom is the imperative we seek if we would know the Truth, in order to become free."

Jing Sheng's expression matched the peaceful Buddha. The energy pulsing from him was so powerful, Liz had to sit a few feet away, and Tom Burns felt as though he was getting a sunburn from being in his presence.

"What does it mean to you to become free?" Burns tried a different tack.

"To be free is to practice non-attachment to the outward physical form. To be free is to know that you are divine spirit; divine spirit and you are one. To know this most fully, you have to let go of ego, which separates you from God, who is love. In the truth, peace, wisdom, and love of God, we can be set free for eternity."

"Mr. Hu, you sound like a preacher rather than a politician; I'm wondering why you came to Washington, D.C.?"

"Preachers belong wherever God's will needs to be done, and God's will is sorely lacking in Washington."

"Well, that's a clear statement of opinion! Thank you, Mr. Hu. Can you tell us what your plans are – what you plan to do next?"

"I will be speaking at The Verizon Center on Sunday afternoon, to explain our mission. The event will be free and open to the public, but only certain media will be allowed to attend."

"There you have it folks: Mr. Jing Sheng Hu will reveal his full mission, his reason for being here in the U.S., at the Verizon Center on Sunday afternoon. Stay tuned to this station for coverage and updates on Mr. Hu's mission."

And so it went. Reporters parried with Jing Sheng to the best of their abilities; he always floated about ten feet above them, which made it seem as though he always came out ahead in the end. At the end, Liz felt exhausted. She wished she could get a glass of red wine and go soak in the Jacuzzi.

Instead, they all went upstairs, ordered dinner in Jing Sheng's room, and after eating, they relaxed as much as they could, and then meditated. They took turns answering Jing Sheng's publicity cell phone, watching the news casts, and responding to the floods of e-mail coming in through the website Darnell and other volunteers had set up. Everything was turned off in order for them to meditate together as a group. Then everyone went to their respective rooms and slept soundly.

Saturday morning, they all met down in the hotel's exercise room where they did some calming yoga and Tai Chi together before engaging in more strenuous work-outs. Liz led the yoga, and Darnell practiced leading the Tai Chi. After showers, Jing Sheng led meditation. Then, breakfast was finally ordered about 8:30 a.m.

The calls and e-mails requesting healings took precedent over other types of meetings, although, in the afternoon, Jing Sheng offered a two-hour meditation workshop.

In the evening, he offered a spiritual growth workshop, and donations were accepted for both classes. The workshops and healings were all set-up in the smallest hotel ballroom. Liz , Daniel and Jing Sheng each performed about 4 healings an hour for three hours Saturday morning, and resumed for another hour-and-a-half in the afternoon. Still, that only covered about 70 people. Liz and Daniel agreed to do healings while Jing Sheng taught his evening class. Darnell and Adam were busy setting up Sunday's event all day.

Part of what had to be factored in was that, when you have 70 people cured instantly of their pain and diseases, the demand will quickly multiply to 100's of additional people, so they planned a morning-long healing session, with the speaking event to start at 2:00 p.m.

So, they took a cab to the Verizon Center, arriving at 9:00 a.m., and scheduled healings from 9:30 to 12:30 – three hours of truly natural spiritual healing energy, which, in-and-of-itself, feels miraculous.

Liz had created brochures, which Adam handed to people as he scheduled them for healings. The brochures explained energy healing, speaking of it as 'universal life force' energy, which comes from God, and that all healing comes from God.

Darnell was busy setting up other aspects of the event, including putting out the word that it was to be a "question-and-answer" session, as well as an opportunity to hear Jing Sheng describe the Exodus 2012 mission to save the earth.

When 2:00 p.m. arrived, Liz Cooper introduced herself, then introduced Jing Sheng as a Chinese Tai Chi master, and added the comment that some people believe that Jing Sheng is a reincarnation of Jesus Christ. She diplomatically explained, "If you listen carefully, you will hear echoes of the truths of Jesus Christ, and certainly you will hear echoes of the truths brought by enlightened masters through the ages. And yet, Master Jing Sheng brings a message for our time and our place, a message for each of us to change ourselves and our lifestyles, in order to save ourselves and our beloved Mother Earth. Please welcome Master Hu Jing Sheng."

Liz bowed in namaste as Jing Sheng came onto the stage, dressed, as always, in his Tai Chi attire. Jing Sheng bowed to Liz and then to the audience. The audience roared with praise and applause, some standing, some waving, some bowing, with others politely clapping, uncertain about what they were getting into.

As the crowd became quieter, the sound track began to play the very old song, "Where have all the flowers gone, long time passing, where have all the flowers gone, long time ago…" The music faded out, and Jing Sheng spoke: "I hope we will never have to ask where have all the flowers gone, but if we do not act, and act soon, we will lose almost all species of life forms upon the earth."

Dead silence stilled the whole auditorium.

"Scientists have been predicting that sixty percent of all species will be gone by the end of this century, unless we halt global warming. I call it global warming rather than climate change, because the term better fits the reality of raised CO_2 levels, and the offense that we have caused to Mother Earth. I realize that climate change best expresses the variability of temperatures and erratic weather patterns and strengthening of storms. I also realize that the warming of the air is not uniform around the entire globe. However, the rising CO_2 levels are also increasing the acidity of the oceans, which, along with their warming temperatures, could eliminate most life forms throughout all the oceans. And so it is that we urgently need to save the Earth.

"I have come to share this mission, which is the mission of Exodus 2012. I have also come to invite your understanding of Exodus 2012. 2012 is the year that the Mayan Calendar ends, a prediction we need to keep in mind when we consider the well-being of life on earth. In addition, Exodus 20:12 is a verse in the Hebrew Bible, which Christians call the Old Testament. The verse is one of the Ten Commandments, and it admonishes: 'honor your father and mother that you may live long in the land.'

Of course, divine love calls us to honor our parents who gave us birth, our biological father and mother. If we are adopted, divine love calls us to honor the parents who adopted us. Tying this concept to living in the land was a two-fold idea in Jewish thought.

First, there is the idea that being faithful to the law of God was what would enable the blessing of living in the land to be fulfilled. Second, there is the idea of Shalom, or wholeness and peace and well-being which encompasses people, God, animals, and the earth.

"What has been left out of the re-telling of this commandment for so many years is the higher spiritual commandment. That higher spiritual command is to love your Heavenly Father as well as your earthly Mother, or Mother Earth if you will. Some of you may have read the Essene Gospel of Peace, in which Jesus commanded a group of men to whom he brought healing that they were to do just that. In that gospel record which was not accepted into the Bible, Jesus acknowledged our earthly Mother and her angels of healing: her angels of the air, her angels of sunshine, and her angels of water.

What Christianity has continued to do throughout the ages is to deny the sacred feminine, that God is both Father and Mother, and that feminine beings are just as divine as masculine beings. Women are equal to men before God. No one is the head of the other.

"If we honor the sacred feminine, we can more readily honor our Mother earth, for she sustains us with energies and material well-being every day.

"However, if we fail to honor the sacred feminine, particularly as it manifests itself in a concern for all life, as well as the life of this planet, then we will face devastating consequences.

"Choose life, life in balance, if you would like to live well in the land, and pass on a healthy earth to your children and grandchildren. Such a choice will mean sacrificing some luxury and some pleasure, but it will also bring much joy."

Jing Sheng bowed, and Liz stepped up and announced that Jing Sheng would now receive questions at the microphones.

A young man was already waiting at a microphone, and Jing Sheng nodded to him.

"Mr. Hu, I am wondering if you realize that your statistics are outrageous. Certainly not all scientists agree that global warming is real, and it is not a common belief that 60% of species will die by the end of this century. I really don't appreciate your version of science – it's nothing but inflammatory, melodramatic, crisis-mindedness."

"I apologize for inadequate instructions, but would you please state your name before making comments or asking questions?" Jing Sheng spoke with respect and peace resonating in his voice.

"My name is Michael Novak, and I'm a biologist, and a Christian, from Grand Rapids, Michigan."

"Mr. Novak, we are neighbors, then, since I have lived in Kalamazoo, Michigan," Jing Sheng replied. "I am fully aware that a few scientists have not embraced the concept of global warming, and that the relatively new predictions of 60% species die-off sound alarming.

"I am also aware that the more information to which one pays attention biologically, climatologically, and chemically around the earth, the more one will become aware of the trends. If one looks only at a few statistics, one will not see the pattern. I also know that some people believe that climate change is a natural phenomenon, which it normally is, but not entirely in this case. I am also aware that some people think it constitutes sheer human arrogance, self-aggrandizement, and anthropocentrism to believe that humans could have so much of an impact on the earth.

"Nonetheless, we have to get ourselves out of denial, face our sins, and look at the reality of how we live our lives. Thank you, Mr. Novak," Jing Sheng bowed his head.

An older woman was at the other microphone, and Jing Sheng nodded to her.

"My name is Eldora Baker, and I am shocked to hear you say that God is a mother. The Bible clearly says that God is our Father – and Jesus himself called God his Father. How could you do blaspheme God's name by suggesting God is a mother?"

"Bless you Eldora Baker, for your forthrightness. Now that you have stated your concerns, we can address them. The Bible is full of the Holy Spirit's message, but the men who heard the Holy Spirit speak to them lived in a patriarchal culture, and so the only way they could hear the Spirit speak was when it sounded as though men were meant to be in control, and women were just there for the needs of men. They could not hear a higher spiritual truth than that, because they were locked into that lower spiritual energy in which one group of people marginalizes another group of people.

"The truth is that Jesus spoke the way they could hear him speak when he was in public, but in private, he gave many teachings, including to women such as Mary Magdalene, who was among his most spiritually attuned disciples. The male disciples were jealous of her, so they painted her as a prostitute, and the rest is history.

"Mrs. Baker, I ask you, are you a mother?"

"Yes, Mr, Sheng, I am."

"And Mrs. Baker, do you believe that you could have been a good mother if God did not already know how to be a good mother?"

"Oh, I'm sure God taught me how to be a good mother and helped me all the time when I prayed!"

"I'm so glad you prayed to be a good mother, Mrs. Baker, your children must be blessed."

Mrs. Baker glowed, beaming at the microphone.

"And Mrs. Baker, since God taught you how to be a good mother, doesn't it make sense that the source of knowing how to be a good mother comes from God because God is, herself, a good mother?"

"I'm sure I don't know what you mean, Mr. Sheng," stammered Mrs. Baker.

"Oh, yes, you do, Mrs. Baker. God is love, so you learned love from God, right?"

"Oh, yes, of course."

"And God is wise, so you learned wisdom from God, is that correct?"

"Yes, naturally.

"And God is a mother, so you learned to be a mother from God, who is the very best mother in the universe, wouldn't you say so?" Jing Sheng pressed gently, smiling at Mrs. Baker all the time.

"Well, now that you put it that way, it does kind of make sense, I guess…" Mrs. Baker did not look convinced.

"Thank you for talking with me, Mrs. Baker," Jing Sheng made every word sound and somehow feel honestly loving.

A young African-American male stepped up to the microphone, dressed in a suit and tie, and looking polished and ready for a public speech.

"Mr. Hu, I am Anthony Green, pastor of Almighty God Church of the Risen Jesus, in Atlanta, Georgia. I would just like to let you know that we Christians find it very offensive that you are stating that you are the reincarnation of Jesus Christ. I would like to ask you to stop making a false claim about our Lord and Savior, who is risen and sitting at the right hand of the Father in heaven."

"Thank you, Pastor Green, for giving us a heaven's view of the situation. Do I understand correctly then, that you have recently visited heaven and have seen Jesus first hand sitting on a throne?" Jing Sheng clasped his hands in front of him – such a human gesture to be made by a god.

"Well, no sir, of course not, but I believe what the Bible tells me."

"And did not the Bible tell you that Jesus would return?"

"Yes, Mr. Hu, of course the Bible tells me Jesus will return some day, but not this way, not Chinese, and certainly not reincarnated." Pastor Anthony Green knew how to put a lot of pastoral certainty into his voice.

"I appreciate your pastoral authority, Pastor Green, but I am equally sure that God did not need to consult with you or any pastors, or Bishops or Arch-Bishops before deciding how Jesus would come back or when. Did you think that the Bible needed to give everyone all the details, or could it be possible that God might have to come up with plan number two if people were really messing things up?"

"Oh, I'm sure we're messing things up, but now that you speak of it, we have much worse problems than global warming. We have young men coming home from war with injuries and combat stress disorder, and we have drugs and racism and too many young black men in prison. God surely does not want you to ignore all those problems does he?"

"Pastor Green, have you been listening to me?"

"Yes, sir, of course."

"Well, are you aware that if 60% of the plant and animal species on earth die, there will be no way to support human life?"

"Well, now that you put it like that, I can see that it is a primary concern to all of us, yes, indeed, a primary concern to all of us."

"Thank you, Pastor Green. If you would like to join my movement, you can decide who I am for yourself, but until you have walked with me for awhile, I doubt that you will be able to see the Truth. I make no claims about myself. Those who have eyes to see, see, as you know from reading your Bible."

"Yes, Mr. Hu, of course. Thank you for the invitation, but now why would I want to join someone who is blaspheming my Lord and Savior?"

"Pastor Green, I have the utmost respect for Jesus Christ – he is an enlightened master, and the only one who suffered as he did in order to make God's love and grace accessible to all, and I mean, to *all* people. But the time has come to understand Christ's message as he truly meant it, not just as it has become abbreviated in the New Testament.

"If you will follow me, you will see that our plan is to invite people around the world into community with one another, so that they can live in peace and harmony – Shalom or Salaam, across ethnicities, national boundaries, gender, and so on. Only by caring for one another's children is world peace going to occur. And only by caring for one another's children are the adults of this planet going to learn how to live in balance with all life on earth."

"Thank you, Mr. Hu," Pastor Anthony Green nodded his head, looking mightily confused. A member of Jing Sheng's followers came and touched the Pastor's arm, encouraging him to come speak with them for more information.

"I think you're just a lunatic cult," an old white lady hobbled up to the space just vacated by Pastor Green. "You should be ashamed of yourself, going and torturing poor innocent people with all these ideas. You have no idea what you're talking about!" She ambled away.

"It is clear to me that many people are confused about what I am saying," Jing Sheng commented, "but we must move on. Two more questions please, and then I would like to unveil our plan for global peace and to save the planet."

A woman stepped up to the other microphone and addressed Jing Sheng: "My name is Marian Taylor, and I am a feminist. I have no idea whether or not you are an enlightened master, but I want you to know that I don't believe for a minute that you are the reincarnation of Jesus Christ. However, I would like to know if you, as a self-styled spiritual master, know why on earth Jesus called that Canaanite woman a dog? I am so angry at Jesus for being so sexist and rude to her – how can you possibly explain it?"

Jing Sheng smiled. "Marian, I thank you for speaking your mind. It is good to hear out loud what is causing you agony so deep inside yourself. Before I answer, I have a question for you: Is it more important to you to be right and to prove you are right, or to learn the truth, whatever that truth might be?"

Marian retorted, "I'm an open-minded woman, I can learn the truth about things I don't know, but I'm also an educated woman with a Ph. D. so I am right about my field of expertise."

"Yes, quite so," Jing Sheng responded. "Your field of expertise is in art history, and so would you admit that you are not an expert on who is an enlightened master and who is not?"

"Wait, how did you know that my field of expertise is art history – did someone tell you that?" Marian fumed into the microphone.

"Marian, my field of expertise is being an enlightened master, which means listening to the voice of God. I have no need to learn these things from someone else."

Jing Sheng paused.

"Well, I never! Are you going to answer my question?" Marian was steaming and flabbergasted and felt embarrassed all at once – a very uncomfortable position to be in when one is standing at a microphone in front of 22,000 people.

"God bless you, Marian, for I see deep inside you the soul which seeks the Truth, even though your mind is absolutely certain that you cannot trust the truth that you are told by someone else." Jing Sheng's words calmed her a little bit.

"So, first of all, let us establish that there is a Truth beyond that which your rational mind can discover by itself. All Truth rests in the consciousness of God. We can access that Truth only by turning to God, who is the source of all Truth.

"Anyone who seeks to know the Truth must have not only a great mind, but also a great heart. Also and above all else, anyone who seeks the Truth must seek from their soul – that part of them which is their greater self – or higher self, which is connected to the Great Spirit, or God. Just as in old-fashioned navigation it was imperative to have three points in order to determine one's location, so also, in navigating towards the Truth, everyone must have mind, heart, and soul in order to locate oneself in the Truth of God. God's Truth will always be out there; the question is do we open ourselves up beyond our own limited mental truth in order to allow God's Truth to dwell within us? Jing Sheng paused while people tried to absorb all this.

"The truth about Jesus the Nazarene speaking to the Syro-Phoenecian woman is this: first of all, she was not really a Canaanite, she was just referred to that way in the gospel of Matthew. Matthew's version of the story shows disrespect to her in a number of ways, most notably by naming the land of her birth incorrectly, and also by making her sound desperate. Mark's version of the story makes the Syro-Phoenecian woman sound determined, rather than desperate, which is closer to the truth. She loved her daughter, and she had faith that this Jesus was the Messiah, and that, as God's representative on earth, he would heal her.

"Jesus admired both her faith, and her wisdom, and the force of love within her which gave her the determination to seek healing for her daughter. When he used the metaphor of dogs, masters, children, and the table, he was using an everyday metaphor, easily recognizable by everyone in that day, to say that the proper order was being overthrown by this woman's request. He was also overturning the natural order of her own society, which considered themselves the children and the Jews to be the dogs. Of course the Jews saw themselves as masters, and the 'Canaanites' as dogs. She brought with her, symbolically, the biases of her own culture that the reverse was true, just as you, Marian, and everyone in this room brings the biases of their own culture.

"Nonetheless, was Jesus' remark, on one level, rude and arrogantly Jewish? Yes, it was. He was tired and seeking to get away from all the people who drew on God's energy through him. He needed a rest, a break, vacation, if you will. And he was still thinking that God had only called him to be the spiritual Messiah of Israel. Jesus did not perceive his role as saving the whole world until he was resurrected and ascended as a master in heaven, which is when God straightened him out."

"Was Jesus being sexist? Perhaps, by the standards of today, he sounded sexist, but by the standards of his day, the very fact that he would listen to a woman speak to him in public was a sign of his utmost respect for women as equals."

There was a pause while that soaked in and everyone found themselves hoping for more explanation. Rather than adding explanations, Jing Sheng sent out a renewed wave of peaceful, loving energy, which apparently even Marian felt.

"Thank you, Master Jing Sheng," Marian replied. Jing Sheng noticed her upgrading his status, and bowed in Namaste to her.

A nervous-looking young man stood at the other microphone, and announced himself, "Master Jing Sheng, my name is Drew Seinfeld, and I have two questions to ask if I may?"

"Not counting that question? Yes, you may." Jing Sheng chuckled.

"Sorry – of course. Well, first, hearing that last discussion, I'd just like to ask, are you saying that enlightened masters are imperfect, and that they still commit 'sin' or whatever you would call it?"

"Yes, Drew, enlightened masters are imperfect by design. They all have a blind spot that keeps them from mistaking themselves for God – or at least that's the divine intention behind our limitations.

Enlightened masters become masters because their intention is to fulfill the will of God in and through themselves, but even so, they are human and make mistakes as well. Jesus himself pointed this out when he said, 'why do you call me good? No one is good but God alone.' So, did Jesus 'sin?' not so much sin as miss the mark of

God's will slightly in a few of his words and actions, which is really what the origin of the word 'sin' means anyway. We all sin when we miss the target of divinely-inspired words and actions. For the most part, Christ's attunement was perfect, but he had a few moments of thinking and acting just as a human being named Jesus, or Yeshua, actually, as his name would have been pronounced in Hebrew and Aramaic."

"Thank you, Master Sheng." Drew leaned into the microphone, as though inexperienced at standing in front of one, and too timid to raise it to the proper level for his height.

"My other question is: do enlightened masters all have many life-times, and do they remember them all?"

Jing Sheng flashed his dependable smile, probably catching Drew's double question. "We do have many life times. Few have made it to enlightened states of being in only a few lifetimes, because our souls choose to suffer so as to learn more about being divine in the face of all circumstances.

"We do remember the lifetimes that we would like to remember, if God allows us to. Please remember that the whole point of life is to become attuned to the will of God and to do it. Looking back is seldom a way to become attuned to God's will, although occasionally it can help us see why we are struggling to get attuned or to carry out our soul's purpose. God allows enlightened masters to remember what is needed, when it is needed."

"Thank you, Master Sheng," Drew replied, bowing and trying to stay close to the microphone at the same time. "Would you permit me one more question, then?"

"Drew, you need to acknowledge that you are my disciple, and come follow me, for your answers are for you – not for everyone."

"Yes, thank-you, Master Sheng!" Drew bowed in Namaste and withdrew from the microphone. Instead of returning to his seat, he left the auditorium to find out how to become one of Jing Sheng's disciples.

"Now, we need to unveil the plan for you to help us restore balance to Mother earth. We have paired up cities, towns, communes, and villages all across America with similarly-sized communities around the world. We are asking that each community exchange four adults and all the children from that community for the period of one month." A gasp was audible throughout the auditorium.

"The communities in other countries have been selected for their economic ties to the American economy. For instance, where there is a manufacturing facility that prepares clothing, or automobile parts, or washers and dryers that then come to America and are sold with American names by American companies, we have obtained agreements for an exchange."

"You're exchanging what!?" Someone stood up at a microphone, shaking their fist. "You're crazy. We're not going to give you our children."

The crowd was noisy and restless, obviously and understandably shocked and upset. Jing Sheng somehow remained calm, and conveyed peace in his voice. He waited for a moment before responding.

"I am not asking you to give me your children. Your children are God's children. All the children of the world are God's children. You can allow your children to be raised in a community by other loving parents, while you care for their children."

"But then our children would have to live in the horrible conditions that those children just came from!"

"Exactly the point of this exercise," replied Jing Sheng. "Or are you saying that your children are more important than the other children of the world?"

"No, but they are our children and you cannot take them away from us!"

"I do hope you will identify yourself soon, as you are probably representing the concerns of many people. However, please understand I will never take 'your' children away from you. If you would like to survive, and make sure that all people on this planet survive, then you need to exchange your children with the children from around the world, so that you can learn, *together*, what it will take to bring your lives back into economic and environmental balance."

"You must be crazy!" yelled a young woman into a microphone. "We're not sending our children to some foreign country to starve in some village!" Turning to the audience next to her she said, "He's crazy!" And into the microphone she shouted: "You cannot send my children away!"

"Are your children more important than the starving children in that village you've obviously heard of?"

"No, but they're my children!"

""Let the children come to me, for to such as these belongs the kingdom of heaven.' God cherishes every child upon the earth. And so it will not matter if your children are there for one month, because you will send adults from your town to look after them.

"If every human being around the world will decide this one thing: that caring for all the children in the world is the most important thing in all of life, then there will be peace on earth, and there will be economic justice for everyone, and there will be an end to global warming and climate change."

"I can't take care of all the world's children by myself!"

"Alone, you cannot, but together with the whole world, every child can be cared for and loved, as every child deserves to be."

"He's crazy!" The young woman yelled again, flailing her hands and looking at the crowd, as if expecting to find support.

"Let the children come to me, for to such as these belongs the kingdom of heaven."

"Yeah, Jesus said that, but you are not Jesus, and he didn't mean we had to give up our children and let them go live in foreign lands!" She was pointing her finger at Jing Sheng and then pointing away to some 'other' place.

"Jesus said, 'as you do it unto the least of these, you do it unto me." Today, and every day, 25,000 children die from poverty – just from poverty, not from wars nor earthquakes nor cancer; just poverty – something that *everyone* here can help prevent."

"But I don't even have children, do I have to be part of your crazy plan?" a young man queried into the other microphone.

"Exodus 20:12 commands everyone to honor their father and mother. What better way is there to honor one's father and mother than to imitate them by being a good father and mother as well? It does not matter whether you have children of your own: the best possible fathers and mothers are those who care for all God's children."

"But how is this going to solve global warming?" an exasperated-sounding middle-aged man spoke up.

"You don't need to *try* to solve global warming. You don't need to *try* to achieve world peace. As soon as the whole world decides this one thing: that we will care for all the children of the world as equally as possible, then there will be no more global warming, there will be no more hunger, there will be no more war. You will find the solutions you need because caring for all children equally will create the solutions you seek. Indeed, it is part of the promise of blessing hidden in Exodus 20:12.

"To honor our Heavenly Father and Earthly Mother, all we have to do is to love and care for all children equally, because what our Heavenly Father and Earthly Mother long for the *most* is that we will seek to love and to take good care of *all* children. When we will provide fairly for *all* the children of the world, then we will truly honor our Heavenly Father and Earthly Mother, and our *children* will live long in the land. That is the full intent of that scripture."

"What about the rich people and the CEO's of multi-national corporations – they're the ones who have really caused this imbalance!" An angry young man yelled into a microphone.

"Ah, thank you for raising an important point. I have a question for you. Do you have a cell phone?" How ludicrous it sounded to most of the crowd that Jing Sheng would ask a 20-something if he has a cell phone.

"Of course!"

"Are you aware of any of the suffering that multitudes of people are experiencing in the eastern part of the Democratic Republic of the Congo, in part, because they are busy extracting coltan for your cell phone and for game systems, laboring as slaves in conditions that are completely intolerable? Are you aware that as many people have died because of conflict minerals in Eastern Congo as ever died in the European Holocaust? That's right: as many people have died in Eastern Congo through the conflict over mineral wealth there, as died in the whole European Holocaust.[4] Even I would not send children to Eastern Congo, unless their own parents are willing to go with them.

However, we do have a great need to send some American adults to live there for a month. And the adults we need to send will need to include physicians who will treat people (including counselors to help the millions of women who have been victims of rape), scientists who will examine the environment, and economists who can report on the economic exploitation." In other areas, the adults you send along with your children can include pediatricians, nurses, and teachers, or whatever leaders you choose from your communities."

Slowly, but surely, this plan began to sound intriguing. Many people started talking and nodding their heads. A murmur of approval began to pass through the crowd, as Jing Sheng merely waited, looking hopefully around at the crowd.

Just when he thought they reached their most positive energy peak, he spoke.

"I thank you for attending today. God will bless you all. Details for this plan are available online at **www.exodus2012.org** , and we have fliers for those who would like further information right away. Thank you, and please be in touch!"

Jing Sheng bowed, the audience stood, applauding in spots, bowing

---

[4] I first heard this statement made at a meeting held by a nonprofit group called Friends of the Congo. For more information, please go to **www.friendsofthecongo.org** .

in places, and storming out the exits in others. Liz and Jing Sheng quietly left the stage.

12. YOU SHALL NOT LESSEN YOUR DAILY NUMBER OF BRICKS

HOW MANY SERVANTS DOES A RICH MAN HAVE?
ENOUGH TO FLOAT HIS GOLDEN BOAT.
STAFF, ASSISTANTS, MANAGERS, WAITERS AND WAITRESSES,
SECRETARIES, WEB DESIGNERS, PARKING ATTENDANTS,
POSTAL WORKERS, DELIVERY PEOPLE, MAIDS, HOTEL
WORKERS, HIGHWAY CONSTRUCTION WORKERS,
ELECTRICIANS, COAL MINERS, CHEFS, NURSES,
FARMWORKERS, AND SO MANY MORE PEOPLE ENABLE A
RICH PERSON TO HAVE THE LIFE THEY LIVE.
AND WHO RECEIVES CREDIT FOR THIS LIFE?

Jing Sheng, Liz, Daniel, Darnell, Adam, and a dozen other volunteers had traveled back to Kalamazoo, where they were all busy creating a worldwide network of seekers and activists for the Exodus mission.

In the meanwhile, new political phenomena arrived on the scene in America - in waves, threatening to flood away basic rights for women, gays and lesbians, poor people, immigrants, and the health of the entire planet.

First, there arrived the Tempest Party, so named because they were as angry as a tempest in a teapot. They were ,bent on liberating their own sense of rights based, so they claimed, on the Constitution, while in fact, many of their views existed in direct violation of some of the main premises of the Constitution, first-and-foremost among them: the responsibility of the U.S. government to promote the general welfare, as well as the protection of the rights of others.

Then, there were Supreme Court assaults on the rights of individual Americans, most notably in declaring a corporation as having the rights of an individual, such that they could make unlimited campaign contributions. *As if that benefited anyone but the rich corporations and the politicians who serve them,* thought Liz. *How is this fair to anyone else? How can we protect the welfare of children and the planet when corporate greed has taken over everywhere?*

Then, the economy fell apart, Wall Street bamboozled politicians into giving big banks a bail-out, and millions of Americans went unemployed, *for years.* Poverty escalated. More children went to bed hungry in America than had since the Great Depression of the 1930's.

Congressional politicians started an onslaught on women's reproductive rights. Congressional politicians began to defund public radio, so that no unbiased news could spread knowledge in the land.

Biased commentators continued to receive funding from large corporations. These commentators continued to spread vitriolic hatred, lies, and mis-information as though their opinions could establish reality once-and-for-all. They falsely accused their opponents of having self-serving and evil motivations that they did not have.

Japan suffered a major flood from an earthquake and resulting tsunami. Then four of its nuclear reactors began to melt down. In the face of this, European countries wisely shut-down nuclear plants for inspection, and chose to emphasize renewable energy instead. America stayed the course with nuclear power being promoted as one of the most promising ways to provide for America's energy future.

Politicians threatened to do away with social security, or at least to privatize it, as though people like Liz's friend Maxie (an older woman) could survive on anything less than the minimal amount of money she now received. Liz felt horrified by the lack of understanding, and downright cruelty of forcing people to live in unsustainable poverty.

A few states mounted attacks on the rights of government workers to organize and negotiate for worker's rights. Some of the states even succeeded by using under-handed tactics. Worker's unions across America revolted, but politicians ignored them, instead, giving big corporations more and more control over America, while giving working Americans less and less power every day. *This is democracy?* Liz wondered. *No way!*

One state even repealed child labor laws, so that parents could send their children to work for a couple of dollars a day, just like in developing countries, where such practices ensure that poverty remains endemic, because then adults workers are displaced, and minimum wages are never enforced.

To top it off, Kalamazoo's own representative led the way to undoing decades of EPA protections of clean air, clean water, and reduction of CO_2 emissions. He and his fellow committee members legislated away top scientific data, saying that climate change cannot be real because in the Bible, God says there will never again be a flood.

"Wait a minute, Jing Sheng," cried Liz, "How can they say that God says there will never again be a flood when the Japanese have just lost thousands of people from flooding? How can they be so naïve, so cruel, so ignorant?"

Her compassion over-spilled and she burst into tears, fell at Jing Sheng's feet, and placed her head on his knee.

Jing Sheng lovingly stroked her hair back from her face.

"Bless you, my child. Thank you for showing us the compassionate face of the Divine Mother. Like a mother, God of course cares for all people, not least the Japanese. Floods occur because nature is free to pursue its own destructive impulses, as well as its life-giving impulses.

"That is part of the double-nature, good and evil, of the quality of Maya, illusion, in the Universe."

"But why?" Liz sobbed. "Why are people so cruel and seemingly stupid?"

"They have been taught a faith that makes the Bible an idol rather than simply seeing it as a revered sacred text. This Biblical idolatry renders an incomplete understanding of God, as well as a false understanding of God's Word.

"*God's Word is a living reality* which is only partially expressed by Biblical words, and which cannot be limited to God's message for long ago, but which must be updated as God's Word for today. We will go address this now in public. Do not lose heart. Above all, no matter what the opposition to God's Way is doing, we must glorify Divine Love through our hearts, our thoughts, our words, and our actions. Are you glorifying Divine Love with your thoughts right now, my child?"

"Probably not. I'm so mad at the people in Congress who are attacking our rights, sending us back to the Dark Ages as far as news and information goes, and ruining our environment – our beautiful Mother Earth."

"Well, they will not hear you as long as you speak like that, will they?"

Liz just let out more sobs, rather than answering Jing Sheng. Finally, she took a deep breath.

"That's better. Now, please go schedule an interview for me with the local public radio station, while they still exist. Thank you."

Liz went to wash her face and place the call.

The next day, she and Adam and Jing Sheng drove to the studio at Western Michigan University to be interviewed on the radio.

The radio commentator wisely chose to ask few questions, preferring to let Jing Sheng have free reign to speak on a variety of topics.

"I understand, Mr. Hu, that you have some concerns about what's happening in the political situation in the world, is that right?"

"Yes," Jing Sheng replied, "but first, let me just reassure everyone that the Divine Mother's heart is breaking along with the hearts of the people of Japan in their current tragedy. Please know that the will of God is that no one suffer. Our suffering simply comes because we have separated ourselves from the Divine, and until we learn to re-unite ourselves fully with our Heavenly Father-Mother, we will continue to suffer. This is true, in part, simply because we will continue to return to earth, where suffering is part of the fabric of reality. The heart of the Divine Mother, however, is compassion, and so as each of us unites ourselves with the Divine Mother, we offer compassion to all who suffer. So, let us give generously to restore, with compassion, what wellbeing can be restored in Japan. Thank you."

"That is very noble of you, Mr. Hu, or may I call you Jing Sheng?"
"You may. Now, I wish to address several issues, if I may briefly do so."

"Of course, you have ten minutes."

"First and foremost, I would like to remind everyone of the Ten Commandments. So many politicians and would-be definers of the American Way consider themselves to be Christians. I call them that because I can see the spiritual truth of their inner being, not because I am wrongly accusing them of anything. That said, I would like to remind all of us of one commandment in particular: the ninth commandment, which states, do not bear false witness against your neighbor.

"Currently in America, there are too many political commentators, as well as politicians who are bearing false witness against their neighbors, as though their political opponents somehow do not count as neighbors. However, if you are Christian, you must know that Jesus calls us to consider even our political opponents to be our neighbors. When you label others negatively, when you accuse others of wrongful motivations they do not have, when you point fingers at them instead of listening to each other, you are violating one of God's most basic commandments.

"It is time to stop.

"I will not name you, but if you do not examine yourself right now to see if you are doing this, then you are serving the Evil One, and not the God of Love, our Supreme Creator. Thou shalt not bear false witness.

"Secondly, if you believe that the Bible is the inerrant and infallible word of God, then you are committing idolatry. The Bible itself says that you should make no graven image – what do you think the Bible is but a graven image? The Bible is the work of men, and I do mean just men, not humankind, the same as any piece of art. While the Bible was written mostly by men (not women) who were inspired by God, nonetheless, it was still written by men. Just like any sermon written today, it is one part human, and only partly divine. To say that the Bible is infallible is to mis-identify the messenger, and therefore, the message, with the Sender of the Message.

"God would not send all the same messages today that God sent yesterday, because people have developed new intellectual and communal awareness. These new forms of awareness lay the groundwork for a new spiritual synthesis, a true harmony of world religions through the Truth of Divine Love.

"When you read the Bible purely from a faith perspective, you deny yourself the intellectual integrity of learning to view it from a historical perspective. When you view the Bible only through the eyes of faith, you also deny yourself the integrity of viewing it from a scientific perspective.

"To hear the Truth requires faith and science and historical understanding. Faith which denies or dismisses historical and scientific understanding is no closer to the Truth than is scientific understanding which is devoid of faith. I pray you stop your idolatry now, and listen to the gentle, but truthful, word of God speaking lovingly in your heart.

"Speaking of hearts, to accuse someone of having a bleeding heart is often akin to recognizing the bleeding of the sacred heart of God in Jesus Christ. Divine Love is indeed the love which bleeds willingly for others, just as Christ willingly bled for others.

"A sure sign that you are listening to the word of God in your heart is that it will confront you and ask you what you are doing to glorify Divine Love, rather than your own agenda, right here, right now, today, even as we speak.

"Thirdly, taking away the rights of others, be they women, children, or gays and lesbians, is to take away your own rights, because as you do unto others it will be done unto you. God's law of karma is the law of the universe; this is why Jesus taught the Golden Rule: do unto others as you would have them do unto you. What has not come through clearly in Christ's words is that, first, you must place yourself in the shoes of the other person, before you decide to do anything unto them. So, always be kind, and restore human rights, whether they benefit you or not.

"Lastly, global warming and the resultant climate change are real, and your own collective human idolatry is causing it. You must begin to take care of the environment. The surest way to do that is always to ask first: is this law, or this business practice, good for all the children of the earth?

"Christ called the children to him and blessed them. His disciples objected because children had no economic value back then. The disciples then, just like so many so-called disciples today, considered economic priorities to be the most important. And yet, the best solutions for all humanity are the ones that benefit children first and foremost.

"I thank you." Jing Sheng bowed in Namaste. There was quiet. The radio commentator was too stunned to speak for a moment.

"Ladies and gentleman, you have been listening to the advice, requests, and concerns of Mr. Hu Jing Sheng, of the Hubei Province of China. Mr. Hu, or Jing Sheng, as his followers call him, is organizing "Exodus 2012: A Mission to Save the Earth." You may find out more at www.jingshenghu.org.

Liz's eyes shone with delight. "How do you do that?" She cried out, "Oh, I know, you are the Christ – of course you can do that! You really do glorify Divine Love. I love you!" And she fell down and hugged his legs.

Adam stood up, and said, "Jing Sheng, you are the best. You are a dream come true. I wish you could run the whole world."

"It is up to each of you to find Christ within yourselves, and to let the consciousness of Christ run you. Then, and only then, will Christ indeed rule the world."

"Mr. Hu, thank you so much. It has been an honor and a privilege. If you wait just a moment, our audio technician will give you a CD of your speech. Again, thank you for coming here. I hope I can help you again."

Jing Sheng smiled, knowing whatever all he did know about everyone's future, which Liz could never guess. "Your services will be needed more when I am gone. Please remain faithful to the vision then. May God be with you and bless you, my son."

Peace surrounded them all and peace accompanied Jing Sheng, Liz, and Adam out the door.

Jing Sheng's following grew. The numbers showing up at Liz's wellness center kept growing every day. Darnell, Liz, Adam, and Daniel had a lot of work to do just to keep up with signing people up for classes and the mission. On top of that, Liz and Daniel and Jing Sheng did a lot of healings as well. They trained a couple of people to run the center, do healings, and teach meditation. That eased up Liz's burdens a bit.

This allowed them to return to New York, where they again stayed in a homeless shelter and performed helpful services and healings and taught classes, which included training people in the mission. A number of individuals and businesses, and even some communities began to put the principles of the mission into practice.

After New York, they returned to Washington, DC, where they once again stayed in a hotel, this time also renting meeting rooms so they could train seekers in meditation, train volunteers in networking and communal work, and do healings as well. Time was very full, in such a pregnant sense, that Liz could only wonder if this could keep going on for more than nine months.

Their work so contrasted with the political machinations of those days that their work never seemed to have an end. But being a force of love in the universe always feels so much better than being a force of evil, for in perfect love, there is never any fear. So wondering aside, Liz found that deeply trusting Jing Sheng gave her the energy, and time, to do everything needed, with deep joy and peace as well.

13. I WILL DELIVER THE ISRAELITES OUT OF THE LAND OF EGYPT

*IN GENESIS, GOD SAYS, "LET US
MAKE HUMANKIND IN OUR IMAGE."
WHO IS 'US'?
DOES IT NOT MAKE SENSE FOR DIVINE LOVE TO HAVE A
PLURALITY OF BEING – A SHARING, COOPERATIVE NATURE?
IF THE DIVINE LOVE IS PLURAL, THEN HARMONIOUS
LIVING MUST ENSUE.
IF THE DIVINE ONES LIVE AS A HARMONIOUS ONE,
THEN HUMANS, MADE IN GOD'S IMAGE, ARE ALSO CREATED
TO LIVE AS A HARMONIOUS ONE.*

"We need to return to Kalamazoo to commence the communal living, and then we will also open an office here in Washington, D.C., or the vicinity, so that we can begin to plan and coordinate the exodus mission," Jing Sheng announced when they returned to their hotel suite.

"Jing Sheng?" Liz looked perplexed.

"Yes, my little dove?" Jing Sheng took her hands and folded them together in his.

"Where are we going to get families who will be willing to do this – I mean, including their children?" Liz sounded very doubtful.

"Would you like to set the example and go first?"

"Well, sure, but you know, my children are grown."

"Then why not be the ones who go to eastern Congo, where you will need a body guard, because you are female, and the incidence of rape is high." Jing Sheng could put a whole roomful of love into a conversation; everyone present felt it, as though they were all personally receiving a blessing.

"I hope you are not expecting me to be her body guard," Darnell hurried to assert in a demanding tone. He felt the love, but his fear of being treated differently for being black and gay was, at that moment, stronger than his ability to absorb Jing Sheng's, that is, God's, love.

After all, despite what many white Americans think, racism is still part and parcel of American culture and values, and Darnell had experienced what felt like discrimination many times, just for being African American, let alone for being gay.

"I would like you to accompany her, Darnell, but we will hire a bodyguard. Are you willing to go to Eastern Congo?"

"Sure. I have no idea what it's like over there, but I am willing to find out." Darnell
looked indifferent, shrugging his shoulders at first, but then planting his feet decisively and squaring his shoulders as he conceded his willingness.

"Darnell, please contact the American embassy in the Democratic Republic of the Congo to request information and to obtain advice about how we handle the mission. Here's a copy of our mission statement, with goals and objectives lined out for gathering information and building relationships in eastern Congo.

Also, please contact TASOK, The American School of Kinshasa, to see if they have anyone in eastern Congo, or know of anyone who would be willing to accompany us and guide us on the trip. Lastly, please contact the State Department, and see if there is anyone in USAID who would meet with us here in D.C. and then also in the Congo."

"Sure thing. I guess I have my homework cut out for me. Adam, let's get going."

Darnell and Adam left to start the assignment right away.

"Liz, please get in touch with your children. Your daughter, as a photojournalist, will be valuable with her gifts on this trip. Your son, as an economist, will be immensely helpful as well. Please have them find out how long they can get away from their jobs and school, obtain passports, expedited if they need to, and so on." Jing Sheng guided gently.

"Daniel, I would like you to help make plans to go to Malaysia, Montenegro, India, and Brazil. We will begin with just those five locations. You may make contacts much like the ones I suggested to Darnell for the Congo, alright?" Jing Sheng smiled at Daniel, peace exuding from every word and every fiber of his being.

"Certainly. How long do I have to get this done?" Daniel smiled cautiously back at Jing Sheng.

"Preliminary plans need to be made while we are here this week. You have easier access to their embassies while we are here. When we return to Kalamazoo, the finer details can be worked out. Among our followers, there are many contacts in each of those countries. Some are eager to be part of the exchange."

Daniel and Liz both wondered how people in other countries had become so eager to follow Jing Sheng at such a long distance, but decided that the televised coverage of his speeches must have been persuasive. *And maybe, just maybe,* Liz thought, *there really is a divine or Holy Spirit floating around that has given many people a sense of urgency to love and care for the earth.* As it was, Daniel was wondering about that as well.

Many contacts were made that week, both with embassies and within the various countries. The Exodus 2012 team also contacted non-profit aid agencies and human rights organizations to determine how to work together within certain countries.

The State Department apparently went on high alert when learning of their plans, and started to perform background checks on all of them.

Liz and Jing Sheng spent the week mostly giving healings and individual counseling sessions, with Liz keeping Jing Sheng's schedule. He also gave news interviews with local commentators, discussing global warming as climate change and his mission more than he discussed spiritual matters. Liz reflected that it was as though spiritual issues somehow did not belong in Washington, DC, or at least they seemed not very popular there.

In the meantime, Liz contemplated contacting her children, as Jing Sheng had requested. Her daughter was a very interesting person; deeply spiritual, but equally deeply in denial about spirituality. Liz would describe her daughter as an old soul revisiting rebellion. She and her ex-husband, who was part Native American, had named her Hopi, meaning 'peaceful.' Hopi and Liz had been blessed to get to travel to Malaysia to visit some old family friends while Hopi was still in high school. This trip had, inevitably, changed Hopi's life, and she had become a photojournalist in order to travel the world and document people's lives, especially the injustices of this world.

In that sense, this trip would be perfect for her, but Liz knew that Hopi would ask a thousand questions which she would not be able to answer. Liz hoped that Darnell would be able to answer them, so she finally broke down and called Hopi, who became very enthusiastic and yet raised every detail imaginable and then some that would have to be considered. Liz really wanted to say, "Let's just trust the Universe to provide guidance and sustenance every step as we go," but she knew that Hopi would simply rebel at such a thought. Instead, she gently suggested that Hopi call Darnell to see if he could fill her in on details, and gave Hopi Darnell's number. *God bless Darnell*, Liz thought.

Next, she had to call her son Cliff. *Oh, boy*, she thought. Cliff was a very old soul, but despite his ancient wisdom and partial Native American ancestry, Cliff, who was studying for a Ph.D. in economics, was manifesting himself as a very Western, white male.

For Cliff, everything had to be rational, compassion was optional, and cerebral experiences were the jewels of life, especially abstract principles, which he believed needed to pop out of one's head as ideas that were completely devoid of social context, and certainly needed no connection to anyone's life story.

Liz, as a feminist, felt horrified at this separation of ideas and principles from the essential matrix of human living, from the environment, and from the womb of being human. She secretly hoped this trip would open Cliff's eyes to the primacy of compassion as the true heart of God come to earth on a very human journey. She called, and Cliff became slightly interested, but even more so when Liz told him that Jing Sheng wanted him as an economist.

"I could do some research while I'm there," Cliff announced, and that was settled. Liz also pointed Cliff in the direction of Darnell for details, thinking she really owed Darnell at this point.

Then she went back to taking phone calls and e-mails for Jing Sheng, keeping his schedule, and accepting healing clients.

At the end of the week, a pastor of a local church invited them to come speak at a pancake breakfast they were having that Saturday morning. The pastor asked him to speak on the concept of the kingdom of God, and what Jing Sheng thought Jesus Christ meant by that. Jing Sheng accepted.

So, Saturday morning found Liz, Darnell, Adam, Daniel, and Jing Sheng all riding the Metro out to a suburban Protestant church in Rockville, Maryland, where they were greeted warmly. Liz had checked out their website, and had shown Jing Sheng how active the congregation was in helping economically-disadvantaged people. Jing Sheng's response was, "Thank you, Liz. I am aware that they are a truly remarkable congregation."

When they arrived in Rockville, they were picked up at the Metro station and driven to the church by the pastor herself, Rev. Babette Fiddmont. "I just wanted to welcome you myself – I'm so grateful to you for taking time to come to our church. I can't thank you enough."

"We are happy to be here, Rev. Fiddmont," Jing Sheng replied.

"I apologize for not requesting your permission, but we did contact the local television station, and they are sending a crew to televise your talk. I hope that is ok…"

"Of course," Jing Sheng replied.

"One of our members will also be videotaping your talk for youtube as well. I hope that's also ok?" Rev. Babette switched from exuding self-confidence to sounding slightly anxious.

"Of course. I just hope that your church will benefit from graciously hosting us. But I must also ask one favor in return." Jing Sheng spoke calmly, as though he were the master of backroom deals.

"Oh, certainly. I'd be happy to help you!" Rev. Babette was all enthusiasm.

Jing Sheng smiled, and apparently let an extra dose of divine love flow through him, for the car was suddenly filled with a sense of peace and joyful love.

"We need your church to become a recruiting station for people to travel overseas to help with our exchange of families. I will need you personally to assist me in screening families and individuals who want to join our mission overseas."

"Wow! When you ask for a commitment, you ask big-time!" Rev. Babette stalled a little bit. "You do remind me of God in that sense – that's for sure!" She laughed.

"Okay, fortunately we have a social worker who will probably help, and I know we have a lot of people who are excited about your idea, but only if the congregation agrees, and only if you agree to come back and coach us on this." Babette reflected out loud and drove the car and seemed to regain control of the situation all in one. *An impressive woman*, thought Liz.

"I will send some of my helpers here to outline the plan. Daniel, Darnell, Adam, and Liz all have specialties that can help you. They are all very professional, responsible, and their spirituality is evolving in a helpful direction." Listening to Jing Sheng's description of themselves, the four helpers found themselves suddenly feeling as though they would need to catch up spiritually to get ahead of the pastor and other potential followers. None of them felt comfortable with the thought of lagging behind other followers when it came to 'getting' Jing Sheng's spiritual message.

When they arrived at the church, the parking lot was crowded.

"Our church members invited a few friends, and we did a little media coverage, so we expect a crowd of about four hundred. That's a lot of pancakes for our crew to fix, but they're up to it – we have a great kitchen, and a great kitchen crew! Oh – and it's an all-vegetarian breakfast, too."

She sure seems to know us, thought Liz. *Or else, she's just all-around amazing anyway.*

They entered the church, and found a standing ovation welcomed them. They were seated at a head table, and served a delicious, better-than-average-church-pancake breakfast. The secret, they learned later, was that the church uses Greek yogurt in their pancakes, along with a blend of oat flour and almond meal. Gourmet health pancakes!

When the pastor introduced Jing Sheng, who actually needed no introduction because he had been so much in the news, she told the congregation that she was in no way urging them to accept Jing Sheng's message, but felt called to invite him to share his message, because she believed that at least some of God's truth was being spoken by him. She urged her parishioners to discern for themselves any message of divine truth which they could hear in Jing Sheng's words.

"Good morning, friends," spoke Jing Sheng with a bow in Namaste. A few people bowed in Namaste back. *They must take yoga lessons,* Liz assumed, and *apparently bowing in Namaste is okay in church if it's outside the sanctuary?* She wondered.

"Rev. Fiddmont has asked me to speak on the subject of the kingdom of God, and what I think Jesus Christ meant by that." Jing Sheng began.

"Let me ask you the one most important question of life." Jing Sheng paused, to let that idea sink in.

"There are, of course, different ways to ask this question, but when we consider life from the perspective of the kingdom of God, there's only one question that matters most.

"If you chose to live as though you were, right now, citizens of the kingdom of God on earth, instead of citizens of your own country, how would you live your life?

"That is the question I must ask you, because our mission, in its essence, is about bringing the kingdom of God on earth. Exodus 2012 is about inviting people to live as though the Reign of God is reality among all humankind.

"If we trust that the Reign of God is real on earth, the question becomes, how are we going to behave? Especially, we need to ask, how are we going to behave towards one another? Jesus Christ told us that the kingdom of God, or the Reign of God, is 'at hand.' By this, Christ means that the possibility of God's reign here on earth is always up to us.

"Indeed, God's spirit, the feminine side of God, already reigns in nature. She gives life and sustains life, and blesses creation with heavenly healing energies through fresh air, fresh water, and through sunshine – that's why you feel so good when you take a shower, go swimming, or spend time outside in nature.

"But as for the Reign of God *on* earth, that always depends on the cooperation of humankind. Each individual has to decide whether or not to let God reign through them and their words, thoughts, and actions every day. That is why the verse in Luke 17:21 can be interpreted as: "The kingdom of God is within you."

"And yet also, each group of people, and indeed all of humanity together, needs to decide how the Reign of Love will guide humanity's economic choices and health care choices, as well as humanity's cultivation of natural resources. How people relate to one another as groups, or as relationship systems, determines whether or not the Reign of Love is happening among them. That is why Luke 17:21 *must* also be understood as saying, "The kingdom of God is among you, and indeed, in the original Greek, that is precisely how this text reads.

"Today, Christ asks you, first: are you willing to live as citizens of the kingdom of God? And second: *HOW* are you willing to live as citizens of the kingdom of God, rather than as adherents to your own cultural values, norms, and legalities?"

Jing Sheng paused, as he looked out at all the serious faces of people who were obviously reflecting deeply. A few people smiled, with an internal sense of joy which also lighted their faces. Some people squirmed a little uncomfortably, reflecting, no doubt, on their lack of 'kingdom of God' thinking in their lives.

"If *every* person is a citizen in the Reign of Love, even if they do not yet know it or accept it, then how are you going to live that reality out together? Why do you think Isaiah wrote about the lion lying down with the lamb? God's reality, or Love's reality, can be so much more than we currently imagine or expect, or even *accept* it to be. Why? Because most of us are not yet ready to allow the Reign of Love to happen in us and through us so fully, that the Reign of Love will become a reality on earth.

"So, I will ask that one question a little differently. Are you ready to allow the Reign of Love to happen through you? Are you ready to allow the Reign of Love to put others first in your life? Are you ready to allow strangers to be among those who bring the Reign of love to reality in your life? Are you ready to let go of your human restrictions, assumptions, judgments, and expectations, in order to let the Reign of Love come first and foremost, no matter what?

"Thank you for your time today. Please let Pastor Babette know if you are willing to help serve on our mission team. We will need a recruitment center set up here in your church building. We will need helpers to screen volunteers for Exodus 2012, a Mission to Save the Earth, and we will need helpers who can assist those volunteers in preparing to travel to the other countries where our mission will be established. Please help bring about the Reign of Divine Love on earth - that is what Christ returns to do. Thank you, and may you find Christ within you, and within each other. So Be It." Jing Sheng bowed.

A hush filled the fellowship hall. Suddenly, people jumped to their feet and started clapping, shouting, dancing even, as a Spirit of Joy overtook the place. As even the organist caught the Spirit, he began to jazzily belt out "What a Friend We Have In Jesus" on the piano. The whole room shone brightly, not just from the sunlight angling in the windows, but as though a hundred angels were dancing in the room as well. *Maybe there are angels here,* Liz mused. *I sure hope they'll protect us all as we travel overseas!*

They spent awhile exchanging contact information and making a few rudimentary plans. Adam finally stepped up and volunteered to be the main contact with the recruitment center. Liz assumed that the fact that this was an open-and-affirming congregation, or one that welcomes gay people, was the primary reason he finally came on board. Although, feeling overwhelmed by Jing Sheng's call to become a citizen of the Reign of Love, she trusted that Adam felt that call deep within himself as well.

After the pancake breakfast, they packed up and headed back to Kalamazoo; not an easy trip by airplane from Washington, D. C. There were too many connecting flights through other cities for it to be convenient, and they had to decide whether to fly all the way to Kalamazoo, or whether to drive from Detroit, Chicago, South Bend, or Grand Rapids. Liz disliked all the options, but preferred flying all the way to Kalamazoo, even though that meant flying on airplanes too tiny for her lack of faith to find comfort.

Whenever she flew, she would sing in her head the refrain of the song "On Eagle's Wings", only she would sing "And God will raise you up on angels' wings," and she used gender-inclusive language for God rather than words like 'his'. For her, God was definitely both divine Father and divine Mother. It was just the only loving and respectful thing that made sense. Loving and respectful both to God and to women and girls, that is.

The flights gave them all plenty of time to think, and the layovers gave them plenty of time to talk.
How are we ever going to launch an international mission from Kalamazoo? Liz wondered while she had time to sit and look out the window at clear blue skies at 30,000 feet. She realized that there were probably plans about which she did not yet know, and relaxed, trusting that God and Jing Sheng had it all under control.

In the airport in Chicago, Daniel and Jing Sheng went off to find some sandwiches together. Daniel was telling Jing Sheng that he had discovered that Croatia had the beautiful Dalmatian coast, and that he thought they should go to Sibenik, on the coast, during the last week of June for the International Child's Festival.

"What a wonderful idea, Daniel. Please look into our getting to make an announcement there. Have you made any contacts with any environmental groups there?"

"Yes, well, I found them online, and if you'd like, I could get in touch with the environmental groups that protect the Krka River and the Krka National Park. There's also the Kornati Islands National Park, which would provide a very rustic retreat setting for any small meetings we might like to have. And Kornati Islands National Park would be a great place for international media coverage, because it is stunningly beautiful."

"Great work, Daniel. Please go ahead and make any and all contacts you feel led to make. I will let Liz know about the timing, so she can place the last week of June on my schedule, and apply for my visa for me."

"Speaking of Liz," Daniel started, and then hesitated.

"Yes, Daniel?" Jing Sheng's eyebrows went up, in a mock-teasing look.

"I really would like to have a chance to have some time alone with her, and the Dalmatian Coast looks like the perfect romantic spot to spend some time together. Could we have a little time together, or couldn't she just stay with me there instead of having to go to such a dangerous place as Eastern Congo? I mean, I looked it up on the internet, and it's a terribly dangerous place to go, especially for women."

"Ahh, Daniel, such is new love. Yes, you may have a week together in Croatia, but not alone, because you will need to set the groundwork there together. Please hire a translator already to start working with you. But Liz is definitely coming to eastern Congo with   me."

"Oh, Jing Sheng, how can you keep her safe there?"

"Is safety all that concerns you, Daniel? Is there not more to life than whether or not we are safe all the time? Isn't a life of danger worth living if you are busy bringing about the Reign of Love on earth?"

"But..." Daniel really did not know what to say. All he knew was that he felt love in his heart, along with this deep longing and passionate desire to be with Liz and to explore the possibilities of their relationship together.

"Daniel, son of my heart, you must know that God holds your love for Liz in God's own heart, and trust that what is meant to be will be."

They had found sandwiches, ordered for everyone, and were just arriving back where Liz, Darnell, and Adam were waiting.

"There is one lesson that we all need to discuss while we eat," announced Jing Sheng, while Daniel parceled out sandwiches and refilled water bottles.

After everyone had paused for a silent grace, Jing Sheng began instructing them.

"It is so important that you become aware that the universe consists of organized consciousness. What used to be referred to as *the ether* may also be called organized consciousness." The others looked up from their sandwiches with inquisitive looks on their faces, although Darnell was actually grinning and nodding in appreciation, as though he had anticipated this thought.

"That organized consciousness comes, originally, from the Divine Source, but it has been parceled out, like our sandwiches, to many beings. Organized consciousness forms patterns through the energy of love and of fear. All consciousness has energy to it, with various frequencies and amplitudes, harmonizing either with the energy of love, which is creative, or with the energy of fear, which is destructive.

"Fear is a distortion of God's original energy of love. Faith, as a form of consciousness, has energy which increases the amplitude of love, that is, both the potential and the actual impact of love. Each of us must choose love, and let go of fear, in order to do our part to energize divine, loving consciousness in the world.

"If we hold on with attachment to a specific outcome, we are not allowing the Divine Spirit the freedom to flow according to the will of Love, or Premier Consciousness. We must choose the energy of love by having the will to love, without limiting its expression by attachment to particular material outcomes, or to particular means of attaining specific outcomes.

"The philosophy of non-attachment allows for the free flow of the energy of love through us, to create with loving intentions both for ourselves, and for others. It is never a matter of control, but it is always a matter of trust."

Silence ensued. Everyone appeared to be munching thoughtfully, or drinking from their lightweight, refillable stainless steel water bottles. Liz even carried a cloth napkin to re-use, and cloth handkerchiefs as well. She had no idea when she would have time to do laundry. *I wish Jing Sheng would think of these practical things more often,* she complained in her own head.

Liz, Liz, always the focus on the mundane, when you could be floating on the spiritual heights. Jing Sheng intruded into her thoughts.

"Oh, I'm sorry, I forgot you could read our thoughts," she spluttered, while trying to keep
a bite of sandwich in her mouth.

"Wow! How did you talk in her mind and in my mind at the same time?" Darnell registered the surprise with his hands and head and voice, all in unison reacting with wonder.

"The point, my friends, is that the universe consists of organized consciousness, and that consciousness is one big whole mind, as it were. It does not matter whose mind the Divine Consciousness is in or where or when, because it lives in all forms of consciousness, or rather, all forms of consciousness exist through the very matrix of Divine Consciousness.

"The differences in consciousness between people, and between animals, rocks, plants, and people, can be explained in part by the limits of one's life-purpose, or intentionality of being, and in part by the degree to which each one is 'tuned in' to divine consciousness, or aware of divine consciousness beyond one's own ego-based awareness.

"To be tuned into divine consciousness is to be fully conscious. To the degree that humans are aware of the mind of God within them, or the Christ-Consciousness within, they can be called conscious. Whenever human beings act out of their limited ego-awareness, they can be referred to as being 'unconscious.' So whenever people are ignorant, or rude, or selfish, they are merely unconscious of the Divine way of being and knowing in that moment. No judgment of them is necessary. It is just necessary to be aware that they are being unconscious – that is, unconscious of Divine Consciousness.

"To increase our awareness, or our Divine Consciousness, we must remain open through open hearts and open minds, to receive an aptitude for awareness beyond our own limited way of being on the earth. That expanded awareness becomes a fully-spiritually-conscious mind when we attain full Christ-Consciousness, or Self-Realization. Self-Realization or God-Realization is a state of being that is fully conscious of the Divine Mind present in creation."

"Wow!" Daniel exclaimed. "This is the best metaphysics I've ever heard."

"It's only natural," Darnell added. "Thank you, Jing Sheng, for explaining what I have long been wondering about."

"And each of you would do well to be able to explain that to other followers as you meet them around the world. But do not worry." Jing Sheng raised a hand as Liz started to shape an objection with her mouth, and only got so far as "ach!"

"I will be with you, in consciousness form, at least, to help you with the wording. All you have to do is to tune into an awareness of me in your heart and mind. Feeling your own love for me will help you to connect with my consciousness. As it does, at least in theory, with everyone, but that's another lesson."

Once back in Kalamazoo, they rented Chenery auditorium, so that the plan could be announced, discussed as a community, and televised, all in one session. Then they realized they were going to have to rent Miller Auditorium at Western Michigan University in order to have enough space, but the costs appeared to be no problem, for donations were pouring in through the Exodus 2012 website.

In addition, people were calling Liz's wellness center to schedule healing sessions along with Tai Chi, yoga, and meditation classes, so plenty of income was flowing in there as well. Liz had her work cut out for her. Jing Sheng was to teach a few classes, lead the early morning Tai Chi, and do some afternoon healings, but other than that, he needed to be free to speak with the media, plan the overseas trips, and respond to people's needs and inquiries on the website.

The order of business seemed humanly impossible, but then, was Jing Sheng merely human? He certainly needed very little sleep – about two to four hours per night was all he ever got. He meditated for an hour before sleep, and for one to one-and-a-half hours after sleeping. So, whether he went to 'bed' and meditated at 11 p.m. or 1 a.m., he was always up and showering at 5:30 a.m. He tended to keep weak (very watery), flavored green tea with him at all times, though it often grew cold.

While Liz was busy keeping Jing Sheng's schedule, doing healings, and teaching yoga, Darnell was busy taking care of "The Mission." He handled much of the website communications, dealt with planning of the trip, stayed informed of the Rockville church's plans to go ahead and form a center for applicants to go on the overseas trips, and communicated with Adam, Daniel, and Liz about all the different parts of the workings of Exodus 2012.

Daniel had to return to work, but Adam alternated between working his traditional job and communicating with the center in Rockville. Eventually, they needed a separate website just for applicants and the center in Rockville. It became known as "The Exodus 2012 Mission Center." There was also the eco-commune movement that was forming, which had its own website as well.

Liz found herself feeling amazed at the combination of central planning and diverse centers of organization, all centered around one common sense of purpose. *Is this how God runs the Universe?* she wondered.

The day came for the presentation and discussion at Miller Auditorium. The seats were sold out, as people came from as far away as Detroit, Chicago, Toronto, Cleveland, and South Bend. The event was called: "The Mission of Exodus 2012." Media coverage was expected from as far away as Toronto and New York. The Canadians were beginning to get on board in large numbers. *Maybe that's part of why Kalamazoo is a good place to start,* thought Liz. *I would expect a lot of Canadians really to get into this.*

This time, the event was presented quite differently, as each of Jing Sheng's close disciples had a lead role in presenting aspects of the mission. The event opened with a local church choir from a nearby Unitarian Universalist Church, which provided some inspirational music about working together for peace and justice on the earth.

A group of children from another local church sang the gender-inclusive version of an old song: "God's Got the Whole World in God's Hands." And a youth group from another church did a skit introducing the different parts of the world where the mission will occur, complete with PowerPoint photos and maps.

Then Darnell came onto center stage to introduce the concept of the mission. Adam entered to a microphone at stage left to explain how to apply online and through the center in Rockville. Daniel spoke at a microphone at stage right about organizing locally to form communal living and communal economic arrangements. Behind them PowerPoint photos and maps flashed up when relevant to the topics at hand. Liz entered and stood with Darnell at center stage and invited people to schedule healings, meditation classes, as well as yoga and Tai Chi sessions. Then she introduced Jing Sheng.

"It is my highest honor to present to you the founder of this mission, a Tai Chi master from China, an Enlightened One, a true Guru who indeed Dispels All Darkness, and quite possibly, as some of us believe, the reincarnation of Jesus Christ: Mr. Hu Jing Sheng!"

The crowd was in an uproar of applause, standing, clapping, rejoicing, cheering, with only a few sullen faces showing the presence of resentment and resistance in the crowd. A couple of people waved signs that said, "Stop pretending to be Jesus – you're just a fraud". They were shouting angrily.

Jing Sheng came onto the stage, waving and smiling pleasantly, bringing with him that incredible light, peace, and love energy which soon actually filled the entire auditorium, touching the four thousand people in attendance.

He bowed in Namaste, and the crowd finally sat down and grew quiet.

"Greetings, Sons and Daughters of Love. Welcome my friends; my heart is warmed to see you here. God is smiling upon us, and I thank you for coming."

The crowd murmured approval. Nods and smiles prevailed.

"I would like to talk with you for a moment about why this mission is so urgent. It was God's design and original intention for life on this earth to be lived in balance, and for tens of thousands of years, humanity did just that, living much like other animals, in harmony with their environment. What an awesome accomplishment to live in harmony with one's environment, not merely because of evolutionary adaptation and instinct, like so many animals, but to do so consciously, tuned into the patterns of nature, and choosing how to survive while protecting the environment which provided humans with their home.

"Now, unfortunately, because of overpopulation and the discovery of fossil fuels, humankind has spent the last century living out of balance, and inharmoniously with nature. It is time to reverse the trend. We need to return to God's original intention of living in harmony with God, with one another, and with the earth herself. This is what Jesus Christ referred to as the kingdom of God. We may call it the Reign of Love. It is time for all people to join together and live into the Reign of Love on earth."

Applause broke out all over the auditorium, and Jing Sheng had to wait for the cheers and the clapping to stop.

"Salvation for humanity will come when we learn to love one another, not just as individuals, but also as part of an economy that spreads around the globe. The natural environment offers a sustainable economy to humankind in reasonable numbers, but it also sets a natural limit on economic growth. It is time to learn to live sustainably with one another – that is the salvation that is needed in this time."

Again, applause and cheers broke up Jing Sheng's speech.

"Jesus Christ commanded us to love our neighbors as we love ourselves, and to accomplish our salvation in this generation, we are going to have to travel around the world, learning more fully how we are going to love our neighbors economically and environmentally."

An angry man had had enough. He stood up in the front row, shook his Bible at Jing Sheng, and yelled so loudly that most of the people in the auditorium could hear and understand him: "Why should we go half way around the world to promote world peace? Aren't you forgetting that all you have to do is to go out and save the world by converting non-Christians to faith in Jesus Christ? That's all God asks us to do. If you are serving Jesus Christ, as you seem to think you are, then all you have to do is to go out and save souls! And that's the truth!"

Jing Sheng fairly sparkled with his calm smile and pleasant demeanor, by contrast to the angry, Bible-thumping man.

"Yes, thank you, sir, you have one piece of the truth in your hand, and in your heart. The fullness of God's Truth is that God has hidden parts of the Truth among all peoples of the earth. In each religion, God planted seeds of truth and love. Among all the peoples of the earth, God spoke, and parts of God's message were heard by every nation upon the earth, throughout human history.

"Christians were only given part of the truth as well. God gave pieces of the truth to each group of people *so that humankind would have to learn to listen to one another in order to hear the whole truth, and thereby to be made whole.* In order for humankind to survive, we will have to go forth and listen to one another's truths, in order to discover the whole truth of God together.

No one people can speak God's entire truth, nor can any single religion speak the whole of God's truth to the world today. We must listen to one another in order to learn the Truth together, across national boundaries, across religions, across races, across lifestyles. When have you ever heard anyone ask, "What is the truth that God taught to the pygmy peoples who live in the forests of the Congo?"

"Salvation, or wholeness, comes from learning the truths of God as presented through each religion, and to each group of people. Neglecting the man-made stuff such as creeds and dogmas, and holding onto truths which promote holiness, wholeness, love, equality, compassion, generosity, caring for the earth, and *justice for all life* is the only thing that will actually bring people both closer to God, closer to their Earthly Mother, and closer to one another.

"It is time to let go of the notion that your religion, whatever it may be, is the only way to please God or the only way to go to heaven. If you have not loved your neighbor, *every neighbor,* then you have not loved God, and heaven will remain distant from you, no matter what you believe. Christ brought this message to earth, so if Jesus Christ truly is your savior, then you know that you must love your neighbors all around the world, as well as your neighbor who is close to home."

"Bunch of nonsense, nothing but a bunch of nonsense." The man left the auditorium, shaking his head. *Ignorance often keeps us from understanding new ideas.* Liz, Darnell, and Daniel were actually sharing the same thought in response to the man. Adam was thinking of the man as unconscious.   Apparently, he had best understood Jing Sheng's airport lesson about divine consciousness.

"It is time to understand the lesson of Exodus 20:12.   Honor your father and mother, so that you may live long in the land.   When we understand that this text speaks not only of our biological parents, but also of our Heavenly Father and our Earthly Mother, then we understand that living long in the land means living peacefully and justly among our neighbors, as well as sustainably in relation to the earth, for the Spirit of the earth is our Divine Mother."

"Why do you always have to say that God is a mother?"   Someone yelled anonymously from the crowd.

"Indeed, thank you for your anonymous question, although your true identity is seen by God, and you would do well to present yourself to the world with your question, as a way of honoring yourself, God, and others."

Liz noticed that Jing Sheng did not make it a point that the person was also failing to honor him by remaining anonymous.   Then she realized that, since Jing Sheng was one with God, it was a moot point. *Oh, maybe that's what happens when we let go of ego and become one with God, we don't have to take offense because if someone is offending our human self, they are also offending God.* Liz wasn't sure how to embody this thought in her daily life yet, but it gave her a sense of peace.

"The Divine Mother brings the incarnate heart of God to earth.   She loves all life as Divine Mother.   She sustains, she gently nurtures, encourages, and guides.   She is the Wisdom of Life, called Sophia in Greek.   She is mentioned in the Bible in the book of Proverbs.   The feminine aspect of all human beings incarnates, to a greater or lesser degree, the Divine Mother's Wisdom and loving heart.

"Therefore, we will be adding a role into our mission: the role of Guru-Doula. A doula, as you may know, is a woman who assists a pregnant woman before, during, and after giving birth. She is not a mid-wife, but she is an assistant.

"A Guru-Doula provides a vital role as One Who Brings the Light in order to assist bringing about, or giving birth to, the Reign of Love among you."

A hush or a sigh went through the auditorium, as though the Divine Mother herself was singing some sort of calming lullaby. Everyone felt it, even the cranky manly-types.

"I will choose mostly women to fulfill this role, although I may select a few men. It is time for all cultures to respect the Divine Mother's presence within each person's heart, and to affirm women as partial incarnations of the Divine Mother herself."

Jing Sheng bowed in Namaste, and all the women of the crowd felt themselves utterly and deeply honored and affirmed; for many of them, it was the first time they felt such deep respect and admiration. The men looked around in bewilderment, although some of them 'got it' and smiled at the women around them.

From the side of the stage, and out-of-view, Liz found herself longing for a man who 'got it,' and then remembered Daniel. She looked over at him, and he smiled and came to her, putting his arm around her and gently kissing her on the cheek. Liz blushed with joy and smiled at Daniel before turning her rapt attention back to Jing Sheng.

"I thank you all for coming today, and I wish you God-speed on your journeys. Please remember that, as you live your life, your life is not about you. Your life is about Love walking the earth in you and through you. In this way, you will all become true Daughters and Sons of Love. God bless you and good afternoon."

Jing Sheng bowed, the crowd jumped to its feet, many people bowing in return, and applause broke out even as the UU choir returned and began to sing, "Let There Be Peace on Earth." Then almost everyone joined in the singing, and there was such an ocean of love and peace and joy in the auditorium, that most people present could feel it, and knew that they had never experienced anything like it before. They all hoped they would experience it again.

At the end of the singing, Darnell went out on stage, thanked everyone for coming, then invited them to get in touch and to get involved. He invited anyone who needed a healing to come down to the stage, and then he wished everyone a good day.

Jing Sheng walked up to Liz and Daniel, smiling at them both, and said, "Liz, I would like to train you to be my first Guru-Doula."
Liz's jaw dropped, and then she bowed in Namaste, "Yes, Jing Sheng, my Light. I thank you." Jing Sheng hugged them both together, and kissed both of them on the cheek. They could feel his incredibly loving, healing, and peaceful energy.

"Come, my love birds, let us give healing to those who are in need." With that, all three returned to the stage, and began to give healings to the 30 or so people who had stayed. Liz could feel the angels and archangels present, helping bring through the mighty energy of God's healing love.

14. PHARAOH'S HEART IS HARDENED

*IF THE ENERGY OF FAITH BLIPS ON AND OFF
LIKE AN OCCASIONAL PARTICLE APPEARING OUT OF
THE WAVE OF LOVE AND FAITH,
THEN THE DUALITY OF EXISTENCE ALLOWS FEAR
TO CREATE INTERACTIONS.
PATTERNS OF FEAR ARE ALL TEMPORARY, LIKE PARTICLES
OF LIGHT,
BUT THEY HURT LIKE SIN
WHEN THE WAVE OF LOVE AND FAITH HAS PASSED ON BY.*

Darnell worked day-and-night updating the website to include the plans: which countries they were going to, what organizations agreed to help, whom to contact to sign up to go to each country. Because the work became so complicated, they divided up responsibility for the countries. Darnell was in charge of the Congo. Adam was in charge of Brazil. Daniel was in charge of Croatia, and Liz was in charge of Malaysia and India.

Only three other people signed up to travel to eastern Congo for a month, and that included no children. Liz called her daughter Hopi and her son Cliff to discuss the situation with them. The hope was that they would be able to create some changes around justice issues relating to mining in eastern Congo, but they had no idea how it would work. Cliff was researching which companies were involved, and found it scary who was benefitting at the expense of poor Congolese people, even at the extreme expense of children.

"We just have to find some children to take with us, Mom," lamented Hopi. "How about if we at least get some college students to go, if not actual children, at least really young adults? That way, they could maybe do some research, or get college credit for writing a paper."

"That's a great idea, Hopi, I'll suggest it to Jing Sheng," answered Liz.

So it was that Darnell added the request for college students to go to Congo on the website, and four signed up. Two of them were young men from Massachusetts Institute of Technology, and two were young women from St. John's College in Annapolis, Maryland.

Well, at least we'll have some smart people along, thought Liz. *Of course, when it comes to traveling in foreign countries, there's smart, and there's wise, two very different things. Oh, well, we'll see what happens.*

So, in the end, the ones scheduled to go to eastern Congo were Darnell, Liz, Hopi, Cliff, a journalist from Huffington Post, a public health nurse from Johns Hopkins, a professor from American University's International Relations program, and the four college students, along with Jing Sheng, of course. Liz had no idea how Darnell and Jing Sheng screened the people who signed up on the website, or how the church in Rockville was involved, but she found out from Darnell that they were selected, not just accepted as volunteers without any screening process. Apparently the church educated them pretty well, also. Somehow, Liz knew, Jing Sheng's guiding hand must have been part of the process, but she had no idea how he kept ahead of every aspect of the mission.

Scheduled to go to Croatia were Daniel, Liz and Hopi (just briefly), and Jing Sheng, along with two families from Philadelphia, Pennsylvania, who apparently had some ancestry in Croatia. The two families included five children between them. They were scheduled to go live in a rural area where the poverty was extreme. In return, two families in Philadelphia had agreed to take in two families from Croatia, including four children.

Scheduled to go to Brazil were Jing Sheng, Adam, and eight adult volunteers from San Diego and Phoenix, with eight children all going as well. There were to be two sites where the exchanges took place in Brazil. Rio de Janeiro was to take in one family, and to send four 'street children' along with four aid workers who needed a break from the stress of dealing with extreme poverty. The second site was kind of poorly defined, due to the nebulous whereabouts of the Guarani people, who needed protection from industries that were destroying their native rainforests. In return, the Guarani people were to send two families, and a representative who would speak about the encroachment of Western businesses into the rainforest, and the devastation resulting.

In Malaysia, Liz, Daniel, Hopi, and Jing Sheng would go along with two families from Austin, Texas, including five children. The main organizational contact there was with Amnesty International, which was helping immigrant workers who had virtually no rights in the country, and who were being exploited by both Malaysian and Western businesses. One of those businesses was Bush Computers of San Marcos, Texas, near Austin, which had a recycling plant in Malaysia. At this recycling 'plant', computers were torn apart for scraps by underpaid workers, including children, who were then exposed to toxic metals. The plan, of course, was for the families to do something about this.

Separate from these exchanges were the beginnings of communes, now referred to as eco-communes, which were also spreading by engaging in international exchanges. Jing Sheng began to train Liz and other women to be Guru-Doulas to live in these communes. He also trained Hopi to be a Guru-Doula, and Daniel became the first male Guru-Doula, which was quite an honor. At the same time, an eco-commune sprang up in Montenegro, as well as ones in Nairobi, Kenya, two in Costa Rica, and one in Bangalore (now Bengaluru), India.

The final trip would take place in Bangalore/Bengaluru in December 2012. All Liz knew was that Jing Sheng only requested that they visit holy sites in two cities. She figured something would turn out to be a surprise. *And with Jing Sheng, anything is possible,* she realized.

The reaction to all this world-wide planning was not just extensive media coverage, but Unconscious, over-reactive, fear-based panic as well. Somehow, the families planning to immigrate to America, although it was just for one year, kept being denied visas, with the State Department giving all sorts of strange reasons as to why they didn't qualify for a visa. In addition, the State Department put a hold on the passports of Darnell, Liz, Daniel, Hopi, Cliff, and Adam. Jing Sheng was told that if he wanted to return to the United States once he left, he would either have to apply for citizenship first, or find an American wife.

The Tempest Party, which ruled over both houses of Congress, passed a law claiming that communes violated fundamental American freedoms, capitalism, and the 'American Way,' (*whatever that is,* thought Liz), and therefore banned them as unconstitutional. So a movement had to get organized, and funded, of course, to fight the ruling. Eventually, the communes won on the basis of freedom to practice a religion.

Certain well-known political commentators started making nasty claims about Jing Sheng and the Exodus 2012 mission – totally misguided comments which completely misunderstood the purpose, motives, and methods of the mission and its participants. Conservative pastors in mega-churches across America preached against Hu Jing Sheng, claiming that he was the Anti-Christ, and deriding the mission, as well as the concepts of global warming, climate change, and of reincarnation.

Unconsciousness and fear ruled the air waves as well as both houses of Congress. The White House remained silent, afraid to get into the controversy in any way. Marches against Exodus 2012 were organized in some cities, while marches for the mission were organized in the towns where families were participating.

Liz, Daniel, and Hopi spent this challenging time traveling to different eco-communes, getting to know people and helping them establish loving, life-respecting processes for all aspects of their lives together. They taught meditation and energy healing, they gave healings, and after a few weeks of getting to know people, selected at least one in each commune for Jing Sheng to train as Guru-Doulas.

Daniel and Liz found themselves spending a lot of time together, enjoying each other's company more and more. Even in the midst of communes, they found alone time. The Exodus 2012 mission funded their basic needs, so they also occasionally went out to eat or to see a movie. They enjoyed hiking wherever they could, and Liz brought Comet with them everywhere, so they had to take a lot of walks. Despite the stalling of the mission overseas, life, for Daniel and Liz, was very happy.

Hopi had been so impressed by Jing Sheng, that she had blossomed into a truly loving young lady, still somewhat shy and ready to hide behind the camera, but much more passionate about incarnating love, and trusting the results, than she had been before. People loved her, especially children, who flocked to her because she loved to play games and sing silly songs. She also taught the young ones to meditate and to accept responsibility for their choices.

After several months of Hopi helping to set up the eco-communes, Jing Sheng inducted her into the training of a guru-doula. Her work with the children and teenagers of the eco-communes blossomed and grew. The teenagers and children even got involved in researching the environmental practices of local stores and companies, and demonstrating against harmful social and environmental policies.

Facebook, Twitter, and YouTube became full of postings, tweets, and videos about companies, stores, and brands to boycott, along with suggestions of websites, brands, and stores which offered environmentally and socially-responsible products along with corporate accountability for their industrial practices. Hopi delighted in being part of all of it, from the research to the boycotts and internet broadcasting, to teaching and leading meditation with the youth.

Cliff was the sole family member not yet fully on board, but he was so busy studying for his Ph.D. that no one could blame him. Hopi visited him and persuaded him to spend a weekend with Jing Sheng. So it was that one Saturday afternoon, Hopi and Jing Sheng greeted Cliff at Baltimore-Washington International airport, and drove him to the hotel in Rockville, Maryland, where Jing Sheng was helping establish the Rockville congregation's involvement in the mission.

Jing Sheng took Cliff out to a restaurant and modeled his vegetarian lifestyle. Seeing that, Cliff launched into a thousand questions. Jing Sheng patiently answered every one of them. Cliff was skeptical about one person making a difference, and valued free will above all else. His deepest fear was that following, or harder yet (he thought) worshiping God would take away his free will.

When Jing Sheng taught him that the universe is made up of God and nothingness, or

Maya – Illusion, and that the nothingness nature of Maya is what led to free will by God's design, Cliff breathed a sigh of relief.

"You mean God does not want to control me?" Cliff answered, kind of red-faced as he drank his beer and ate his steak.

"Cliff, where do you think you will encounter God?" Jing Sheng returned.

"I don't know. I have no idea because heaven makes no sense to me, because there is no such place in the universe." Cliff felt a slight sense of relief at being able to speak bluntly and honestly to Jing Sheng, whose calm, loving demeanor usually made people feel free to say anything.

"Right, just so, heaven is not on this earth plane. Heaven is in another energetic dimension. Mind and energy determine whether we are here or in heaven. Of course, energy is determined in large part by our spiritual karma.

 "But I repeat: where do you expect to find God?"

"You're serious, aren't you? You do realize that most of us here in America don't expect to ever encounter God, right?" Cliff's tone was, unfortunately, disdainful and distrustful.

"Actually, there are many people in this society who expect to see God, or at least Jesus, when they die, but unfortunately for them, their understanding of God and Christ will leave them surprised at what they will experience along with God and Christ when they die. For instance, many of them will be surprised to meet Jewish people and Muslims and Buddhists and Hindus in heaven." Jing Sheng's tone was notably sad.

"What do you mean?" Cliff would never have been the author of the Cliff Notes series, as his mother and sister used to tease him.

"Cliff, my intelligent little one, you have much to learn about spirituality, but it is best to approach the spiritual life through the eyes of the heart rather than through the eyes of the mind. I repeat my question: where do you expect to find God?"

Realizing that he seemed rather rude for not answering Jing Sheng's question, and that, karmically speaking, Jing Sheng therefore owed him no further answers, Cliff paused and thought awhile. He gazed at the candle lighting their table as he slowly chewed steak and sipped his beer.

"Sometimes I see what I might call God in the sunrise or the sunset, or in a bird soaring high in the sky," Cliff managed. "Sometimes I see what makes me think of God when someone does something really loving for someone else."

"Good, my son." Jing Sheng was about ten years older than Cliff in his physical body, so visually, this statement seemed a little jarring to one's sense of reality.

"Now, where do you long most to find God?" Jing Sheng's directness definitely made Cliff feel put on the spot on the one hand, and yet, on the other hand, it made him feel as though Jing Sheng could lovingly look right through him and see what Cliff needed more deeply than he himself was aware. After a delay, Cliff realized that any sense of false modesty would not help this discussion, and so he answered boldly.

"I long to find God within myself, so that I can know the reality of God within my own mind all the time."

"Touché, my friend," Jing Sheng honored Cliff more than he realized. "That is almost a perfect answer. A better answer would be: so that I can know the reality of God within my own heart, soul, mind, as well as the temple of my body all the time."

"And how do I get closer to accomplishing that?" Cliff ventured.

"That is a perfect question!" Jing Sheng laughed, as though Cliff could possibly share his sense of humor. It was almost as if Jing

Sheng were laughing at him, which would be the view someone would have if they looked at the situation through the eyes of their ego. However, as anyone who considered Jing Sheng's laughter through the eyes of their soul could see, Jing Sheng was simply delighting joyfully in Cliff's spiritual progress.

"Please allow me to teach you Raja Yoga meditation, and then Kriya Yoga meditation, and sooner or later, you will find God within." Jing Sheng bowed in Namaste to Cliff.

Cliff felt a little silly that Jing Sheng would be bowing to him, when obviously he was the one who should be bowing to Jing Sheng.

"Of course!" Cliff bowed awkwardly in Namaste to Jing Sheng.

And so it was that Jing Sheng and Cliff spent the next 24 hours practicing meditation together. Jing Sheng's ability to see into the depths of a person left Cliff in a daze. He became a little more open, wondering what was real, and decided that maybe he did not have all the answers, and that maybe he did not *have* to have all the answers. That was significant progress. The next evening, Cliff boarded a plane to return to his Ph.D. work, having begun a new course of study in life with his brand new practice of meditation.

In the meantime, the public tirades against the eco-communes increased, especially as the folks who were living communally got organized and started advocating for environmentally-responsible choices in their communities. They took on recycling, transportation, housing, air pollution standards, toxic waste sites, environmental justice (the dismantling of environmental racism) and every issue they could discover around them that had a negative impact on the environment.

They also sought to create green spaces and to honor animals as living beings that deserved ecosystems and habitats just as much as humans do. Of course, this made them very unpopular, and corporations funded politicians and commentators who would speak all kinds of evil against them falsely.

Jing Sheng went from community to community among the eco-communes, teaching, healing, and speaking out publicly for a changed way of life. He had to hire a bodyguard. Darnell and Adam often traveled with him, but they needed bodyguards as well. When Jing Sheng would visit Liz, Daniel and Hopi, Liz always felt such relief and joy, as though God really had walked into her life and made everything all better.

What does it take for people to open up and see God when God is standing right in front of them? Liz wondered.

15. The Plagues of God

IF THE FOCUS OF OUR DAILY CONCERNS
MOST HOURS OF THE DAY
IS OUR OWN WELLBEING,
WITHOUT GIVING THOUGHT TO OTHERS,
WHAT IS THE KARMIC RESULT OF THE FOCUS OF OUR
THOUGHTS?
IF WE NEGLECT TO FOCUS ON THE WELLBEING OF
OTHERS, WHAT IMPACT DOES OUR CONSCIOUS ENERGY
HAVE ON THE WELLBEING OF CREATION?
CAN WE REALLY BLAME ANYONE ELSE FOR THE STATE OF
THE WORLD,
WHEN OUR LIVES ARE SO ALL-CONSUMED WITH SELF?

Meanwhile, while 'Pharaoh' stalled and wouldn't grant the visas to let the people's exchanges occur, the plagues began. Birds dropped by the thousands over the skies of several cities in Arkansas. Fish washed up dead by the thousands in rivers in Missouri, all along the Mississippi, in rivers in Maine, and in Washington State.

A lightning storm hit Washington, D.C. harder than anyone could remember a lightning storm ever hitting anywhere ever before. Over a hundred pedestrians were killed before the news alerts went out and people stayed off the street. Those who were killed and injured included some congressional staff people and even some senators and representatives, as the lightning struck mostly around the capitol.

Out west, mudslides pestered Californians while wildfires raged through parts of Texas, Oklahoma, and Kansas. Florida was hit by two hurricanes in a row.

A few newscasters actually reminded people that one of the predictions of global warming is climate change that will cause harsher and harsher storms, with more unpredictability in the process. After all, weather is a chaotic system which is incredibly sensitive to environmental changes. What an inconvenient fact to remember at a time like this.

After decades of warning that it might occur, a huge ice shelf in Antarctica finally slid off of the continental shelf and crashed right into the ocean. Satellite images were all that was available, because the ship of scientific observers got too close and was capsized by the tidal wave that resulted. The tip of South America was hit so hard by the tidal wave that the wave just continued up both coastlines of South America, causing flooding and untold damage, deaths, and suffering for thousands of miles.

An earthquake hit Japan, causing a tsunami which traveled in both directions across the Pacific, causing flooding not only in Japan, but also Korea, the Philippines, and so many other places, the news media could hardly keep track. Nuclear reactors in both Japan and Korea were damaged, and radioactive waste started leaking into both the air and the Pacific Ocean. People all around Southeast Asia began to get sick from the radiation, and hundreds of thousands of people in Japan and Korea actually died within months. Environmental groups could not even keep accurate estimates of the loss of animal life.

While European countries responded by shutting down nuclear plants, inspecting some, and permanently closing others, the corporate PAC-infected congress insisted that the U.S. should expand its nuclear energy supply, and that nothing more than routine inspections were needed, even at aging plants.

In Africa, drought was drying up crops and people were starving to death in the tens of thousands, perhaps millions, but Westerners usually can't be bothered to count Africans, no matter what's happening to them. More people had already died as a result of conflict minerals in Eastern Congo than had died in the entire holocaust, but only a few Westerners actually were aware of this fact. As predicted by global warming models, the band of rain around the equator was shifting northward, drying out even rainforests that have existed as stable ecosystems for tens of thousands of years. The loss of rainforest led to a loss of oxygen as well as a loss of animal habitat and a loss of human life that reached truly inestimable numbers. The sheer magnitude of loss was staggering.

In southern Asia, flooding occurred in Pakistan, Bangladesh, and India, as a result of the ice shelf dropping off of Antarctica. Droughts inland in all three countries led to starvation on a massive scale, of both humans and animals.

South Africa also lost cities and millions of people in the flooding resulting from the ice shelf separating from Antarctica. The whole country was devastated together – people of all colors suffering, dying, and finally rescuing each other when faced with the reality that nothing really did separate them as human beings.

In China and Mongolia, drought and fires plagued large parts of the land. In Siberia and northern Europe, rain was intense and caused horrendous flooding, again costing thousands of people their lives, their homes, and their towns. Coastal towns were flooded by the combination of rain and melting ice caps. More hundreds of thousands of people died.

In the Middle East, drought was also causing problems, but the wealth of oil money was delaying the intensity of what the ruling class experienced, even as lower class people suffered and died by the thousands.

Class warfare was apparent everywhere as people struggled to survive, and intense fear ruled in so many lands. Those who survived but lost homes in the floods became homeless nomads by the tens of thousands. People were too afraid to remain close to the now changed coastline. Only the wealthy could afford new homes and transportation, so poor people by the hundreds would invade their property and take what they needed.

In most places, there was no way for police or military police to maintain order, and in most cases, no one had the heart to shoot and kill anyone else, because so many people had already died. Except for in a few places in the world, the exceptions tending to be among the wealthy, most people laid down their weapons and simply sought to help others or to share what they had.

The coastal areas of North America also flooded, losing towns, cities, crops, and causing desperation that no amount of Federal Emergency Relief could repair. Churches, synagogues and temples of all faiths became sanctuaries and meccas for homeless people. Fundamentalist pastors preached that God must be punishing people for sinfulness, and about repentance so that God would not harm people anymore. The mainline, liberal pastors preached about going to the aid of our neighbors around the world who were suffering.

News media around the world began to change their studios into comforting, sanctified spaces with lighted candles and sacred images of all faiths. It was the only way that most news commentators could cope with reporting the *staggering* losses of both life *and hope* on the planet.

Jing Sheng began to spend more time in prayer and meditation, as did his followers. He got to meet with South American elders, who honored him, and whom he greatly honored, because of the ancient wisdom they had retained, and by which they chose to live. Together, they meditated, prayed, sang, chanted, danced, drummed, and prayed some more. Perhaps that is what saved the earth.

Media coverage of the event led people in virtually every city and town around the world to hold 'Prayer-ins' during which people fasted, prayed, danced, sang, meditated, drummed, or whatever their hearts led them to do as a group, to ask humbly for divine forgiveness and assistance in surviving the plagues.

Many Christian preachers, especially in America, started preaching about the end times, and warned people to convert, lest they be 'left behind.'

I'd rather be left behind than have to hear you preach for a thousand years, thought Liz, as she briefly listened to a televangelist. *I would gladly listen to Jing Sheng for a thousand years, though.* She changed the channel to a news station with 24-hour news, and watched as people in Africa made a plea for food assistance. The U.N. was swamped with disasters, and not likely to be able to respond.

As you do it unto the least of these, you do it unto me, Liz remembered Christ's words, and wondered how so many white American Christians conveniently managed to forget those words as they preached about 'taking care of our own first,' meaning their own kind of people in their own churches and their own communities, and that probably did not include people living in severe poverty nor people of color, for the most part, and it certainly did not include non-Americans.

In the most densely populated area of Eastern Europe, an outbreak of SARS occurred, and it spread worldwide before any of the Eastern European countries could get precautionary measures in place. After about two weeks, precautionary measures began to be taken everywhere, which meant that many people withdrew into their own homes and mostly stayed there until the epidemic had passed.

From the end of 2008 through the beginning of 2012, over four billion people worldwide died from one catastrophe or another. The repercussions crippled the global economy, and world food production plummeted. Many people lived on the edge of starvation, as famine and lack of medical care exacerbated the existing catastrophes. Transportation and communications suffered, and every aspect of government work slowed to a snail's pace.

Social disruption led to outbreaks of fundamentalist religion, while peace-communes formed in public spaces in cities around the world. Those who hung out in the peace communes camped there, with some of them being demonstrators, and some of them joining in simply because they were homeless, hungry, and desperate.

16. THE PASSOVER OF GOD

HEAVEN IS NOT AS MUCH A PLACE AS IT IS
A STATE OF BEING,
A CONDITION OF THE MIND AND HEART
THAT REQUIRES LOVE.
HEAVEN IS FILLED WITH LIGHT AND LOVE,
AND SO LIFE BECOMES TRANSFORMED INTO SOMETHING
MORE LIKE
WHAT WE HOPE FOR, LONG FOR, DREAM OF,
BUT ONLY BECAUSE
WE LEAVE BEHIND FEAR, DESPAIR, ANGER, AND HATE.

During this time, Jing Sheng and his followers awaited their passports, and the international exchange families awaited their visas. What had begun as a political delay tactic had taken much longer as the world had literally fallen apart. The whole mission team planned to travel beginning in June 2012, starting with the International Children's Festival in Sibenik, Croatia.

As the world situation worsened, they all spent more and more time in prayer, fasting, and meditation. The eco-communes became mini-retreat centers for people who also sought to fast, meditate, and pray.

Eventually, people began to ask, "For what should we pray? An end to global warming? An end to the tyranny of profit, greed, material comforts? An end to the plagues hitting humankind, or to the causes of human sin?" Even the followers of Jing Sheng Hu became confused about what to pray for.

Jing Sheng called a conference, returned to Kalamazoo, and drew Darnell, Adam, Liz, and Daniel to him.

"You four represent the four winds of change, the four directions of the earth. I will ask you to pray for peace around the earth. Darnell, you will pray for North America and the Arctic. Adam, you will pray for South America, the Antarctic, and the Pacific islands. Liz, you will pray for Europe, the Middle East, and Africa. Daniel, you will pray for Russia, central Asia, southern Asia, and Southeast Asia. You will all pray for the peoples of the lands I have given you. By the way, that is what God meant when he told Abraham that he was giving him land – it was to pray for the people of the land and to live peaceably among them. So you, too, will pray for the people of the land, for their safety, for the end of the plagues, and for peaceful living among themselves. You may gather eco-communes to pray with you. Please spend one week in prayer.

"I will pray that God will Passover the communities which have agreed to make an exchange of families, and I will pray for God to Passover the eco-communes, and to provide food for them all."

And so it was, that on February 14th, 2012, Valentine's Day, Jing Sheng held a Prayer Conference, which was televised worldwide, to ask God to Passover the eco-communes, the communities willing to exchange families, as well as all families of the earth.

That day, mild weather came to all the exchanging communities as well as all the communities that were home to the eco-communes. Anonymous donors brought food to each commune as well as to each community where an exchange was to occur.

After that, a rainbow was seen all the way around the earth, at 3:00 o'clock in the afternoon of February 14th. It actually followed the sun around the entire earth, so that, no matter where it turned 3:00 p.m., there was, quiet inexplicably, a rainbow visible in the sky. So God so loved the world that God gave the whole world a rainbow.

A gift is a gift and a sign is a sign. People repented of their selfish, self-concerned ways and in droves flocked to churches, temples, and synagogues. Many atheists converted to something – anything positive and non-judgmental that meant there was really a loving source of the universe; this largely meant that the Baha'is, the Buddhists, and the Unitarian Universalist Churches benefitted greatly from the influx of atheists and former atheists.

People shared their food with others. People took homeless people into their own homes. All around the world, kindness and generosity broke out. Was this the way the world was meant to be? People stopped dressing for success, or to one-up the Joneses or to impress or impersonate, or for whatever reason than just to look nice and clean and presentable for the day. Instead, they gave away clothes to the less fortunate, who now outnumbered the fortunate many times over. The less fortunate also shared and gave and worked to help out. And virtually everyone found something for which to be grateful.

The U.N. declared an International Day of Thanksgiving for March 1st, and asked people to celebrate it by being less materialistic, and by giving away generously everything they possibly could.

Pretty soon, people were laughing and adults were playing with children, even children they didn't know, but who lived just down the street or even out on the street. Houses and apartment buildings were crowded, but people decided they had better get outside and plant gardens together. No businesses allowed anyone to work long hours; everyone understood the importance of going home, cherishing families, and then volunteering in the community instead.

Wall Street was stunned. Traders were in a daze. The market dropped, but nobody seemed to care. Everyone was just happy to be alive. Even on Wall Street, a co-op formed to consider ways to end world hunger and global warming.

Many people chose to leave the U.S. and form eco-communes in other countries. So it was that Costa Rica, Uruguay, Mexico,

Tanzania, Kenya, Ghana, Australia, South Africa, India, Turkey and Europeans start to get involved as well with developing eco-communes and earth co-ops.

Fair trade began to proliferate across the earth, especially as music and food and celebrations moved across continents and oceans, with whole groups of Exodus 2012 "hippies" celebrating life and getting to know one another across international boundaries. Internationally, yoga centers and eco-communes began to celebrate 'bliss days' during which they offered day-long yoga and meditation sessions with vegetarian feasts after sundown, like Ramadan.

Native Americans began to get involved, at first mostly by holding sweat lodges with traditional prayer ceremonies at eco-communes spread across the earth. In this way, Native Americans helped other people learn about honoring the earth mother in spiritual ceremonies which honored walking in beauty upon the earth. Native Americans from the tribes who owned large casinos in Michigan began to purchase large sections of foreclosed properties in places like Detroit, and transformed them into spiritual communes practicing both traditional ceremonies such as sweat lodges and dances, and yoga, Tai Chi, and meditation.

A Lakota medicine man traveled to Egypt to meet Egyptian elders who retained the ancient teachings, even in the midst of modern day turmoil. They spent time together exchanging ancient wisdom, both spiritual and practical wisdom such as herbal lore and healing.

Together, they next traveled to meet elders and Shamans in Central and South America. Out of a month-long ceremony in which they worshiped, honored the earth, and learned each other's traditions, they decided to share the best of their ceremonies and wisdom with the world. They hired some young techies, and taped a message for youtube together. Of course the Global Elder Video immediately 'went viral.'

For a few months, gratitude, cooperation, generosity, and even peace and love reigned among human beings around the planet.

17. THE EXODUS – CROSSING THE SEA OF REEDS

WHAT IS LIFE ALL ABOUT? WHY LIVE IT? WHY LIVE HERE ON EARTH?
WHO ARE YOU? WHAT IS YOUR LIFE PURPOSE?
IF WE CANNOT ANSWER THESE QUESTIONS, WHAT IS THE POINT OF ALL KNOWLEDGE?

Eventually, after people resumed regular work schedules, the visas were granted, and the passports were released. Daniel, Liz, Hopi, the two families, and Jing Sheng headed to Sibenik, Croatia in time to get there before the International Children's festival. They started out on the Kornati Islands, where Hopi took photographs and videos to show the delicate balance of nature and to document how carefully that pristine environment has been maintained by the local people and governments. With the help of the translator Daniel had hired, she interviewed people from local environmental conservation groups in Croatia. There were several such groups, and an eco-commune had been formed near Sibenik, along the Krka River.

The first day of the International Children's Festival, Jing Sheng was scheduled to give an opening keynote address, which was to be televised locally. Media coverage came from far-and-wide, though, as did crowds of people, to hear him speak. The speech was to be given right in front of St. James Cathedral, the most prominent landmark and tourist attraction of the city.

"My friends," started Jing Sheng, and then paused for the translators to translate into five different languages – Croatian, Bosnian, French, Japanese, and Spanish. He himself spoke in Mandarin after he spoke in English.

"I would like to thank the people of Croatia for sponsoring the International Children's Festival – what a God-given idea that was.

<pause> I also would like to thank the people of Sibenik for hosting this festival. <pause>

"All peoples of the world can live in peace, indeed, we have just witnessed that it is possible for all people to live in peace for a few weeks.   <pause, and scattered applause broke out> If people of every nation and of every community will simply decide to put children first, <pause> and to care about all children on the earth, then we can live in peace. <pause>

"If people all around the world will trouble themselves to find out how the children all around the world are living, <pause> then global warming will gradually be reversed as well, because greed and excessive materialism, <pause> at the expense of poor people around the world, is what causes global warming. <pause> Yes, fossil fuels are the direct cause, but it is greed and the idolization of material comfort which drives the excessive use of fossil fuels. <pause>

Let us all, today, commit ourselves to cherishing our children – all our children – more than we cherish material comfort. <pause> Let us, today, commit ourselves to saving the earth. <pause> The message of Exodus 2012 is: if we will honor our Heavenly Father and our Earthly Mother, <pause> by loving all the children of the earth, then we will all live long in the land. So be it." Jing Sheng bowed in Namaste.

Applause broke out profusely all around. Some people jumped up-and-down and shouted "Djeca Prva!" (Children First!)   Music began to play and the band marched by, on camera, for millions of people around the world to get to join in, for the first time in history, in celebrating children all around the world, Croatian-style.

What a joy-filled day it was for everyone present. Daniel, Liz, Jing Sheng and the adults who came to stay for a month met with local leaders about the mission, while Hopi took the children in tow, taking photos and videos and having fun with the children to her heart's content. She also posted videos of their activities on youtube. The next day, they were all scheduled to go visit an eco-commune, and then travel to where the two families would live, meeting the families who would travel to the U.S. for the first time in an exchange of homes.

Fortunately, they had good weather for travel. They hired a small bus and driver, so that there was room for everyone to travel together, including the translator, who now offered to act as tour guide. They drove over the Krka River, and he told them about local conservation efforts to keep the area pristine.

It's so pristine already, thought Liz, *I wonder why they are worried about it. If only we Americans valued pristine areas of nature as much as this – everywhere looks so beautiful!*

As they drove into the eco-commune, they noticed farm fields and greenhouses of various kinds, some of them having earthen berms on the north sides. They arrived at the cooperative house, only to discover that it, too, was built into a hillside in order to be partially sheltered by the earth. Atop its own hillside, the housing structure had solar panels feeding it energy on sunny days. On another hillside nearby were two large wind turbines. They produced enough electricity for not only the cooperative, but also the whole valley, which included three other farms, and two other homes, nestled along the Krka River. Only one cell phone tower was in sight, and that was placed as far from the river as possible.

"What a beautiful setting!" Liz remarked to Daniel.

"How peaceful it is, too," Daniel echoed her praise. He took her hand as they walked toward the house. Hopi was busy taking pictures. Jing Sheng was speaking quietly with the families as he walked with them.

"I admire you so much," Daniel confessed to Liz.

"Me? Why? I'm just a follower of Jing Sheng – he's the one we all need to admire!" Liz exclaimed.

"Just so – you are humble, extremely intelligent, passionate, compassionate, and you care deeply about the earth and her peoples. And you are beautiful inside and out! And I could go on... but maybe words are not the best way to express it!" Daniel took both her hands, and turned to face her. Looking into the depths of her eyes, he leaned forward and slowly, passionately, kissed her.

Liz delightedly returned the favor. Then, looking into his eyes, she choked up saying, "I admire you, too, for much the same reasons, only, you're so gorgeous!"

Daniel laughed, and they moved on, knowing that other people needed them to commune with them socially, building bridges cross-culturally and across languages as well.

The work in Croatia went well, and the Croatian families traveled to America, settling in Philadelphia, Pennsylvania. From there, they were easily able to take trips to New York, and Washington, DC, so that they could speak at eco-communes and large rallies.

Speak out they did, too, especially as they encountered, for the first time, this Philly-style version of the American attitude, "Let's help out at home before we help anywhere else. We have plenty of Americans who need help, so let's help out in our own neighborhoods."

The Croatian families responded with speeches about American tribalism causing rifts in global harmony, and the importance of recognizing that all humankind is in the same boat, and all humankind is equally important, as well as equally dependent on one another. They also pointed out that Americans had no one but themselves to blame for poverty in their own backyards, because of the capitalistic competition and emphasis on individual rather than communal responsibility for well-being.

One poignant question they asked was, "What if all nations were to cease doing trade with America, to cease sending goods to America, simply because they wanted to put their own people first?"

They just kept questioning: "What goods would Americans have, since almost nothing is made in America anymore? Do you really think that you don't depend entirely on the rest of the world? Where do you get such arrogance, that you think you are better than everyone else? How do you manage to think that you are more important than people in the streets of Iraq, or people in the jungles of the Congo? Do you even know any of these other people? How can you decide to put yourself first, without being simply selfish and self-serving? What kind of example is this to the rest of the world?

"In fact, the rest of the world sees Americans as selfish and greedy, even exploitative. The whole history of Western culture is one of exploitation and domination. Is that really advancement, or is it decline?

"Cooperation is truly one of the highest, most advanced elements of human society. Co-operation as the basis for human relations is far more advanced, and far more demanding of wisdom and abilities than is domination. Any bully can dominate, but who can lead a cooperative, just global economy? That nation is the leader of today."

And so it was that, in Philadelphia, the birthplace of democracy in America, freedom and truth and a voice for the common good rang anew, but with a global and environmental voice in the 21st century. True democracy was recognized as being global, based on fair trade between and among equal partners, rather than on the basis of domination by multi-national corporations whose assets rivaled the GDP of some Third World nations. Furthermore, true democracy was now recognized as including human habitats, which, as environmental bio-systems, became honored as the actual foundation of human society that they truly are.

The Croatian families in America gave voice to the possibility of a new world order, where the Promised Land was no longer just an American possibility, but a global vision for a truly global reality.

Imagine the whole earth becoming the Promised Land. Liz wondered if that wasn't what God had always intended.

♥ ♥ ♥

18. WANDERING IN THE DESERT

WHAT BECOMES IMPORTANT WHEN YOU ARE WANDERING
IN A DESERT?
IS IT WHO YOU KNOW, OR WHAT YOU KNOW?
IS IT LIFE? OR IS IT DEATH?
WHERE IS YOUR FAITH WHEN YOUR LIFE IS AT STAKE?
IS THE WORLD A FRIENDLY PLACE, A CRUEL PLACE, OR AN
IMPARTIAL PLACE? IF GOD CREATED THE WORLD, THEN
CAN IT NOT BE
THE BEST POSSIBLE PLACE FOR US RIGHT NOW?

As the Mission expanded, the travels continued on the part of Jing Sheng and his disciples. Jing Sheng had to remain outside the country until the U.S. government decided to allow him to return, or until he got married, whichever came first. Daniel stayed with him in Croatia while Liz and the other disciples gathered briefly in Washington, DC, to organize the next trip, with the help of the church in Rockville.

This next trip was to be to Brazil, and Daniel would get to return 'home' to Kalamazoo while Jing Sheng and Adam traveled with the exchange families to Rio de Janeiro. Apparently, Adam had brushed up on his Portuguese, because he had long been fascinated with the ancient tribes of Brazil, in particular the Guarani people, who lived in complete harmony and balance with the rain forests of Brazil, rather than destroying them as the supposedly 'advanced' Western cultures were doing.

What is so 'advanced' about dominating other cultures and destroying habitats and peoples? Liz wondered. *Isn't respect for diversity and living in harmony far more advanced than destroying things like some two-year-old who likes to see things fall apart and hear them go 'bang'? Or a two-year-old who sees something new and immediately grabs it saying, "Mine!"?*

So, Adam and the families from San Diego and Phoenix gathered at the church in Rockville, where they prepared for the cultural, linguistic, and survival differences they would encounter traveling and living in Brazil, especially the ones who planned to find the Guarani people. Those who planned to live in Rio began to communicate, with the help of Adam, with the families with whom they would be staying.

They managed to plan access to health care, thanks to Doctors Without Borders, in case the children, especially, would need it. They also planned mission work and speaking tours on which Jing Sheng would spread the mission of Exodus 2012. Adam became responsible for travel arrangements as well as Jing Sheng's schedule, and he was the main translator. Darnell began to worry about Adam having too much to do.

August 10, 2009 was their scheduled departure date, and Jing Sheng flew to Rio to meet them on August 11th.

The family that planned to stay in Rio de Janeiro went to the home of the family which was ready to move to San Diego. Together, they all drove to a near-by church, where a group of Jing Sheng's Brazilian followers gathered to discuss the mission in Rio. The focus was to be on reaching the street children of Rio.

Several NGO's (non-governmental organizations, that is, charities) were present to advise and to work with the mission to improve the lives of the street children of Rio. Unfortunately, only two slum areas could be targeted immediately to work with the children, providing health care, food, shelter, education, and a sense of home and family. Some volunteers actually left their own homes to live with and raise the children in boarding school-type settings.

Jing Sheng greeted and blessed this group, while the other group rested before traveling out into the rainforest to find the Guarani people. Jing Sheng spent two days with the Rio de Janeiro group, teaching, healing, and meditating with them, so that they became blessed in every way.

The following day, Jing Sheng, Adam, several followers, and the other family left with some local followers who were to guide them in search of the Guarani people in the rainforest. They first flew in small airplanes, then traveled by rustic, run-down buses.

The scenery was beautiful, though they were struggling to adapt to the rough, potentially dangerous, and inconvenient lifestyle that came with traveling through tropical rainforests.

The group that went out into the rainforest to find the Guarani people stayed in touch for a week, letting Darnell and Liz know their whereabouts, but all of a sudden, their communications went silent. Darnell became almost frantic with fear and worry for Adam's well-being.

Liz reminded him, "Darnell, you are the one who already knew that stuff about the universe being comprised of organized consciousness and patterns of energy from either fear or love. Why are you creating patterns of fear in your consciousness?"

"Oh sure, now you go all enlightenment on me!" Darnell retorted. "I know, I know – you're right, it's just that … I don't want to live without Adam in my life."

"Darnell, you know God-in-the-flesh in Hu Jing Sheng, and you still don't find yourself ready to live without a particular human being?" Liz sounded a little incredulous, because the presence of Jing Sheng in her life seemed to preempt every other priority, longing, desire, and fear.

"Well, who knows how long he'll be with us?" Darnell threw back at her.

"That's true, but we all had that little invitation to live in the Reign of Divine Love, or have you forgotten that?"

"Sometimes it would seem so much easier if I could just feel that love, instead of having to have faith enough to imagine it first," Darnell explained.

"I know what you mean," Liz answered slowly, staring in space as if she were in a daze. "Having Jing Sheng here makes life seem so much easier emotionally. I don't know how well I will do if or when he's gone."

"Exactly!" Exclaimed Darnell.

"Well, let's pray and meditate, then, and see what comes. I'm sure it will bring you peace." Liz spoke with a sense of authority, but the reality was that she found comfort in praying and meditating with Darnell, rather than having to pray and meditate alone.

Meditators around the world are familiar with the sense of peaceful energy that pervades the room or space around a group of people meditating. For Liz, it was more than that, though. She had spent years having to meditate alone in her own home, and so she felt grateful to meditate with other people, instead of being by herself all the time.

"Okay," Darnell conceded the wisdom of meditating, and found comfort in Liz's presence as well.

Why is it that we don't automatically realize that what we appreciate in one another is in fact the very presence of God in another human being, Liz wondered. *What a great reminder that God is always with us – inside ourselves, in who we are, as well as within the very nature of each person's soul.*

Liz and Darnell were staying at the home of Pastor Bobette Fiddmont in Rockville, and so they asked if she would pray with them.

"Of course, of course!" She eagerly replied. "But first, let me call and start the prayer chain at our church, so others will join us in praying for the safety of Jing Sheng, Adam, and the whole Exodus group in Brazil." Pastor Bobette had a way of calming every situation right down.

They re-grouped in her living room, sitting on cushions and lighting candles to honor the divine presence with and within them. Darnell started an "Aum" chant, and Bobette and Liz joined him. When he stopped, Pastor Bobette began to pray.

"Oh, Lord, gracious God, we come before you in prayer now for our friends in Brazil. We lift up especially your servant Jing Sheng, and your servant Adam, and ask that you continue to hold them in your care. Guide them, keep them safe, along with the whole Exodus mission group, for they only seek to serve you and others with your love. Return them home safely to us, and bless your mission with the Guarani people. Bless also your mission to save the earth, and us her people, that we may have wisdom to care for your Creation. Thank you, thank you, thank you. In Jesus' name we pray."

"God," Darnell began, and then hesitated, "Send your Spirit of Love and Wisdom to Adam, and fill him with love so he will never feel lonely or afraid. Send him guides and whatever he needs for safety. I thank you for Master Hu Jing Sheng, and ask you to keep him safe as well. Please bless our mission with the Guarani people. Thank you for the Guarani people and their wisdom of living in harmony with the earth. Thank you for their non-materialistic ways. Help us to be more like them, and to honor you by honoring the earth. Amen."

There was silence in the room. Liz chose not to break the silence, because she strongly disliked praying out loud, even though she was the one who suggested it. She prayed in her own head, and then meditated.

Silence reigned for 30 minutes, and a peaceful energy pervaded the room. The phone then rang, and Pastor Bobette rose to answer it. She spoke quietly so as not to disturb Darnell and Liz. Obviously, it was a pastoral work call.

She returned to sit and meditate with them, only she sat in a chair, rather than cross-legged on a cushion.

Another 30 minutes went by. Liz rose, went to the kitchen for some water, then the bathroom, and then returned and sat cross-legged on a cushion on the floor again. An hour went by. Pastor Bobette rose to make some coffee and tea, and brought both Liz and Darnell some flavored green tea, while she herself drank coffee. She sat down again, and resumed the quiet vigil with them.

Darnell stirred. He looked at Pastor Bobette and Liz, and spoke quietly.

"I just had a sense of Jing Sheng's presence," he said. "I saw him sitting by a campfire in a village in the rainforest, surrounded by trees, and listening to people whom I could not understand. Adam was sitting by the fire too – it was as though I could see him through Jing Sheng's eyes. Adam looked fine, just a little too thin, and maybe dehydrated a bit."

Darnell paused, then closed his eyes, raised his hands in Namaste to his forehead, then bowed slightly, praying, "I thank you for this vision, Jing Sheng. I thank you and I honor you."

Pastor Bobette remained respectfully quiet. Liz, ever the practical and direct one, said, "Do we need to keep praying and meditating? Or is it alright to go to bed now? Oh, are there any other messages?"

"Why don't we meditate for a little while longer, and see if any news or anything else comes to us," Darnell suggested.

Liz nodded, Pastor Bobette put down her coffee cup. Liz sipped some tea with a soft, gentle slurping sound because it was still too hot for her, and then they all meditated together again. Pastor Bobette had learned the Raja Yoga meditation that Jing Sheng taught everyone who was willing to learn.

The quiet sense of peace deepened in the room. It was as though angels had descended and were keeping them company. Or to put it quite simply, peace and hope and a gentle sense of joy permeated everything and everyone. Another half hour passed.

"We need to start focusing on the Congo mission," Darnell spoke abruptly. "I just got an urgent sense from Jing Sheng that we need to gather everyone and prepare, and finalize the plans and communications with people in the Congo. Oh, especially, we need to find protocol officers to meet us at the airport – apparently that is extremely important when flying into the Congo."

Liz wondered how Darnell did that – get the messages so directly from either God or Jing Sheng. *Maybe he asks,* the thought came into her head like a message from Jing Sheng, and all she could do was laugh and inwardly say, "Thank you!"

Of course, then she had to explain to the others why she was laughing. "God and Jing Sheng have such a way of getting me to laugh at myself. It always makes me think of the laughing Buddha. But really, who knew that what is so important on the spiritual path is laughing at oneself?"

"Please come here and let me show you something," Pastor Bobette urged Liz. She walked down the hallway toward her bedroom. Liz joined her, and Pastor Bobette paused in front of a black-and-white portrait of Jesus laughing.

"I often look at this portrait of Jesus, and it always seems to me that he is both loving me intensely, and getting me to laugh at my paltry spirituality at the same time − as though my silly humanness was both lovable and funny all in one."

"Yes!" Exclaimed Liz, excited that someone else shared this same experience.

"Alright, though, I think we all need to go to bed and get a good night's sleep. Especially if we're going to begin the next adventure," Pastor Bobette sounded both down-to-earth and intuitively wise about the workings of the mission.

"Of course," replied Liz, yawning. "Good night Pastor Bobette. Good night, Darnell."

"Good night" chorused all around. And with a sense of reassurance from Jing Sheng in everyone's heart and mind, it was a good night.

The next day, Darnell went to the station set up at the church in Rockville, and began communications to finalize the trip to the Congo. Liz went to the church and gave healings, taught meditation, and checked email from the Exodus 2012 website. They stopped for a vegetarian lunch at a near-by Whole Foods market. Liz had fallen in love with Whole Foods stores, which didn't exist in the tiny city of Kalamazoo. Their salad and lunch buffet offered a large variety of deliciously-flavorful vegetarian dishes which were also really healthy, too.

The afternoon resumed with a pause for meditation. Then Liz's cell phone rang.

"Jing Sheng!" She cried out, loud enough for everyone in half of the church building to hear. "How are you?" She nodded, smiled, and then even grinned. Darnell came over to her, sat down to await the news, crossing his arms, and looking just a touch resentful that she, rather than he, was receiving this call. Liz looked over at Darnell, smiled and nodded again, and closed the call with, "I will – yes, I will. Be careful!"

Feeling kind of silly about this last remark, she sat down across from Darnell, and shook her head at him.

"Really? After last night's intuitive connection with Jing Sheng, you manage to feel even a slight bit of resentment towards me for Jing Sheng's phone call?"

"Well, I mean, a phone call is real, but how do we ever know that our intuitions and visions are right?"

"Oh, come on, Darnell, you know that 'right' is not the appropriate word there. Intuitions and visions are about love, insight, and affirmation, rather than rightness, which could be verified with some objective test. The only way to know the truth about intuitions and visions is to experience the results of living them out. You know – "we walk by faith, not by sight." So you are right on target with your intuitions and visions – you just have to trust them and yourself enough to live them out!"

Darnell smiled, stood up, and gave Liz a hug. "I'm glad you're my sister on this journey, even if you are a much older sister," he jabbed at her about his own youth.

"You little bugger – just like a little brother!" She laughed and jabbed his arm gently. "I think we are a spiritual family because we're so good for each other – we help each other make spiritual progress."

"I know that's right!" Darnell laughed, and walked back to his desk to resume the planning of the Congo trip.

Liz emailed her kids about preparations for the trip, and checked on the vaccinations they would need, scheduling a visit to the local health department for their vaccinations.

Suddenly, Darnell ran into the room and exclaimed, "I got an email from Adam. They found the Guarani people. They confronted the large corporation that has been running them off the rainforest land where they have lived for tens of thousands of years, and they got media coverage on CNN and the BBC, as well as some other international coverage, to raise awareness and support for the Guarani people. And Adam is fine – he just had a bout with diarrhea, but he's better now." Darnell sunk into a chair and sighed with relief.

"So, we'd better add something to the website about this part of the mission. Can we get a video or link to the news coverage and add it?" Liz inquired eagerly.

"Oh, yeah, thanks for reminding me to do my job. I'll look for a video link now!" Darnell switched to excitement in a heartbeat. "I just feel so relieved that Adam and Jing Sheng are on their way home now. Well, first they have to stop in Rio and check in on the mission there. They may do a media spot there as well."

While Darnell focused on the mission, Liz shifted her focus back to Spring of Life Healing Center back in Kalamazoo. It had become part of the mission in a sense, as well. She had spent time training healers to meditate, and then to heal the way Jing Sheng taught her.

People flocked from across the mid-west to the center in order to learn meditation, often in hopes of glimpsing Jing Sheng, sometimes to join the mission, and sometimes just to be healed of some infirmity, whether cancer or arthritis or whatever they experienced as suffering. She had had to hire an accountant. Things were hopping, and, in fact, had become quite lucrative. Of course that had not been her goal, but it was a nice side-benefit, because she could focus on the mission, and she could afford to fly to places like Croatia and the Congo.

When she got off the phone, she realized there was a loud commotion outside the church. She joined Pastor Bobette, the church secretary, the custodian, and Darnell at the front door, where the custodian had locked out some protestors.

"What's going on?" Liz inquired.

"We seem to have attracted some protestors because of our support for the Exodus 2012 Mission," Pastor Bobette replied.

"Those people are crazy!" exclaimed Ruth, the church secretary. She went on to explain that they had been calling the church, complaining that it was supporting the anti-Christ, yelling at her, and telling her that only those who had not accepted Jesus as the one-and-only true Christ as their Savior were going to die in Armageddon, or be left behind while the real saints of Christ would go to heaven with him.

"If those protestors are actual saints who go to heaven, I'll be quite content to go somewhere else when I die," Ruth added.

"We'll have to organize a prayer service," Pastor Bobette declared.

"Ruth, please call the prayer chain, the moderator and vice-moderator, and explain what's going on, and that I feel we need a prayer service. Ask the moderator to call our attorney, and I'm going to call the news media, and then go into the sanctuary and start praying. Oh, I'll see if John is still in the choir room and would come up and play the organ while I pray. Barry, thanks for locking the front door. Please check to make sure the other entrances are secure. If the protestors start to damage the property any, will you please call the police?"

"Sure thing, Pastor Bobette!" Barry shook his head, grabbed his cleaning cart, and rolled it on down the hall. Pastor Bobette called out her thanks to him as he walked away.

Wow! She's efficient, thought Liz. "I'll come and pray with you. Darnell, would you like to put word out on the website, along with prayer requests? What else do we need to do?"

"Well, I'll try to reach Adam and let him know," Darnell jumped at the excuse to call Adam. "I'll also send out emails to supporters. If I can get a video of the protestors somehow, I'll also post that online as well."

Liz wondered if they were safe inside the church, but she decided the best thing to do was to pray, and this time, her prayers would be not only to God, but also to Jing Sheng. She decided that if Darnell could hear Jing Sheng in his prayers during the tough, scary times, she probably could too, if she'd just stop feeling so inadequate about her part in all this. By 'all this', as she thought of it, she meant the Exodus 2012 Mission.

She waited by the sanctuary for Pastor Bobette to return from the choir room. When she returned with John, the organist, Liz smiled at him, although he just looked dazed, concerned, and confused back at her. *Maybe he's blaming me, or us, for all of this,* Liz realized. *I guess not everyone at this church really agrees with Pastor Bobette's support of our mission. That's too bad, but maybe John will soften as he sees that what we do, unlike the protestors, is love, serve, heal, and meditate, and pray.*

Liz proceeded to sit down front in the sanctuary, where she immediately started thinking of and visualizing Jing Sheng, even talking with him in her mind.

"Little dove," Jing Sheng's voice calmly caressed her in her mind. "Be not afraid. I will send a message to the protestors from Rio de Janeiro. God will protect you, and much of the world will see through their anger and hatred, knowing that Christ would never demonstrate with anything but service, prayer, and love." Liz felt immediately calm and reassured. She knew that by prayer, Jing Sheng also meant meditation, because that is the part of prayer in which we listen to God, rather than talking at or to God.

So, Liz began to meditate. Soon, church members began to appear. John quietly played the organ. From time to time, Pastor Bobette or a church member would read a Psalm or other scripture from the lectern. Most of the church members quietly prayed at their seats. At six o'clock, Pastor Bobette led a prayer from the pulpit, and then announced that a light meal of soup and bread was available in the fellowship hall for those who needed to take a break before returning to prayer.

Liz realized that somehow this had become a prayer vigil. She joined those who went to the fellowship hall for supper. A basket for a free-will offering for supper had been placed on the buffet table. Liz could afford to be generous, and as she felt a wave of deep gratitude for Pastor Bobette, the church, and its members, she placed a $20 bill in the basket. She realized that she should write the church a check, and ask Darnell if the mission were also paying the church. She knew he had probably handled it, but she wanted to know, so she could support the church as well, if needed.

The fellowship hall was very quiet, as people discussed the situation in hushed tones. Liz realized that some of the church members felt afraid and unhappy with the situation. She found Darnell and spoke with him. He confirmed that he had given the church a generous financial contribution for their work in support of the mission. Then he turned to her and said:

"I really think you should go out there and talk with those people. If anyone can reason with them, you can."

"Reason with protestors? That never works, does it? I mean, they haven't taken hostages or anything – oh, my, I hope they don't think of that! Well, I don't know why they would take hostages...Darnell, I'm babbling, and you think I could possibly be articulate with them? How about Pastor Bobette?"

"No, someone from the Mission needs to talk with them, to find out their concerns."

"Oh, my, what do you think Jing Sheng would want us to do?"

"Call him. He should be available by phone now."

"You don't think I should just pray and ask him?"

"It's up to you." Darnell shrugged. He looked around the room at the church members present for the prayer vigil. Liz did the same. Then she rose, spoke with Pastor Bobette, and the two went upstairs to the front door.

"Let's ask for police to come, because they are actually blocking our front door," Pastor Bobette suggested. "I'll call, and then you can go out."

Oh, Jing Sheng, please show me what to do, Liz thought fervently, if not entirely prayerfully. She did picture him in her mind.

All of a sudden, she heard his voice speaking to her in her mind:

"Liz, little dove, fly peacefully before the foe, for this is the time to be wise as a serpent, and innocent as a dove. Yes, find out their grievances, but stay clear of their physical agenda, because the hatred in their hearts comes from the evil one – that is the ego that tears all human hearts away from their roots in divine love."

Liz waited until the police drove up, and a police officer strode through the protestors to the front door.

"You have to remain 200 feet away from the entrance. You cannot legally block the entrance." The police officer waved the protestors back from the door, and slowly a wave pressed backwards so that the front door became clear for almost 200 feet.

Liz opened the front door, emerged slowly, and deliberately walked over to the police officer.

"Hi, I'm Liz Cooper. Thank you for coming to the church."

"Certainly, Ma'am, I'm Officer Green. I understand you want to talk to the protestors? Ma'am, I advise against it."

"I know, I know, but I just need to find out their grievances."

"Okay, Ma'am, but I don't want to have to be calling for a back up, now."

"I know. Let me just get one of those reporters to get us on camera," Liz replied. She waved at one of the news camera crews, and then motioned for them to come closer. As they approached, she explained what she was going to do, and requested that they film her speaking with the protestors. They were only too happy to oblige.

Then Liz approached the protestors. For a moment she stood still, and those who knew her well would have known she was praying. How handy it was to have a direct connection with Jing Sheng, although not many were as convinced as Liz that he could affect the situation from a distance.

"Welcome to this house of God, where all people who enter in peace to worship and serve God are welcome. I am Liz Cooper, here to represent the Mission of Exodus 2012. If anyone from your group would like to list your grievances, please address them now to me." Liz's legs shook a little because she could not quite help feeling a little afraid in the face of such an angry crowd, who were yelling and shaking their fists at her, all supposedly in the name of god. Obviously this was not in the name of God, who is love. Then Liz remembered that these people NEEDED Love, and she felt a little calmer, allowing God to love them through her.

A grizzled, old man in a flannel shirt and a baseball cap approached her. Another man in a decades-old suit with a narrow tie (*1950's vintage?* wondered Liz) also approached Liz.

"I'm elder Jonah White, and this here's our pastor, Pastor Donald Hickman. You'd best show him no disrespect," the man in flannel addressed Liz with a Southern twang.

The man in the really old suit and tie puffed up his chest as though he always deserved to be announced, and spoke towards the camera, ignoring Liz entirely.

"We're here from the Grace of Jesus Church in Montgomery, Alabama to be the voice of Christian values, which this group disrespects like the anti-Christ. As a matter of fact, we believe that this man Jing Sheng Who IS the anti-Christ. Why, I never heard such a bunch of nonsense in my entire life. This man obviously does not know his Bible, and the Bible is god's word of TRUTH."

"What language was the Bible written in, originally?" asked Liz.

"It makes no never mind what language the Bible was written in – in all of its translations, it speaks god's *truth*!" Pastor Hickman retorted.

"Okay, what language did Jesus speak?" Liz asked.

"That doesn't matter either! Obviously you have not been studying your Bible, because if you had, you would never be following this China-man who is committing Blasphemy claiming to be Jesus Christ! And to think he mentions Jesus Christ and reincarnation in the same breath! That's the worst blasphemy there is!" Pastor Hickman had grown very red in the face and his finger pointing had actually caused the cameraman to back up.

"Pastor Hickman, I'm Preeti Singh from CNN, and I'm wondering if you have any grievances against the Exodus 2012 Mission?" The reporter held the microphone in front of Pastor Hickman, but she remained close to the cameraman, her high heels pointed somewhat pigeon-toed and one arm across her waist, as though she needed to keep herself protected from the anger pouring out of the protestors.

"You heard me, they are blaspheming Jesus Christ, and they are blaspheming the Holy Spirit, which is an unforgivable sin! The Bible says so! We will never forgive this sin, because god will never forgive this sin!"

"I see, so your grievance is blasphemy against the historical figure of Jesus Christ…." Preeti Singh did her best to sound even-toned and reporter-like, although her eyebrows were unavoidably raised at the incredulous nature of their upset.

"Mr. Hu Jing Sheng never claims to be Jesus Christ. He never claims to be the reincarnation of anyone. Some of us followers consider him to be the reincarnation of Jesus Christ, precisely because we have read our Bibles, and Hu Jing Sheng sounds exactly like Christ returned on earth to us." Liz seemed to glow with loving confidence.

"Thank you for making us aware of your grievances. I will go now." Liz's brevity surprised the pastor, and he watched, open-mouthed as Liz returned to the door and whisked inside the door which was being held open for her by Darnell.

"Well done. I thought for a moment you were going to get cooked!" Darnell shook his head. "Let's go back and pray."

"Wait," Liz pleaded, "I think Jing Sheng will speak on the news from Rio. Can we turn on the news, please?"

"Sure, let's just go to the office where we have the internet and TV set up." Pastor Bobette led the way.

They turned on CNN where they watched the report with Liz and Pastor Hickman. Then a news anchor announced a breaking news report from Rio de Janeiro.

The TV flashed a beautiful view of Rio before them, with the towering statue of Jesus Christ shining bright white and copper-y in the setting sun. There, perched on Jesus' head, was Jing Sheng Hu, no longer dressed in his snazzy black Tai Chi costume, but rather a shiny, white silk martial arts-style jacket and pants. He glowed white against the statue of Christ.

"Oh, my gosh! How did he do that?" Liz exclaimed while Darnell uttered, "What the…?!" Pastor Bobette just uttered, "Oh, my heavens!"

A helicopter circled around the figure of Jesus, with a microphone cord dangling above Jing Sheng's head.

"Beloved People of God, I call on you to hear Words of Love, for Love is the Greatest TRUTH there is," Hu Jing Sheng announced with his loudest, most radio-announcer voice. Somehow, his voice could caress the masses at full-volume from 1,000s of feet up in the air.

"The apostle Paul wrote, 'faith, hope, and love abide, these three, but the greatest of these is love.' What use is it if a person has faith that Jesus is the Christ, and yet fails to love his or her neighbor? If you cannot or will not love a person, you are standing behind Christ with Satan, rather than representing God who is Love. Christ himself was accused of blasphemy by the religious authorities of his day. Christ overturned tables in the temple in a very angry-seeming way. Depending on how we look at Jesus Christ, he could appear to have been a sinner. Certainly, from the perspective of the religious authorities of his day, he was a blaspheming sinner. Yet Christians often tell us that Christ 'knew no sin.' Hmmm. Jesus was, after all, human. Again, as the apostle Paul wrote, 'all have sinned and fallen short of the glory of God.' All human beings sin, and yet God asks us to love each and every human being ever – all sinners, including ourselves."

Jing Sheng paused as the helicopter circled a little wider with a gust of wind. He himself visibly braced himself against the wind. All of a sudden, angels appeared around him, visible to many, even on camera, as Liz and Darnell could see clearly. Many people thought it was a theatrical spectacle or special effect. Many people could not see the angels, because they so deeply denied the existence of them. It was as though the energy of the angels made them visible only through the energy-consciousness of faith.

"The only way to blaspheme the Holy Spirit is through resentment, because if you are resenting reality, you are living as though the Holy Spirit is not working in your life. In fact, the Holy Spirit constantly works to shape your reality, and while the Holy Spirit does not cause the negativities you resent, the Holy Spirit stands ready to help you when you accept whatever you are facing in life. Once you accept your present reality, then you can work with the Holy Spirit to bring greater wisdom, peace, love, and service into each and every situation.

"Only resentment, hatred, and despair kill the workings of the Spirit. Fear puts a damper on it, and anger misguides its work. So, if you sin by getting angry, feeling afraid, feeling depressed, resentful, or lacking hope and faith, then you are blaspheming the Holy Spirit, because you are thinking, believing, speaking, and acting as though the Holy Spirit is inactive, rather than active in all creation.

"Your anger, your fear, your depression, and your resentment are all your own responsibility to work on. Only by trusting that the Holy Spirit is constantly working in your life will you be able to make your life better at all. So, trust constantly that the Holy Spirit is working in your life, let go of fear, anger, hatred, and resentment, and you will surely be blessed."

Jing Sheng made a slight bow in Namaste. The helicopter lowered a ladder, and Jing Sheng deftly climbed up the ladder and aboard the helicopter.

Liz let out a sigh when he made it safely into the helicopter. She watched the angels disappear from her sight as the helicopter flew away.

CNN segued to newscaster Preeti Singh standing outside the Rockville church where the protestors were visible, loud, and angry-sounding. The interview with Liz ran again, with the contrast between Jing Sheng's message of love and the hatred and anger of the protestors becoming starkly visible to everyone who had attained a certain level of spiritual evolution.

Other people couldn't hear the Words of Love as TRUTH because they were stuck in fundamentalist beliefs about the truth of their religious texts, no matter how unloving those texts could sometimes be. Others were too materialistic and self-absorbed to care about anything besides success for themselves in this lifetime, and others still were not yet selfless enough to care about loving others to that degree. And so it was that Words of TRUTH which spoke of love, were only understood by about one-fourth of humanity.

Liz somehow sensed this, and despaired. Sighing, she decided to do some pranayamic breathing in order to raise her subtle energy level, and thus to raise her spiritual awareness level to a higher plane. And then, of course, she realized that her despair was, according to Jing Sheng's message, a form of blasphemy. *Alright*, she thought, *I will accept what is, and hope for a better future anyway, and offer myself in service to creating that future. 'That's the way, my little dove,'* she heard Jing Sheng reply in her thoughts.

Darnell came into the office quietly and tapped Liz on the shoulder. They both stood up, and Darnell told Liz that he had received a call and an email with the itinerary for the four street children from Rio, the four aid workers accompanying them, as well as the two Guarani families and their messenger.

"They are all arriving at BWI tomorrow morning. We need to go get them, welcome them here at the church, spend a few days with them, and then send them to Phoenix and San Diego so that they can settle in for awhile."

"Oh, gosh, they need a place to stay here, then?" Liz inquired somewhat foggily.

"Yes," Darnell replied firmly, looking at her with the expectation that she would find the solution to their housing needs.

Liz couldn't read his mind, but she got the message from his look.

"Ok. Do we have funds that we can spare to put them in hotel rooms?"

"Not much, maybe a night or two." Darnell replied, equally firmly.

"Ok....Pastor Bobette, do you have any church families that might be willing to take in the children and aid workers, or the Guarani families?"

"We have two families who have joined two different eco-communes in the area. Why don't I contact them and see if the eco-communes could take them in?" Pastor Bobette sounded as gracious and self-assured as ever.

"Fantastic. Thank you," Liz returned enthusiastically. "Is there anything I can do to help?"

"Well, meeting the families and transporting them here and contacting the news media would be your role, I hope?" Pastor Bobette could be direct and gentle at the same time.

"Yes, right!" Liz answered, thinking to herself, *I wonder if Hopi can help me*. So, she called her daughter, who jumped at the opportunity, and offered to contact news media as well.

So it was that Liz and Hopi greeted the children, aid workers, and families at the airport near Baltimore the next day. Through the interpreter/messenger, they found out what needs everyone had for food, shoes, clothes, medicines, and so on. Then they drove them to the eco-communes, where they were given a night and half a day to rest, before the news media showed up at 2:00 the next afternoon.

Liz and Hopi and Darnell were there, and helped array everyone for the media shoot. Several different media were represented: American Morning News Hour sent Roberta Robins and CNN sent Preeti Singh, both of whom were avid followers of Exodus 2012. The Washington Post sent a reporter and photographer, and USA Today did as well. Conspicuously absent was FOX news, because Hopi refused to subject the Brazilians to what she considered to be their exploitative and biased reporting.

The children were dressed in their original Brazilian street clothes, and whatever footwear they had, or didn't have. (Church members had volunteered to go shopping for the children's clothes.) The Guarani people dressed in their own attire, which was unacceptable according to the nudity laws of the United States. (They would also be given clothing suitable for the tastes of Western culture.) The aid workers and the translator/messenger all wore their best-looking clothes, as they understood what was actually going on.

Roberta Robins interviewed Liz first.

"Liz Cooper, ladies and gentleman, represents the Exodus 2012 Mission, and is a close disciple of Mr. Hu Jing Sheng, leader of the group, whom we have met before. Mr. Hu remains in Brazil at this time, working, as I understand, with eco-communes forming chiefly in and around Rio de Janeiro, but also in other cities in Brazil." Both Darnell and Liz thought of Adam, who was significantly helping to set up these communes. His knowledge of Portuguese was coming in handy.

"Liz," continued Roberta Robins, "I understand these people came here from Brazil as part of the Exodus 2012 mission. Can you please explain to us why they are here?"

"Certainly, Roberta." Liz paused, trying not to think of the millions of people who could be watching her right now. "The four children you see live on the streets of Rio de Janeiro, and they represent the exploitation of workers overseas. Every time an American or European corporation exports jobs overseas, the workers are usually paid less than a living wage. As a result, families cannot support their children, and many are sent into prostitution or merely left to wander the streets, in the thought that they will be able to survive somehow, instead of staying with the family which cannot provide them enough food to eat."

"Now, to be fair, there have been street children longer than there have been Western corporations sending jobs overseas, so this cannot all be just from the recent trend to send jobs overseas!" Roberta played the fence-walking game.

"Of course, Roberta, there have been street children ever since Western white people traveled to South America and exploited the resources, killed native peoples, nearly destroyed their cultures, and disrupted their lifestyles. The point is that we Westerners have got to stop exploiting the resources of other peoples at their expense, so that they can live lives of integrity and well-being according to their own cultural values." Liz was prepared, and gave it right back. Hopi felt proud of her mom, although she could not show it. Hopi would have loved to speak, but in her professional role as a photojournalist, she could not take sides. She did, however, take some remarkable photos which mostly made it online to places like Huffington Post and BBC.

"I see, so is that why these people are dressed as they are?" Roberta tried a different tactic.

"*These people*, as you refer to them, are two Guarani families from deep in the rainforest of Brazil, and they have come here with a message about freedom and democracy for the American people."

"Well, now that is unexpected. How could anyone have anything to teach Americans about freedom and democracy?" Roberta meant it as a rhetorical question, of course, but again, Liz was ready.

"Let's hear the message firsthand from their interpreter/messenger, whose name is Piedro."

Piedro stepped up and introduced himself and the family members, explaining that they had been forced to become semi-nomadic people, traveling around the rainforest to stay away from the parts that were being destroyed by Western multi-national corporations.

"Their message today is simple," Piedro announced with a lovely accent. "They have come to challenge the American people to do what they say they believe in: to spread freedom and democracy to the Brazilian rainforests, where the local people have lost their freedoms, and rather than having self-rule over their regions, they are ruled by foreign businesses who buy the very land on which they live and destroy the native people's habitat, which they need for survival. So, not only do Americans and Europeans still practice genocide and the stealing of resources from traditional peoples, they also destroy the freedom and democratic rights of traditional peoples as well. So, we stand here today to ask the American people: do you believe in freedom and democracy for all, or just for those who can afford it?"

Silence reigned, as no one knew how to respond wisely to that question.

"I see you have no answer," Piedro wisely responded himself. "Perhaps you were unaware of reality. Perhaps now that you are aware of reality, you will make different choices. If not, you will surely destroy the earth and all her peoples." Piedro paused.

"We have brought with us three precious children from our two families. One is just a baby. In order for this baby to survive in the rainforest, we need the freedom to move about a large area of intact rainforest, as we have for thousands of years, to find the resources we need. Please do not take our land from us, destroy our forests, and kill this child."

Wow! thought Liz. *It's so refreshing to do away with white culture's polite rules of 'don't really tell it like it is because you might hurt someone's feelings' when you tell it with love and truth. Oh, yeah, Jing Sheng would say that Love is TRUTH.*

Darnell walked over to the families, on camera, and asked if he could hold the baby. Then, he touchingly took the baby in his arms, and held it up for all to see. No doubt some people were reminded of that similar scene in the Lion King, and Liz couldn't help thinking how wonderful it would be if this child were king, well, queen, actually, of the rainforest. *Could this child rule the rainforest and therefore protect it?*

"There you have it, folks, the message from the Guarani people of the rainforests of Brazil," closed Roberta Robins.

Preeti Singh did a similar close, and concluded the day with a taped interview of both Liz and Darnell, which she used as her intro for CNN.

Americans in large numbers began to think about what freedom and democracy actually did mean for other people, and *how they might export freedom and democracy economically or culturally, rather than mostly through war*. A new way of thinking was emerging in America, and finally, it had some True elements of global Consciousness.

♥ ♥ ♥

The time came to go to the Congo. Liz realized that she had been unconsciously dreading it. In other words, she was holding onto a consciousness of fear. *Oh, my gosh, how am I supposed to transform my fear of being raped, injured, sick, or killed in Eastern Congo into some kind of loving consciousness?!* Liz really had no idea how to do that. But she found herself thinking about Jing Sheng, and immediately heard his voice in her head.

Liz, my little dove, on whom are your thoughts focused? If you are thinking only about yourself, of course you will feel fear. If you think about bringing love to the people of the Eastern Congo, then you will be in line with the work of God's Spirit, and you will be filled with love, rather than fear. So, why not stop focusing on yourself so much? And remember: be wise as a serpent, but innocent as a dove. In other words, use precautions that your ego would wisely use, but also hold pure intentions of loving service.

That certainly made sense to Liz, although she found it easier to think about than actually to do. She traveled back to Kalamazoo to spend a few days packing and enjoying Daniel's company. She got the necessary vaccinations, bought hand sanitizer, a water purification drinking bottle, insect repellant in a variety of forms, travel toilet paper, as well as a mosquito net. Liz was determined to survive the Congo. As mom, she also purchased all of the above items for Hopi and Cliff, and told them to leave room to pack these items. Daniel flew with her to DC, in order to see her off and to help Adam replace Liz and Darnell at the Rockville mission center.

The journalist from Huffington Post, the public health nurse from Johns Hopkins, and the professor from American University's International Relations program all gathered at the Rockville center of the Exodus 2012 Mission to meet Liz, Darnell, Hopi, Cliff, and the four college students. Jing Sheng, of course, had to stay out of the country because the U.S. government had refused to give him a visa.

At the Rockville center inside the Rockville church, all of the participants planning to go to the eastern, conflict-mineral part of the Democratic Republic of the Congo gathered to be briefed on the situation in eastern Congo. Two body guards were paid to accompany the group. They were both former members of special forces units in the U.S. military, although they were prohibited from bringing weapons other than knives and clubs on this trip. No lethal force was to be used, according to Jing Sheng, except against wild animals, in the remote chance that would be necessary when the animals were confronted with love rather than fear.

The four college students had already met with Jing Sheng and learned to meditate months ago, while he was traveling around helping establish eco-communes. Once in Rockville, they asked Darnell and Liz about a thousand questions about Jing Sheng and the mission.

Liz had had her doubts about extremely intelligent college students being able to get into the spirituality of Jing Sheng's message, partly because she knew what a struggle she had had sharing a spiritual worldview with her son Cliff, who had always scored at the 99th percentile on every achievement test. But these four seemed fascinated by the mission, Jing Sheng's message, and everything they could learn from Darnell, Liz, and even Pastor Bobette, who was only too happy to speak with them about possible Biblical perspectives on Jing Sheng's life and message.

Well, that was intended to be, thought Liz as she considered the four college 'kids' learning about the connection between Jing Sheng and Jesus' own message. *They must have been drawn to this mission in order to be drawn to Jing Sheng. Obviously, they are disciples as well. So much for my doubts that people with brains couldn't be touched by Jing Sheng's holiness. I just hope that Cliff will also be deeply moved by the reality of Jing Sheng.*

And by 'the reality of Jing Sheng,' Liz really meant the reality of God walking the earth through a human being.

19. THE TEN COMMANDMENTS

WHAT IS A COMMANDMENT FROM GOD?
SINCE GOD IS LOVE, A COMMANDMENT IS A GUIDELINE
FOR STAYING WITHIN THE CIRCLE OF LOVE,
NOT JUST AS INDIVIDUALS, BUT ALSO TOGETHER,
FOR LOVE IS ALWAYS LARGER THAN ANY ONE PERSON.
THE TEN COMMANDMENTS,
RE-ENVISIONED, FORM THE ORIGINAL,
GOD-GIVEN, CIRCLE OF LOVE – LOVE'S GUIDE TO LIFE –
ABUNDANT LIFE FOR EVERYONE!

After four days of learning about the Congo and building teamwork through spending time getting to know one another, by meditating together, and by sharing what the mission means to each person, the Exodus to Congo Mission Team got on board a flight to Brussels, Belgium, from which airport they would then fly first to Douala, Cameroon, and then on to land in Kinshasa, the capital of the Democratic Republic of the Congo, where they would meet Jing Sheng before traveling to the eastern part of the Congo.

Since the D.R. Congo had been a Belgian colony, ties between the two countries still existed, although it was Belgium's King Leopold who had first plundered the Congo of its wealth, amassing a personal fortune, while also committing the first major genocide of almost the 20th Century there (it was in the 1890's).   King Leopold was responsible for the killing of 10 million Congolese people in order to gain access to a lucrative supply of rubber.   This genocide of the 1890s was known as the 'Red Rubber Trade.'   One hundred years later, the second mass genocide began.   The West was still plundering the Congo for its mineral wealth, although this time it is for its 'coltan,' a mineral used in cell phones and video game systems.   Warlords obtained weapons, and vied for control of the mineral-rich area.

Cliff was going to explore the actual mining and wealth extraction going on in eastern Congo, and the Huffington Post reporter would report on his findings. Liz hoped the reporter would emphasize the Congolese Holocaust of the last few decades, including the rape of millions of women, and report on its various root causes.

The total flight/trip time was to be about 30 hours, and Liz found herself struggling to enjoy the trip. She had begun to take a malaria preventative, and it had already begun to have side effects. Mostly, she found herself unable to think clearly, and feeling somewhat irritable because of the mental fog she was experiencing. She also wished with all her heart that Daniel could be on the trip with her. Finally, she told herself that everything would be alright because she would see Jing Sheng soon.

And then the turbulence began. Tropical thunderheads appear beautiful as fluffy, white mountains in the sunshine, but the up and down drafts associated with them can cause some heavy wind sheer. All of a sudden, the cabin dropped, and food trays flew up a couple of feet in the air.

Oh, dear, God, thought Liz, *please help us now! Holy Archangel Michael, protector, please keep us safe. Thank you!* She thought of Jing Sheng, and again, she found comfort.

Liz decided to try looking out the window as a distraction, only to see that they were descending below the clouds into what appeared to be tropical rainforest. All she could see was green. *Oh, my gosh! I hope there is a landing strip really close, really soon.*

The captain came on the loudspeaker and announced in French and English that they were descending into Douala, Cameroon. They were only taking time to allow passengers to disembark and for new passengers to embark so that they could continue on to Kinshasa quickly. That was going to put them into Kinshasa at about 9:00

p.m. local time. From having lived in the tropics, Liz knew it would be totally dark by then. At the equator, the sun sets quite quickly because of the greater relative curvature of the earth, at around 6:00 p.m. year-round.

I hope the protocol officer is on time. Liz could worry about anything and everything, when it came to travel in developing countries.

They took off quickly from Douala, and headed south to Kinshasa. The sunset among the tropical thunderheads was stunningly beautiful with purple and orange hues lighting the sky and the interior of the cabin. Liz thought it was better than having a movie to watch.

As they began to descend to land in Kinshasa, Liz found herself excited that they were going to see Jing Sheng. Hopi and Cliff were seated together, and began to chatter excitedly. Liz was sitting next to the reporter and the public health nurse, Susan. She took up looking out the window again, and was rewarded with seeing the lights of a city. Then all of a sudden, she saw runway lights, but they were headed the other direction than the plane was. The plane suddenly lurched back upwards, climbing steeply and banking around to the right. As they came back around, they started to descend again, this time apparently in the right direction to land on the runway.

Their Congo adventure had begun.

The landing was particularly bumpy, because the airport tarmac had been poorly maintained for years. The airplane stopped near the airport building, and a portable set of stairs was wheeled up to the side of the plane.

Liz found it difficult to descend in the dark with her luggage in hand and holding onto the railing at the same time. Just when she thought she might stumble, one of the bodyguards, a big man named Jerry came up beside her and caught her arm to steady her. He went on down the steps onto the pavement ahead of her. The other bodyguard, Tyrone, took up the rear behind the rest of the group.

Jerry and Liz led the way into the airport, where they had to go through customs. Liz knew that all sorts of bad things, like expensive bribes, theft, delays, and accusations of illegal items could occur if they did not encounter their protocol officer, who would pay small bribes for them to get them through smoothly.

There was no sign of their protocol officer. Several men began to yell at Liz in French and gestured for her to go through the customs line, but she stopped dead still, refusing to move until the protocol officer got there. Unfortunately, she had no idea how to communicate about this choice, so the men just kept yelling at her. Jerry stood at her side, and the group gathered behind her. A few eternal seconds passed, when the protocol officer finally appeared to their right, speaking English (*thank God!* thought Liz).

He took their bags, and told them to proceed off to the right, and that he would meet them on the other side of customs. Liz knew they would each have to pay him about $30 to cover bribes and his own fees.

Half an hour later, they were walking out the front entrance of the airport. Hopi and Cliff had placed themselves closer to their mother, as that old sense of security, comfort and familiarity seemed necessary in this wildly unpredictable setting.

Sure enough, outside the front entrance, a young Gendarme was walking back-and-forth with a rifle. Hopi had never seen a soldier strolling around with a rifle before, and commented to her mom.

"That's to be expected, honey," Liz replied. "You might as well get used to it; although I hear that the young boy soldiers are the most unpredictable and therefore the most dangerous." Hopi felt anything but reassured.

A small, European-style bus was waiting for them out front, and there, beside the bus, stood Jing Sheng.

Liz dropped her bags and threw her arms around him, and then bowed in Namaste and touched his feet.

"Oh, Jing Sheng, I'm so glad to see you!" Liz realized she had given into fear, regretted it, but still felt immense relief at seeing and feeling the peaceful presence of Jing Sheng. She picked up her bags, staring longingly at him.

"Little dove, you have no need to fear, for God is with you, no matter how troublesome or painful life might become." Jing Sheng's words were not particularly comforting to the ego, although they were healing for the soul. The ego longs for ease and comfort, while the soul longs for the presence of God.

Jing Sheng bowed in Namaste to everyone in the group, and most put down their bags and bowed in Namaste in return. The reporter and Susan both shook hands with Jing Sheng, as did also Jerry and Tyrone. Darnell hugged Jing Sheng and touched his feet like Liz.

On the bus, Cliff and Hopi again sat together, the four college students sat together, while Liz and Darnell got as close to Jing Sheng as they could. The three of them sat right behind the bus driver, with the protocol officer sitting across from them. They headed out to the Intercontinental Hotel, an old hotel atop the hill where the old dictator Mobutu had built himself a palace overlooking the massive Congo River and its impassable rapids. Near the airport, the river is several miles wide and has islands in the middle.   Below the main part of the city, the rapids become impassable, but the city itself has a port where river boats travel north and east as the major means of commerce.   The protocol officer was giving them a verbal introduction to the city, even though it was too dark to see.

When they arrived at the hotel, they could see that it had become quite dilapidated, with worn carpet, questionable air conditioning, and a touch of mildew-y, tropical smells.   Liz realized she was hungry, but she had brought water bottles and power bars on the plane with her.   She ate as soon as she and Hopi got to the room they were sharing.

Darnell and Cliff shared a room with Jing Sheng.   Jing Sheng chose to sleep on the floor, for the few hours that he would sleep.   He didn't need much.   Before they went to bed, though, Darnell, Liz, Hopi, and Cliff all chose to meditate with Jing Sheng.   The rest of the night most of them slept heavily because they were exhausted from the trip.

In the morning, Jing Sheng greeted everyone with a knock on their door and an invitation to join him for breakfast.   They all went downstairs to a patio dining area, where they ate fresh mangoes, papayas, scrambled eggs, and croissants.   Not quite the French Riviera, but a pretty good breakfast with a great view of the Congo River.

They rode in the bus to the American School of Kinshasa, TASOK, so that they could meet a couple of people who were going to lead them in their travels.   One person was the high school economics teacher, Dave Schmidt.   The other was the Belgian Assistant Director of TASOK, who saw this as an opportunity for media coverage for the school.   The Director had agreed, and gave permission for the Assistant Director to join them on the trip.

Jing Sheng, however, had an amendment to their plans.

"Before we go east, I wish to travel southwest to the hill where the Kimbanguists expect Jesus to return – the hill marked with three wooden crosses." How Jing Sheng could possibly know about something like that mystified even Liz and Darnell, who decided it was just more proof that he is indeed the reincarnation of Jesus himself.

"Alright, we can do that if we rent the bus for a two-day trip, south towards the port city of Matadi," the Assistant Director replied, as though suddenly he was in charge of their trip. "We'll need overnight accommodations in Mbanza-Ngungu, which was called Thysville by the Belgians, and was considered a resort town. Fortunately, there's still one old hotel left that will probably fit all of us."

"Thank you," Jing Sheng replied, being ever humble, but certainly in charge of the entire mission.

So it was that, after a 30-hour trip and a massive sense of jet lag, they had 24 hours of recovery time before climbing on board a bus that, well, would not have passed inspection in the U.S. of A., as Liz saw it.

The young people were excited. *Oh, good*, Liz thought, *I'm glad someone can get excited about going to a spot where people literally believe that Christ will appear out of the clouds and land on a hill. How did missionaries manage to have that effect on them?*

"Mom, I did an internet search on the Kimbanguists, and found that Simon Kimbangu was a prophet and Baptist minister who healed people of every infirmity and even raised a girl from the dead! He developed such a large following that the Belgians threw him in jail and tried to execute him for sedition. He ended up with a life sentence in jail instead. Can you imagine? He was a healer and he got thrown in jail for it."

"Ouch, that's awful!" Liz replied, feeling remorse for her own mistaken judgmentalism about the Kimbanguist movement. *Maybe they deserve to have Jing Sheng appear on their hill, after all*, she thought.

Cliff and Hopi were making friends with the four college students. Liz and Darnell hung close to Jing Sheng and each other, while the reporter and nurse stayed together as well. The bus drove them through the outskirts of Kinshasa, a massive slum-like area with giant potholes and tons of dirt and dust everywhere.

They turned onto a two-lane paved road, well, once-upon a time it had been paved, but that was apparently long ago. The pot-hole ridden road wound around the hills that shaped the Congo River's twists and turns as they headed southwest towards the coast.

About five hours later, they arrived at Mbanza-Ngungu. The first view that greeted them were three wooden crosses on a hill, the actual site on which Jesus was to return for the rapture, for those who believe in the rapture and the second coming of Christ, at least, according to the Kimbanguist version of the story.

Jing Sheng asked everyone to leave their belongings in the hotel, and then to join him on the hilltop. He quickly left his belongings at the hotel, and then went straight to the church down the hill, where he met the pastor, and explained the Exodus 2012 Mission, and why he wanted to speak on the hilltop.

The pastor was a bit doubtful about the whole mission. Like many well-educated Congolese, he followed international news from well-informed European and African sources on a regular basis, in both French and English, so he was well aware of the mission, if not yet convinced to be supportive of it. Nonetheless, he could tell that Jing Sheng was a sincere man of God, so he agreed to accompany Jing Sheng up the hill.

That led to a growing following among the local people as, one after another, they saw the pastor walking with Jing Sheng. Soon, about one hundred people were gathered on the hill with Jing Sheng and his followers.

The Huffington Post reporter took on the role of video-recorder, and an event was staged for a world-wide audience. Jing Sheng was dressed in his silky, glowing white Tai Chi uniform with a white silk sash. He positively glowed, with white light constantly beaming down on him from above, from some invisible source.

Jing Sheng stepped in front of the crosses, with the local audience circled entirely around the crosses and Jing Sheng.

A woman stepped forward, holding a very sick child in her arms, and knelt down, asking Jing Sheng to bless her child in Lingala, the trade language spoken in most of the Congo. Jing Sheng placed his hand on the child's head, prayed silently, the white light beaming through his hand and visibly surrounding the child.

The child stirred, sat up in her mother's arms, and smiled at Jing Sheng. The mother broke into a joyful high-pitched ululation with her tongue wagging back-and-forth rapidly, the Congolese-style celebratory announcement of good news. Others joined in the ululation, which sounded like a chorus of joy.

People lined up in front of Jing Sheng for healing. A formerly crippled boy got up and walked away on his own, singing and clapping a joyful hymn of praise to God.

Nothing announces the presence of God better than curing the sick, thought Liz. *This is good!*

Jing Sheng raised his hands, and asked the Assistant Director to translate his words into Lingala.

"Please, let us take a moment to pray to God, and to hear God's word. We will resume the healings after dinner on the front porch of the hotel, with my assistant Liz Cooper helping me as well.

"Gracious God, Redeemer of all peoples, we thank you for your glory and for your healing power. Thank you for healing these people. Now we ask that You heal our hearts with your love, heal our minds with your wisdom, and heal our bodies with your grace. Thank you, Amen.

"And now, I would like to thank the Kimbanguist people for offering this hill for Christ's return to earth. Thank you for your faithfulness to Christ's mission.

"Today, I would like to announce from this hill, the mission of Exodus 2012, which is to save the earth by honoring our Heavenly Father and our Earthly Mother by caring for all children on earth."

Jing Sheng continuously paused for the Assistant Director of TASOK to translate his words into Lingala.

The Huffington Post reporter recorded every word and panned the audience with the video recorder during the translation, to show people's reactions to Jing Sheng's words. Some people frowned, some people smiled, and some people nodded.

Jing Sheng resumed his speech: "The time has come to renew the 10 Commandments with the loving message that they speak to us for today.

And so, I re-present the 10 Commandments of Love and Holiness to you in Today's English Translation:

1. *Cherish no other god but Love.*
2. *Let nothing become more important to you than love*; neither money nor any material object, nor any human allegiance to family, religion, team, or nation, nor any choice, thought, action, feeling, or pleasure; instead, always put unconditional love first.
3. *Always be conscious of the holiness of love*, and never let your words stray from that holy love, always expressing respect and devotion for the Creator who imparts life and love in all beings.
4. *Remember to make time for holiness and to renew yourself in divine ways of being*, trusting that God will provide for you rather than idolizing your own work and pleasure.
5. *Honor your Heavenly Father and your Earthly Mother by caring for one another*, so that all children of God will live together peacefully in the land.
6. *Practice non-violence and reverence for all life*; for everything that lives is a temple of divine spirit, which breathes life into all beings.
7. *Respect vows of faithfulness*; that your love will always cherish and honor the one with whom you are called to share life, as well as respecting the intimacy shared by others.
8. *Respect the property of others*; never let material well-being become your god; rather *seek to give more than you receive*.
9. *Speak truthfully yet lovingly about the actions and speech of others;* for the way you treat others will become the way you yourself are treated.
10. *Let go of all desires that might diminish others in any way*, whether by objectifying them, or their possessions, or their loved ones; *rather, seek to desire love, peace and joy, the eternal jewels of life, for yourself and for everyone else.*

When the Assistant Director finished translating the Ten Commandments of Love and Holiness into Lingala, silence ensued for a full two minutes. No one knew what to say. Everyone got the point that, rather than focusing on what not to do, these commandments focused on how we are to serve Love faithfully with our words and actions.

Jing Sheng continued: "When you keep these 10 Commandments of Love and Holiness, you will live the Reign of Love on earth. That is how the Kingdom of God will come into this world. This is the TRUE return of Christ: when Christ reigns in each and every human heart, for this is the only way that suffering will end on earth, when everyone allows Christ, or Divine Love & Wisdom, to reign through them fully for the sake of others' well-being.

I stand here on Christ's hill, calling each and every human being to allow the Reign of Love to come on earth. This is the same as having Buddha-Consciousness. This is the same as winning the Greater Jihad – the struggle between goodness and evil within each person. This is the same as the Hindu concept of Self-Realization. All faiths speak to this in their own way, because this is the purpose of the Universe: to live in love and harmony with one another, and to incarnate God's peace on all levels of being. Please allow the Reign of Love to begin in you and through you right now. Thank you."

Jing Sheng bowed in Namaste. Everyone sensed that something really important had just happened here. The reporter got so excited, that she forgot to wait for the Lingala translation before she began to save the video file so that she could send it as soon as possible to the Huffington Post.

Silence reigned for a moment, and then the Kimbanguists began to sing a hymn, in traditional African 3-part harmony, a haunting sound that brought joy and sadness and a deep sense of reverence all at the same time. Many people came and bowed before Jing Sheng one-by-one. Most people left very quietly, touched with their own personal call to holiness and wholeness as a way of living.

When the Mission team returned to the hotel, they had many healings to do. Nonetheless, they ended at 9 p.m. The next morning, Jing Sheng and Liz gave healings until 11 a.m.. While Jing Sheng and Liz gave healings, Darnell had posted the 10 Commandments of Love and Holiness on the website. Cliff, Hopi, and the four college students went to visit some nearby caves and stopped in the local marketplace to buy local craft items. Susan, the nurse, accompanied by the reporter, donated some medical and pharmaceutical items to the local health clinic. Together, Darnell, Liz, and Jing Sheng, aided by the Assistant Director's translations, left an Exodus 2012 Mission station set-up where once the Baptist mission station had been. The change of theology was staggering, but the important point to most of the Congolese was that healings still occurred, because Jing Sheng had blessed a couple of people to become healers.

When the mission team returned to Kinshasa, they stopped at the American School, where a small group had gathered to join them in their travels to eastern Congo. Among them were a Methodist physician, a USAID (United States Agency for International Development, part of the State Department) director, whom Liz expected would probably interfere with as much as help the mission, and a CNN reporter who had gotten wind of their whereabouts and planned to go with them.

Jing Sheng spoke to the group: "Our purpose in eastern Congo is to identify the injustices to the Congolese people, as well as the destruction of the environment. The particular focus is to be the impact on the local children, both in terms of economic impact, and loss of natural habitat. Please assess the economic situation, the health of the children, the health of the environment, as well as what can be done to change the situation. Please also assess the violence, the rebel groups or war lords, and the multinational corporations and governments which are exploiting the situation for their own ends.

"Please look for paths to forgiveness, as well as paths to wholeness, with an emphasis on placing the well-being of children in the communities first-and-foremost. Where there is a need for healing, please let me and Liz as well as Susan and Dr. Miller know.

"Thank you for your cooperation. Darnell will be updating the Exodus 2012 Mission website based on your findings, so please share them with him. Media attention to the realities on the ground are critical to transforming the situation. Again, I thank you."

And so everyone went to their rooms to prepare for the trip, which was to begin the day after tomorrow.

Cliff and Hopi and the college students asked Jing Sheng if they could spend the next day touring Kinshasa and seeing the Congo River. Arrangements were made. The following morning, most of the team went downtown near the U.S. embassy to what is still called the Ivory Market, although ivory is illegal to sell there as it is in international trade.

The array of items sold delighted everyone, from the artwork to the jewelry, to the fabrics and scrap metal toys. For lunch they went to a local restaurant, and enjoyed palm sauce with rice and chicken, or the traditional river fish and greens cooked with palm oil.

That afternoon, they rode in the bus to the island in the middle of the Congo River where a rock quarry was decades old. Everyone walked across a little bridge that looked very much in need of re-engineering. They walked around the island to the side of the island facing the biggest rapids of the Congo River.

The rapids were essentially impassable; only once had they been traversed safely in known human history, and that was with the aid of a hover craft. The river was massive beyond anyone's expectations.

That evening, Jing Sheng led Liz, Darnell, Hopi, Cliff, and the college students to a little chapel on the Congo River, where they attended Wednesday evening services, and then Jing Sheng offered healings. The tropical sunset over the Congo River was beautiful, with the floating islands of water hyacinths creating a peaceful foreground beneath the orange glow of the sky, the lavender blossoms of an ironwood tree, and the bright flaming blossoms of several flamboyant trees. Liz was reminded of her childhood in Malaysia, and felt a deep sense of peace and contentment come over her.

They completed their evening with dinner at the home of a missionary family that lived across the street. Dinner consisted mostly of rice and vegetables with palm sauce, and was rounded out with fresh tropical fruit and peanuts, but the pièce-de-résistance was green mango pie, served not with ice cream, but a slice of cheese, which keeps more easily in a tropical climate.

At least they were well fed before the big adventure began.

The next day, the whole group rode in the bus to the airport, where a small local, privately-owned jet awaited them. Liz was very uncomfortable flying on such a small plane, but had no choice. Once they were in the air, she enjoyed the view of the Congo River, grassland areas, and tropical rainforest areas very much. Unfortunately, areas of environmental devastation were also clearly visible, but she knew they were nothing compared with the destruction of rainforest areas of Brazil.

Late afternoon found them circling above the northern end of Lake Kivu, one of the Great Lakes of Africa, with a view of the nearby volcano close to the border of Rwanda. They landed at the airport in Goma, and found themselves in a very different world than any to which they had ever been before. The sense of isolation – or was it violence? – was palpable.

Signs of NGOs mixed with the presence of UN Peace-Keeping forces and local military police, which Liz could not distinguish from a rebel group if her life depended on it. Signs of the old colonial days with villas surrounded by walls covered with flowering bougainvilla vines spoke of a prosperity that seemed distant today.

Poverty was everywhere: children wearing tattered clothing, people carrying burdens while walking for miles, the main form of transportation being bicycles that were old and beat up. Men and boy soldiers strolling along with rifles or machine guns were common sights. Trucks and SUV's serving non-profit groups such as Doctors Without Borders, Amnesty International, and World Wildlife Fund were also visible from time to time. But tension seemed pervasive in the air everywhere. Liz wondered if she just felt nervous, or if decades of conflict and exploitation, rape and murder had left a tangible feeling of evil.

Maybe the people are constantly on edge, she wondered, *and that's what I feel.*

They all climbed on board an old, rusty bus, which took them to the remnants of an old colonial hotel, now run by a local family that obviously had some connections to one of the more illicit sources of wealth in the area.

Cliff whispered to Liz: "I bet they have a hand in the arms trade somehow; see the Russians staying here? The largest suppliers of weapons around here are the Russians."

Liz got a sinking feeling in her gut on top of her case of nerves. Jing

Sheng seemed as calm and peaceful as ever, although his smile was more reserved and less boisterous than usual.

Darnell and the Assistant Administrator from TASOK made the arrangements, explaining that they might be staying there a couple of weeks. Liz felt a slight sense of panic as she wondered if they would get out of this place alive. The voice of intuition in her head laughingly said, *this time, the work is definitely not about you!*

The body guards, Jerry and Tyrone, began to stay with the group, where before they had remained in Kinshasa, because there was no expected need for them until now. They took turns staying up during the night and guarding the rooms by patrolling the hallway and walking around the little hotel in the dark. They had been hired because Jerry spoke French and Tyrone spoke Swahili, which were the main languages spoken here in eastern Congo.

Jing Sheng invited everyone who wanted to do so to join him in his hotel room to meditate, either sitting on the bed, a chair, or the floor. Liz was unwilling to go for a spot on the floor, so she shared the bed, choosing to sit cross-legged at the foot of the bed. Jing Sheng chose this opportunity to levitate in order to make more space available for everyone who joined in.

The feeling of peace in his room comforted everyone. Jing Sheng invited everyone to pray for the safety and efficacy of the mission, to pray for peace in Goma and the surrounding area while they were there, and to pray for guidance so that what was needed would be accomplished for the greater good of all. As they meditated, the sound of music and singing came in the window from a group of people gathered around a campfire nearby.

Liz couldn't tell if the singing was religious or just for fun, but it was definitely uplifting. She loved the sound of the drums, rhythmically beating reassurance that life is good and worth celebrating all the time. At least, that's the message she heard in the drums.

Only because of extreme fatigue and the peaceful meditation time was Liz able to sleep at all. She hung her mosquito net above her bed, sharing a room with Hopi, who did the same thing. Darnell and Cliff shared a room next door, so she and Hopi were sandwiched between Jing Sheng and the guys, bringing her a smidgen of a sense of safety. The footsteps of first Jerry and then Tyrone pacing the hallway gave her a small measure of comfort as well. The hotel itself was very quiet. *Having no TVs will do that for you*, thought Liz. She slept a few hours, anyway.

The tropical sunrise always happens around 6 a.m. all year, so bright sunshine greeted them very early the next day. Everyone arose early, and bathed or showered the best they could, given the rudimentary facilities. Some meditated before breakfast, although Liz managed to acquire a cup of tea first, and then meditated. Some meditated after breakfast.

Everyone, including the Methodist physician and the CNN reporter, gathered in Jing Sheng's small room at 9 a.m. to create a plan of action. Only the USAID officer chose not to join them. Liz was grateful that she did not have to be part of the data collection team, nor take photos, nor intentionally observe anything. She and Jing Sheng would visit the local hospital, followed by churches and missions, greeting people and offering healings where needed.

Before the day was over, she discovered that this work was overwhelming enough. So many people, including children, had been injured by violence over the past two decades. Too many women had been raped. Too many children were orphaned. She decided to ask Hopi to spend at least one day taking photos with them, although she knew that Hopi was taking important photographs elsewhere. So, Liz resorted to taking a few photos with her phone. It was really all she could do. The stories of people they met often moved her to tears, which of course was not helpful, but at least she bonded with people.

They felt touched by her tears, knowing she felt their pain. Many people, including children, had been attacked with machetes, so they had lost hands or feet or legs or arms. She did offer them healing, referring to it as "prière de guérison" or "prayer of healing."

Jing Sheng had a way of naturally comforting everyone. The children flocked to him, even the crippled children who had to crawl to sit at his feet. He picked up as many as wanted to be picked up, holding them, placing his hand on their heads, healing and blessing them.

At 1:00 p.m., they gathered back at the hotel for lunch. Lunch was only marginally helpful for recovering from their draining work, as they could only manage fresh fruit, peanuts, and some cheese at the hotel. In the old days, a plate of fresh fruit and cheese was the customary after-dessert 4th course for lunch after a three-course meal French or Belgian-style. Bread and soup or salad with a main course followed by pastry and then the fresh fruit and cheese formed a typical lunch, or dejeuner forty years ago in this area.

The topics of conversation at lunch were all shocking. Cliff had made a list of 12 violations of international law by the various mineral and mining companies. He also made a list of multinational corporations connected with the mining companies, and political connections with the various groups and companies working in the area.

Well, on the first day, he began the lists, but the 12 violations had been quick and easy to spot, because the working conditions of the miners, including children, were so horrible. The Huffington Post reporter had accompanied Cliff, and had counted multiple human rights violations, which of course Amnesty International had already reported, but no one had listened. The four college students talked with UN Peace-keeping forces, as well as with anyone holding a gun and wearing army fatigues. Their translator told them the stories of how and why the men and boys started doing what they're doing. One of the students was writing a report on child soldiers, while another was reporting on the lives of UN Peace-Keeping troops.

Hopi and the public health nurse had followed Cliff, taking pictures and noting what kind of health conditions existed in the mining industry. Jerry accompanied Hopi as bodyguard everywhere she went. Hopi and Susan planned to spend the afternoon visiting NGOs and gathering information from them.

Finally, when it came time for Liz and Jing Sheng to share about their morning, Jing Sheng spoke about the conditions which led to the wounding, killing, and raping of so many people. He actually shared what he had learned from people's stories to him. Liz shared about how the children had been drawn to Jing Sheng, and that he had spent over an hour just healing children.

Fortunately, the particular group gathered for the mission all understood the importance of healing and blessing children, rather than just focusing on the bigger picture. They were grateful that Jing Sheng and Liz were present to do that, while the rest of them focused on the bigger picture and what could be done to transform it.

After lunch, they rested for half an hour.

At two o'clock, they gathered in Jing Sheng's room and meditated for 20 minutes, then got ready to go back out and face the sad challenges of life in and around Goma. They left the rooms at 2:30, which only gave them three-and-a-half hours until sunset.

Liz and Jing Sheng, accompanied by Tyrone and a French translator, went straight to the biggest church in town, which was a Seventh-Day Adventist Church, school, and university. They walked into the office, where they were greeted cordially. They asked to speak to the head pastor. After sitting in the waiting area for 15 minutes, they were shown into an office where the head pastor, a Congolese man in his fifties, rose and came to greet them. Pastor Albert Mwenye[5] seemed very calm and friendly.

With the help of their translator, they carried on a conversation half in French, half in English, although Tyrone did greet the pastor in Swahili, in which language the pastor returned the greeting and then spoke with Tyrone for a few minutes. Tyrone seemed both to warm the pastor to their presence, and alert him that something unexpected and uncontrollable was going on.

So many people of faith develop belief systems that are bogged down by dogmatic thinking because they are only shaped by the past, reflected Liz. I think they desire some sort of control over reality, or have a high need for control, because they constantly force reality to fit into their paradigm, even when others have no desire to fit into their paradigm. Oh, dear, I suppose that criticism could be reflected back at me. Ugh, it's the mirror affect! I had better just listen, and try not to judge!

Darnell began the introduction of Jing Sheng and the Exodus 2012 Mission. The French-speaking translator translated. He explained that Jing Sheng was a Chinese Tai Chi master, and that he had begun the world-wide mission in order to save the earth by inviting the earth's peoples to live out the commandment by caring for all the children on earth equally.

Pastor Mwenye nodded, and asserted that he had heard about the mission, and had heard about its good work for children, for the

---

[5] "Mwenye" is a name that means "owner" or "lord" in Swahili

environment, and its concern for the people of the Congo. "That is all good," he said, as translated, "But I have heard that you also claim, or that your followers claim, that you are the reincarnation of Jesus Christ. I'm afraid that you must be wrong, and I question that you are a man of God, because you do not remain faithful to the Word of God. The Bible tells us that Jesus will come again on a cloud, and that the faithful will be raised up to heaven at that time."

Jing Sheng began his response by congratulating the pastor on what a success the mission and the schools were, and how high the attendance at his church was every Sunday. Liz knew that Pastor Mwenye would just assume that Jing Sheng had heard these facts from someone else, or read about the mission. But then Jing Sheng broke out and did what only Jing Sheng could do.

"However, I know that you have been siphoning off an early retirement fund for yourself and your wife, with plans to retire to the Bahamas in one year's time. And do not worry, no one told me about this information. As a man of faith, I'm sure you know that being faithful to God means being honest and never coveting nor stealing - two of the ten commandments in the Word of God. I have come on a mission, so people are welcome to think of me as whomever they please; I am here simply to fulfill a mission. You may consider me a prophet, if you like, and my prophetic message to you is to repent and to restore what is not rightfully yours. If God asks or allows you to suffer with your people, how can you glorify God – that is, how can you exemplify Love, if you provide yourself with wealth and a better life than that which you provide for God's people?

"Go, repent, and restore to God's people what is theirs, so that they will have a better life. Then, trust that God will provide for you. And ask Christ's forgiveness and grace to be shared with you."
Pastor Mwenye just sat there with big eyes while Jing Sheng spoke. Obviously he was contemplating continuing in his dishonesty, but

Jing Sheng had pulled enough divine love into the room that the gentleness of it moved Pastor Mwenye to tears. He knelt down then and there and prayed to God for forgiveness.

Slowly he rose off his old knees, painful from kneeling on the simple concrete floor, and he turned to Jing Sheng.

"I don't know who you are. Obviously, you are a man of God. I just have one question for you. Why is it that you do not simply preach to the people of China, and turn their hearts to Christ?"

Jing Sheng smiled at Pastor Mwenye, and gestured for him to sit down again. The Pastor moved behind his desk and sat down with his eyes glued on Jing Sheng.

"The people of China are forbidden to practice any form of spirituality or religion. To do so is to invite death and torture for oneself and one's loved ones. Tai Chi and Qi Gong are the limited forms in which the expression of spirituality is accepted in China.

"However, a movement has arisen of a form of meditation that is being practiced widely in China. This form of meditation, known as Falun Gong, and introduced by spiritual master Li Hongzhi, is indeed from God, although its practitioners do not always believe in God. Falun Gong is, however, God's way of reaching people in China with peace, with the fruits of the Spirit such as self-control, gentleness, peace, and even miraculous healing. Yet, even practicing this meditation has led to persecution by the government of China.

"The time will come when the masses of humanity will move together to bring God's light and love to China, but the time is not yet now." Jing Sheng smiled peacefully at the group gathered in the office, including Pastor Mwenye.

"So, now, Pastor Mwenye, I trust that your knees are feeling better?"

Pastor Mwenye looked startled, reached down and touched his knees, then stood up and bent his knees in a partial squat, and then blurted out in Swahili, "What did you do? I mean, did you do that?"

Tyrone translated.

"Love is the Supreme Force in the Universe, Pastor Mwenye. What does it mean to you if Love heals your knees today?"   Jing Sheng smiled at the bewildered pastor.

"I... I... it means I must serve God!"

"Indeed, Pastor, I hope you will serve God. As Christ once said, those who worship God must worship God in Spirit and in Truth. We, too, are here to serve God by bringing the Mission of Exodus 2012: Honor your Heavenly Father and your Earthly Mother by caring for all children of the earth so that the earth herself will be saved, and all life will be able to live long in the land.

"Will you join us on this mission?"

"What are you asking me to do?" Pastor Mwenye managed to bring doubt and fear back into the situation despite the fact that Love still filled the room.

"I am asking you to allow and to support the presence of international visitors to monitor mining activities in Goma, while engaging in an exchange of children and families to help create a sense of what is needed for all people in this situation."

"Yes, I can see that you care deeply. I do not think that I have the budget to guarantee the safety of these people who will come."

"Never fear, Pastor Mwenye, we have the budget, all you have to do is oversee the care, protection, and housing of these children and families, as well as the exchange of children and families from this community."

"In that case, yes, I will be honored to be part of this mission to save all God's children on earth." Pastor Mwenye bowed slightly, an awkward look for him, Liz thought.

"Thank you. I will leave Darnell and the translator here to work out the details with you."

Jing Sheng rose, and Liz and Tyrone rose to accompany him.

The mission proceeded according to plan, with only a few scary incidents. Hopi and Susan were visiting an NGO when some rebel soldiers burst in and demanded money. Hopi told them that if they would turn over their guns and leave peacefully, she would give them $100. A translation was made, and the men laid down their guns by the door. One man returned, and stuck out his hand in front of Hopi. She noticed that he used a local gesture of respect, placing his left hand on his forearm while holding his right hand out, palm up. She realized that the rebel soldiers were mostly like everyone else: scared little boys inside, who just needed reassurance of safety and to have their own needs met.

Cliff was poking around a mine when some security guards asked him to leave at the point of a gun. Jerry was with him, and the situation calmed down when Jerry assured them that they would leave immediately, while also holding out a couple of $100 bills. Money talks everywhere, in every language.

Data gathered, photos taken, traumatized women and children healed, contacts made, the group gathered seven days later to take a flight from Goma back to Kinshasa, and then all the way back to

Washington, D.C. They shortened the trip from two weeks to one week in order to spread the word more quickly.

Families would be screened, prepped, and sent later both from and to the mission station set up at the Adventist school and church, thanks to Pastor Mwenye. Families from around the world would also come to the mission station to begin eco-communes, teach meditation, and be community organizers for fair mining practices and to protect the wealth and natural resources for the people of the Congo. Renewable energy sources such as wind and solar were to be part and parcel of the mission.

Liz felt exhausted, and longed to see Daniel, with whom she had had very little contact, just a couple of phone calls while they were in the Congo, and four email messages. When they reached Kinshasa for an overnight rest, she and Darnell managed to set-up Skype on a computer and talk face-to-face, as it were, with Daniel and Adam. That made the trip home much easier for both of them.

Cliff and Hopi came to Liz's room before the group meditation time.

"Mom, we don't know how to say this, really, but thank you for being our mom, and thank you for getting us into this mission with Jing Sheng. This is the best thing that could possibly happen to the earth, and we are grateful that we get to be part of it," Hopi hurriedly gushed on behalf of both of them.

"Yeah, Mom, thanks," Cliff echoed. "I plan to do everything I can to get this information out. The world needs to know about the injustices in the Congo, and I plan to tell them."

"Oh, you two, I'm just so grateful that I get to be your Mom. You're both such gifts from God to me! What a blessing you both are to the whole world, even if the whole world does not yet know it!"

A group hug ensued, and then they all went to meditate together with Jing Sheng and the other mission trip participants. Even the Huffington Post reporter and bodyguards and translators had begun to meditate with them. Liz felt safer than ever.

20.   ARRIVAL AT THE PROMISED LAND

WHAT IS LOVE? A FEELING? A THOUGHT?
AN ACTION VERB?
A DESIRE? A SACRIFICE OF SELF-GIVING?
ALL OF THE ABOVE?
LOVE, LIKE LIGHT, IS A WAVE OF ENERGY IN MOTION.
LOVE HAS A CONSCIOUSNESS TO IT
WHICH CAN EXPAND OR NARROW IN FOCUS, BECOMING
CONCENTRATED OR EXPANSIVELY INCREASING IN ENERGY
AND SCOPE.
LOVE TRAVELS IN GLOBE-LIKE CIRCLES,
LIKE SOME KIND OF MAGNETIC FIELD THAT DRAWS
OTHERS INTO ITS OWN CIRCLE OF BEING.

If Liz had ever doubted Margaret Meade's wonderful quote about it only taking a small group of people to change the world, she certainly saw results this time from their trip to the Congo. Liz did reflect on the fact that Margaret Meade had made the comment long before social media helped pass ideas more rapidly than wildfire, and wondered what she would have to say today.

The return from the Congo brought internet reports, twitters, facebook and youtube movements, as well as global efforts on all levels to stop the exploitation of people in the Congo. Boycotts of certain key corporations were organized on college campuses and online. The movement grew until Congress and the President had to act, sending an advisory panel to eastern Congo to check it out. A UN special envoy went along with the Congressional panel, to explore the United Nation's options for increasing peace while maintaining productivity.   Thousands of young Americans volunteered to be human rights witnesses. A fund was set-up to send and support them while they went to catalog any human rights violations they saw. Of course, this means that visible, observable human rights violations diminished rapidly.

Cell phone companies began to compete for business by proclaiming that they were investing in the communities in Eastern Congo where coltan was extracted for use in cell phones. Businesses around the world began to realize that social, environmental, and corporate responsibility really, truly, actually was the best way to make a profit – *with the return on investments being of benefit to everyone, including the environment.* Sustainability finally became not only 'cool,' but also, in the short as well as the long run, more profitable.

In the meantime, the Exodus 2012 Mission had to prepare for their trip to Malaysia. Liz felt excited to go home. Well, to her childhood home. She was also excited that she would get to travel with Daniel this time. When she returned to Kalamazoo, she landed at the tiny airport, and met Daniel by the curb. He got out of the car, she dropped her bags, and they fairly leaped into each other's arms. Neither one wanted to let go, but Daniel gently slid his hands down her arms and stood back just enough to kiss her softly. Then he whispered, "We have to go – we're standing at an airport." They both laughed, and placed her bags in the trunk. They held hands in the car.

So much for spiritual non-attachment, thought Liz. *Well, maybe incarnational attachment is good sometimes, because that's what love really is. Of course, love also gives the other freedom and trusts the Universe, so the best form of love includes freedom, which requires a degree of non-attachment. When did I learn to think like this!?* Liz smiled at Daniel, who turned to look at her while driving, and smiled back, mirroring a joy that can only be shared.

The next day, Liz and Daniel met Adam and Darnell at the Spring of Life Wellness Center so they could all do Tai Chi and meditate together. Jing Sheng still had to remain out of the country, so he had flown to Paris, where great progress was being made with eco-communes and fair trade businesses. Jing Sheng spent the next month opening up Exodus 2012 Mission Centres in Paris, Madrid, and London. He also swung by to visit friends along the Dalmatian Coast, which had become one of his favorite spots, especially the Krka River. He lived so simply that the money to support him paid easily for the trips on top of his meager need for food, drink, and modest accommodations.

Everywhere Jing Sheng went, he performed healings, gave talks, and taught meditation. Money flowed towards him and the Mission constantly. Translators always appeared when necessary, and Jing Sheng blessed many women, and a few men, to become Guru-Doulas. They always came from and became part of his inner circle of disciples – a crowd within a crowd who followed Jing Sheng. Many people followed the Mission, without being direct disciples of Jing Sheng. That was okay with him, for he knew that God exists in everyone, and the important thing was for each person to find God within themselves, and then to be able to see God in others – all others.

That was the salvation of the earth. That was also salvation on earth. Finding God within oneself and manifesting that unconditionally loving Self instead of ego-self is the essence of Christ, of incarnation, of the reason for It All – meaning the entire Universe existed for this purpose. That salvation, or wholeness, was happening more and more across the earth.

The Mission seemed to be taking forever to Liz. What started in August 2008 had developed nicely, but was still going on and they were just starting to finalize plans for the Malaysia trip in October 2012. The plan was to spend the first week of December there, and to leave two families in a community on the edge of Kuala Lumpur. Liz and Darnell checked out the State Department website for warnings and information on Malaysia, and Liz realized that it had changed so much since she grew up there, becoming more and more dominated by Islam and Sharia Law.

"Look, they cane people, even women, although their federal law opposes it!" Liz exclaimed.

"Yeah, being gay can't be good in Malaysia," Darnell retorted.

"They caned people just for being in close proximity to someone of the opposite sex. I don't want to know what they do to homosexuals!"

"I guess that's why Jing Sheng didn't include you and Adam in the plans for going to Malaysia. Oh, my, Darnell, we're going to have to be careful enough as it is, because there are criminal groups that have kidnapped Americans, and they have detained tourists who don't have their passports on them at all times. It sounds as though we have to stay away from eastern Malaysia, where I grew up, because travel can be dangerous there, and foreigners can get arrested and detained indefinitely. So, it's not just dangerous, but we might get thrown in jail if we offend someone, and let's face it, the Exodus 2012 Mission offends people all the time!"

"You know that's right!" Darnell agreed. "Let's find an Amnesty International contact, and also see if Jing Sheng is okay with our letting the American Embassy know when we arrive there."

Liz and Darnell had their hands full planning. Jing Sheng, however, chose this particular time to remind Liz that he needed her to write a book for the sake of the Mission. So it was that she began nightly excursions to her office at Spring of Life Wellness Center to sit at her desk and type up transcripts of recordings of Jing Sheng's speeches, and put them into a travelogue sort of account of the Mission. That left so little time for her and Daniel to spend together, except that they met five times a week with Darnell and Adam to meditate and join together on a conference call with Jing Sheng.

Good news came like a karmic kick-back, just in time to allow Liz to relax and prepare for Thanksgiving and Christmas: Adam, who had been tending the Exodus 2012 Mission website, discovered there were eco-communes that had formed in Malaysia, just as they had in much of the world. He also found that some of the people in the eco-commune nearest to Kuala Lumpur actually spoke English in addition to Malay.

So, plans were made to teach meditation and do healings at some of the eco-communes, and families were selected to make the switch with the two families from Austin, Texas. Everything was on a roll. Liz and Daniel got more time to themselves after that. They planned to spend Thanksgiving together.

Jing Sheng went to Malaysia ahead of the rest of the group, just before Thanksgiving, to spend a week with the main eco-commune in the outskirts of Kuala Lumpur.

Hopi and Cliff came home for Thanksgiving, along with Hopi's boyfriend Krishna and Cliff's girlfriend Susan. Daniel brought his young adult daughter, Clarissa, her husband, Chris, and their two children to Liz's house for the Thanksgiving meal. Liz, Hopi and Cliff had become quite a team preparing the Thanksgiving feast.

Krishna brought a special form of incense for ceremonial blessing of everyone, while Susan brought music CDs from all the places on the Exodus 2012 mission. Clarissa and Chris brought some wine, while Daniel brought a beautiful floral centerpiece, complete with golden beeswax candles and porcelain candleholders.

Although they planned to enjoy the day, they also planned to volunteer at Ministry with Community before actually eating their own feast. The whole family volunteered, including the children, and then returned to Liz's house to take the turkey out of the oven.

Everyone was getting along beautifully, when they decided to take a football break and kitchen clean-up break before enjoying pumpkin pie. When everyone gathered in the living room to enjoy pumpkin pie and homemade whipped cream, Daniel asked if they could turn off the TV for a few minutes. He stood up, got a small box out of his pocket, and turned to Liz.

"Liz, I love you, and I love your family. In front of your family and mine, I would like to ask you to do me the honor of marrying me, so that I get to spend the rest of my life loving you."

Then Daniel knelt down by Liz, opened the box, and inside she could see a gold necklace shaped in the Sanskrit sign for OM.

"Oh, Daniel, of course! I love you, too," Liz managed as she scooted carefully forward on the couch with a plate of pumpkin pie in one hand, and her other hand touching Daniel's arm gently. They kissed.

Daniel put the necklace around Liz's neck, explaining "The necklace is fair trade from India, and reflects the fact that our lives together are centered around the very presence of God in us and with us and among us all."

The family celebrated noisily and joyously, and then went back to eating pumpkin pie.

Two days later, on the Saturday after Thanksgiving, while most Americans were doing their holiday shopping, the Exodus team met at the airport in Los Angeles to head on to Malaysia. At least this year, many American shops offered environmentally-conscious products and reusable shopping bags. More malls had begun to use their own renewable energy sources, including photovoltaic cells located on the expansive roofs of the malls.

After an exhausting trip, in which they stopped briefly in Australia, the Exodus 2012 team landed at the airport in Kuala Lumpur. They were greeted cheerfully by Jing Sheng and a kind man named Nizam Merican, who was one of the leaders at the eco-commune in which they would be staying.

Nizam had arranged for a small bus to take them all, along with their luggage, to the eco-commune, where they would meet the families who were leaving, and spend a couple of days with them before they went on to the U.S.

When Jing Sheng, Liz, Daniel, Hopi, and the two families from Texas arrived at the eco-commune, they discovered a group of media reporters and camera crews outside, and a banner saying 'welcome' hanging along the side of the house. The whole community of families from the eco-commune had gathered to wave and greet them as they arrived.

Reporters flocked around Jing Sheng, Liz, Daniel, and Hopi. They felt welcomed more than confronted; it was a celebration of unity and hope, because so many people in Malaysia had apparently become involved with environmental protection, confronting child labor, and spiritually purifying themselves, no matter what their religion.

The State Department missed a few details in its report on Malaysia, or else the Malaysian government is seeking to keep this movement quiet, thought Liz.

Jing Sheng stepped up on the front porch of the house, requested a microphone, and addressed the crowd.

"Greetings, favored ones," he began, "I come in peace, to bring you a message of hope, which you yourselves may live out with your own power of personal choice.

"The time has come to win the Greater Jihad, the battle between goodness and evil within each human being. I invite you to learn how to win that battle." Jing Sheng paused, and actually took time to look each individual person present in the eyes. They were all, of course, looking at him. Some people bowed when he looked at them.

"The only way, I repeat, the only way to win the Greater Jihad is through the power of love. Love is the greatest force on earth, because earth is composed not only of material that decays in a few days or a few millennia, but earth is composed of Spirit, and Spirit is composed of Love.

"To win the Greater Jihad, each person must cease judging his or her neighbor, and begin simply to love. Love does set limits. Love does choose healthy boundaries. Love can be strong, but love is also gentle and meek, sharing power rather than coercing or wielding power over others.

"To love without fear requires seeing through the Maya, or illusion and duality of this natural world, and breaking on through to the other side, where one realizes that Spirit is the Infinite Source of possibilities for life and love. The future is shaped more by love and hope and faith and service than it is by fear.

"Out of which would you rather create your future: fear, judgment and hatred; or love, peace, and kindness? The Greater Jihad requires no judgment, no hatred of supposed infidels, no fear. Rather, the Greater Jihad IS love, peace, and kind service to Allah and others.

"The only real infidel is fear." Jing Sheng paused and allowed this idea to stand on its own. "There is no other infidel; fear alone is the one infidel which must be overcome.

"Everyone who hates and everyone who kills, also commits the murder of their own hearts, by first killing love within themselves.

"Perfect love casts out fear because fear is the opposite of love. And underneath all anger lies either fear or hurt, or both.

"Misunderstanding creates both judgment and fear, while judgment and fear in turn create anger and hatred.

"Fear is the infidel that must be cast out of everyone's heart, mind, and soul, because fear is the infidel who steals Allah, who is Love, out of human hearts. Fear is the only infidel. If you would serve Allah, then first you must love your neighbor, and first you must love yourself as a servant of Love. The main commandment of Allah is to cast out the infidel of fear, and the only way the human race can do that is by loving one another as one family of God's people, as one family of all religions united in Perfect Love.

"Would you rather fear, and let that painful energy create your future? Or would you rather Love, and let peace and harmony heal your lives and your world?"

Jing Sheng paused again. "Thank you. Namaste." Jing Sheng bowed.

Everyone bowed. Some people kneeled. Some people applauded. Some had tears streaming down their faces. Liz, Daniel, and Hopi got down on their knees on the steps going up to the porch. Even reporters were hushed. Most of the camera people held the cameras on Jing Sheng because they themselves felt so overcome, but then they slowly panned to show the crowd's response around Jing Sheng.

Jing Sheng waved, and turned to go inside. Nizam Merican opened the door for him.

Liz, Daniel, and Hopi followed them into the eco-commune. There they met a lovely variety of people, some of whom were Muslim like Nizam, some of whom were Hindu, some of whom were Buddhist, and a few of whom were Christian. There were families, monks, older persons, formerly homeless poor people, including orphaned children who had been living out on the streets. Everyone lived there in harmony, seeking to help and serve as much as possible for the good of all. No one complained about cooking, cleaning, or washing dishes. Even the toilets were constantly cleaned.

Jing Sheng and his American followers, including the families from Austin, were served a light meal, shown where the meditation room was, and then shown to some sleeping quarters.

Liz awakened in the middle of the night, and used her flashlight to make her way quietly to the meditation room, where she found Jing Sheng meditating all alone. A few minutes later, Daniel came in. They meditated for half an hour, and then Jing Sheng began to OM. When he had finished, he quietly rose and addressed Liz and Daniel.

"Please do me the honor of allowing me to perform your wedding at the Batu Caves in front of the famous golden statue of Lord Murugan. We will be going there in two days to arrange for the coming Thaipusam Festival to include the blessing of children from around the world and from all faiths. I will await your answer tomorrow." Jing Sheng bowed.

Liz and Daniel returned the Namaste, and then looked at one another. Obviously, they had some talking to do. Quietly, they rose and went out onto the front porch, and after talking softly for a few minutes, came to their decision.

The next day, the whole traveling group rose at different times because their jet lag was so strong. Liz and Daniel looked for Jing

Sheng after they had showered and eaten breakfast. They bowed before him, and sat down with him.

"We have made our decision," announced Liz.

"We humbly thank you and accept your kind offer to perform our marriage at the Batu Caves holy site," Daniel added.

Jing Sheng grinned, placed one hand on each of their heads, and said, "Bless you, my children. Cliff, Susan, Clarissa, Chris, and Krishna will all be joining us this afternoon. I have found guides who will accompany each of you to find appropriate attire this afternoon. The other arrangements have been made.

Liz and Daniel laughed and joked that it was a good thing they had said "yes" instead of "no, thank you".

Two days later, the whole group took a train north from Kuala Lumpur to the Batu Caves, where a Hindu woman saint, a Muslim Imam, a Buddhist monk, and a Catholic priest had all agreed to bless the wedding and the family as a symbol of world unity, love, and peace.

The media had gathered, and local on-lookers flocked to see what the commotion was all about. Of course, local on-lookers in this setting includes a variety of bats and monkeys, the latter being very curious about humans and their activities. So, it was a colorful, exotic setting for a marriage; certainly not what most Americans envision. The civil, legal ceremony would be done back in Kalamazoo, but Liz and Daniel found themselves delighted at the variety of human and non-human participants in the occasion.

Jing Sheng placed himself at the foot of the 141-foot tall statue of Lord Murugan, commemorated here for defeating Surupadman, an evil, greedy, materialistic Asura, or powerful being. The various holy men and women gathered to his left and right. Daniel and Liz came and stood before them, flocked on either side by their family members. A macaque monkey strolled through the group, pulled at Liz's dress, then ran off. Hopi, being the photographer for the occasion, got a photo of the monkey just as it grabbed at the extra flounce of colorful fabric on Liz's sari-inspired dress.

The media and crowd followed in, close behind the group. Jing Sheng faced the crowd, with his back to the golden statue. Cameras were rolling as he began to speak.

"Friends, family of God around the earth, we are gathered here in this holy place to commemorate the gift of Love, and to celebrate the gift of Life, especially life lived in community, where love alone unites, while selfishness and materialism divide.

"And so we remember here, in this holy shrine, that long ago, the divine Lord Murugan defeated the evil Asuras for their greedy, materialistic ways. Lord Murugan was created from the powerful love of Lord Shiva. Indeed, it is divine love which creates, and selfish materialism which destroys.

"And so, in this sanctified place, we come to confront the Asuras of today. Together, united in love, we must confront and defeat the evils of greed, materialism, and selfishness. This is a world-wide necessity; defeating greed and materialism and the selfishness that insists on personal comfort at the expense of others and at the expense of the earth has become a dire necessity.

"I challenge each and every one of you to defeat greed and materialism and selfishness within yourself. I also challenge you to defeat these Asuras in our world today. With courage and confidence, just like Murugan, I challenge you to confront the power of evil, defeat the Almighty dollar and its billionaire adherents. Confront the power of money everywhere it rules, for it is like an evil Asura. Free of concerns about wealth, you are called to be a Servant of God, or a Deva, who serves God's people rather than just a handful of greedy men.

"Those who exist primarily for themselves do not exist for God. How can those who exist first and foremost for themselves then expect God to exist for them?

"We celebrate today the gift of marriage, as a symbol of the embodiment of divine Love dwelling within and among human beings. Liz and Daniel, we celebrate today your commitment to God and to one another, and I ask you: will you be an example to the world with your love, serving one another and letting love be your guide in this relationship and in all your relations? If so, please answer: 'I will, with the help of God.' "

Liz and Daniel both repeated the vow.

"Liz and Daniel, the earth exists through the life of God, which provides you with the means of life in community with other human beings and with all life. And so I ask you: do you affirm your commitment to one another, to God, and to the earth? If so, please answer: 'I do, with the help of God.' "

Again, Liz and Daniel replied, affirming their vow.

Jing Sheng invited the other holy people to speak, and a half hour ensued in which many spiritual blessings were poured out, prayed for, and lifted up, both for Daniel and Liz, and also for the entire human community, including the earth.

Jing Sheng concluded: "Liz and Daniel, I now pronounce you husband and wife; you may kiss one another!" He grinned.

Liz and Daniel kissed in front of potentially millions of people around the world. They heard cheering in the background, and then music began to play. They waved at the crowd and the media, and then walked towards the closest building so that they could get away from the crowds and have a personal moment. Neither one of them resented their wedding becoming an opportunity for a message during the Exodus 2012 Mission, because both of them had rather expected it. They actually liked Jing Sheng's message very much, along with the blessings of many faiths.

"Do we have some special burden to live our lives a certain way?" asked Liz. "I mean, we're both guru-doulas, and had a special marriage ceremony. It seems to me that we need to run eco-commune training centres or something."

"I don't know, my inspiring one; you may be right," Daniel replied, "but I trust that all will be revealed to us in good time, just like the wedding which was planned for us. We always have free will, but we'd rather do what God and Jing Sheng are asking us to do, so no worries. I'm guessing we need to ask Jing Sheng what he would like us to do next, after our stay in Malaysia." Daniel's faith inspired Liz.

The day was complete with a walk up the 272 stairs to the top of the mountain, where the temple complex included an astoundingly beautiful view. Dinner would come later in Kuala Lumpur; in the meantime, most everyone just snacked on the bananas and peanuts, like the local monkeys, who tried to steal their food away from them. Hopi was, of course, the one person who ignored the advice to avoid feeding the monkeys, because they might bite you. She had a grand time, although she was being extremely careful, and had a little help from Krishna, who kind of rescued her by throwing a bunch of bananas and peanuts off to the side, and then grabbed her out of the midst of the monkeys.

The next day, the two families from Austin were escorted to a slum area, where they exchanged places with two local families. The two local families came to the eco-commune to prepare to go to the United States. They filled the evening meal with tales of life in the slums of Kuala Lumpur.

The following day, the two families left for America along with Cliff, Krishna, Clarissa, and Chris.

Along with Nizam Merican, Jing Sheng, Liz, and Daniel rode a bus to go to the Amnesty International headquarters, and spent the day making plans there. The following day, they all left to tour the site where Bush Computers had a manufacturing and recycling plant, both of which heavily polluted the environment, and where the workers had experienced significant health issues from the toxic pollutants. In addition, these workers had no health insurance, and not enough income to access health care. Only the management workers had access to health care.

Jing Sheng made sure that they brought the media with them. Several of the world's major TV networks did follow the Exodus 2012 Mission wherever they went as it was already.

When they finished seeing what they could of the Bush Computers compound, Jing Sheng asked the media to hear him speak.

"I invite my good friend Bob Woodson from Amnesty International to share with us, on the record, the practices of Bush Computers, which is headquartered in beautiful Austin, Texas, but which manufactures and recycles computers right here outside of Kuala Lumpur."

Bob Woodson spoke about the toxic pollution, the health effects on the workers, the lack of health care for them, and the fact that they could be easily exploited, because they were, like so many workers in Malaysia, immigrants who had no legal status. He called on Bush Computers to change their ways immediately, or for a boycott to take place.

Jing Sheng stepped up to the microphone.

"Friends, family of God around the world, we must care for all people of the earth equally. How we employ one another matters. How we live with one another in our home matters. Each and every human being is a child of God, born on this earth with a soul's purpose. If you mistreat one child of God, you mistreat God's own Self. I call on everyone to stop buying Bush Computers until they have mended their ways. Thank you."

So it was that Bush Computers got a lot of negative publicity, and had to change their ways as sales immediately dropped.

The rest of the week was spent traveling to the eastern part of Malaysia, where Liz had grown up in the main city of Kuching. Her parents had both been medical missionaries, serving in a local hospital there. The British influence in Kuching had been very strong, and yet the culture there was diverse, with many ethnic groups adding to the cultural milieu. She couldn't wait to see what life is like in Kuching now.

They were meeting up with an employee of Habitat for Humanity, to show what basic housing around the world could look like for families, to promote giving to Habitat and similar groups, and to discuss how Habitat's approach could be adopted to build eco-communes. The most exciting possibility, though, was that two different environmental groups were meeting with Habitat for Humanity to develop housing from recycled materials that were commonly available world-wide, or at least, could be available world-wide. Jing Sheng committed to supporting the development of this type of housing by promoting it through the Exodus 2012 Mission website and by mentioning it in media presentations.

Liz and Daniel hired a taxi to take them in search of Liz's childhood home and other favorite spots. When they drove up to the house in which she had grown up, the familiarity almost overwhelmed her with a sense of loss. She felt grateful, however, that the house had a new coat of paint, and, even after three decades, was well-maintained. The most joyful part for her, though, was seeing three Malaysian children playing happily in the same yard where she herself had played. However, as Liz and Daniel drove around the city, the pollution, poverty, and excess trash evident in many areas grieved her very deeply.

Liz went into a different and personal mental zone: one part memory lane, one part excitement at sharing with Daniel the place of her childhood, and one part lament as she experienced her age and the negative changes of the world. Of course, at least the latter part motivated her to commit her life even more to the cause of Exodus 2012. She realized that much of this lament and stroll down memory lane was her ego, and so she pulled herself out of it after a couple of days.

The second part of this trip to eastern Malaysia involved exploring and exposing oil exploration and extraction practices, which were causing devastation on surrounding environments, including the South China Sea. In addition, destruction of the rainforests by logging companies was to be documented and exposed.

Jing Sheng once again spoke to the media, and called yet again for caring for our Earthly Mother. This time, he called for a boycott of two major oil companies, and asked people to begin to fund a search for alternative energy sources more than ever.

I do hope we listen, Liz thought. *Maybe we can call for wind turbines right here along the coast of the South China Sea.* She spoke to Jing Sheng, and then they began to organize work around that idea, contacting as many local groups as they could. Liz began to feel hopeful. They even organized a local eco-commune around the concept of promoting renewable energy in Sarawak.

At the end of their week in Malaysia, they flew back to Kuala Lumpur, and rested in a resort hotel for a night before flying on to India.

Early the next day, they began the last leg of their international tour, flying north of Indonesia across the Bay of Bengal to the Babatpur Airport outside of Varanasi. They took the Babatpur Railway to Varanasi, and chose to stay in the Golden Buddha Hotel. Varanasi is one of the centers of holy sites in India, with famous Ghats along the Ganges River. They arrived in time for the last of the annual holy festivals ending in December.

After their travels, they rested and then ate dinner close to the Ganges. They strolled down to the closest place where they could walk down the stone steps into the Ganges. Jing Sheng led them in a simple Tai Chi routine that they could do while balancing on the steps. He then stripped off his outer garments, and clad in dark grey silk boxer shorts, he stepped into the Ganges, ducked his head under water, and rose out of the water with his hands praying Namaste. He flipped his hair back, smoothed it down, and climbed, dripping wet, back up the steps to retrieve his clothes. He sat down to rest.

People flocked around them in curiosity. Jing Sheng rose and bowed in Namaste to a local Saddhu, a holy man who was scantily clothed himself, in a simple loin cloth befitting his status as a renunciant of worldly goods. The Saddhu gently touched Jing Sheng's forehead, marking it with red sandalwood paste. He then bowed in Namaste and reverently touched Jing Sheng's feet. Jing Sheng blessed him, touching his head and speaking to him in a language Liz did not know, but guessed was Hindi. Suddenly, Jing Sheng was swarmed with people seeking healing, or bringing babies and elderly loved ones to him to be healed.

Liz and Daniel joined in greeting people with Namaste, and then placing their hands on peoples' heads to heal them. Singing broke out, chant-like and eerily mystical to match the twilight and the last rays of the setting of the sun behind the Ganges. Liz had never experienced anything so sacred, so poignantly holy, so intimate yet universal, so earthly and yet so heavenly all at the same time.

The next day, they arose at 6 am to bathe in the Ganges at sunrise. Liz was a little concerned about this, because friends had told her there were dead bodies floating in the Ganges. That didn't make sense to her, since the local practice was to cremate bodies and then float them on the river. When she dipped herself under the water, she felt the cool rush of energy both physically and energetically. When she rose out of the water, she did feel refreshed and cleansed, purified and forgiven. She had been told that bathing in the Holy Ganges leads to forgiveness and purification so that one can attain Nirvana. She wasn't sure what Nirvana would feel like, but she did feel fantastic and joyful.

They then proceeded to the Kashi Vishwanath Temple for Darshan meditation at 7 a.m. They sat and meditated for an hour, and then departed for the hotel for breakfast and to get dressed for a holy festival.

During the Holy Festival, they followed a procession from the Ghats to the temple, and sat and meditated again, with chanting and Om-ing resounding all around them. Liz felt as if she were in a daze. She was seeing light in her Third Eye, and felt as though she and the universe were one, and all that existed was Love. Purple energy seemed to swirl around her, followed by green and blue and pink.

Then a bright, golden white light surrounded her, and she heard a voice saying:

"Welcome, my daughter, you have found your Path to the Infinite. Stay the course, and we will be One."

The next thing she knew, a Hindu Swami dressed in ocher robes was inviting Jing Sheng to stand on a raised dais. Jing Sheng invited those who needed healing to come. Liz and Daniel were also escorted up front, and again gave healings to those who were in need. Word spread, so they spent a couple of hours giving healings before the Swami and priests of the temple led them to a dining room where they were given cups of water and then served lunch.

Jing Sheng spent the afternoon in the temple speaking with the Swami and the temple priests. Liz wondered why women weren't also in charge. She did find a statue that honors the Mother Goddess, and she felt better. The sacred feminine and the sacred masculine seemed sometimes more in balance in India than America, sometimes less, but overall healthier somehow.

They departed the next day for Bengaluru, or Bangalore, as Americans name it. Jing Sheng insisted on calling it by its ancient name, with a wistful, faraway look in his eyes as if he had once been a visitor there in the ancient days when the temples themselves were founded. *Maybe he was*, thought Liz.

In Bengaluru, they visited the gardens of Lal Bagh, which Liz absolutely loved, especially enjoying walking hand-in-hand with Daniel through them. They skipped the temple of Krishna Consciousness – to Liz, neglecting to visit it seemed like quite a potent statement. When Liz asked Jing Sheng why they did not go there, Jing Sheng replied:

"I honor the original consciousness of Lord Krishna. True light is interior and is visible without a veneer of outer glitter. Yet this veneer of glitter has been added for the sake of those who come here from the West. Those who seek glitter on the outside still need to seek perfection on the inside. Do not expect perfection outside if inner perfection has not yet been attained; only inner perfection can be a true and permanent route to outer perfection, while outer perfection does not necessarily lead one to inner perfection at all. Nevertheless, may Love bless the devotees of Krishna Consciousness at the Temple of Lord Krishna."

Liz assumed that Jing Sheng might have been referring to the polished and westernized functionality of the Krishna Consciousness temple, which differed markedly in its attraction from the ancient temples. It seemed to Liz that the Lord Krishna Temple almost marketed spirituality, much the same as some Western churches seemed to do in Liz's opinion.

It seems practical to me, she thought. *How else do you let people know you exist and draw them to you?* She was wondering that idly, rather than addressing it to either God or to Jing Sheng, so no obvious answer popped into her head.

Jing Sheng chose, instead, to meditate at the Someshwara Temple. This Temple marks where Abbakka Rani, a 16th century princess, worshiped at a time when the Portuguese were seeking to dominate the province. Princess Rani resisted their decrees, choosing to divorce her husband and give up her life rather than submitting to the Portuguese. Jing Sheng meditated, greeted the holy men and women at the site, and asked permission to speak. They sounded a gong, and Jing Sheng stood at the entrance of the temple, as people gathered to hear and see what was happening. The news media had caught up with them, and cameras rolled.

All of a sudden, a motorcade drove up, and out of two limousines climbed the CEOs of two major multinational bank corporations, two major computer conglomerates, and two major oil companies. They approached Jing Sheng.

"We understand that you are responsible for bringing us here. What do you want?" One of them rudely inquired.

"Please join with your equals who have come to hear Truth, and to worship Love. Can you join them as equals, also seeking Truth and worshiping Love?"

"Well, I never!" one of the men retorted. They *were* all *men*, as Liz noted. The executives stood off to one side, looking impatient and, well, *snooty*, Liz decided.

"How do you measure the true worth of a human being? Is it the suit he or she wears, or the money listed after their names? True worth is the spiritual worth of a human being within and beyond this lifetime. True worth is never measured in dollars and cents, but rather in the Love and Light one pays forward for the sake of others. True worth is the inner Love and inner Light which can be drawn upon as a gift to be shared with others.

"True light draws light. Let the light within you be complete and whole, by focusing on your inner eye, your Third Eye, which is the seat of Krishna-Consciousness, Christ-Consciousness, and Buddha-Consciousness. I am grateful to the wise and holy men and women who keep the witness to the Divine Light here in these temples. Long ago, the Light here was very bright, and taught me what I needed to know.

"Now, I call all people to turn from their materialistic ways, and to sacrifice their egos at the altar of Love, where only the gift of Self can be fully given, and fully received. Give yourself for others, and you will be filled with Light. Worry not at all about receiving material well-being, for Divine Light sustains all life. Light draws

Light. Love heals all that is not love. There is nothing in you that cannot be healed by Love. Let yourself be healed, let yourself be given. Let yourself be loved, and Love in return. Give the gift of life to others, and you will receive abundant life as well. OM. So be it." He bowed in Namaste.

Many of the people in front of the temple bowed in Namaste, and then came forward to touch Jing Sheng's feet. Of course, this quickly turned into another healing session. The executives on the sidelines looked uncomfortable. One of them seemed to be thinking this was a waste of time. Nonetheless, Liz thought that the love in the air was even more palpable here than it had been elsewhere.

Suddenly, Jing Sheng walked over to the group of executives, and placed his hands on the head of one of the men. The man actually shuddered and shook as the energy of Love moved to him and through him. He collapsed on his knees, groaning, moaning, and writhing.

"No, I can't give in to love – I have to win! No one can make me vulnerable like that!"

The other men were backing up, looking terrified. They started glancing around to try to see how far off the limousines had driven, but they were out of sight.

Jing Sheng just kept his hands on the man's head. Liz could see the waves of loving, healing energy moving from Jing Sheng's heart chakra to the man, as though the man was being surrounded by the glow of light which surrounded Jing Sheng. Liz realized that it looked as though the healing energy could not or would not penetrate the man, because he was afraid of "losing."

"Release your fear, and you will feel no pain. Letting go of fear creates room for love. I will never betray you, as others have. You no longer need to fear and dominate others, for you have access to the Love you need any day, all day and night. Simply call on my name, and you will be at peace."

At that, the man slumped forward, and rolled over on the ground unconscious. Liz and Daniel both went over to help lift his head gently, and carry him to the steps, where they sat with him.

"What did you do to him? We could sue you!" screamed one of the other executives.

Jing Sheng said, "Thank you. You have nothing to fear. Why do you fear anything? Has your money never removed the fear from your mind? Then why do you pursue it as though it will save you from everything that you do fear? If money does not take away fear, then what good is it? Only Love casts out fear. I invite you to allow Love to heal you."

Jing Sheng slowly stepped one or two steps towards them. The man he had already healed suddenly sat up, with his face glowing peacefully, a serene smile on his lips.

"Let him heal you. It feels so good to be free of fear at last, finally, and I hope for good!"

The other men looked puzzled, but one by one, they came forward, approaching Jing Sheng. Jing Sheng placed his hands on the head of the one who was closest to him, and he shuddered mightily, and collapsed slowly to his knees as well. All of a sudden, a glow appeared on his face, and he grinned. "Oh my gosh, I see Light! I do! I see the Light! I feel the Love! Thank you!" He leaned over and kissed Jing Sheng's feet.

The other men moved closer, and one by one, they received healing and blessing from Jing Sheng.

"Gentlemen, what are you going to do to give your lives for others?"

"I'm going to turn our bank into a cooperative credit union – following all the rules and principles to make money and savings accessible to everyone!"

"I'm going to give up the search for new oil and focus on renewable energies, so that we can save the earth!"

"I don't know yet, but I will invite a group of holy men and women to advise our board."

And so it went, the transformation of "successful," fear-driven men into loving souls, just as they had been when they entered the earth through their mother's womb.

"You must enter the Kingdom of God as a child. Children have no economic power, only good hearts, willing hands, and Love. Seek to be as honorable as an innocent child, and all will be blessed. I thank you for coming." Jing Sheng bowed to the men, who bowed in return. Just then, their limousines conveniently drove up.

"If you choose, please join me at Gandhi Bhavan, all who are interested. Would you care to offer a ride to the crowd?" The executives invited people to join them in the limos, and a few people quietly accepted, bowing in Namaste as they climbed in.

And so, Jing Sheng led a mass visit to Gandhi Bhavan, the memorial center which honors Mahatma Gandhi. Here, after touring and honoring Gandhi, Jing Sheng chose again to speak. The crowd gathered, the media recorded, and Liz and Daniel flanked his sides.

"I thank you for joining me in honoring a true saint, the honorable Mahatma Gandhi. In his honor, I would like to introduce as part of the Exodus 2012 Mission, a commitment to fasting once a week as a

329

way of giving of one's own life for the life of the earth, and for the life of others. Spiritual disciplines must be recovered if human life is going to thrive in loving communities around the earth.

"Spiritual sustenance is the true essence of life, and so humans need to set the example of drawing on that true life in order to maintain all life on earth. Please remember the peaceful and self-sacrificing example of Mahatma Gandhi, and give of yourself and of your own resources to provide for the well-being of others. Thank you. Namaste." Jing Sheng bowed.

The crowd again climbed into the limos, which dropped them back at the temple. Jing Sheng, Liz, and Daniel returned to their hotel, where Jing Sheng asked them to come to his room to meditate with him.

"This is the last time I will meditate with you, my little doves."

"What?! No!" cried Liz.

"Jing Sheng, I hope you are not serious!" exclaimed Daniel.

"My lovebirds, I cannot remain with you forever. My mission is almost fulfilled. Let us plan to meet in Palenque, Mexico, with Adam and Darnell, and all who would join us there. My love for you is strong, but it cannot always keep me on the earth. Love will always bless you, my little ones."

Liz sobbed, knelt down in front of Jing Sheng and grabbed his feet.

"I cannot imagine a world without you, Jing Sheng!" she cried, and then had to sit up and blow her nose.

"Love with always be with you, and where Love is, I AM." Jing

Sheng smiled at them lovingly. "Let us find our peace together." He was inviting them to meditate, ever the Master, ever the Teacher.

Eventually, even Liz found peace as they meditated together for the last time.

♥ ♥ ♥

21.   THE DEATH OF MOSES

WHAT IS LIGHT? WHAT IS LIFE? WHAT IS ETERNITY?
IS THIS THE TRINITY WE SEEK? WHAT IF
LIGHT/LIFE/ETERNITY ARE ONE?
WHAT IF GOD IS ALL THREE?
LIGHT IS A WAVE OF CONSCIOUSNESS WHICH EMANATES
OUTWARD, CREATING LIFE THROUGH LOVE, AND THEN
ETERNALLY RETURNING THAT LIFE INTO THE FOLDS OF ITS
OWN GLORIOUS BEING.
LIGHT FROM LIGHT.
TRUE GOD FROM TRUE GOD.
THAT LIGHT IS THE LIFE OF ALL PEOPLE,
NOW AND FOREVER.

One December 20th, 2012, Jing Sheng, Adam, Darnell, Liz, Daniel, Hopi, and Cliff arrived in Palenque, Mexico. Many disciples traveled with them. The regular retinue of media attendants followed as well, but they had become quite the faithful group. At 6:00 a.m. the following morning, they walked to the ruins of the Mayan holy site there. Local people also followed.

Jing Sheng climbed atop a monument. He looked down with his face serenely glowing; his eyes full of love. He spoke with a peaceful smile, and yet with just the slightest hint of sadness mixed in with joy. Gratitude transformed that hint of sadness into a greater joy. His voice was amplified by the natural backdrop of the ruins.

"My friends, this is one of the places where the ancient Elders wisely recorded the wisdom of the stars and planets which guided them, even as it guides us on this Mission. I have come here to pay them homage, to thank them for passing on that ancient wisdom in such a permanent message that earth's people could hear it in time for many to be saved, and for the earth itself to be saved. You are doing well at living together in Love. You are doing much better at saving the earth. And so I have come here to say good-bye."

Audible gasps and cries of "No!" in many languages could be heard from the crowd.

"Look Within to find Wisdom and Love . . . Share that Wisdom and Love with one another . . . Respect the Sacred Feminine and the Sacred Masculine within each person . . . . . Seek, above all, to live in harmony with that Wisdom and Love within yourself, to live in harmony with one another, and to live in harmony with the Earth. This is the Way, the Dao, the path to Enlightenment. The Way *is* the Promised Land.

"Love the Spirit of God within all visible Creation; She is your Mother. Love the Spirit of God beyond all visible Creation; He is your Father. Embody Her and Him within yourself by blessing children and by honoring, nurturing and protecting all life. This is your work to do upon the Earth. This work is your blessing. Blessings are never received simply for ourselves; blessings are always meant to be shared. Love is never Love unless it is shared. The sharing of Love is wholeness; let that wholeness be your salvation.

"The Presence of Love is always within you. Let this knowledge be your Peace.

"I love you, and I leave you with my Peace, within and among you all. So be it, my friends. May love always bless you."

Jing Sheng quickly rose straight up in the air about a thousand feet, hovered there, turned a full circle to look in every direction around the earth, and then kept rising, until he vanished from sight.

A solar flare flashed so fast and so bright that it surrounded the Earth. The Earth's magnetic shield, which had become weak, shimmered red and gold, and the Earth itself shook in one big aftershock.

It was the beginning of the End. It was the beginning of the Golden Age of human life upon the Earth. Light danced around the Earth, and people laughed and hugged, and took care of one another.

The Light had come for good. People found that Light within themselves. They saw the Light glowing in others. They rejoiced in finding that Light everywhere on Earth. The Light was visible everywhere. In that light, all that glimmered gold was Love.

ABOUT THE AUTHOR

Carol Richardson was born Carol Elizabeth Dodson on the equator in what was then the Belgian Congo in 1958. She grew up traveling back-and-forth between the U.S.A. and Africa during her whole childhood, living in different parts of the Congo, as well as Texas, New York, Tanzania, Maryland, and the Ivory Coast.

Carol was first told she had the ability to "cure animals with her hands" by a mystic from India whom she met when she was just 13. Since no mentoring program was available to her for learning healing at that age, her road to becoming a healer was long indeed.

She graduated high school in 1977 at TASOK, the American School of Kinshasa, where she also originally had attended kindergarten. She received a B.S. in psychology from Texas Christian University in 1981.

After being turned down for the Peace Corps because of a severe problem with her knees, she worked with autistic children in San Antonio, Texas, where she met her late husband, David Wayne Richardson.

They moved to Houston, and were married in 1982. Together, they had a daughter and then a son, while Carol was working on a master's degree in public health at UT Health. David died of a cerebral aneurysm at the age of 34, leaving 28-year-old Carol with a 22-month-old daughter and a 7-month-old son.

This led Carol to a sense of call to ministry. After completing her M.P.H., she and the children moved to Nashville, Tennessee. She attended Vanderbilt University Divinity School, taking five-and-a-half years as a widow and single mother to get the three-year degree. She received the Newcombe Prize for her senior project along with her Master of Divinity degree. She was ordained into the Christian Church (Disciples of Christ) in 1994.

Rev. Richardson served churches mostly in Michigan. In 1996, Carol learned Raja Yoga and Kriya Yoga meditation, along with animal healing, from teachers who came over from the UK. From 1999 to 2002, Carol traveled four times to England to pursue spiritual training in Progressive Counseling, and Natural Spiritual Healing. Subsequently, she studied Reiki at Spirit of Wellness in Michigan.

With the benefit of all these spiritual studies as well as pharmaceutical grade nutritional supplements which greatly benefitted her knees, in 2009, Carol found herself aging rather well. She felt so shocked by the death of Michael Jackson, who was the same age as she was, that she felt deeply moved and inspired to write the book: *Aging Well – Be Your Best Self Forever!*

On May 27, 2010, Carol had an Enlightenment Vision in which she was blessed by Enlightened Masters of many faiths. This vision was life-changing, and launched her onto the path of seeking Self-Realization as a yogini. The term Guru-Doula was given to her during a time of prayer and meditation, as was the title of this book.

In 2011, Carol moved to Washington, DC to become a spiritual wellness practitioner. She offers energy therapy (healing), hypnotherapy, life coaching, and meditation classes.

The views expressed in this novel belong solely to Rev. Richardson, and in no way are they meant to represent the views, teachings, or beliefs of any other earth-bound human being, institution, church, or organization. In the character of Hu Jing Sheng, Rev. Richardson seeks to honor God and Jesus Christ, to whom her gratitude is eternal.

www.ingramcontent.com/pod-product-compliance
Lightning Source LLC
Chambersburg PA
CBHW050036030726
47506CB00001B/304